Novellas — that satisfyi_ ...~y point between short stories and novels — have a fine tradition in New Zealand writing, and several of this country's most important writers have done their best work in this genre. This anthology groups work from seven top writers to form a concise introduction to New Zealand fiction, spanning 80 years from the expatriate modernism of Mansfield at the start of the twentieth century, to Peter Wells and Elizabeth Knox at the end of the century.

Peter Simpson is associate professor of English at the University of Auckland. Born in Takaka, he has a masters degree from the University of Canterbury and a PhD from the University of Toronto. He has taught at universities in New Zealand and Canada since the 1960s. He is the author of *Ronald Hugh Morrieson* (OUP, 1982) and *Answering Hark: McCahon/Caselberg: Painter/Poet* (Craig Potton Publishing, 2002). He has edited several books and writes frequently for journals on New Zealand literature and art. He is also a curator and the managing editor of The Holloway Press.

seven
new zealand
novellas

edited by
Peter Simpson

REED

Established in 1907, Reed Publishing (NZ) Ltd
is New Zealand's largest book publisher, with over 300 titles in print.

For details on all these books visit our website:
www.reed.co.nz

Published by Reed Books, a division of Reed Publishing (NZ) Ltd,
39 Rawene Rd, Birkenhead, Auckland.
Associated companies, branches and representatives throughout the world.

ISBN 0 7900 0896 3

Cover designed by Richard Killeen
Text designed by Graeme Leather

First published 2003

Printed in New Zealand

contents

introduction

Everybody knows what a 'novel' is and what a 'short story' is, but what about a work of fiction which is both too long to be a short story and too short be a novel? Sometimes such prose narratives are called 'long stories', sometimes they are called 'short novels', but the form is distinctive enough to warrant a term of its own. Over the past century *novella* has increasingly come to be used for such narratives. A recent definition of novella is: 'a fictional tale in prose, intermediate in length and complexity between a short story and a novel, and usually concentrating on a single event or chain of events, with a surprising turning point'.[1]

How long is a novella? Mary Doyle Springer, author of one of the few critical studies exclusively devoted to the form, offers this definition: *'the novella is a prose fiction of a certain length (usually 15,000 to 50,000 words), a length equipped to realize several distinct formal functions better than any other length.'*[2] All seven novellas collected here fall within these parameters except Patricia Grace's *Valley* which — at a little over 10,000 words — is shorter than most though in structure it resembles a novella rather than a short story. Frank Sargeson's *That Summer* is the longest example at about 35,000 words.

I have always enjoyed the novella as a form of fiction. At high school one of my favourite books was *Short Novels of John Steinbeck*, which consisted of six novellas, including *Cannery Row*, *Of Mice and*

---

1. Christopher Baldick, *The Concise Oxford Dictionary of Literary Terms* (Oxford University Press, Oxford, 1996).
2. Mary Doyle Springer, *Forms of the Modern Novella*. (The University of Chicago Press, Chicago and London, 1975): 9.

Men, and *The Pearl*. I found something peculiarly satisfying about a story which could be read in an hour or two but which offered more narrative interest and depth of character than is possible in most short stories. Later I discovered that many of the world's great writers had contributed to the novella form including Leo Tolstoy (*The Death of Ivan Illych*), Fyodor Dostoevsky (*Notes from Underground*), Herman Melville (*Billy Budd*), Joseph Conrad (*Heart of Darkness*), Henry James (*The Turn of the Screw*), D.H. Lawrence (*The Fox*), William Faulkner (*Spotted Horses*), Franz Kafka (*The Metamorphosis*), Thomas Mann (*Death in Venice*), Katherine Anne Porter (*Pale Horse, Pale Rider*), Carson McCullers (*The Ballad of the Sad Café*), Alexander Solzhenitsyn (*One Day in the Life of Ivan Denisovich*), and many others.

In this book seven novellas by New Zealand writers are collected. The earliest, Katherine Mansfield's *Prelude*, was first published in 1918, and the most recent, Elizabeth Knox's *Pomare*, in 1994 — a span of nearly 80 years. As well as introducing readers to fine examples of the novella my further purpose has been to provide a kind of short history of New Zealand fiction through some of its finest practitioners.

New Zealand writers have excelled at the novella. Both Katherine Mansfield's and Maurice Duggan's finest work was done in this form — neither ever completed a novel, though both aspired to do so, but as C.K. Stead has remarked: 'the failure can be seen in both cases as a kind of artistic scrupulousness'.[3] That is, they allowed their material to find the form which best suited it. Frank Sargeson was another who turned to the novella again and again, as has Elizabeth Knox in more recent times. This collection by no means exhausts the list of those who have written novellas of distinction in New Zealand. Others include Greville Texidor, A.P. Gaskell, O.E. Middleton, Janet Frame, John Caselberg, Maurice Shadbolt, Maurice Gee, C.K. Stead, Ian Wedde, Witi Ihimaera, Keri Hulme, Alan Duff, Michael Morrissey, Mike Johnson and Chad Taylor.

---

3. C.K. Stead, 'Introduction' Maurice Duggan, *Collected Stories*. (Auckland University Press, Auckland, 1981): 8.

Katherine Mansfield's *Prelude* was vitally important both in her own artistic development and in the development of modern fiction in general. She began writing it soon after a memory-stimulating reunion with her younger brother, Leslie, in London in 1915 shortly before he was killed as a soldier in France. In Paris she 'fell into the open arms of my first novel' (as she told her partner John Middleton Murry),[4] a story which imaginatively reconstructed events that had occurred half a world away when she was five and her family shifted in 1893 to a new and larger house.

After Leslie's devastating death Mansfield travelled to the south of France seeking relief from her painful grief. She wrote in her journal:

> Now — now I want to write recollections of my own country. Yes, I want to write about my own country till I simply exhaust my store. Not only because it is a 'sacred debt' that I pay to my country because my brother and I were born there, but also because in my thoughts I range with him over all the remembered places ... Oh, I want for one moment to make our undiscovered country leap into the eyes of the Old World. It must be mysterious, as though floating ...[5]

Soon afterwards she rediscovered the 'novel' she had begun in Paris (at this stage called *The Aloe.*) She wrote:

> I *found The Aloe* this morning ... *The Aloe* is right. *The Aloe* is lovely. It simply fascinates me, and I know that it is what you would wish me to write. And now I know what the last chapter is. It is your birth — your coming in the autumn ...[6]

She completed *The Aloe* before returning to England in March 1916, but *Prelude* as eventually published in 1918 not only has a

---

4. Vincent O'Sullivan & Margaret Scott, eds, *The Collected Letters of Katherine Mansfield,* vol. I. (Clarendon Press, Oxford, 1984): 167.
5. J. Middleton Murry, ed., *The Journal of Katherine Mansfield 1904–1922.* (Constable, London, 1954): 93–94.
6. *Ibid.*: 97–98. As it happens the narrative turned out differently from how she predicted; it was not until her later novella *At the Bay* that her brother appears as a character.

different title, it is also considerably shorter.[7] She changed the story by cutting out unnecessary episodes and details, telling a friend:

> What form is it? you ask. Ah. Brett, its so difficult to say. As far as I know its more or less my own invention.[8]

Mansfield was convinced that the 1914–18 war had changed everything so utterly that writing too must change.[9] In making changes from *The Aloe* to *Prelude* Mansfield was acting on this conviction. What started out as a 'novel' became a novella as she chopped out much of the detail a conventional novel might have provided and offered mere glimpses of her characters, shifting the narrative perspective continuously from consciousness to consciousness, creating a multi-faceted portrait of a family at a significant moment of change.

Antony Alpers has suggested that in *Prelude* Linda Burnell is already pregnant as the story starts.[10] I believe, however, that Linda becomes pregnant on the night the family arrives at the new house, a suggestion obliquely conveyed by Linda's dreams and fears. I am convinced that *Prelude* honours the dead brother by incorporating his conception secretly into the subtext of the story, so that it becomes indeed the 'prelude' to his life.

The two decades which separated Mansfield from Sargeson constituted a watershed in New Zealand's cultural development. As an artist of the colonial era, Mansfield inevitably looked to the metropolitan centre of London as the locus of artistic achievement. Like

---

7. Readers can compare the two versions in Vincent O'Sullivan, ed., Katherine Mansfield, *The Aloe,* edited by Vincent O'Sullivan, (Port Nicholson Press, Wellington, 1982), which places *The Aloe* and *Prelude* side by side on facing pages. I have made considerable use of this edition in my account of *Prelude*.
8. *Collected Letters*, vol. I: 330–31.
9. 'I feel in the profoundest sense that nothing can ever be the same that as artists we are traitors if we feel otherwise: we have to take it into account and find new expressions, new moulds for our thoughts & feelings.' KM to J.M. Murry, *Collected Letters*, vol. III (Clarendon Press, Oxford, 1993): 82.
10. 'Perhaps some present day readers might not realise (so discreet are the numerous hints, beginning with the third line of the first paragraph) that Linda is meant to be pregnant in the story.' Antony Alpers, ed., *The Stories of Katherine Mansfield*, (Oxford University Press, Auckland, 1984): 558.

other gifted New Zealanders of her generation she became a permanent expatriate.[11] Sargeson was very differently placed. Lacking the
resources to support an independent life as a writer in Europe, he was
forced to return to New Zealand after his brief obligatory excursion
overseas to confront the difficult reality of becoming a writer in New
Zealand, a task to which he committed himself with remarkable courage
and tenacity. His career became exemplary in demonstrating that you
did not have to leave New Zealand to pursue an artistic career.

That Summer, Sargeson's first novella, was achieved after a decade
of ceaseless experimentation, as recorded in his autobiographical
writings.[12] Sargeson abandoned his first attempt at an autobiographical novel in London in the late 1920s when he realised it was a dull
copy of James Joyce's *Portrait of the Artist as a Young Man.* Back in
New Zealand his second attempt failed because it was written in the
formal language of the English novel that was insufficiently
connected to the New Zealand life he was describing. He began
exploring the possibility of an appropriate idiom in very short
sketches collected in *Conversation with My Uncle* (1936). He wrote:
'I was as much excited by the thought of the advance I had made
towards bringing an appropriate New Zealand language to light, as I
was by the substance of the story'.[13]

Armed with this technical discovery Sargeson set out on his third
attempt at a novel, *That Summer,* which took him three years to
complete, though it turned out shorter than he had hoped. As with
Mansfield, his novel had metamorphosed into a novella.

Modern readers are as much likely to be intrigued by the subtleties
and evasions of Sargeson's account of the homosexual love affair
between Bill, the emotionally and verbally inarticulate narrator, and
the older man Terry, as they are by his technical advances, especially
since Michael King's 1995 biography revealed the full details of

---

11. The painter Frances Hodgkins is another prominent example.
12. Notably in *More than Enough*, the middle volume of his autobiographical
   trilogy, and in his contribution to the series of essays called *Beginnings* in the
   journal *Landfall,* later published in book form.
13. Robin Dudding, ed., *Beginnings: New Zealand Writers Tell How They Began
   Writing,* (Oxford University Press, Wellington, 1980): 40.

Sargeson's sexual history and the arrest and trial (obliquely replicated in *That Summer*) which lay behind his decision to change his name and his life, a subject which was carefully concealed in his autobiographies.[14]

Maurice Duggan was one of the many New Zealand writers of the next generation who benefited directly from Sargeson's example and encouragement, though his early stories were written in an elaborately artificial style which was in stark contrast to the older writer's austerely disciplined idiom. Eventually he began, partly under Sargeson's influence, to write more simply and to abandon the 'habit of rhetoric': 'If it was to be strong, it had to be simple; the language must be a focusing glass and not, as had up to now been the case, a sort of bejewelled and empty casket'.[15]

His first book, *Immanuel's Land* (1956), demonstrated the results of this process, especially in brief stories like 'A Small Story' which was dedicated to Sargeson. But as he matured Duggan began to loosen up and his stories became longer and more elaborate in style. Having starved himself of his natural eloquence in order to learn his craft he was able progressively to indulge it without fear of losing himself in the empty rhetoric of his early experiments.

O'Leary's Orchard, one of his last stories (first published in 1967 when Duggan was 45), reveals the splendour of his fiction when he was at full stretch. No New Zealand writer (unless perhaps Janet Frame) has written with such subtlety, strength and assurance as Duggan in this novella that took him more than three years to complete.

Like Mansfield before him Duggan found his true home in the novella, of which he wrote two splendid examples: *Riley's Handbook*, a fierce and excoriating work that owes something to Samuel Beckett, and *O'Leary's Orchard*. The latter is a lyrical but unsentimental

---

14. See Michael King, *Frank Sargeson: a Life* (Viking, Auckland, 1995); and for a discussion of the sexual theme in *That Summer*, John Newton, 'Homophobia and the Social Pattern: Sargeson's Queer Nation,' *Landfall* 199, March 2000: 91–107.

15. *Beginnings*: 96.

exploration of the brief and doomed love affair between an ageing man and a much younger woman. In exploring the complexities of sexual love, frequently through the antiquated imagery of alchemy (O'Leary was formerly a chemist), the novella achieves something of the linguistic subtlety and analytical complexity associated with the fiction of Henry James.

A year after Maurice Duggan died Patricia Grace produced her first collection of stories, *Waiariki*, including the short novella *Valley*. It was the first collection of stories by a Maori woman writer and came just three years after Witi Ihimaera had produced his first collection. This was the beginning of the literary manifestation of the so-called Maori renaissance, a process that has completely transformed the landscape of New Zealand literature in the last three decades.

Set in a rural school, *Valley* follows the school year from summer through to summer, each of the four seasons given a 'chapter' to itself. As is typical of much fiction by Maori writers, and in strong contrast to the Pakeha tradition that often centres on solitary individuals, the focus of *Valley* is on the communal life of the school and the wider community which sustains it. Emphasis is given to communal activities such as galas, auctions and tangi, events in which both children and adults participate. The tone is warmly empathetic; Grace seems animated by the dual aims of offering to Maori readers an affirmative mirror of their own culture and to Pakeha readers the opportunity to see a functioning community free of the negative stereotypes which so often colour the presentation of Maori in the media.

But while the spirit of *Valley* is sympathetic it is by no means sentimental. During the course of the story the children are confronted by death — as when one the teachers collapses with a heart attack and subsequently dies ('Mrs Kaa, she fell down') — and also by the presence of violence in human relations. The artistically talented boy Hiriwa smashes with his fist the clay cricket he has cleverly modelled. His behaviour seems unaccountable until later we meet him again, the side of his face covered in bruises. The connection is not explicit but is unmistakable.

Throughout, *Valley* is enlivened by the dialogue and poetry of very young children instilling humour and vitality into a novella that throbs with life in all its variety and complexity.

Just as New Zealand fiction has been revitalised by the emergence of Maori writers so, in recent decades, it has also been enriched by immigrant voices from the Pacific. The precursor and in many ways the source of this enrichment has been the writing of Albert Wendt. Born in Samoa, Wendt has lived for extensive periods in New Zealand, first in the 1950s and 1960s and again since 1988 when he returned to settle here. Initially his writing dealt primarily with Samoa, though his first novel *Sons for the Return Home* was set largely in New Zealand, and his more recent novels and stories often have New Zealand settings.

Flying-fox in a Freedom Tree, however, is wholly Samoan in setting. The title story of his first collection published in 1974, it later emerged with the publication of Wendt's epic novel *Leaves of the Banyan Tree* (1979) as part of a larger structure. It stands alone as a work in its own right but in *Leaves* it forms the central section of a three-part novel. Through several generations of the same family *Leaves* recounts the history of a Samoan community since European colonisation.[16]

The central figure in *Leaves* is Tauilopepe, the father of Pepe whose narrative of his life constitutes the substance of *Flying-fox*. The title of the first section of the novel, 'God, Money and Success' sums up Tauilopepe's attitude to life; he becomes rich and powerful by embracing wholeheartedly the culture of the colonisers, in particular Christianity and capitalism. Pepe totally repudiates his father's value system, and adopts an anarchic and rebellious approach to life that owes something to writers like Albert Camus as well as to elements in Samoan mythology. The structure of the novel is dialectical, for the generation that comes along after Pepe's death is represented by the curious figure of Galupo who tries to reconcile the antithetical opposites of Tauilopepe and Pepe.

---

16. In this respect *Leaves of the Banyan Tree* has much in common with Chinua Achebe's *African Trilogy*, which performed a similar role for the Ibo people of Nigeria.

The sardonic and lively narrative of the dying Pepe represents a kind of dystopian inversion of those narratives of the paradisal South Pacific so beloved by Western writers from Herman Melville to James Michener. Pepe presents himself as an ironic reincarnation of Robert Louis Stevenson, a *tusitala* (teller of tales) who also died of tuberculosis. The dwarf Tagata, the 'flying-fox' of the title, represents an intensification of the plight of Pepe himself and forms a vivid exemplar of the values of courage, rebellion and humour with which the narrator faces his inevitable death.

In the last decades of the twentieth century New Zealand fiction was characterized by increasing diversification from the critical realism of (mostly male) Pakeha writers which dominated the earlier post-Second World War decades. A somewhat monolithic literary culture was progressively subverted by the emergence of more and more groups asserting their sense of difference in literary terms. Women writers, Maori and Polynesian writers, immigrant writers from Asia and Europe, gay and lesbian writers all contributed to this process. There was a corresponding emancipation of subject matter and literary forms within fiction. Increasingly New Zealand writers began locating their fiction outside the mainstream culture of Pakeha New Zealand and outside the realistic modes with which it had mostly been recorded in the past.

Some of these tendencies are evident in Peter Wells' novella *Of Memory and Desire* in his first book, *Dangerous Desires* (1991). In some ways this novella represents a surprising departure from the material with which Wells is most commonly identified. Wells is New Zealand's first explicitly gay writer, and edited (with Rex Pilgrim) the first anthology of gay writing in New Zealand, *Best Mates* (1997). He has recently written an extensive memoir, *Long Loop Home*, about growing up as a homosexual in New Zealand. There had been gay writers before in New Zealand such as Frank Sargeson, but, as in *That Summer*, the gay content is conveyed by subtle hints and inferences as compared to the explicitness of Wells' approach in, for example, *One of THEM!*, a second novella in his first book.

As if to demonstrate his versatility and refusal to conform to the stereotype of the 'gay writer', in *Of Memory and Desire* Wells presents a moving heterosexual love story which frankly explores the sexual negotiations of a newly-wed Japanese couple, Sayo and Keiji, who spend their honeymoon in New Zealand with tragic consequences. Loosely based on a real event, *Of Memory and Desire* remarkably demonstrates Wells' ability to enter imaginatively into the lives of characters remote from his own culture.

In her longer fiction Elizabeth Knox has increasingly participated in the expansion of fictional possibilities discussed above, as, for example, in her internationally successful novel *The Vintner's Luck* (1998), set in nineteenth-century France, in which an angel (with wings) plays a central part. But in her trilogy of novellas collected as *The High Jump* (2000), of which *Pomare* is the first (though it was published after *Paremata*, the second novella in the trilogy), Knox demonstrates her fictional versatility by writing realistically about a New Zealand childhood which in many ways looks back to Katherine Mansfield in method and material.

In fact — allowing for the differences between the New Zealand of the 1890s and the 1960s, which the respective novellas vividly evoke — the parallels between *Prelude* and *Pomare* are considerable. Both are set in Wellington; both focus on the relationships within a family, and especially between parents and children; in both families there are three young girls; in both the impact of death on young minds is explored — in *Prelude* by means of the duck-killing episode, in *Pomare* through the actual death of a child from cancer. In both the narrative perspective shifts fluidly from one character to another. The parallels could be considerably extended. There is even a broad similarity in the ages of the authors and their distance from the autobiographical events reconstructed in the two novellas.

These two novellas, then, serve as appropriate bookends for a collection which records the variable and exciting use made by New Zealand writers of the novella form throughout the last century.

Peter Simpson
February 2003

katherine mansfield
prelude

I

THERE was not an inch of room for Lottie and Kezia in the buggy. When Pat swung them on top of the luggage they wobbled; the grandmother's lap was full and Linda Burnell could not possibly have held a lump of a child on hers for any distance. Isabel, very superior, was perched beside the new handy-man on the driver's seat. Hold-alls, bags and boxes were piled upon the floor. 'These are absolute necessities that I will not let out of my sight for one instant,' said Linda Burnell, her voice trembling with fatigue and excitement.

Lottie and Kezia stood on the patch of lawn just inside the gate all ready for the fray in their coats with brass anchor buttons and little round caps with battleship ribbons. Hand in hand, they stared with round solemn eyes first at the absolute necessities and then at their mother.

'We shall simply have to leave them. That is all. We shall simply have to cast them off,' said Linda Burnell. A strange little laugh flew from her lips; she leaned back against the buttoned leather cushions and shut her eyes, her lips trembling with laughter. Happily at that moment Mrs Samuel Josephs, who had been watching the scene from behind her drawing-room blind, waddled down the garden path.

'Why nod leave the chudren with be for the afterdoon, Brs Burnell? They could go on the dray with the storeban when he comes in the eveding. Those thigs on the path have to go, dod't they?'

'Yes, everything outside the house is supposed to go,' said Linda Burnell, and she waved a white hand at the tables and chairs standing on their heads on the front lawn. How absurd they looked! Either they ought to be the other way up, or Lottie and Kezia ought to stand on their heads, too. And she longed to say: 'Stand on your heads, children, and wait for the storeman.' It seemed to her that would be so exquisitely funny that she could not attend to Mrs Samuel Josephs.

The fat creaking body leaned across the gate, and the big jelly of a face smiled. 'Dod't you worry, Brs Burnell. Loddie and Kezia can have tea with by chudren in the dursery, and I'll see theb on the dray afterwards.'

The grandmother considered. 'Yes, it really is quite the best plan. We are very obliged to you, Mrs Samuel Josephs. Children, say "thank you" to Mrs Samuel Josephs.'

Two subdued chirrups: 'Thank you, Mrs Samuel Josephs.'

'And be good little girls, and — come closer —' they advanced, 'don't forget to tell Mrs Samuel Josephs when you want to. . . .'

'No, granma.'

'Dod't worry, Brs Burnell.'

At the last moment Kezia let go Lottie's hand and darted towards the buggy.

'I want to kiss my granma good-bye again.'

But she was too late. The buggy rolled off up the road, Isabel bursting with pride, her nose turned up at all the world, Linda Burnell prostrated, and the grandmother rummaging among the very curious oddments she had put in her black silk reticule at the last moment, for something to give her daughter. The buggy twinkled away in the sunlight and fine golden dust up the hill and over. Kezia bit her lip, but Lottie, carefully finding her handkerchief first, set up a wail.

'Mother! Granma!'

Mrs Samuel Josephs, like a huge warm black silk tea cosy, enveloped her.

'It's all right, by dear. Be a brave child. You come and blay in the dursery!'

She put her arm round weeping Lottie and led her away. Kezia followed, making a face at Mrs Samuel Josephs' placket, which was undone as usual, with two long pink corset laces hanging out of it. . . .

Lottie's weeping died down as she mounted the stairs, but the sight of her at the nursery door with swollen eyes and a blob of a nose gave great satisfaction to the S.J.'s, who sat on two benches before a long table covered with American cloth and set out with immense plates of bread and dripping and two brown jugs that faintly steamed.

'Hullo! You've been crying!'

'Ooh! Your eyes have gone right in.'

'Doesn't her nose look funny.'

'You're all red-and-patchy.'

Lottie was quite a success. She felt it and swelled, smiling timidly.

'Go and sit by Zaidee, ducky,' said Mrs Samuel Josephs, 'and Kezia, you sid ad the end by Boses.'

Moses grinned and gave her a nip as she sat down; but she pretended not to notice. She did hate boys.

'Which will you have?' asked Stanley, leaning across the table very politely, and smiling at her. 'Which will you have to begin with — strawberries and cream or bread and dripping?'

'Strawberries and cream, please,' said she.

'Ah-h-h-h.' How they all laughed and beat the table with their teaspoons. Wasn't that a take in! Wasn't it now! Didn't he fox her! Good old Stan!

'Ma! She thought it was real.'

Even Mrs Samuel Josephs, pouring out the milk and water, could not help smiling. 'You bustn't tease theb on their last day,' she wheezed.

But Kezia bit a big piece out of her bread and dripping, and then stood the piece up on her plate. With the bite out it made a dear little sort of a gate. Pooh! She didn't care! A tear rolled down her cheek, but she wasn't crying. She couldn't have cried in front of those awful Samuel Josephs. She sat with her head bent, and as the tear dripped slowly down, she caught it with a neat little whisk of her tongue and ate it before any of them had seen.

II

After tea Kezia wandered back to their own house. Slowly she walked up the back steps, and through the scullery into the kitchen. Nothing was left in it but a lump of gritty yellow soap in one corner of the kitchen window sill and a piece of flannel stained with a blue bag in another. The fireplace was choked up with rubbish. She poked among it but found nothing except a hair-tidy with a heart painted on it that had belonged to the servant girl. Even that she left lying, and she trailed through the narrow passage into the drawing-room. The Venetian blind was pulled down but not drawn close. Long pencil rays of sunlight shone through and the wavy shadow of a bush outside danced on the gold lines. Now it was still, now it began to flutter again, and now it came almost as far as her feet. Zoom! Zoom! a blue-bottle knocked against the ceiling; the carpet-tacks had little bits of red fluff sticking to them.

The dining-room window had a square of coloured glass at each corner. One was blue and one was yellow. Kezia bent down to have one more look at a blue lawn with blue arum lilies growing at the gate, and then at a yellow lawn with yellow lilies and a yellow fence. As she looked a little Chinese Lottie came out on to the lawn and began to dust the tables and chairs with a corner of her pinafore. Was that really Lottie? Kezia was not quite sure until she had looked through the ordinary window.

Upstairs in her father's and mother's room she found a pill box black and shiny outside and red in, holding a blob of cotton wool.

'I could keep a bird's egg in that,' she decided.

In the servant girl's room there was a stay-button stuck in a crack of the floor, and in another crack some beads and a long needle. She knew there was nothing in her grandmother's room; she had watched her pack. She went over to the window and leaned against it, pressing her hands against the pane.

Kezia liked to stand so before the window. She liked the feeling of the cold shining glass against her hot palms, and she liked to watch the funny white tops that came on her fingers when she pressed them hard against the pane. As she stood there, the day flickered out and dark came. With the dark crept the wind snuffling and howling. The windows of the empty house shook, a creaking came from the walls and floors, a piece of loose iron on the roof banged forlornly. Kezia was suddenly quite, quite still, with wide open eyes and knees pressed together. She was frightened. She wanted to call Lottie and to go on calling all the while she ran downstairs and out of the house. But IT was behind her, waiting at the door, at the head of the stairs, at the bottom of the stairs, hiding in the passage, ready to dart out at the back door. But Lottie was at the back door, too.

'Kezia!' she called cheerfully. 'The storeman's here. Everything is on the dray and three horses, Kezia. Mrs Samuel Josephs has given us a big shawl to wear round us, and she says to button up your coat. She won't come out because of asthma.'

Lottie was very important.

'Now then, you kids,' called the storeman. He hooked his big thumbs under their arms and up they swung. Lottie arranged the shawl 'most beautifully' and the storeman tucked up their feet in a piece of old blanket.

'Lift up. Easy does it.'

They might have been a couple of young ponies. The storeman felt over the cords holding his load, unhooked the brakechain from the wheel, and whistling, he swung up beside them.

'Keep close to me,' said Lottie, 'because otherwise you pull the shawl away from my side, Kezia.'

But Kezia edged up to the storeman. He towered beside her big as a giant and he smelled of nuts and new wooden boxes.

III

It was the first time that Lottie and Kezia had ever been out so late. Everything looked different — the painted wooden houses far smaller than they did by day, the gardens far bigger and wilder. Bright stars speckled the sky and the moon hung over the harbour dabbling the waves with gold. They could see the lighthouse shining on Quarantine Island, and the green lights on the old coal hulks.

'There comes the Picton boat,' said the storeman, pointing to a little steamer all hung with bright beads.

But when they reached the top of the hill and began to go down the other side the harbour disappeared, and although they were still in the town they were quite lost. Other carts rattled past. Everybody knew the storeman.

'Night, Fred.'

'Night O,' he shouted.

Kezia liked very much to hear him. Whenever a cart appeared in the distance she looked up and waited for his voice. He was an old friend; and she and her grandmother had often been to his place to buy grapes. The storeman lived alone in a cottage that had a glasshouse against one wall built by himself. All the glasshouse was spanned and arched over with one beautiful vine. He took her brown basket from her, lined it with three large leaves, and then he felt in his belt for a little horn knife, reached up and snapped off a big blue cluster and laid it on the leaves so tenderly that Kezia held her breath to watch. He was a very big man. He wore brown velvet trousers, and he had a long brown beard. But he never wore a collar, not even on Sunday. The back of his neck was burnt bright red.

'Where are we now?' Every few minutes one of the children asked him the question.

'Why, this is Hawk Street, or Charlotte Crescent.'

'Of course it is,' Lottie pricked up her ears at the last name; she always felt that Charlotte Crescent belonged specially to her. Very few people had streets with the same name as theirs.

'Look, Kezia, there is Charlotte Crescent. Doesn't it look different?' Now everything familiar was left behind. Now the big dray rattled into unknown country, along new roads with high clay banks on either side, up steep, steep hills, down into bushy valleys, through wide shallow rivers. Further and further. Lottie's head wagged; she drooped, she slipped half into Kezia's lap and lay there. But Kezia could not open her eyes wide enough. The wind blew and she shivered; but her cheeks and ears burned.

'Do stars ever blow about?' she asked.

'Not to notice,' said the storeman.

'We've got a nuncle and a naunt living near our new house,' said Kezia. 'They have got two children, Pip, the eldest is called, and the youngest's name is Rags. He's got a ram. He has to feed it with a nenamuel teapot and a glove top over the spout. He's going to show us. What is the difference between a ram and a sheep?'

'Well, a ram has horns and runs for you.'

Kezia considered. 'I don't want to see it frightfully,' she said. 'I hate rushing animals like dogs and parrots. I often dream that animals rush at me — even camels — and while they are rushing, their heads swell e-enormous.'

The storeman said nothing. Kezia peered up at him, screwing up her eyes. Then she put her finger out and stroked his sleeve; it felt hairy. 'Are we near?' she asked.

'Not far off, now,' answered the storeman. 'Getting tired?'

'Well, I'm not an atom bit sleepy,' said Kezia. 'But my eyes keep curling up in such a funny sort of way.' She gave a long sigh, and to stop her eyes from curling she shut them. . . . When she opened them again they were clanking through a drive that cut through the garden like a whip lash, looping suddenly an island of green, and behind the island, but out of sight until you came upon it, was the house. It was long and low built, with a pillared verandah and balcony all the way round. The soft white bulk of it lay stretched upon the green garden like a sleeping beast. And now one and now another of the windows leaped into light. Someone was walking through the empty rooms carrying a lamp. From a window downstairs the light of a fire flickered. A strange beautiful excitement seemed to stream from the house in quivering ripples.

'Where are we?' said Lottie, sitting up. Her reefer cap was all on one side and on her cheek there was the print of an anchor button she had pressed against while sleeping. Tenderly the storeman lifted her, set her cap straight, and pulled down her crumpled clothes. She stood blinking on the lowest verandah step watching Kezia who seemed to come flying through the air to her feet.

'Ooh!' cried Kezia, flinging up her arms. The grandmother came out of the dark hall carrying a little lamp. She was smiling.

'You found your way in the dark?' she said.

'Perfectly well.'

But Lottie staggered on the lowest verandah step like a bird fallen out of the nest. If she stood still for a moment she fell asleep, if she leaned against anything her eyes closed. She could not walk another step.

'Kezia,' said the grandmother, 'can I trust you to carry the lamp?'

'Yes, my granma.'

The old woman bent down and gave the bright breathing thing into her hands and then she caught up drunken Lottie. 'This way.'

Through a square hall filled with bales and hundreds of parrots (but the parrots were only on the wall-paper) down a narrow passage where the parrots persisted in flying past Kezia with her lamp.

'Be very quiet,' warned the grandmother, putting down Lottie and opening the dining-room door. 'Poor little mother has got such a headache.'

Linda Burnell, in a long cane chair, with her feet on a hassock, and a plaid over her knees, lay before a crackling fire. Burnell and Beryl sat at the table in the middle of the room eating a dish of fried chops and drinking tea out of a brown china teapot. Over the back of her mother's chair leaned Isabel. She had a comb in her fingers and in a gentle absorbed fashion she was combing the curls from her mother's forehead. Outside the pool of lamp and firelight the room stretched dark and bare to the hollow windows.

'Are those the children?' But Linda did not really care; she did not even open her eyes to see.

'Put down the lamp, Kezia,' said Aunt Beryl, 'or we shall have the house on fire before we are out of the packing cases. More tea, Stanley?'

'Well, you might just give me five-eighths of a cup,' said Burnell, leaning across the table. 'Have another chop, Beryl. Tip-top meat, isn't it? Not too lean and not too fat.' He turned to his wife. 'You're sure you won't change your mind, Linda darling?'

'The very thought of it is enough.' She raised one eyebrow in the way she had. The grandmother brought the children bread and milk and they sat up to the table, flushed and sleepy behind the wavy steam.

'I had meat for my supper,' said Isabel, still combing gently.

'I had a whole chop for my supper, the bone and all and Worcester Sauce. Didn't I, father?'

'Oh, don't boast, Isabel,' said Aunt Beryl.

Isabel looked astounded. 'I wasn't boasting, was I, Mummy? I never thought of boasting. I thought they would like to know. I only meant to tell them.'

'Very well. That's enough,' said Burnell. He pushed back his plate, took a tooth-pick out of his pocket and began picking his strong white teeth.

'You might see that Fred has a bite of something in the kitchen before he goes, will you, mother?'

'Yes, Stanley.' The old woman turned to go.

'Oh, hold on half a jiffy. I suppose nobody knows where my slippers were put? I suppose I shall not be able to get at them for a month or two — what?'

'Yes,' came from Linda. 'In the top of the canvas hold-all marked "urgent necessities".'

'Well you might get them for me will you, mother?'

'Yes, Stanley.'

Burnell got up, stretched himself, and going over to the fire he turned his back to it and lifted up his coat tails.

'By Jove, this is a pretty pickle. Eh, Beryl?'

Beryl, sipping tea, her elbows on the table, smiled over the cup at him. She wore an unfamiliar pink pinafore; the sleeves of her blouse were rolled up to her shoulders showing her lovely freckled arms, and she had let her hair fall down her back in a long pig-tail.

'How long do you think it will take to get straight — couple of weeks — eh?' he chaffed.

'Good heavens, no,' said Beryl airily. 'The worst is over already. The servant girl and I have simply slaved all day, and ever since mother came she has worked like a horse, too. We have never sat down for a moment. We have had a day.'

Stanley scented a rebuke.

'Well, I suppose you did not expect me to rush away from the office and nail carpets — did you?'

'Certainly not,' laughed Beryl. She put down her cup and ran out of the dining-room.

'What the hell does she expect us to do?' asked Stanley. 'Sit down and fan herself with a palm leaf fan while I have a gang of professionals to do the job? By Jove, if she can't do a hand's turn occasionally without shouting about it in return for . . . .'

And he gloomed as the chops began to fight the tea in his sensitive stomach. But Linda put up a hand and dragged him down to the side of her long chair.

'This is a wretched time for you, old boy,' she said. Her cheeks were very white but she smiled and curled her fingers into the big red hand she held. Burnell became quiet. Suddenly he began to whistle 'Pure as a lily, joyous and free' — a good sign.

'Think you're going to like it?' he asked.

'I don't want to tell you, but I think I ought to, mother,' said Isabel. 'Kezia is drinking tea out of Aunt Beryl's cup.'

IV

They were taken off to bed by the grandmother. She went first with a candle; the stairs rang to their climbing feet. Isabel and Lottie lay in a room to themselves, Kezia curled in her grandmother's soft bed.

'Aren't there going to be any sheets, my granma?'

'No, not to-night.'

'It's tickly,' said Kezia, 'but it's like Indians.' She dragged her grandmother down to her and kissed her under the chin. 'Come to bed soon and be my Indian brave.'

'What a silly you are,' said the old woman, tucking her in as she loved to be tucked.

'Aren't you going to leave me a candle?'

'No. Sh-h. Go to sleep.'

'Well, can I have the door left open?'

She rolled herself into a round but she did not go to sleep. From all over the house came the sound of steps. The house itself creaked and popped. Loud whispering voices came from downstairs. Once she heard Aunt Beryl's rush of high laughter, and once she heard a loud trumpeting from Burnell blowing his nose. Outside the window hundreds of black cats with yellow eyes sat in the sky watching her — but she was not frightened. Lottie was saying to Isabel:

'I'm going to say my prayers in bed to-night.'

'No you can't, Lottie.' Isabel was very firm. 'God only excuses you saying your prayers in bed if you've got a temperature.' So Lottie yielded:

Gentle Jesus meek anmile,
Look pon a little chile.
Pity me, simple Lizzie
Suffer me to come to thee.

And then they lay down back to back, their little behinds just touching, and fell asleep.

Standing in a pool of moonlight Beryl Fairfield undressed herself. She was tired, but she pretended to be more tired than she really was — letting her clothes fall, pushing back with a languid gesture her warm, heavy hair.

'Oh, how tired I am — very tired.'

She shut her eyes a moment, but her lips smiled. Her breath rose and fell in her breast like two fanning wings. The window was wide open; it was warm, and somewhere out there in the garden a young man, dark and slender, with mocking eyes, tip-toed among the bushes, and gathered the flowers into a big bouquet, and slipped under her window and held it up to her. She saw herself bending forward. He thrust his head among the bright waxy flowers, sly and laughing. 'No, no,' said Beryl. She turned from the window and dropped her nightgown over her head.

'How frightfully unreasonable Stanley is sometimes,' she thought, buttoning. And then, as she lay down, there came the old thought, the cruel thought — ah, if only she had money of her own.

A young man, immensely rich, has just arrived from England. He meets her quite by chance. . . . The new governor is unmarried. . . . There is a ball at Government house. . . . Who is that exquisite creature in *eau de nil* satin? Beryl Fairfield. . . .

'The thing that pleases me,' said Stanley, leaning against the side of the bed and giving himself a good scratch on his shoulders and back before turning in, 'is that I've got the place dirt cheap, Linda. I was talking about it to little Wally Bell to-day and he said he simply could not understand why they had accepted my figure. You see land about here is bound to become more and more valuable . . . in about ten years' time . . . of course we shall have to go very slow and cut down expenses as fine as possible. Not asleep — are you?'

'No, dear, I've heard every word,' said Linda. He sprang into bed, leaned over her and blew out the candle.

'Good night, Mr Business Man,' she said, and she took hold of his head by the ears and gave him a quick kiss. Her faint far-away voice seemed to come from a deep well.

'Good night, darling.' He slipped his arm under her neck and drew her to him.

'Yes, clasp me,' said the faint voice from the deep well.

Pat the handy man sprawled in his little room behind the kitchen. His sponge-bag, coat and trousers hung from the door-peg like a hanged man. From the edge of the blanket his twisted toes protruded, and on the floor beside him there was an empty cane bird-cage. He looked like a comic picture.

'Honk, honk,' came from the servant girl. She had adenoids.

Last to go to bed was the grandmother.

'What. Not asleep yet?'

'No, I'm waiting for you,' said Kezia. The old woman sighed and lay down beside her. Kezia thrust her head under her grandmother's arm and gave a little squeak. But the old woman only pressed her faintly, and sighed again, took out her teeth, and put them in a glass of water beside her on the floor.

In the garden some tiny owls, perched on the branches of a lace-bark tree, called: 'More pork; more pork.' And far away in the bush there sounded a harsh rapid chatter: 'Ha-ha-ha . . . Ha-ha-ha.'

V

Dawn came sharp and chill with red clouds on a faint green sky and drops of water on every leaf and blade. A breeze blew over the garden, dropping dew and dropping petals, shivered over the drenched paddocks, and was lost in the sombre bush. In the sky some tiny stars floated for a moment and then they were gone — they were dissolved like bubbles. And plain to be heard in the early quiet was the sound of the creek in the paddock running over the brown stones, running in and out of the sandy hollows, hiding under clumps of dark berry bushes, spilling into a swamp of yellow water flowers and cresses.

And then at the first beam of sun the birds began. Big cheeky birds, starlings and mynahs, whistled on the lawns, the little birds, the goldfinches and linnets and fantails flicked from bough to bough. A lovely kingfisher perched on the paddock fence preening his rich beauty, and a *tui* sang his three notes and laughed and sang them again.

'How loud the birds are,' said Linda in her dream. She was walking with her father through a green paddock sprinkled with daisies. Suddenly he bent down and parted the grasses and showed her a tiny ball of fluff just at her feet. 'Oh, Papa, the darling.' She made a cup of her hands and caught the tiny bird and stroked its head with her finger. It was quite tame. But a funny thing happened. As she stroked it began to swell, it ruffled and pouched, it grew bigger and bigger and its round eyes seemed to smile knowingly at her. Now her arms were hardly wide enough to hold it and she dropped it into her apron. It had become a baby with a big naked head and a gaping bird-mouth, opening and shutting. Her father broke into a loud clattering laugh and she woke to see Burnell standing by the windows rattling the Venetian blind up to the very top.

'Hullo,' he said. 'Didn't wake you, did I? Nothing much wrong with the weather this morning.'

He was enormously pleased. Weather like this set a final seal on his bargain. He felt, somehow, that he had bought the lovely day, too — got it chucked in dirt cheap with the house and ground. He dashed off to his bath and Linda turned over and raised herself on one elbow to see the room by daylight. All the furniture had found a place — all the old paraphernalia — as she expressed it. Even the photographs were on the mantelpiece and the medicine bottles on the shelf above the wash-stand. Her clothes lay across a chair — her outdoor things, a purple cape and a round hat with a plume in it. Looking at them she wished that she was going away from this house, too. And she saw herself driving away from them all in a little buggy, driving away from everybody and not even waving.

Back came Stanley girt with a towel, glowing and slapping his thighs. He pitched the wet towel on top of her hat and cape, and standing firm in the exact centre of a square of sunlight he began to do his exercises. Deep breathing, bending and squatting like a frog and shooting out his legs. He was so delighted with his firm, obedient body that he hit himself on the chest and gave a loud 'Ah.' But this amazing vigour seemed to set him worlds away from Linda. She lay on the white tumbled bed and watched him as if from the clouds.

'Oh, damn! Oh, blast!' said Stanley, who had butted into a crisp white shirt only to find that some idiot had fastened the neck-band and he was caught. He stalked over to Linda waving his arms.

'You look like a big fat turkey,' said she.

'Fat. I like that,' said Stanley. 'I haven't a square inch of fat on me. Feel that.'

'It's rock — it's iron,' mocked she.

'You'd be surprised,' said Stanley, as though this were intensely interesting, 'at the number of chaps at the club who have got a corporation. Young chaps, you know — men of my age.' He began parting his bushy ginger hair, his blue eyes fixed and round in the glass, his knees bent, because the dressing table was always — confound it — a bit too low for him. 'Little Wally Bell, for instance,' and he straightened, describing upon himself an enormous curve with the hairbrush. 'I must say I've a perfect horror . . . .'

'My dear, don't worry. You'll never be fat. You are far too energetic.'

'Yes, yes, I suppose that's true,' said he, comforted for the hundredth time, and taking a pearl pen-knife out of his pocket he began to pare his nails.

'Breakfast, Stanley.' Beryl was at the door. 'Oh, Linda, mother says you are not to get up yet.' She popped her head in at the door. She had a big piece of syringa stuck through her hair.

'Everything we left on the verandah last night is simply sopping this morning. You should see poor dear mother wringing out the tables and the chairs. However, there is no harm done —' this with the faintest glance at Stanley.

'Have you told Pat to have the buggy round in time? It's a good six and a half miles to the office.'

'I can imagine what this early start for the office will be like,' thought Linda. 'It will be very high pressure indeed.'

'Pat, Pat.' She heard the servant girl calling. But Pat was evidently hard to find; the silly voice went baa-baaing through the garden.

Linda did not rest again until the final slam of the front door told her that Stanley was really gone.

Later she heard her children playing in the garden. Lottie's stolid, compact little voice cried: 'Ke — zia. Isa — bel.' She was always getting lost or losing people only to find them again, to her great surprise, round the next tree or the next corner. 'Oh, there you are after all.' They had been turned out after breakfast and told not to come back to the house until they were called. Isabel wheeled a neat pramload of prim dolls and Lottie was allowed for a great treat to walk beside her holding the doll's parasol over the face of the wax one.

'Where are you going to, Kezia?' asked Isabel, who longed to find some light and menial duty that Kezia might perform and so be roped in under her government.

'Oh, just away,' said Kezia. . . .

Then she did not hear them any more. What a glare there was in the room. She hated blinds pulled up to the top at any time, but in the morning it was intolerable. She turned over to the wall and idly, with one finger, she traced a poppy on the wall-paper with a leaf and a stem and a fat bursting bud. In the quiet, and under her tracing finger, the poppy seemed to come alive. She could feel the sticky, silky petals, the stem, hairy like a gooseberry skin, the rough leaf and the tight glazed bud. Things had a habit of coming alive like that. Not only large substantial things like furniture but curtains and the patterns of stuffs and the fringes of quilts and cushions. How often she had seen the tassel fringe of her quilt change into a funny procession of dancers with priests attending. . . . For there were some tassels that did not dance at all but walked stately, bent forward as if praying or chanting. How often the medicine bottles had turned into a row of little men with brown top-hats on; and the washstand jug had a way of sitting in the basin like a fat bird in a round nest.

'I dreamed about birds last night,' thought Linda. What was it? She had forgotten. But the strangest part of this coming alive of things was what they did. They listened, they seemed to swell out with some mysterious important content, and when they were full she felt that they smiled. But it was not for her, only, their sly secret smile; they were members of a secret society and they smiled among themselves. Sometimes, when she had fallen asleep in the daytime, she woke and could not lift a finger, could not even turn her eyes to left or right because THEY were there; sometimes when she went out of a room and left it empty, she knew as she clicked the door to that THEY were filling it. And there were times in the evenings when she was upstairs, perhaps, and everybody else was down, when she could hardly escape from them. Then she could not hurry, she could not hum a tune; if she tried to say ever so carelessly — 'Bother that old thimble' — they were not deceived. THEY knew how frightened she was; THEY saw how she turned her head away as she passed the mirror. What Linda always felt was that they wanted something of her, and she knew that if she gave herself up and was quiet, more than quiet, silent, motionless, something would really happen.

'It's very quiet now,' she thought. She opened her eyes wide, and she heard the silence spinning its soft endless web. How lightly she breathed; she scarcely had to breathe at all.

Yes, everything had come alive down to the minutest, tiniest particle, and she did not feel her bed, she floated, held up in the air. Only she seemed to be listening with her wide open watchful eyes, waiting for someone to come who just did not come, watching for something to happen that just did not happen.

VI

In the kitchen at the long deal table under the two windows old Mrs Fairfield was washing the breakfast dishes. The kitchen window looked out on to a big grass patch that led down to the vegetable garden and the rhubarb beds. On one side the grass patch was bordered by the scullery and wash-house and over this whitewashed lean-to there grew a knotted vine. She had noticed yesterday that a few tiny corkscrew tendrils had come right through some cracks in the scullery ceiling and all the windows of the lean-to had a thick frill of ruffled green.

'I am very fond of a grape vine,' declared Mrs Fairfield, 'but I do not think that the grapes will ripen here. It takes Australian sun.' And she remembered how Beryl when she was a baby had been picking some white grapes from the vine on the back verandah of their Tasmanian house and she had been stung on the leg by a huge red ant. She saw Beryl in a little plaid dress with red ribbon tie-ups on the shoulders screaming so dreadfully that half the street rushed in. And how the child's leg had swelled! 'T — t — t — t!' Mrs Fairfield caught her breath remembering. 'Poor child, how terrifying it was.' And she set her lips tight and went over to the stove for some more hot water. The water frothed up in the big soapy bowl with pink and blue bubbles on top of the foam. Old Mrs Fairfield's arms were bare to the elbow and stained a bright pink. She wore a grey foulard dress patterned with large purple pansies, a white linen apron and a high cap shaped like a jelly mould of white muslin. At her throat there was a silver crescent moon with five little owls seated on it, and round her neck she wore a watch-guard made of black beads.

It was hard to believe that she had not been in that kitchen for years; she was so much a part of it. She put the crocks away with a sure, precise touch, moving leisurely and ample from the stove to the dresser, looking into the pantry and the larder as though there were not an unfamiliar corner. When she had finished, everything in the kitchen had become part of a series of patterns. She stood in the middle of the room wiping her hands on a check cloth; a smile beamed on her lips; she thought it looked very nice, very satisfactory.

'Mother! Mother! Are you there?' called Beryl.

'Yes, dear. Do you want me?'

'No. I'm coming,' and Beryl rushed in, very flushed, dragging with her two big pictures.

'Mother, whatever can I do with these awful hideous Chinese paintings that Chung Wah gave Stanley when he went bankrupt? It's absurd to say that they are valuable, because they were hanging in Chung Wah's fruit shop for months before. I can't make out why Stanley wants them kept. I'm sure he thinks them just as hideous as we do, but it's because of the frames,' she said spitefully. 'I suppose he thinks the frames might fetch something some day or other.'

'Why don't you hang them in the passage?' suggested Mrs Fairfield; 'they would not be much seen there.'

'I can't. There is no room. I've hung all the photographs of his office there before and after building, and the signed photos of his business friends, and that awful enlargement of Isabel lying on the mat in her singlet.' Her angry glance swept the placid kitchen. 'I know what I'll do. I'll hang them here. I will tell Stanley they got a little damp in the moving so I have put them in here for the time being.'

She dragged a chair forward, jumped on it, took a hammer and a big nail out of her pinafore pocket and banged away.

'There! That is enough! Hand me the picture, mother.'

'One moment, child.' Her mother was wiping over the carved ebony frame.

'Oh, mother, really you need not dust them. It would take years to dust all those little holes.' And she frowned at the top of her mother's head and bit her lip with impatience. Mother's deliberate way of doing things was simply maddening. It was old age, she supposed, loftily.

At last the two pictures were hung side by side. She jumped off the chair, stowing away the little hammer.

'They don't look so bad there, do they?' she said. 'And at any rate nobody need gaze at them except Pat and the servant girl — have I got a spider's web on my face, mother? I've been poking into that cupboard under the stairs and now something keeps tickling my nose.'

But before Mrs Fairfield had time to look Beryl had turned away. Someone tapped on the window: Linda was there, nodding and smiling. They heard the latch of the scullery door lift and she came in. She had no hat on; her hair stood up on her head in curling rings and she was wrapped up in an old cashmere shawl.

'I'm so hungry,' said Linda: 'where can I get something to eat, mother? This is the first time I've been in the kitchen. It says "mother" all over; everything is in pairs.'

'I will make you some tea,' said Mrs Fairfield, spreading a clean napkin over a corner of the table, 'and Beryl can have a cup with you.'

'Beryl, do you want half my gingerbread?' Linda waved the knife at her. 'Beryl, do you like the house now that we are here?'

'Oh yes, I like the house immensely and the garden is beautiful, but it feels very far away from everything to me. I can't imagine people coming out from town to see us in that dreadful jolting bus, and I am sure there is not anyone here to come and call. Of course it does not matter to you because —'

'But there's the buggy,' said Linda. 'Pat can drive you into town whenever you like.'

That was a consolation, certainly, but there was something at the back of Beryl's mind, something she did not even put into words for herself.

'Oh, well, at any rate it won't kill us,' she said dryly, putting down her empty cup and standing up and stretching. 'I am going to hang curtains.' And she ran away singing:

> How many thousand birds I see
> That sing aloud from every tree . . .

'. . . birds I see That sing aloud from every tree. . . .' But when she reached the dining-room she stopped singing, her face changed; it became gloomy and sullen.

'One may as well rot here as anywhere else,' she muttered savagely, digging the stiff brass safety pins into the red serge curtains.

The two left in the kitchen were quiet for a little. Linda leaned her cheek on her fingers and watched her mother. She thought her mother looked wonderfully beautiful with her back to the leafy window. There was something comforting in the sight of her that Linda felt she could never do without. She needed the sweet smell of her flesh, and the soft feel of her cheeks and her arms and shoulders still softer. She loved the way her hair curled, silver at her forehead, lighter at her neck, and bright brown still in the big coil under the muslin cap. Exquisite were her mother's hands, and the two rings she wore seemed to melt into her creamy skin. And she was always so fresh, so delicious. The old woman could bear nothing but linen next to her body and she bathed in cold water winter and summer.

'Isn't there anything for me to do?' asked Linda.

'No, darling. I wish you would go into the garden and give an eye to your children; but that I know you will not do.'

'Of course I will, but you know Isabel is much more grown up than any of us.'

'Yes, but Kezia is not,' said Mrs Fairfield.

'Oh, Kezia has been tossed by a bull hours ago,' said Linda, winding herself up in her shawl again.

But no, Kezia had seen a bull through a hole in a knot of wood in the paling that separated the tennis lawn from the paddock. But she had not liked the bull frightfully, so she had walked away back through the orchard, up the grassy slope, along the path by the lace bark tree and so into the spread tangled garden. She did not believe that she would ever not get lost in this garden. Twice she had found her way to the big iron gates they had driven through the night before, and then had turned to walk up the drive that led to the house, but there were so many little paths on either side. On one side they all led into a tangle of tall dark trees and strange bushes with flat velvet leaves and feathery cream flowers that buzzed with flies when you shook them — this was the frightening side, and no garden at all. The little paths here were wet and clayey with tree roots spanned across them like the marks of big fowls' feet.

But on the other side of the drive there was a high box border and the paths had box edges and all of them led into a deeper and deeper tangle of flowers. The camellias were in bloom, white and crimson and pink and white striped with flashing leaves. You could not see a leaf on the syringa bushes for the white clusters. The roses were in flower — gentlemen's button-hole roses, little white ones, but far too full of insects to hold under anyone's nose, pink monthly roses with a ring of fallen petals round the bushes, cabbage roses on thick stalks, moss roses, always in bud, pink smooth beauties opening curl on curl, red ones so dark they seemed to turn black as they fell, and a certain exquisite cream kind with a slender red stem and bright scarlet leaves.

There were clumps of fairy bells, and all kinds of geraniums, and there were little trees of verbena and bluish lavender bushes and a bed of pelagoniums with velvet eyes and leaves like moths' wings. There was a bed of nothing but mignonette and another of nothing but pansies — borders of double and single daisies and all kinds of little tufty plants she had never seen before.

The red-hot pokers were taller than she; the Japanese sunflowers grew in a tiny jungle. She sat down on one of the box borders. By pressing hard at first it made a nice seat. But how dusty it was inside! Kezia bent down to look and sneezed and rubbed her nose.

And then she found herself at the top of the rolling grassy slope that led down to the orchard. . . . She looked down at the slope a moment; then she lay down on her back, gave a squeak and rolled over and over into the thick flowery orchard grass. As she lay waiting for things to stop spinning, she decided to go up to the house and ask the servant girl for an empty match-box. She wanted to make a surprise for the grandmother. . . . First she would put a leaf inside with a big violet lying on it, then she would put a very small white picotee, perhaps, on each side of the violet, and then she would sprinkle some lavender on top, but not to cover their heads.

She often made these surprises for the grandmother, and they were always most successful.

'Do you want a match, my granny?'

'Why, yes, child, I believe a match is just what I'm looking for.'

The grandmother slowly opened the box and came upon the picture inside.

'Good gracious, child! How you astonished me!'

'I can make her one every day here,' she thought, scrambling up the grass on her slippery shoes.

But on her way back to the house she came to that island that lay in the middle of the drive, dividing the drive into two arms that met in front of the house. The island was made of grass banked up high. Nothing grew on the top except one huge plant with thick, grey-green, thorny leaves, and out of the middle there sprang up a tall stout stem. Some of the leaves of the plant were so old that they curled up in the air no longer; they turned back, they were split and broken; some of them lay flat and withered on the ground.

Whatever could it be? She had never seen anything like it before. She stood and stared. And then she saw her mother coming down the path.

'Mother, what is it?' asked Kezia.

Linda looked up at the fat swelling plant with its cruel leaves and fleshy stem. High above them, as though becalmed in the air, and yet holding so fast to the earth it grew from, it might have had claws instead of roots. The curving leaves seemed to be hiding something; the blind stem cut into the air as if no wind could ever shake it.

'That is an aloe, Kezia,' said her mother.

'Does it ever have any flowers?'

'Yes, Kezia,' and Linda smiled down at her, and half shut her eyes. 'Once every hundred years.'

VII

On his way home from the office Stanley Burnell stopped the buggy at the Bodega, got out and bought a large bottle of oysters. At the Chinaman's shop next door he bought a pineapple in the pink of condition, and noticing a basket of fresh black cherries he told John to put him a pound of those as well. The oysters and the pine he stowed away in the box under the front seat, but the cherries he kept in his hand.

Pat, the handy-man, leapt off the box and tucked him up again in the brown rug.

'Lift yer feet, Mr Burnell, while I give yer a fold under,' said he.

'Right! Right! First-rate!' said Stanley. 'You can make straight for home now.'

Pat gave the grey mare a touch and the buggy sprang forward.

'I believe this man is a first-rate chap,' thought Stanley. He liked the look of him sitting up there in his neat brown coat and brown bowler. He liked the way Pat had tucked him in, and he liked his eyes. There was nothing servile about him — and if there was one thing he hated more than another it was servility. And he looked as if he was pleased with his job happy and contented already.

The grey mare went very well; Burnell was impatient to be out of the town. He wanted to be home. Ah, it was splendid to live in the country — to get right out of that hole of a town once the office was closed; and this drive in the fresh warm air, knowing all the while that his own house was at the other end, with its garden and paddocks, its three tip-top cows and enough fowls and ducks to keep them in poultry, was splendid too.

As they left the town finally and bowled away up the deserted road his heart beat hard for joy. He rooted in the bag and began to eat the cherries, three or four at a time, chucking the stones over the side of the buggy. They were delicious, so plump and cold, without a spot or a bruise on them.

Look at those two, now — black one side and white the other — perfect! A perfect little pair of Siamese twins. And he stuck them in his button-hole. . . . By Jove, he wouldn't mind giving that chap up there a handful — but no, better not. Better wait until he had been with him a bit longer.

He began to plan what he would do with his Saturday afternoons and his Sundays. He wouldn't go to the club for lunch on Saturday. No, cut away from the office as soon as possible and get them to give him a couple of slices of cold meat and half a lettuce when he got home. And then he'd get a few chaps out from town to play tennis in the afternoon. Not too many — three at most. Beryl was a good player, too. . . . He stretched out his right arm and slowly bent it, feeling the muscle. . . . A bath, a good rub-down, a cigar on the verandah after dinner. . . .

On Sunday morning they would go to church — children and all. Which reminded him that he must hire a pew, in the sun if possible and well forward so as to be out of the draught from the door. In fancy he heard himself intoning extremely well: 'When thou did overcome the *Sharp*ness of Death Thou didst open the *King*dom of Heaven to *all* Believers.' And he saw the neat brass-edged card on the corner of the pew — Mr Stanley Burnell and family. . . . The rest of the day he'd loaf about with Linda. . . . Now they were walking about the garden; she was on his arm, and he was explaining to her at length what he intended doing at the office the week following. He heard her saying: 'My dear, I think that is most wise.' . . . Talking things over with Linda was a wonderful help even though they were apt to drift away from the point.

Hang it all! They weren't getting along very fast. Pat had put the brake on again. Ugh! What a brute of a thing it was. He could feel it in the pit of his stomach.

A sort of panic overtook Burnell whenever he approached near home. Before he was well inside the gate he would shout to everyone within sight: 'Is everything all right?' And then he did not believe it was until he heard Linda say: 'Hullo! Are you home again?' That was the worst of living in the country — it took the deuce of a long time to get back. . . . But now they weren't far off. They were on the top of the last hill; it was a gentle slope all the way now and not more than half a mile.

Pat trailed the whip over the mare's back and he coaxed her: 'Goop now. Goop now.'

It wanted a few minutes to sunset. Everything stood motionless bathed in bright, metallic light and from the paddocks on either side there streamed the milky scent of ripe grass. The iron gates were open. They dashed through and up the drive and round the island, stopping at the exact middle of the verandah.

'Did she satisfy yer, Sir?' said Pat, getting off the box and grinning at his master.

'Very well indeed, Pat,' said Stanley.

Linda came out of the glass door; her voice rang in the shadowy quiet. 'Hullo! Are you home again?'

At the sound of her his heart beat so hard that he could hardly stop himself dashing up the steps and catching her in his arms.

'Yes, I'm home again. Is everything all right?'

Pat began to lead the buggy round to the side gate that opened into the courtyard.

'Here, half a moment,' said Burnell. 'Hand me those two parcels.' And he said to Linda, 'I've brought you back a bottle of oysters and a pineapple,' as though he had brought her back all the harvest of the earth.

They went into the hall; Linda carried the oysters in one hand and the pineapple in the other. Burnell shut the glass door, threw his hat down, put his arms round her and strained her to him, kissing the top of her head, her ears, her lips, her eyes.

'Oh, dear! Oh, dear!' said she. 'Wait a moment. Let me put down these silly things,' and she put the bottle of oysters and the pine on a little carved chair. 'What have you got in your buttonhole — cherries?' She took them out and hung them over his ear.

'Don't do that, darling. They are for you.'

So she took them off his ear again. 'You don't mind if I save them. They'd spoil my appetite for dinner. Come and see your children. They are having tea.'

The lamp was lighted on the nursery table. Mrs Fairfield was cutting and spreading bread and butter. The three little girls sat up to table wearing large bibs embroidered with their names. They wiped their mouths as their father came in ready to be kissed. The windows were open; a jar of wild flowers stood on the mantelpiece, and the lamp made a big soft bubble of light on the ceiling.

'You seem pretty snug, mother,' said Burnell, blinking at the light. Isabel and Lottie sat one on either side of the table, Kezia at the bottom — the place at the top was empty.

'That's where my boy ought to sit,' thought Stanley. He tightened his arm round Linda's shoulder. By God, he was a perfect fool to feel as happy as this!

'We are, Stanley. We are very snug,' said Mrs Fairfield, cutting Kezia's bread into fingers.

'Like it better than town — eh, children?' asked Burnell.

'Oh, yes,' said the three little girls, and Isabel added as an after-thought: 'Thank you very much indeed, father dear.'

'Come upstairs,' said Linda. 'I'll bring your slippers.'

But the stairs were too narrow for them to go up arm in arm. It was quite dark in the room. He heard her ring tapping on the marble mantelpiece as she felt for the matches.

'I've got some, darling. I'll light the candles.'

But instead he came up behind her and again he put his arms round her and pressed her head into his shoulder.

'I'm so confoundedly happy,' he said.

'Are you?' She turned and put her hands on his breast and looked up at him.

'I don't know what has come over me,' he protested.

It was quite dark outside now and heavy dew was falling. When Linda shut the window the cold dew touched her finger tips. Far away a dog barked. 'I believe there is going to be a moon,' she said.

At the words, and with the cold wet dew on her fingers, she felt as though the moon had risen — that she was being strangely discovered in a flood of cold light. She shivered; she came away from the window and sat down upon the box ottoman beside Stanley.

* * *

In the dining room, by the flicker of a wood fire, Beryl sat on a hassock playing the guitar. She had bathed and changed all her clothes. Now she wore a white muslin dress with black spots on it and in her hair she had pinned a black silk rose.

> Nature has gone to her rest, love,
> See, we are alone.
> Give me your hand to press, love,
> Lightly within my own.

She played and sang half to herself, for she was watching herself playing and singing. The firelight gleamed on her shoes, on the ruddy belly of the guitar, and on her white fingers. . . .

'If I were outside the window and looked in and saw myself I really would be rather struck,' thought she. Still more softly she played the accompaniment — not singing now but listening.

. . . 'The first time that I ever saw you, little girl — oh, you had no idea that you were not alone — you were sitting with your little feet upon a hassock, playing the guitar. God, I can never forget. . . .' Beryl flung up her head and began to sing again:

> Even the moon is aweary . . .

But there came a loud bang at the door. The servant girl's crimson face popped through.

'Please, Miss Beryl, I've got to come and lay.'

'Certainly, Alice,' said Beryl, in a voice of ice. She put the guitar in a corner. Alice lunged in with a heavy black iron tray.

'Well, I have had a job with that oving,' said she. 'I can't get nothing to brown.'

'Really!' said Beryl.

But no, she could not stand that fool of a girl. She ran into the dark drawing-room and began walking up and down. . . . Oh, she was restless, restless. There was a mirror over the mantel. She leaned her arms along and looked at her pale shadow in it. How beautiful she looked, but there was nobody to see, nobody.

'Why must you suffer so?' said the face in the mirror. 'You were not made for suffering. . . . Smile!'

Beryl smiled, and really her smile *was* so adorable that she smiled again — but this time because she could not help it.

VIII

'Good morning, Mrs Jones.'

'Oh, good morning, Mrs Smith. I'm so glad to see you. Have you brought your children?'

'Yes, I've brought both my twins. I have had another baby since I saw you last, but she came so suddenly that I haven't had time to make her any clothes, yet. So I left her. . . . How is your husband?'

'Oh, he is very well, thank you. At least he had a nawful cold but Queen Victoria — she's my godmother, you know — sent him a case of pineapples and that cured it im-mediately. Is that your new servant?'

'Yes, her name's Gwen. I've only had her two days. Oh, Gwen, this is my friend, Mrs Smith.

'Good morning, Mrs Smith. Dinner won't be ready for about ten minutes.'

'I don't think you ought to introduce me to the servant. I think I ought to just begin talking to her.'

'Well, she's more of a lady-help than a servant and you do introduce lady-helps. I know, because Mrs Samuel Josephs had one.'

'Oh, well it doesn't matter,' said the servant carelessly, beating up a chocolate custard with half a broken clothes peg. The dinner was baking beautifully on a concrete step. She began to lay the cloth on a pink garden seat. In front of each person she put two geranium leaf plates, a pine needle fork and a twig knife. There were three daisy heads on a laurel leaf for poached eggs, some slices of fuchsia petal cold beef, some lovely little rissoles made of earth and water and dandelion seeds, and the chocolate custard which she had decided to serve in the paua shell she had cooked it in.

'You needn't trouble about my children,' said Mrs Smith graciously. 'If you'll just take this bottle and fill it at the tap — I mean at the dairy.'

'Oh, all right,' said Gwen, and she whispered to Mrs Jones: 'Shall I go and ask Alice for a little bit of real milk?'

But someone called from the front of the house and the luncheon party melted away, leaving the charming table, leaving the rissoles and the poached eggs to the ants and to an old snail who pushed his quivering horns over the edge of the garden seat and began to nibble a geranium plate.

'Come round to the front, children. Pip and Rags have come.'

The Trout boys were the cousins Kezia had mentioned to the storeman. They lived about a mile away in a house called Monkey Tree Cottage. Pip was tall for his age, with lank black hair and a white face, but Rags was very small and so thin that when he was undressed his shoulder blades stuck out like two little wings. They had a mongrel dog with pale blue eyes and a long tail turned up at the end who followed them everywhere; he was called Snooker. They spent half their time combing and brushing Snooker and dosing him with various awful mixtures concocted by Pip, and kept secretly by him in a broken jug covered with an old kettle lid. Even faithful little Rags was not allowed to know the full secret of these mixtures. . . . Take some carbolic tooth powder and a pinch of sulphur powdered up fine, and perhaps a bit of starch to stiffen up Snooker's coat. . . . But that was not all; Rags privately thought that the rest was gun-powder. . . . And he never was allowed to help with the mixing because of the danger. . . . 'Why if a spot of this flew in your eye, you would be blinded for life,' Pip would say, stirring the mixture with an iron spoon. 'And there's always the chance — just the chance, mind you — of it exploding if you whack it hard enough. . . . Two spoons of this in a kerosene tin will be enough to kill thousands of fleas.' But Snooker spent all his spare time biting and snuffling, and he stank abominably.

'It's because he is such a grand fighting dog,' Pip would say. 'All fighting dogs smell.'

The Trout boys had often spent the day with the Burnells in town, but now that they lived in this fine house and boncer garden they were inclined to be very friendly. Besides, both of them liked playing with girls — Pip, because he could fox them so, and because Lottie was so easily frightened, and Rags for a shameful reason. He adored dolls. How he would look at a doll as it lay asleep, speaking in a whisper and smiling timidly, and what a treat it was to him to be allowed to hold one. . . .

'Curve your arms round her. Don't keep them stiff like that. You'll drop her,' Isabel would say sternly.

Now they were standing on the verandah and holding back Snooker who wanted to go into the house but wasn't allowed to because Aunt Linda hated decent dogs.

'We came over in the bus with Mum,' they said, 'and we're going to spend the afternoon with you. We brought over a batch of our gingerbread for Aunt Linda. Our Minnie made it. It's all over nuts.'

'I skinned the almonds,' said Pip. 'I just stuck my hand into a saucepan of boiling water and grabbed them out and gave them a kind of pinch and the nuts flew out of the skins, some of them as high as the ceiling. Didn't they, Rags?'

Rags nodded. 'When they make cakes at our place,' said Pip, 'we always stay in the kitchen, Rags and me, and I get the bowl and he gets the spoon and the egg beater. Sponge cake's best. It's all frothy stuff, then.'

He ran down the verandah steps to the lawn, planted his hands on the grass, bent forward, and just did not stand on his head.

'That lawn's all bumpy,' he said. 'You have to have a flat place for standing on your head. I can walk round the monkey tree on my head at our place. Can't I, Rags?'

'Nearly,' said Rags faintly.

'Stand on your head on the verandah. That's quite flat,' said Kezia.

'No, smarty,' said Pip. 'You have to do it on something soft. Because if you give a jerk and fall over, something in your neck goes click, and it breaks off. Dad told me.'

'Oh, do let's play something,' said Kezia.

'Very well,' said Isabel quickly, 'we'll play hospitals. I will be the nurse and Pip can be the doctor and you and Lottie and Rags can be the sick people.'

Lottie didn't want to play that, because last time Pip had squeezed something down her throat and it hurt awfully.

'Pooh,' scoffed Pip. 'It was only the juice out of a bit of mandarin peel.'

'Well, let's play ladies,' said Isabel. 'Pip can be the father and you can be all our dear little children.'

'I hate playing ladies,' said Kezia. 'You always make us go to church hand in hand and come home and go to bed.'

Suddenly Pip took a filthy handkerchief out of his pocket. 'Snooker! Here, sir,' he called. But Snooker, as usual, tried to sneak away, his tail between his legs. Pip leapt on top of him, and pressed him between his knees.

'Keep his head firm, Rags,' he said, and he tied the handkerchief round Snooker's head with a funny knot sticking up at the top.

'Whatever is that for?' asked Lottie.

'It's to train his ears to grow more close to his head — see?' said Pip. 'All fighting dogs have ears that lie back. But Snooker's ears are a bit too soft.'

'I know,' said Kezia. 'They are always turning inside out. I hate that.'

Snooker lay down, made one feeble effort with his paw to get the handkerchief off, but finding he could not, trailed after the children, shivering with misery.

IX

Pat came swinging along; in his hand he held a little tomahawk that winked in the sun.

'Come with me,' he said to the children, 'and I'll show you how the kings of Ireland chop the head off a duck.'

They drew back — they didn't believe him, and besides, the Trout boys had never seen Pat before.

'Come on now,' he coaxed, smiling and holding out his hand to Kezia.

'Is it a real duck's head? One from the paddock?'

'It is,' said Pat. She put her hand in his hard dry one, and he stuck the tomahawk in his belt and held out the other to Rags. He loved little children.

'I'd better keep hold of Snooker's head if there's going to be any blood about,' said Pip, 'because the sight of blood makes him awfully wild.' He ran ahead dragging Snooker by the handkerchief.

'Do you think we ought to go?' whispered Isabel. 'We haven't asked or anything. Have we?'

At the bottom of the orchard a gate was set in the paling fence. On the other side a steep bank led down to a bridge that spanned the creek, and once up the bank on the other side you were on the fringe of the paddocks. A little old stable in the first paddock had been turned into a fowl house. The fowls had strayed far away across the paddock down to a dumping ground, in a hollow, but the ducks kept close to that part of the creek that flowed under the bridge.

Tall bushes overhung the stream with red leaves and yellow flowers and clusters of blackberries. At some places the stream was wide and shallow, but at others it tumbled into deep little pools with foam at the edges and quivering bubbles. It was in these pools that the big white ducks had made themselves at home, swimming and guzzling along the weedy banks.

Up and down they swam, preening their dazzling breasts, and other ducks with the same dazzling breasts and yellow bills swam upside down with them.

'There is the little Irish navy,' said Pat, 'and look at the old admiral there with the green neck and the grand little flagstaff on his tail.'

He pulled a handful of grain from his pocket and began to walk towards the fowl-house, lazy, his straw hat with the broken crown pulled over his eyes.

'Lid. Lid — lid — lid — lid —' he called.

'Qua. Qua — qua — qua — qua —' answered the ducks, making for land, and flapping and scrambling up the bank they streamed after him in a long waddling line. He coaxed them, pretending to throw the grain, shaking it in his hands and calling to them until they swept round him in a white ring.

From far away the fowls heard the clamour and they too came running across the paddock, their heads thrust forward, their wings spread, turning in their feet in the silly way fowls run and scolding as they came.

Then Pat scattered the grain and the greedy ducks began to gobble. Quickly he stooped, seized two, one under each arm, and strode across to the children. Their darting heads and round eyes frightened the children — all except Pip.

'Come on, sillies,' he cried, 'they can't bite. They haven't any teeth. They've only got those two little holes in their beaks for breathing through.'

'Will you hold one while I finish with the other?' asked Pat. Pip let go of Snooker. 'Won't I? Won't I? Give us one. I don't mind how much he kicks.'

He nearly sobbed with delight when Pat gave the white lump into his arms.

There was an old stump beside the door of the fowl-house. Pat grabbed the duck by the legs, laid it flat across the stump, and almost at the same moment down came the little tomahawk and the duck's head flew off the stump. Up the blood spurted over the white feathers and over his hand.

When the children saw the blood they were frightened no longer. They crowded round him and began to scream. Even Isabel leaped about crying: 'The blood! The blood!' Pip forgot all about his duck. He simply threw it away from him and shouted, 'I saw it. I saw it,' and jumped round the wood block.

Rags, with cheeks as white as paper, ran up to the little head, put out a finger as if he wanted to touch it, shrank back again and then again put out a finger. He was shivering all over.

Even Lottie, frightened little Lottie, began to laugh and pointed at the duck and shrieked: 'Look, Kezia, look.'

'Watch it!' shouted Pat. He put down the body and it began to waddle — with only a long spurt of blood where the head had been; it began to pad away without a sound towards the steep bank that led to the stream. . . . That was the crowning wonder.

'Do you see that? Do you see that?' yelled Pip. He ran among the little girls tugging at their pinafores.

'It's like a little engine. It's like a funny little railway engine,' squealed Isabel.

But Kezia suddenly rushed at Pat and flung her arms round his legs and butted her head as hard as she could against his knees.

'Put head back! Put head back!' she screamed.

When he stooped to move her she would not let go or take her head away. She held on as hard as she could and sobbed: 'Head back! Head back!' until it sounded like a loud strange hiccup.

'It's stopped. It's tumbled over. It's dead,' said Pip.

Pat dragged Kezia up into his arms. Her sun-bonnet had fallen back, but she would not let him look at her face. No, she pressed her face into a bone in his shoulder and clasped her arms round his neck.

The children stopped screaming as suddenly as they had begun. They stood round the dead duck. Rags was not frightened of the head any more. He knelt down and stroked it, now.

'I don't think the head is quite dead yet,' he said. 'Do you think it would keep alive if I gave it something to drink?'

But Pip got very cross: 'Bah! You baby.' He whistled to Snooker and went off.

When Isabel went up to Lottie, Lottie snatched away.

'What are you always touching me for, Isabel?'

'There now,' said Pat to Kezia. 'There's the grand little girl.'

She put up her hands and touched his ears. She felt something. Slowly she raised her quivering face and looked. Pat wore little round gold ear-rings. She never knew that men wore ear-rings. She was very much surprised.

'Do they come on and off?' she asked huskily.

X

Up in the house, in the warm tidy kitchen, Alice, the servant girl, was getting the afternoon tea. She was 'dressed'. She had on a black stuff dress that smelt under the arms, a white apron like a large sheet of paper, and a lace bow pinned on to her hair with two jetty pins. Also her comfortable carpet slippers were changed for a pair of black leather ones that pinched her corn on her little toe something dreadful. . . .

It was warm in the kitchen. A blow-fly buzzed, a fan of whity steam came out of the kettle, and the lid kept up a rattling jig as the water bubbled. The clock ticked in the warm air, slow and deliberate, like the click of an old woman's knitting needle, and sometimes — for no reason at all, for there wasn't any breeze — the blind swung out and back, tapping the window.

Alice was making water-cress sandwiches. She had a lump of butter on the table, a barracouta loaf, and the cresses tumbled in a white cloth.

But propped against the butter dish there was a dirty, greasy little book, half unstitched, with curled edges, and while she mashed the butter she read:

'To dream of black-beetles drawing a hearse is bad. Signifies death of one you hold near or dear, either father, husband, brother, son, or intended. If beetles crawl backwards as you watch them it means death from fire or from great height such as flight of stairs, scaffolding, etc.

'Spiders. To dream of spiders creeping over you is good. Signifies large sum of money in near future. Should party be in family way an easy confinement may be expected. But care should be taken in sixth month to avoid eating of probable present of shell fish. . . .'

How many thousand birds I see.

Oh, life. There was Miss Beryl. Alice dropped the knife and slipped the *Dream Book* under the butter dish. But she hadn't time to hide it quite, for Beryl ran into the kitchen and up to the table, and the first thing her eye lighted on were those greasy edges. Alice saw Miss

Beryl's meaning little smile and the way she raised her eyebrows and screwed up her eyes as though she were not quite sure what that could be. She decided to answer if Miss Beryl should ask her: 'Nothing as belongs to you, Miss.' But she knew Miss Beryl would not ask her.

Alice was a mild creature in reality, but she had the most marvellous retorts ready for questions that she knew would never be put to her. The composing of them and the turning of them over and over in her mind comforted her just as much as if they'd been expressed. Really, they kept her alive in places where she'd been that chivvied she'd been afraid to go to bed at night with a box of matches on the chair in case she bit the tops off in her sleep, as you might say.

'Oh, Alice,' said Miss Beryl. 'There's one extra to tea, so heat a plate of yesterday's scones, please. And put on the Victoria sandwich as well as the coffee cake. And don't forget to put little doyleys under the plates — will you? You did yesterday, you know, and the tea looked so ugly and common. And, Alice, don't put that dreadful old pink and green cosy on the afternoon teapot again. That is only for the mornings. Really, I think it ought to be kept for the kitchen — it's so shabby, and quite smelly. Put on the Japanese one. You quite understand, don't you?'

Miss Beryl had finished.

That sing aloud from every tree . . .

she sang as she left the kitchen, very pleased with her firm handling of Alice.

Oh, Alice was wild. She wasn't one to mind being told, but there was something in the way Miss Beryl had of speaking to her that she couldn't stand. Oh, that she couldn't. It made her curl up inside, as you might say, and she fair trembled. But what Alice really hated Miss Beryl for was that she made her feel low. She talked to Alice in a special voice as though she wasn't quite all there; and she never lost her temper with her — never. Even when Alice dropped anything or forgot anything important Miss Beryl seemed to have expected it to happen.

'If you please, Mrs Burnell,' said an imaginary Alice, as she buttered the scones, 'I'd rather not take my orders from Miss Beryl. I may be only a common servant girl as doesn't know how to play the guitar, but . . . .'

This last thrust pleased her so much that she quite recovered her temper.

'The only thing to do,' she heard, as she opened the dining-room door, 'is to cut the sleeves out entirely and just have a broad band of black velvet over the shoulders instead. . . .'

XI

The white duck did not look as if it had ever had a head when Alice placed it in front of Stanley Burnell that night. It lay, in beautifully basted resignation, on a blue dish — its legs tied together with a piece of string and a wreath of little balls of stuffing round it.

It was hard to say which of the two, Alice or the duck, looked the better basted; they were both such a rich colour and they both had the same air of gloss and strain. But Alice was fiery red and the duck a Spanish mahogany.

Burnell ran his eye along the edge of the carving knife. He prided himself very much upon his carving, upon making a first-class job of it. He hated seeing a woman carve; they were always too slow and they never seemed to care what the meat looked like afterwards. Now he did; he took a real pride in cutting delicate shaves of cold beef, little wads of mutton, just the right thickness, and in dividing a chicken or a duck with nice precision. . . .

'Is this the first of the home products?' he asked, knowing perfectly well that it was.

'Yes, the butcher did not come. We have found out that he only calls twice a week.'

But there was no need to apologise. It was a superb bird. It wasn't meat at all, but a kind of very superior jelly. 'My father would say,' said Burnell, 'this must have been one of those birds whose mother played to it in infancy upon the German flute. And the sweet strains of the dulcet instrument acted with such effect upon the infant mind . . . . Have some more, Beryl? You and I are the only ones in this house with a real feeling for food. I'm perfectly willing to state, in a court of law, if necessary, that I love good food.'

Tea was served in the drawing-room, and Beryl, who for some reason had been very charming to Stanley ever since he came home, suggested a game of crib. They sat at a little table near one of the open windows. Mrs Fairfield disappeared, and Linda lay in a rocking-chair, her arms above her head, rocking to and fro.

'You don't want the light — do you, Linda?' said Beryl. She moved the tall lamp so that she sat under its soft light.

How remote they looked, those two, from where Linda sat and rocked. The green table, the polished cards, Stanley's big hands and Beryl's tiny ones, all seemed to be part of one mysterious movement. Stanley himself, big and solid, in his dark suit, took his ease, and Beryl tossed her bright head and pouted. Round her throat she wore an unfamiliar velvet ribbon. It changed her, somehow — altered the shape of her face — but it was charming, Linda decided. The room smelled of lilies; there were two big jars of arums in the fire-place.

'Fifteen two — fifteen four — and a pair is six and a run of three is nine,' said Stanley, so deliberately, he might have been counting sheep.

'I've nothing but two pairs,' said Beryl, exaggerating her woe because she knew how he loved winning.

The cribbage pegs were like two little people going up the road together, turning round the sharp corner, and coming down the road again. They were pursuing each other. They did not so much want to get ahead as to keep near enough to talk — to keep near, perhaps that was all.

But no, there was always one who was impatient and hopped away as the other came up, and would not listen. Perhaps the white peg was frightened of the red one, or perhaps he was cruel and would not give the red one a chance to speak. . . .

In the front of her dress Beryl wore a bunch of pansies, and once when the little pegs were side by side, she bent over and the pansies dropped out and covered them.

'What a shame,' said she, picking up the pansies. 'Just as they had a chance to fly into each other's arms.'

'Farewell, my girl,' laughed Stanley, and away the red peg hopped.

The drawing-room was long and narrow with glass doors that gave on to the verandah. It had a cream paper with a pattern of gilt roses, and the furniture, which had belonged to old Mrs Fairfield, was dark and plain. A little piano stood against the wall with yellow pleated silk let into the carved front. Above it hung an oil painting by Beryl of a large cluster of surprised looking clematis. Each flower was the size of a small saucer, with a centre like an astonished eye fringed in black. But the room was not finished yet. Stanley had set his heart on a Chesterfield and two decent chairs. Linda liked it best as it was. . . .

Two big moths flew in through the window and round and round the circle of lamplight.

'Fly away before it is too late. Fly out again.'

Round and round they flew; they seemed to bring the silence and the moonlight in with them on their silent wings. . . .

'I've two kings,' said Stanley. 'Any good?'

'Quite good,' said Beryl.

Linda stopped rocking and got up. Stanley looked across. 'Anything the matter, darling?'

'No, nothing. I'm going to find mother.'

She went out of the room and standing at the foot of the stairs she called, but her mother's voice answered her from the verandah.

The moon that Lottie and Kezia had seen from the storeman's wagon was full, and the house, the garden, the old woman and Linda — all were bathed in dazzling light.

'I have been looking at the aloe,' said Mrs Fairfield. 'I believe it is going to flower this year. Look at the top there. Are those buds, or is it only an effect of light?'

As they stood on the steps, the high grassy bank on which the aloe rested rose up like a wave, and the aloe seemed to ride upon it like a ship with the oars lifted. Bright moonlight hung upon the lifted oars like water, and on the green wave glittered the dew.

'Do you feel it, too,' said Linda, and she spoke to her mother with the special voice that women use at night to each other as though they spoke in their sleep or from some hollow cave — 'Don't you feel that it is coming towards us?'

She dreamed that she was caught up out of the cold water into the ship with the lifted oars and the budding mast. Now the oars fell striking quickly, quickly. They rowed far away over the top of the garden trees, the paddocks and the dark bush beyond. Ah, she heard herself cry: 'Faster! Faster!' to those who were rowing.

How much more real this dream was than that they should go back to the house where the sleeping children lay and where Stanley and Beryl played cribbage.

'I believe those are buds,' she said. 'Let us go down into the garden, mother. I like that aloe. I like it more than anything here. And I am sure I shall remember it long after I've forgotten all the other things.'

She put her hand on her mother's arm and they walked down the steps, round the island and on to the main drive that led to the front gates.

Looking at it from below she could see the long sharp thorns that edged the aloe leaves, and at the sight of them her heart grew hard . . . . She particularly liked the long sharp thorns. . . . Nobody would dare to come near the ship or to follow after.

'Not even my Newfoundland dog,' thought she, 'that I'm so fond of in the daytime.'

For she really was fond of him; she loved and admired and respected him tremendously. Oh, better than anyone else in the world. She knew him through and through. He was the soul of truth and decency, and for all his practical experience he was awfully simple, easily pleased and easily hurt. . . .

If only he wouldn't jump at her so, and bark so loudly, and watch her with such eager, loving eyes. He was too strong for her; she had always hated things that rush at her, from a child. There were times when he was frightening — really frightening. When she just had not screamed at the top of her voice: 'You are killing me.' And at those times she had longed to say the most coarse, hateful things. . . .

'You know I'm very delicate. You know as well as I do that my heart is affected, and the doctor has told you I may die any moment. I have had three great lumps of children already. . . .'

Yes, yes, it was true. Linda snatched her hand from mother's arm. For all her love and respect and admiration she hated him. And how tender he always was after times like those, how submissive, how thoughtful. He would do anything for her; he longed to serve her. . . . Linda heard herself saying in a weak voice:

'Stanley, would you light a candle?'

And she heard his joyful answer: 'Of course I will, my darling,' and he leapt out of bed as though he were going to leap at the moon for her.

It had never been so plain to her as it was at this moment. There were all her feelings for him, sharp and defined, one as true as the other. And there was this other, this hatred, just as real as the rest. She could have done her feelings up in little packets and given them to Stanley. She longed to hand him that last one, for a surprise. She could see his eyes as he opened that. . . .

She hugged her folded arms and began to laugh silently. How absurd life was — it was laughable, simply laughable. And why this mania of hers to keep alive at all? For it really was a mania, she thought, mocking and laughing.

'What am I guarding myself for so preciously? I shall go on having children and Stanley will go on making money and the children and the gardens will grow bigger and bigger, with whole fleets of aloes in them for me to choose from.'

She had been walking with her head bent, looking at nothing. Now she looked up and about her. They were standing by the red and white camellia trees. Beautiful were the rich dark leaves spangled with light and the round flowers that perch among them like red and white birds. Linda pulled a piece of verbena and crumpled it, and held her hands to her mother.

'Delicious,' said the old woman. 'Are you cold, child? Are you trembling? Yes, your hands are cold. We had better go back to the house.'

'What have you been thinking about?' said Linda. 'Tell me.'

'I haven't really been thinking of anything. I wondered as we passed the orchard what the fruit trees were like and whether we should be able to make much jam this autumn. There are splendid healthy currant bushes in the vegetable garden. I noticed them to-day. I should like to see those pantry shelves thoroughly well stocked with our own jam. . . .'

XII

'My Darling Nan,

Don't think me a piggy wig because I haven't written before. I haven't had a moment, dear, and even now I feel so exhausted that I can hardly hold a pen.

Well, the dreadful deed is done. We have actually left the giddy whirl of town, and I can't see how we shall ever go back again, for my brother-in-law has bought this house "lock, stock and barrel", to use his own words.

In a way, of course, it is an awful relief, for he has been threatening to take a place in the country ever since I've lived with them — and I must say the house and garden are awfully nice — a million times better than that awful cubby-hole in town.

But buried, my dear. Buried isn't the word.

We have got neighbours, but they are only farmers — big louts of boys who seem to be milking all day, and two dreadful females with rabbit teeth who brought us some scones when we were moving and said they would be pleased to help. But my sister who lives a mile away doesn't know a soul here, so I am sure we never shall. It's pretty certain nobody will ever come out from town to see us, because though there is a bus it's an awful old rattling thing with black leather sides that any decent person would rather die than ride in for six miles.

Such is life. It's a sad ending for poor little B. I'll get to be a most awful frump in a year or two and come and see you in a mackintosh and a sailor hat tied on with a white china silk motor veil. So pretty.

Stanley says that now we are settled — for after the most awful week of my life we really are settled — he is going to bring out a couple of men from the club on Saturday afternoons for tennis. In fact, two are promised as a great treat to-day. But, my dear, if you could see Stanley's men from the club . . . rather fattish, the type who look frightfully indecent without waistcoats — always with toes that turn in rather — so conspicuous when you are walking about a court in white shoes. And they are pulling up their trousers every minute — don't you know — and whacking at imaginary things with their rackets.

I used to play with them at the club last summer, and I am sure you will know the type when I tell you that after I'd been there about three times they all called me Miss Beryl. It's a weary world. Of course mother simply loves the place, but then I suppose when I am mother's age I shall be content to sit in the sun and shell peas into a basin. But I'm not — not — not.

What Linda thinks about the whole affair, per usual, I haven't the slightest idea. Mysterious as ever. . . .

My dear, you know that white satin dress of mine. I have taken the sleeves out entirely, put bands of black velvet across the shoulders and two big red poppies off my dear sister's *chapeau*. It is a great success, though when I shall wear it I do not know.'

Beryl sat writing this letter at a little table in her room. In a way, of course, it was all perfectly true, but in another way it was all the greatest rubbish and she didn't believe a word of it. No, that wasn't true. She felt all those things, but she didn't really feel them like that.

It was her other self who had written that letter. It not only bored, it rather disgusted her real self.

'Flippant and silly,' said her real self. Yet she knew that she'd send it and she'd always write that kind of twaddle to Nan Pym. In fact, it was a very mild example of the kind of letter she generally wrote.

Beryl leaned her elbows on the table and read it through again. The voice of the letter seemed to come up to her from the page. It was faint already, like a voice heard over the telephone, high, gushing, with something bitter in the sound. Oh, she detested it to-day.

'You've always got so much animation,' said Nan Pym. 'That's why men are so keen on you.' And she had added, rather mournfully, for men were not at all keen on Nan, who was a solid kind of girl, with fat hips and a high colour — 'I can't understand how you can keep it up. But it is your nature, I suppose.'

What rot. What nonsense. It wasn't her nature at all. Good heavens, if she had ever been her real self with Nan Pym, Nannie would have jumped out of the window with surprise. . . . My dear, you know that white satin of mine. . . . Beryl slammed the letter-case to.

She jumped up and half unconsciously, half consciously she drifted over to the looking-glass.

There stood a slim girl in white — a white serge skirt, a white silk blouse, and a leather belt drawn in very tightly at her tiny waist.

Her face was heart-shaped, wide at the brows and with a pointed chin — but not too pointed. Her eyes, her eyes were perhaps her best feature; they were such a strange uncommon colour — greeny blue with little gold points in them.

She had fine black eyebrows and long lashes — so long, that when they lay on her cheeks you positively caught the light in them, someone or other had told her.

Her mouth was rather large. Too large? No, not really. Her underlip protruded a little; she had a way of sucking it in that somebody else had told her was awfully fascinating.

Her nose was her least satisfactory feature. Not that it was really ugly. But it was not half as fine as Linda's. Linda really had a perfect little nose. Hers spread rather — not badly. And in all probability she exaggerated the spreadiness of it just because it was her nose, and she was so awfully critical of herself. She pinched it with a thumb and first finger and made a little face. . . .

Lovely, lovely hair. And such a mass of it. It had the colour of fresh fallen leaves, brown and red with a glint of yellow. When she did it in a long plait she felt it on her backbone like a long snake. She loved to feel the weight of it dragging her head back, and she loved to feel it loose, covering her bare arms. 'Yes, my dear, there is no doubt about it, you really are a lovely little thing.'

At the words her bosom lifted; she took a long breath of delight, half closing her eyes.

But even as she looked the smile faded from her lips and eyes. Oh God, there she was, back again, playing the same old game. False — false as ever. False as when she'd written to Nan Pym. False even when she was alone with herself, now.

What had that creature in the glass to do with her, and why was she staring? She dropped down to one side of her bed and buried her face in her arms.

'Oh,' she cried. 'I am so miserable — so frightfully miserable. I know that I'm silly and spiteful and vain; I'm always acting a part. I'm never my real self for a moment.' And plainly, plainly, she saw her false self running up and down the stairs, laughing a special trilling laugh if they had visitors, standing under the lamp if a man came to dinner, so that he should see the light on her hair, pouting and pretending to be a little girl when she was asked to play the guitar. Why? She even kept it up for Stanley's benefit. Only last night when he was reading the paper her false self had stood beside him and leaned against his shoulder on purpose. Hadn't she put her hand over his, pointing out something so that he should see how white her hand was beside his brown one.

How despicable! Despicable! Her heart was cold with rage. 'It's marvellous how you keep it up,' said she to the false self. But then it was only because she was so miserable — so miserable. If she had been happy and leading her own life, her false life would cease to be. She saw the real Beryl — a shadow . . . a shadow. Faint and unsubstantial she shone. What was there of her except the radiance? And for what tiny moments she was really she. Beryl could almost remember every one of them. At those times she had felt: 'Life is rich and mysterious and good, and I am rich and mysterious and good, too.' Shall I ever be that Beryl for ever? Shall I? How can I? And was there ever a time when I did not have a false self? . . . But just as she had got that far she heard the sound of little steps running along the passage; the door handle rattled. Kezia came in.

'Aunt Beryl, mother says will you please come down? Father is home with a man and lunch is ready.'

Botheration! How she had crumpled her skirt, kneeling in that idiotic way.

'Very well, Kezia.' She went over to the dressing table and powdered her nose.

Kezia crossed too, and unscrewed a little pot of cream and sniffed it. Under her arm she carried a very dirty calico cat.

When Aunt Beryl ran out of the room she sat the cat up on the dressing table and stuck the top of the cream jar over its ear.

'Now look at yourself,' said she sternly.

The calico cat was so overcome by the sight that it toppled over backwards and bumped and bumped on to the floor. And the top of the cream jar flew through the air and rolled like a penny in a round on the linoleum — and did not break.

But for Kezia it had broken the moment it flew through the air, and she picked it up, hot all over, and put it back on the dressing table.

Then she tip-toed away, far too quickly and airily. . . .

frank sargeson

that summer

IT was a good farm job I had that winter, but I've always suffered from itchy feet so I never thought I'd stick it for long. All the same I stayed until the shearing, and I quit after we'd carted the wool out to the station, just a few bales at a time. It was just beginning December and I had a good lot of chips saved up, so I thought I'd have a spell in town which I hadn't had for a good long time, and maybe I'd strike a town job before my chips ran out.

The old bloke I was working for tried hard to get me to stay but there was nothing doing. I liked him all right and the tucker was good, but him and his missis were always rowing, and there was just the three of us stuck away there with hardly any company to speak of. I had to sleep on an old sofa in the kitchen because it was only a slab whare they lived in with two rooms, and I got a bit sick of hearing them fighting every night when they'd gone to bed. The old bloke told me he'd had money enough to build a decent house long ago, but his missis said if he did she'd be there for keeps. So she wouldn't let him, but they'd gone on living there just the same.

I had to get up early to walk the six miles to catch the train, and I never saw the old bloke but his missis came out just when I was going. She had a little bag of sovereigns that I'd never seen before and she made me take one, only she said it was to keep and not to spend so as I'd always remember her. And when I got down the road she came running along and grabbed hold of me for a kiss, and then she stood in the road and waved. She looked a bit of a sketch I can tell you, with her hair hanging down and her old man's coat on over her nightgown. I felt a bit sorry and wished in a way I wasn't going, because the farm away back there in the valley looked sort of nice and peaceful with the sun just getting up on such a fine morning, and only a sheep calling out now and then, and the dogs barking because I hadn't let them off the chain when I started down the road. And I looked at the hills and thought what a hell of a good worker I was to have cut all the fern and scrub I had in the winter. But I thought no, I've got to be on the move. Many a time I've wished I didn't have my itchy feet, but it's never much good wishing for things to be any different.

So I caught the train all right, but I had a few minutes to spare and I talked to the porter. He'd been to a dance the night before, he was yawning his head off and looked as if he needed a wash.

The old bloke giving you a spell? he said.

No, I said, I'm going out for good.

What, he said, turning it in. You'll never get another job.

I'll be O.K. I said.

So he told me about how he'd got a letter from his sister, and her husband was out of a job and things couldn't be worse in town. But he hadn't finished telling me when the train came in. So I got on board, but it was a slow train that stopped to shunt all the way along the line, and I was pretty fed-up by the time I got into town early that afternoon.

I left my bag at the station and after I'd had a feed I just walked about the streets looking at the shops and the people. I thought to myself, now I'll have a good time. I thought maybe I'd pick up with a girl, and with the chips in my pocket I knew I could kick around for a good many weeks before I'd need to think about getting a job. I thought I'd go to the flicks, but it seemed better just to be in the streets. I'd have plenty of time to do all the things I wanted to do, so there wasn't any need to go rushing things. Because things never turn out as good as you think they will, so it's always just as well to get all the fun you can out of thinking what they're going to be like beforehand. I went and sat in the park, and whenever there was a girl came past that I thought might have me on I'd watch out to see if she'd look me over. But there was nothing doing. And I said to myself well, a knock-back from one of yous isn't going to make me lose any sleep. But I hoped it wouldn't be long before I had a bit of luck all the same.

After I'd had another feed I thought I'd better look for a place to sleep, so I went and got my bag from the station, and then I found a joint that was kept by a Mrs Clegg and I thought it would be O.K. It was a two-storeyed place standing in between a butcher's shop and a brick warehouse. You paid for your bed and had to get your meals out, but there was a gas ring at the top of the stairs, and Mrs Clegg said I could borrow a spare teapot and make myself a cup of tea if I wanted to. So I thought that would suit me fine, because I could buy myself a couple of buns and have a lie-in some mornings just for a change after the farm.

Mrs Clegg was quite a decent sort, but she had a glass eye that was cracked right down the middle, and it was funny the way she sort of looked out at you through the crack. Her old man was out of a job and that was why she was running the joint, though seeing she only had three rooms to let she said she wasn't making a fortune.

When she'd fixed my bed up she took me down to the kitchen to give me the teapot, and her old man was reading the paper, and their little girl was saying pretty boy to a budgie that was answering her back. Though sometimes it would ring a little bell instead. Mr Clegg told me he'd been a cook on a boat but now he couldn't get a keel. It was hard, he said, because he liked being at sea, though I thought by the look of him it must have been only a coastal or even a scow he'd worked on. He was pretty red too, though he said he hadn't been until he'd had experience of being on relief.

Of course it was the sort of talk I'd heard a good many times knocking around, so I didn't take much notice. Mrs Clegg kept on chipping in and they'd squabble a bit though not as bad as the old couple on the farm, and the little girl left off talking to the budgie and started asking her mother if she could have some money to spend. She asked about fifty times before her mother said no, and asked her if she thought money grew on trees. So then she began to ask if money did grow on trees, and when she'd got to about the fiftieth time I chipped in myself and said I'd have to go.

But it was only to go down the street and buy what I wanted so I could lie-in if I felt like it, and then I turned in, because walking about the town in my good shoes had made me feel tireder than if I'd done a day's work on the farm. And I thought I wouldn't need any rocking to get to sleep, but my room was right over the kitchen and I could hear the pair of them going it hammer and tongs, and then the youngster got spanked and the way she yelled gave me the dingbats. It was too much like what I'd been used to, and for the first time that day I didn't feel so good about throwing up my job and coming to town. Because I thought there wasn't any sense in having itchy feet if they only got you out of a steady job and into a place like Mrs Clegg's. And there wasn't any sense in having them anyhow, because they never gave you any peace. Yet all the time I was thinking like that I was asking myself whether I'd get up and clear out right away, or whether I'd wait until daylight, and I knew that wherever I went I wouldn't go back to the farm. But while I was trying to decide I must have gone to sleep because I don't remember anything more.

But it turned out I never shifted from Mrs Clegg's, not for a long time as I'll tell you.

The first morning I stayed in bed, and I thought nobody could be any better off than I was. It was a good bed to lie on after the sofa on the farm, I had my chips, and there wasn't a job I wouldn't take on if I got the chance. But for a while I was going to have a good time just kicking around. I laughed when I heard Mrs Clegg chase her old man out of the house, and I tried to get an earful when I heard somebody out on the landing place. There were only two other rooms upstairs but Mrs Clegg hadn't said if they were let. I didn't see anyone that first morning anyhow, because every time I told myself I'd better get up I thought no, it's too good where I am. Though once I sat up to look out the window, and the weather was good, but there was nothing much to see except the butcher's backyard on one side and the wall of the warehouse on the other, and Mrs Clegg's washing hung out in between.

It wasn't until late that I'd had my tea and was all flossied up, and by that time there was no one about the house except the little girl, and she was hanging the budgie's cage on a nail on the front of the house. She was the thinnest kid you ever saw, with legs like sticks, and a real old woman's face. She said her name was Fanny and asked me what mine was. So I told her to call me Bill, and she said, Does money grow on trees Bill?

It might do, I said. I couldn't say for certain.

We've got a tree, she said, so you can mind the house while I go and look.

No, I said, but hang on until tomorrow and we'll both have a look. See you mind the house, I said, because I don't want anyone to break into my room.

Then just along the street I passed Mr Clegg. He had a waistcoat on over his flannel, and he was leaning up against the wall of a pub talking to the taxi-drivers. I bought a newspaper and one of the taxi-drivers asked me if I wanted to take a double, so I took a half dollar one even though all the good ones were filled up. Because taxi-drivers are good blokes to keep in with, they usually know of a house to take you to if you don't happen to know of one yourself. And I thought I ought to stand Mr Clegg a drink, but what with the taxi-drivers there were too many around, so I put it off until another time. You could tell by the look of him he got a good few anyhow.

There wasn't much I could do before it was time to eat, so I went into the park to read the paper, but instead I watched an old man who was having a wash in the fountain. After he'd finished washing he looked in the water and spent a lot of time combing his hair, then he came past my seat and asked me if I'd done with the paper, so I said I had and gave it to him. But a young joker got up from the next seat and said he wished I hadn't done that, because he was going to ask me for the paper himself.

Stiff luck, I said.

He said he'd had a date with a sheila the Sunday before but she hadn't turned up. It was right there where he'd been sitting, and he'd been waiting at the same time every day ever since. She might have put an ad in the paper, he said. I felt like telling him to forget it but he was taking it pretty bad, so instead I asked him if he'd come and eat, because by the look of his clothes I'd have said he was up against it.

I shouted him a bob dinner and I could tell by the way he ate he was in need of a binder, but he never said whether he was out of a job or not. He just wanted to tell me what a great sheila she was that had let him down, so to shut him up I said we'd go to the flicks. But it was a mistake, because after the lights went out a girl came and sat in the seat next to me, and when I put my leg over her way she was willing. I pushed and she pushed back, and it wasn't long before I had hold of her hand, and what with holding her hand and wondering how I'd get rid of this fellow Sam if she looked any good when the lights went up I never had much idea what the first part of the programme was about.

Well, the lights went up and she certainly looked good. She gave me the onceover and maybe she thought I didn't look so bad either, but she could tell I was with Sam and Sam didn't look so good. I said if he liked he could take my tin and go out and roll himself one, but he said no, he could wait till after. He just wanted to talk about his sheila, she was a bit like the girl in the big picture he said. It made me properly narked but I hadn't got the heart to tell him off. Me and the girl got to work again while the big picture was on and this Sam was that thick in the head I bet he never guessed a thing, but soon as the lights went up she went for her life while Sam was saying he'd have a fag if it was O.K. with me. So I gave him my tin, and I thought that's that, but I could have crowned him all the same. He wanted to get going about his sheila again but I said, To hell with all that, let's go and have a drink.

So we got in a pub and we both had a good few in by closing time, and then they said we could carry on upstairs if we liked, so it wasn't long before we were properly canned. Sam talked about his sheila and once I'd got canned I didn't mind. I didn't mind doing all the paying either, though I spent a lot more money than I intended, and when it was about ten o'clock we took a taxi and went to a dance that Sam knew about. It was a pretty flash turnout with a lot of streamers and balloons, but what with Sam looking like a proper bum and the both of us being canned they wouldn't let us in. So we went to another place that was a lot tougher, and nobody said anything, not even when we started butting in on other blokes' sheilas. We got a couple of them to come outside for a spot, but they went crook when we spilt beer over their skirts, and in the end there was nothing doing. And so far as I was concerned it didn't matter because I was that canned I wouldn't have had a hope of doing anything. And I don't remember getting home to Mrs Clegg's but I was there the next morning when I woke up.

It was Sunday and the church bells were ringing, but after the night before I didn't feel so hot until I had a drink out of a bottle I found in my pants' pocket. Then I felt better, and I looked out the window and the weather was still good, and Mrs Clegg's washing was still hanging on the line. I thought I might go and lie on the beach in the sun, but Fanny came and asked if I'd go and look at the tree to see if there was any money.

There was nobody about upstairs but Mrs Clegg was in the kitchen, and her old man had put his chair on the bricks outside and was reading the paper. Fanny and I went down to the fence where there was a pretty good smell, because a heap of sawdust out of the butcher's shop was over the other side. We couldn't see any money hanging on the tree and Fanny was disappointed, but I said maybe it was the wrong time of the year. Fanny said perhaps it had fallen in the grass, it would if it was ripe, she said. So we looked and I had my fingers on a sixpence in my pocket, and then I thought no, I'll give the kid a real thrill, I'll make it a bob. So I dropped the bob and so help me if it wasn't the sovereign the old lady had given me on the farm. I put my foot out but Fanny was too quick. She didn't know what to make of it but she wouldn't let me have a look, and before I could stop her she'd run up the bricks singing out that it was a money-tree. Her old man looked over the top of his paper and held out his hand, but Mrs Clegg suddenly showed up and got in first. And then there was a proper hullabaloo, the two of them going it hammer and tongs, and Fanny howling and jumping up and down on the bricks.

Come on Fanny, I said, those legs of yours will snap off at the knees if you're not careful.

I got her to come back and we had another look, and I took jolly good care it was only a sixpence this time. Her old man wanted to take it off her but Mrs Clegg wouldn't let him, so there was another hullabaloo. And Fanny wanted to keep on looking but Mr Clegg said if he caught her near the tree again he'd tan her hide.

Well, I felt a bit sore over the sovereign, but I thought if Mrs Clegg put it towards buying a new glass eye I wouldn't mind so much. Fanny had just about decided I was her property and wanted me to play penny catches, but her mother came out and started to weed round a row of tomatoes she had growing up against the fence, and I said if she'd tell me where the spade was I'd make a proper job for her. Fanny went to get the spade but Mr Clegg came out and said he was going to do a bit of digging himself.

You're going to do a bit of digging, Mrs Clegg said, but he didn't say anything.

It was under the tree that he went to dig and off and on he'd be down there for a good few weeks after.

I wished I'd gone to the beach because the sun was real hot and there wasn't a cloud. It had been a dry spring and everybody said it was going to be a hot summer. There was the yarn they always say about how the Maoris had said so. Though it was getting a bit late in the day to go off to the beach so I played penny catches with Fanny, but the ball kept on banging into the washing and in the end Mrs Clegg went crook, though she needn't have done because her clothes weren't as clean as all that. So then I told Fanny I hadn't any more time to go on playing, but it was really because I'd seen a smart-looking piece of goods drying her face and having a bo-peep out the bathroom window, which was upstairs next to mine. I went up the stairs about six at a time and she was crossing the landing place with only a sort of kimono-thing on. Hello, I said, but she only said, How do you do, and went inside and slammed the door of her room. She didn't look nearly so good as she'd looked through the window anyhow, she was a little piece that somehow made you think of a kid's doll and not my type at all. So of course I told myself I couldn't be worried.

I began to feel empty so I went down town and had some dinner in a place that was run by a Dalmatian. Being Sunday there wasn't much doing, so he brought out his two little boys to show me, though one was so shy he got behind his father's legs and only put his head out now and then. And when his missis brought the tucker he said how she wouldn't learn to speak English. You could only grin at her, though I talked to the kids and they were great kids, the sort of little blokes I wouldn't mind if I had myself.

My wife thinks always of our country, the Dally said. She says that if she learns to talk here I will not take her back to our country.

And will you? I said.

Yes I will, he said. But first I must have a lot of money. My wife she wants us to go now but I say no. It is lonely for her when she will not talk but she has her little boys and soon they will take her shopping which she will not go now, because she does not talk.

Anyhow *he* talked, and I liked listening to him, and I'd grin at the wife now and then just to sort of include her in the conversation, and the kid that wasn't shy sat on a chair with his legs stuck out and took it all in. I thought they were a real nice family, I promised I'd go there again, and when I came out I was wishing in a way I was settled down myself, because here I was in town all on my own, and that afternoon I felt at a bit of a loose end. Sunday afternoons on the farm when there was nothing else doing I'd go and shoot pigeons away up in the bush, and I wouldn't feel as much on my own as I did now in a town full of houses and people. But it's no good letting those things get you down, so I went back to Mrs Clegg's to lie on my bed and read a True Story. I read them sometimes though the yarns are all a lot of baloney, nothing like real life at all. But I'd hardly got started when Fanny came in and I didn't shoo her out because I wanted to do a bit of fishing.

Fanny, I said, who lives here besides me?

Terry, she said.

Terry? I said. Isn't there a lady?

That's Mrs Popeye, she said.

That's a funny name, I said.

Mr Popeye doesn't live here, she said, because he's a sailorman. But he comes sometimes.

I see, I said. And I got the idea all right but I didn't have a chance to ask her any more because Mr Clegg came up and asked if I felt like having a drink. He'd had a shave and put on a collar, though without any tie.

Yes, I said. But can you get one?

Come on, he said. And you clear away out of here, he said to Fanny. Look at her legs, he said.

I've got nice legs, Fanny said, and she pulled her dress up to her waist to show me.

Of course you have, I said. Only you want to be careful they don't snap off.

Her old man told her off for pulling her dress up, and we left her talking to the budgie which was kidding to itself in a piece of looking-glass. But all the way along to the pub Mr Clegg kept on about her legs.

You look at them, he said, it just shows you the way a working man gets it put across him every time.

Too right, I said, but I wasn't anxious to start talking politics.

We went along to the pub where I'd seen Mr Clegg the day before and the pub-stiff that was on the door told us to go upstairs where there was quite a few, including all sorts, men and women. And we hadn't been there long when the barman got the tip and we were all shoved up a little stairway on to the next floor. But that was the only scare, nobody was caught, and by the time it was dark the pair of us had a good few in, and each time I paid because there never was a time when Mr Clegg even looked like paying. And things being what they were I was beginning to feel like calling it a day, only just then a bloke came in that was a cobber of Mr Clegg's.

He was a cook off a boat too, a tremendous big man, but dressed more like a stoker in dungarees that would hardly button across his chest. He didn't have any singlet on underneath and his chest was all hair, and when he'd had a few drinks he started to sweat, and you could see it oozing out and running down under the hair until it soaked into his trousers. I shouted him and Mr Clegg and he shouted back, and then I got talking to the barman and dropped out while the cook went on shouting Mr Clegg. The both of them talked politics and the cook sounded a good deal more bolshy than Mr Clegg was. And then a tall bloke joined in. He'd been sitting there on his own listening, and he started off by saying he didn't see anything wrong with capitalism. Well, that got the cook going good and proper, he paid for whiskies for the three of them and they went on and had one after another, the cook always paying and calling the big nobs that run the world for all the names he could think of. Me and the barman just listened, and after the cook had spent about a quid him and Mr Clegg went off together, and then the tall bloke came over and asked the barman what the cook's name was. But the barman said he didn't know.

Come on, he said, you know.

I don't know, the barman said.

You heard what he was talking about?

Sure, the barman said.

He's a bolshy.

Maybe, the barman said.

What do you reckon's wrong with capitalism? the tall bloke said, but the barman wouldn't answer. What's the name of his cobber? he said.

I don't know, the barman said.

Well, instead of saying anything more he went downstairs and the barman winked at me and said he was a demon, and I wasn't surprised because I'd picked there was something wrong with him right from the start. But it wasn't long before he came back with the boss.

Terry, the boss said, you know the name of that big fellow.

I don't know, the barman said.

You better tell.

No I don't know, the barman said, and considering the way they were picking on him I felt like having a go at cleaning up the pair of them.

Anyhow the boss saw it was no good so they went out and I asked the barman to have a drink. You could see it had shaken him up and we both had double gins. And seeing there was nobody else there just then he said we'd have another two on the house. It would be good for his cough, he said. He had an awful cough. And once having got started we kept on for quite a while. He was a lot older than me, with one of those hard faces all covered with wrinkles like Aussies have, but I sort of had the feeling he was a decent bloke.

You've got a hard dial, I said, but I bet you've got a kind heart.

I'll say, he said.

I bet you have, I said. But of course I was stunned. Anyhow, I said, isn't your name Mr O'Connor?

Sure, he said.

Well, I wanted to tell him I'd been sort of trying to place his face right from the jump, and now I'd suddenly remembered. One time when I was working on a farm he brought out a racehorse to graze. It was a good while ago but I knew he was the same bloke, though I didn't get the chance to make certain because a crowd came in and he had to get busy. He pushed me over one more double gin which he only pretended to ring up on the peter, but there wasn't a chance to talk. So I thought I'd better shove off or I'd be ending up tight as I was the night before. I said so long to the barman and that I'd be seeing him, and it was only when I was trying to walk straight along the street, just to see how tight I was, that I remembered the boss had called him Terry. Which made me pull up while I tried to figure out whether he might be the same bloke as Fanny's Terry. I thought maybe I'd go back and find out, but instead I kept on along the street to find out how tight I was. I could walk straight all right but it didn't mean anything, because sometimes you get head-drunk, and sometimes you get leg-drunk, and there's a lot of difference between the two.

I thought I'd better cry off the booze for a bit, so all next week I went to the beach. It was too good to miss, specially as it was so baking hot round the streets. The asphalt went soft and there were marks of motor tyres all over the road, and away in front of you the heat made it look as if water was lying on the road, so you'd naturally think of the beach. And it was certainly great to be out there. I'd go on a tram as far as it went, and then I'd walk on to a quiet bit of beach that I knew about.

Most days nobody'd come around, but I had company, because the first morning on the tram I met a bloke named Ted who was doing the same as myself. I'd meet him every day, and I'd always bring a couple of riggers and he'd buy some buns, and it was certainly nice to have his company. He never had much to say so I couldn't make out hardly anything about him, though I thought he looked a bit of a hard-shot. He wasn't a rangy specimen like me, no, he was nuggety, with one of those faces that is flat on the front of your head. And being dark he didn't get sunburnt nearly so bad as I did. To kick off with we'd fool about in the water, and if there was nobody around we wouldn't worry about any togs. Then we'd fool about on the beach and lie in the sand, and when it was time for the buns and the beer they'd go down well, and in the afternoon we'd just about go to sleep. It was a great life I can tell you, though coming home in the tram we'd be properly tired out, which is what lying in the sun always does to you. Ted'd say, So long, see you again tomorrow, and I'd be too tired for anything except a feed and a talkie, and if the talkie wasn't any good I'd just about go to sleep. And one night the joker sitting next to me had to poke me in the ribs because I was snoring.

Well, it was like that for a whole week, and some nights my sunburn was that bad I could hardly sleep. By Sunday I thought I'd better give it a rest, but the weather was still holding out so I thought no, the going's good, I'll give it one more pop.

And that day Ted was there as usual but he had his girl with him. I didn't feel like butting in but he called me over and gave me a knock-down, and she was certainly the goods, a good-looker and a great figure, sort of streamlined all over, though you could tell she had a temper. She wasn't like Ted, she was a mag, and all the way along until we got to our beach she talked about how nice the water looked, and she'd make us stop to pick up shells and look in the pools to see things. But it wasn't long before we were undressed and in the water, and nearly all morning we had a great time just fooling about. Mavis was the girl's name and she'd brought a thermos and plenty of sandwiches, and she made me have some. I'd brought my riggers as usual but Mavis wouldn't have any, because she said drink only brought sorrow into people's lives. Ted said he was willing to take the risk so we drank the beer between us, and then Ted lay on his back with his togs rolled down and said this sort of life would do him for keeps. Mavis kept on looking his way and you could tell she was nuts on him, but I knew there was something wrong because she couldn't help picking on him every chance she got.

Yes, she said, you can be a sand-boy every day while I go and work in that damn shop.

Forget it kid, Ted said.

Listen to him Bill, she said. The first time we made a date he turned up tight in a taxi. He was broke too, and I had to pay five shillings for the fare.

And instead of saying anything to that Ted just rolled over and curled himself round Mavis.

Don't make out you're a smoodger, she said, because you're not.

If anyone knows anything better than this sun lead me to it, Ted said.

He's a baby over the cold Bill, Mavis said. Last winter I knitted him a woolly and he used it to go to bed in, with his underpants on too. And what's the good of a man when he goes to bed like that?

Ted rolled away from her then, he lay on his side with his back to the pair of us.

Look at that sea, he said.

But Mavis couldn't stop herself from trying to put nasty ones across him, though I bet she knew she was making him feel sore.

Yes, she said, it's all right for you, but what's a hot day in that damn shop. It only means us girls have to let our stockings down to try and keep cool. If they didn't let you go home at night you might just as well be in gaol.

You'll get over it kid, Ted said.

Listen to him Bill, Mavis said. He works about three months a year, so where would he be if he hadn't got me?

You get your money's worth sweetie, Ted said.

Listen to him Bill, Mavis said. That's what he says. When I knitted him a woolly and he used it to go to bed in.

Well, Ted got up and went away and tried to see how far he could throw stones up the cliff. And Mavis kept on talking, but I pretended to go to sleep and when I gave a few snores she didn't say anything more. But I looked and she was crying, though when I looked again she was reading a True Romance, but it wasn't long before she gave that up and just stretched herself out in the sun. Ted came back and stretched himself out too, with his arm round Mavis, and we must have all gone to sleep because for a long time nobody moved or said anything.

But when we were sitting up and talking again Mavis must have temporarily got all the dirt out of her system, because instead of picking on Ted she made us laugh with yarns about people she served in the shop, and the way they talked and carried on, and what she'd do with the money if she ever won an Art Union. And afterwards we all went in for another swim, and Ted said he'd bet me I wasn't game to swim round a buoy that was anchored a good way out from the shore. So I took him on, but when I was out there hanging on to the buoy for a rest I got a bit of a surprise, because they'd both gone out of the water and were just about dressed. I swam back fast, but by the time I touched bottom they'd climbed nearly to the top of the cliff, and I could hear Ted swearing at Mavis and telling her to come on. And when I sang out for them to wait Ted sang out that they'd wait at the tram.

Well, I didn't hurry myself. If they waited at the tram that would be all right, but if they didn't that would be all right too. Because I thought it wouldn't be long before Mavis was picking on Ted again, and I wasn't anxious to be there when she started. And it was only when I'd finished dressing that I found out my money was gone.

Of course it was a knock and I certainly felt bad. I thought well, I hope poor old Mavis gets her whack, but Ted being the sort of joker I'd gathered he was I didn't suppose she would. She probably wasn't in the joke. What's money anyhow, I thought. I'd been in town just over a week and had a good time, even if I hadn't had any luck so far as a girl was concerned. To hell with Ted and Mavis, I thought.

But it was hard all the same. I thought I could go into every shop in town until I found out where Mavis worked. But I knew I wouldn't do that. Ted might be no good but I could tell she was nuts on him, and it'd be rocking it into her properly to put the police on to him. I'd never be able to prove anything anyhow, and my idea of the johns is that a man wants to keep well away from them no matter what goes wrong.

My sugar's gone, I thought, that's all there is to it. Now I've got to look for a job.

Well, it wasn't the first time I'd been broke, and I knew I'd feel better if I went home and slept on it. The main thing was to stop myself from doing any more thinking. I didn't have the price of a tram fare because Ted had left me a skinner, so I started to walk into town. But I didn't hurry myself, and I kept stopping to look at everything I saw going on in the streets just to keep my mind occupied.

And as it turned out it wasn't long before I got a notion. I went past a house that was hidden behind some trees and just over the fence there was a garden. So I walked up and down and when there was nobody in sight I hopped over the fence and pulled up a plant that looked as if it might be growing into a little tree. I wrapped it in a sheet of newspaper I was keeping because of the acceptances, and I'd only gone a few more streets when I met a lady that looked as if she might do a bit of business.

Excuse me lady, I said, but maybe you're interested in gardening.

Yes, she said, I am.

Well, I said, I'm off a boat and I got this in Jamaica.

Why, she said, it looks like a something or other.

I don't know what you call them, I said, but I've never seen them out here and you never saw such a pretty flower.

So she asked me if it had got long red petals.

No, I said, the flower's blue-coloured and as big as my head. You don't see many of them even in Jamaica, I said, so I reckon it ought to be worth a good five bob out here.

So then she said she hoped I wasn't telling her a story.

Oh no lady, I said, I wouldn't do that.

We had a bit more barney and finally she took it for three and six, and soon as I'd got the sugar in my pocket I didn't lose any time in shifting along. But I didn't take a tram, no, I kept on walking and slowed down again after a while, and got into town pretty late, so although I was feeling a bit empty I went straight home to bed and was lucky enough to get to sleep before I had a chance to start doing any more thinking.

And next morning I woke up early and the weather still looked good, though of course I didn't think it looked quite so good as it had other mornings. I hadn't anything to eat but I made a cup of tea, then I thought I'd better get down town to see about a job. I looked at the paper in the Library but there was nothing doing, and I spent the morning going round the registry offices but there was nothing doing in any of those places either. And in the afternoon it was just the same. I tried all the registry offices again, and when it was time for the afternoon paper to come out I waited outside where they always stick up the front page to let people see the ads. But I could hardly get near for the crowd, and when I did get a bo-peep there weren't any jobs that I thought I'd have a chance of getting. So I went inside to look at the file, because I'd missed seeing the results of the double I had on with the taxi-driver, and what with going to the beach all the week before, and having plenty of chips in my pocket, I hadn't worried. Well, I'd picked a first and a second, and the second had only got beat by a head. It was the first time I'd ever got so close and I got a bit excited, because I thought if I could get that close I could pick two winners, so I decided I'd see the taxi-driver and take another instead of breaking into my three and six, which I hadn't done even though I was feeling pretty empty inside.

But first I hung round the streets a bit longer, standing on the corners to roll cigarettes and watch the crowd, though seeing I have my itchy feet I never can stand still for very long, particularly when everyone else is on the move. Then I went up to see the taxi-driver but he wasn't on the stand. His cobbers said he'd be back soon so I waited but he didn't turn up, and I had to go into the pub because I wanted to pick up a bit of counter-lunch. I saw Mr Clegg there with a half-handle in front of him and he looked as if he was making it last a good long while, but I dodged about in the crowd to keep him from seeing me and asked for a half-handle myself. The eats were late coming out and I had to make my drink last a lot longer than I thought I would, but when the trays did come I was one of the first to be in, and I finished up by putting away quite a good feed. The barman took my half-handle to fill it again but I said, Wait a minute, where can I see Terry?

Terry? he said, Terry's left here.

All right, I said, fill her up. Where's he working now? I said.

The barman didn't know, so I had my drink and came out. The taxi-driver was there and I took the double, and he said I was lucky because it was a new chart he'd just got out. There were hardly any taken certainly, so I picked a good one, but at the last moment I decided I wouldn't cough up the sugar just then. The taxi-driver didn't look any too pleased but he said O.K. boy, I'm a sport.

Then I didn't know what to do. I didn't know whether to blow in a bob on a talkie or not, so to put off trying to decide I thought I'd go and have a lie-down on my bed. But Fanny was just taking the budgie inside, and she showed me the way it could swing a ping-pong ball that was tied to the top of its cage. She'd bought it with the money from the money-tree, she said.

The old man isn't home yet, Bill, she said, so we can go and look.

No, I said, not just now.

But she pulled me by the hand, so I gave in and we had to walk on the ground that Mr Clegg had dug to get under the tree, but it was only a tray bit that I dropped. Fanny danced up and down and went to show her mother and I went upstairs, and when the old man came home I heard them having a row. And later on I looked out the window and he was down there digging.

But being all on my pat up there that evening somehow gave me the dingbats properly. I couldn't decide what to do to fill in the time, and I couldn't keep my mind off thinking about a job. I tried reading my True Story but it was no good. I'd just lie on my bed but that was no good either, and I'd have to keep getting up to walk up and down. I'd stop in the middle of the floor to roll a cigarette and listen to them downstairs. I'd think, my God I've got to have someone to talk to, but even after I'd turned out the light and had my hand on the doorknob I'd go back and just flop on the bed. But the last time I flopped I must have dozed off, because I woke up lying in my clothes, and I wondered where the hell I was. I'd been dreaming, and I still seemed to be in the dream, because there wasn't one sound I could hear no matter how hard I listened. Then somebody started coughing and I knew where I was, but next minute I was back in the dream again, and I kept on dreaming and waking up right until it began to get light, though the last time I dropped off I slept a long time and never dreamt a thing.

It doesn't matter what sort of night you have, things are always different in the morning. I didn't waste any time hopping out of bed because I didn't want to give myself a chance to start doing any more thinking. And I didn't have much of a chance anyhow, because while I was mucking about getting my bed made, I heard Mrs Clegg come upstairs and start giving somebody a tongue-banging. It developed into a real ding-dong row, and so help me if the other voice didn't sound like Terry O'Connor's, and so far as I could tell he was giving just about as good as he got.

Shut the door, was the last thing he sang out. And Mrs Clegg sang out, Shut it yourself.

So I went out to get an eyeful and there was Terry sitting up in bed reading the paper.

Gee, I said, so this is where you hang out.

Hello boy, he said, and I went and sat on his bed and said I'd heard he'd left the pub.

That's right, he said.

You know Terry, I said, I remember you. You remember Mr Fletcher's farm?

Sure, he said.

Well, I said, I remember when you brought out a horse.

That's right, he said. Well, he said, it looks like another scorcher, and he threw the paper away and did a big stretch and we yarned for a bit and I asked him who the dame was that lived next door.

That's our Maggie, he said.

She's not my type, I said.

No, Terry said, nor mine either, and he said he wouldn't have her on if she was hung with diamonds. Well, he said, I suppose a man's got to rise and shine.

I've got to go and look for a job, I said. And Terry said he was looking for a job too, and while he was getting dressed I looked in the paper but there didn't seem to be any jobs going. We went down town together anyhow, and I thought it was certainly great to have a bit of company. We passed a coffee and sandwich place and Terry asked if I felt like a bite.

Not specially, I said, but I'll have one.

So we had coffee and sandwiches, and I paid because the girl was waiting and Terry just went on eating. And when we came out we ran right into the taxi-driver that had the double chart.

Hello Terry, he said, how's things?

A box of birds, Terry said, and the taxi-driver brought out his chart. But Terry said he was stiff because the one he would have picked had been taken. Too bad, the taxi-driver said, and I told Terry the double I'd picked, and he said I'd beaten him to it and I'd be in the money there was nothing surer.

So that was all right, Terry made me think my luck was going to be in, and we went round all the registry offices together but there was nothing doing. So I asked Terry if he couldn't go to his Union, but he said it wouldn't be any good.

I had something to say about the Union boss last meeting, he said, and that's why I'm on the street. That and not letting that bloody dee bulldoze me.

Gee, I said, that's hard.

But Terry said it was best to forget it, and I asked him to come to the Dalmatian's for a feed. So we went along and the place was pretty full, but the Dally was working the peter and he remembered me.

You are back again, he said. That is good for me.

Good for me too, I said, because I want to eat.

Good, he said, good. It is good to eat.

Too right, I said.

Well, we had three courses and it certainly felt good afterwards, and after we'd rolled cigarettes I told Terry to wait because I wanted to speak to the Dally. Terry said O.K. and I barged into the kitchen and the Dally didn't look any too pleased.

What do you want? he said.

Well, I said, sort of embarrassed a bit.

Be quick, he said.

Well, I said, I suppose you couldn't give me a job.

No, he said, I cannot give you a job. Already I have too many to pay. They are not too many for the work, but they are too many to pay.

Yes, I said, but I thought if anybody turned it in.

You think somebody will walk out, he said. But nobody will walk out. It is always easy to walk out but today it is hard to walk in, so today nobody will walk out even if it is easy.

Then his missis put her head in the door and he told me to wait a minute. And soon as he'd gone the cook, who was a fat little joker and walked like a proper queen, came over and asked if it was a job I was after.

You come back tomorrow, he said. And when I asked him why tomorrow he said the bloke they had washing dishes out in the pantry would have to go to the quack.

What's he got? I said.

You know, the cook said. He showed me this morning and he's got it pretty bad.

Good, I said, and thanks for the tip.

And then the boss came back. You are still here, he said, but I cannot give you any work.

Never mind, I said.

You can pay now, he said. One dinner one shilling, and he held out his hand.

No, I said, two dinners two shillings, and I'll pay you tomorrow.

And he certainly didn't look any too pleased over that, but I walked out the door and picked up Terry, and the Dally came after us right on to the street but he never said anything. Then just to get out of the streets for a bit the pair of us went down on the wharves, and half-way along one wharf we watched while a lot of wharfies worked on a boat that was unloading guano.

There's your chance, Terry said. You get extra pay for working that stuff.

What about you? I said.

No, he said, the dust's no good to me.

I asked a man and he told me to go on board and ask, and I went on board but I couldn't find the man I had to ask for. I looked down the hold and the wharfies were shovelling the stuff into bags, but you could hardly see them for dust. They looked as if they hadn't got a stitch on and they were sweating properly and the dust was sticking to the sweat, and it was certainly a sight because all you could see was a tangle of bodies nearly the same colour as the guano, except that the colour was darker where the sweat was collecting and running down. The stuff smelt like the bird-dung it was too, it got up my nose and all over me just looking down, so I went back to Terry.

I can't find the man, I said, but the job don't look any catch.

I bet it don't, Terry said, and we walked on to the end of the wharf and sat on the edge with our legs hanging down. And it was great to be sitting there too. For the first time for days a wind had got up and you could sit in the sun without feeling too hot. There were big woolly clouds in the sky, and blowing up against the tide the wind was making the sea choppy, and I thought no man whose belly was full could have said it wasn't good to be alive. I wondered if Terry was thinking the same way, but a man never does ask those sort of questions, so instead I asked him if he'd have a smoke, and he made one but it made him cough. He threw it away and I asked him hadn't he got rid of his cold.

It's not a proper cold, he said.

No? I said.

It was the war, he said.

I didn't say anything but I thought it was rotten. Terry looked hard and tough, but his face was sunk in, and maybe the wrinkles didn't improve it either, and there was only enough of him to cover his bones and nothing over. But when things are rotten like that what can a man say? But it sort of made it not so good to be just sitting there on the end of the wharf, and so help me if I didn't begin to start thinking about how I was broke, which I didn't want to do.

Come on, I said. And I wanted to do the registry offices again but Terry said once a day was enough and we had an argument, and in the end I said I was going to do them anyhow, so Terry came along and waited outside. And so help me if there wasn't a job going at the second one I tried. It was a farm job a good way out of town and you had to pay your own fare, but I knew if I took it on I'd get there all right. But I somehow just couldn't say I'd take it on, and it was mainly because I couldn't help thinking of Terry waiting for me in the street outside. So I got the woman to promise she'd keep it open for me if I came back inside a couple of hours. And I never said a word to Terry but when he stopped outside the next registry place I said no, because I'd got to go back to the last place later on. So to pass the time we went and had a lie-down in the park and Terry put his hat over his face and went to sleep.

But I didn't feel like sleeping. I kept looking at Terry and I kept wondering what the hell would become of him, and I couldn't make out why he wasn't racing horses any more. He looked sick anyhow, and I was practically certain he was a skinner. Of course it was none of my business, but I thought he was a decent bloke and it was certainly nice to have his company. I thought damn it all, it's none of my business, but I couldn't make my mind up all the same. Then while I was wondering what the hell was wrong with me there was a joker came and sat on the grass right alongside.

I say mate, he said, could you give me the lend of a bob.

No, I said, and you needn't wake my cobber up.

Sorry mate, he said, and he went and sat further off.

Well, I thought that showed a sort of nice feeling so I went over.

I'm on the beach myself, I said, but I can make it a deener.

Never mind mate, he said.

No, I said, you take the dough.

God bless you mate, he said.

That's all right, I said.

Then he got talking and he said he felt like calling me Bill, because I reminded him of a mate of that name. It was quite a yarn he got telling me. This Bill was a pretty good mate, he said, and when they were up against it he didn't mind going shares with any money he got. Though later on it was different, it was the joker telling me the yarn that usually did the shelling out. He didn't mind, he said, though he reckoned he shelled out a lot more than Bill ever did. And Bill would admit that. Bill'd say never mind, because he'd make it up when his ship came home. Well, it finally turned out that once when he was away in the country looking for a job he read in the paper how Bill had won a prize in an Art Union. And it made him think. He'd been thinking he'd like to make the break with Bill if he could without letting him down, so now was a good opportunity. He was up against it at the time and Bill had promised to make it O.K. with him when his ship came home, but he had the feeling that a man can say those things, but it's different when you actually have the dough. So he thought of a stunt, he thought he'd do Bill one last good turn. He sent him a letter and said he'd heard of a job away down south, so he'd decided to go and so long and good luck, and he never mentioned a thing about the Art Union. But he'd hardly posted the letter when he got one from Bill saying so long and good luck because he was getting out of the country and sailing that night. And Bill never mentioned a thing about the Art Union either.

It just shows you, he said.

Yes, I said.

A man wants a mate that won't let him down, he said.

Yes, I said. But I wasn't paying much attention because Terry had woke up.

I've got to go, I said.

Wait a minute mate, he said.

No, I said, I've got to go.

Listen mate, he said.

No sorry, I said, and I went back to Terry, and we went down town again and Terry waited while I went in and told the woman I wasn't taking the job. When I came out I told Terry there was nothing doing and he said I was stiff.

It's O.K. I said, and when I turned into the first pub we came to Terry said he knew of a better one, and it was certainly a good one for a feed. The counter-lunch had just come out, and for the price of our half-handles we put away just about as much as we could hold. Then we had another two half-handles which meant I hadn't a razoo left. Terry said let's go, and to finish up the day there was nothing to do except kick around the streets. We'd stand in shop doorways and

Terry'd pipe off everyone that went past, and outside the picture theatres he'd make me wait to watch people getting out of their cars.

See that old duchess, he'd say, she wants you to look at her now she's got her feathers pruned, but when she wakes up in the morning she won't look so hot, she won't want anybody looking at her then.

I bet she won't, I'd say, and I'd forget about being broke thinking what a funny joker Terry was. He didn't seem to be worrying about anything, and we carried on joking all the way up to Mrs Clegg's.

But when we got to the top of the stairs it was different, because all Terry's gear was in a heap outside his door and the door was locked. And Terry got excited and said he'd bust in the door. But I said he'd better not, he could doss in with me, I said, and have it out with Mrs Clegg in the morning. So while I made us a cup of tea he put his things in my room, and then we managed to get pretty comfortable in the bed even though it was a pretty tight fit.

Terry didn't waste any time going right off to sleep either, but I couldn't get to sleep. After all, considering the two of us were broke, and what with turning down a job, a man would have been lucky to get to sleep without doing any thinking. It was one of those hot nights too, and I started to roll round and woke Terry up. So I tried to lie still but when I got the cramp I thought no, this is no good. I waited until Terry was snoring again and then I managed to get out without disturbing him. I went and leaned out the window and I could see Fanny's money tree in the moonlight, and maybe that's what gave me the notion how to pick up a little money before morning. I got into my clothes and borrowed a pair of sandshoes that were among Terry's gear, and out in the street it was nice and quiet and a lot cooler. And a clock said it was going on for one o'clock.

I did a long trek out to one of the suburbs and then I didn't waste any time getting round the back of the houses to clean up any money that had been left out for the milkman. Some places I couldn't find any billy, or a dog would bark and put the wind up me properly, but I kept on until I got nearly ten bob all told. Then it wasn't so good doing the long trek back again, and I couldn't stop myself from worrying a bit over pinching money. But I thought when a man's in a jam he oughtn't to let himself be worried, and besides, there were the two of us to consider. Then when I got back to Mrs Clegg's I knew as soon as I was inside the room that Terry was awake. So when I got back into bed I said I'd had to do a job for myself, and when I was nearly asleep Terry said that sort of job didn't usually take several hours to do.

Oh I don't know, I said, they say a dog will travel five miles.

No, Terry said, more than that.

Well, you mightn't believe it, but I woke up early feeling just like a box of birds. And it was certainly great to have somebody to talk to, though Terry didn't look any too good so I told him to stay in bed, and while the kettle was boiling I went out to buy him a newspaper, and we looked at the jobs but there didn't seem to be any going. So Terry sat up and read the news out while we had our tea. Then I told him I'd be back in a minute, and I went downstairs and barged right into the kitchen where Mrs Clegg was getting the breakfast.

Mrs Clegg, I said, Terry's shifted his gear into my room.

Then he can shift it out again, she said.

No, it's stopping there, I said, and I suppose you don't happen to have another bed.

Who's paying the rent? she said, and I said I was.

All right mister, Mrs Clegg said, only it'll be extra for the room.

Good, I said, but what about the bed?

Well, we fixed it up. Mrs Clegg said we could have Fanny's bed and Fanny could sleep on the floor. And seeing it was just a stretcher we could fold it up for more room during the day if we liked. I said wasn't it a bit tough on Fanny, but Fanny jumped about and said she *wanted* to sleep on the floor.

So that was all right, and when I went back to Terry there was Mrs Popeye sitting on the bed in her kimono-thing.

Our Maggie's come to see us, Terry said.

Good, I said. How are you Maggie?

I'm feeling fit, she said, and the way she sort of slowly blinked her eyes made me think of a kid's doll.

We know what you're fit for, Terry said.

That's right, Maggie said, and she asked how was her back hair.

Bitch, Terry said, and he went on reading the paper.

That's no way to talk to a lady, Maggie said. Me being a married lady too.

Well, Terry said something pretty rude to her then but she didn't seem to mind. What with her fringe she certainly looked like a sort of cheap doll, though she showed real rabbit's teeth when she giggled.

Fancy you two boys sleeping here together, she said.

That's all right Maggie, I said.

Yes, she said, two's always better than one if you don't like a crowd.

I don't get you Maggie, I said, but just then Terry hit her whack over the head with the paper.

Get out, he said.

But Maggie didn't seem to mind. She said she'd be seeing us again and cleared off to her room, and I told Terry I wouldn't mind trying her out even though she wasn't my type, though her being married made a bit of difference. And Terry said she was no more married than he was, and anyhow he wouldn't have her on if she was hung with diamonds.

I thought it was about time I was getting along to the Dally's, so I told Terry I wanted to get down town but he needn't worry about getting up until he was ready, and I told him about what I'd fixed with Mrs Clegg.

I'll meet you at the Dally's at twelve o'clock for dinner, I said, and I gave him half a dollar. And I went off whistling and feeling life was good when a man had a cobber like Terry to kick around with, and maybe I was feeling good because I was thinking what a hell of a good joker I was. Though if I was I was kidding myself, because when all said and done I was only doing what I was to please myself, though it might have been a roundabout way of doing it.

I went along to the Dally's anyhow, and besides everything else the weather was still staying good, so I didn't leave off whistling, and the Dally was standing in front of the peter with his hands in his pockets. And he looked a bit worried.

Hello, I said, here I am and I'm after a job.

He looked a bit more cheerful when he saw me but he looked suspicious.

How did you know? he said.

Know what? I said, sort of innocent.

Never mind, he said, but what do you know? Have you ever done the work? he said.

Sure, I said, I've helped the cook in camps out in the bush.

It's not the same, he said, but he told me to come with him and he took me out the back and told me to get busy on a bag of potatoes.

Wait a minute, I said, what are the wages and how long do I work?

He didn't look too pleased over that, and instead of telling me he said it was no good me starting if I hadn't got an apron. But just then the cook came out of the kitchen and said he'd lend me an apron, so the Dally said what the hours and wages were, and then I got the apron from the cook and got busy on the spuds. And by the time I'd done a few benzine tins full time was getting on, and I had to get the sink all clear to be ready for the twelve o'clock rush. And when the whistles blew I went outside and Terry was waiting, so I gave him the works and told him to meet me when I knocked off. Then I had to get inside again and get busy, and what with being new to the work, and except for time off to get outside the two meals that were thrown in with the pay, I was kept busy without hardly a minute to spare right until the time I knocked off.

It was good having the job though. I came out feeling everything was O.K. and I met Terry and after we'd splashed on a talkie we went home and the two beds were all set, and Terry had cleaned up the room and made everything real tidy. There was hardly any room to move about certainly, but we didn't let that worry us, no, we made us cups of tea before we went to bed and I said it'd be beer once I got my pay. And I wasn't long going to sleep, though I remember Terry woke me up several times with his coughing, and each time I could see the red dot of a cigarette in the dark, and I supposed he felt the need of it but it only made him cough all the worse.

Then each morning it was the same. I'd wake up feeling good and I'd put the kettle on and go and buy Terry a paper, and maybe Maggie would come hanging around cadging cigarettes, and sitting on the beds while she talked. And I wouldn't have minded taking it easy but

I'd have to get off to the Dally's, and the morning I went after I'd given Terry my last half dollar I was a bit worried because it was still a good few days to payday, and Terry hadn't managed to pick up any sort of job. He just kicked about the town all day and came into the Dally's for his meals, and I didn't blame him if he wasn't trying much for a job because every day he looked more sick, and at night the way he coughed was something awful. I thought if I could get Maggie on her own I might ask her for the lend of a few bob, but I changed my mind because I thought of another stunt.

I got up before it was light and Terry never woke up, and this time I picked on a different locality. It was just getting daylight when I got there, and I picked on a street that ran off the main road from near a bus-stop, and sure enough the papers had been delivered. So I collected the lot and parked them in a heap in a shop doorway, then when the buses began to run I stood at the bus-stop with the papers under my arm, and it wasn't long before I'd nearly sold out. Of course I thought the stunt was a good deal more risky than the last one, specially as a good few jokers came out of the street I'd been down, and went very crook about their papers not being delivered. So between buses I put what was left back in the shop doorway, all except one which I kept for Terry, and then I had to do the long trek back because I didn't like the idea of being seen on a bus. And it took longer to do because I kept off the main road as much as I could. So it was late when I got back to Mrs Clegg's, and I only had time to look in and give Terry the paper and half a dollar and then get along to the Dally's. And I felt a bit windy all the rest of the day, and off and on for a few days after. But nothing happened, so I was lucky, and what with a half-dollar I borrowed from Maggie Terry didn't go short of any meals before payday.

But by the time my second payday came round I was well sick of working for the Dally. He was certainly tough to work for. He was tight with the hot water, and it was hard to make a job of the dishes when there was grease floating thick on the top of a sink full of dirty water. And there were things I saw that put me right off the tucker. If the pumpkin wouldn't cook the cook'd put it out on a big dish and work it through his fingers until he'd squeezed all the lumps out. And a man hardly had time to wipe off his own sweat, let alone roll a cigarette, so for a spell I used to go out the back and pretend to do a job for myself. But I couldn't do that too often, because if there wasn't any cleaning up to do there was always the spuds to keep ahead with. You had to put them in a machine and turn the handle to knock the worst of the skin off, and with the weather like it was it certainly made a man sweat doing the turning.

I never got much chance to talk to any of the girls either, and it was a disappointment because there were several good-lookers among them, and I wouldn't have minded trying to fix a date. But with all of us going for the lick of our lives there'd only be time for a wisecrack now and then, though one of them began pinching me on the backside every chance she got. I didn't mind, though I'd rather have done the pinching myself, but the cook got my goat when he started trying to do the same thing. He was a tonk all right, just a real old auntie, and I'd met the sort a few times before. Right from the jump he'd come hanging round me if the boss wasn't about. He'd want me to let him do things for me, so just to keep him quiet I brought along a big bundle of washing which included Terry's as well, and so help me if instead of turning it down he didn't do the best job I've ever seen done. And it was then he started doing the pinching, which made it mighty awkward for me seeing I'd let him do the washing. And what with working alongside him every day he had me a bit worried, and what with the tough work I knew my feet would get itchy and I wouldn't be able to stick it out at the Dally's for long.

And I haven't mentioned it before but it was coming on to Christmas, and it worked out that payday came just the day before. So after I'd knocked off me and Terry had a spree up in our room. We got Maggie to come and be in as well, and so help me if she didn't know how to drink beer. And when the party was going properly we got Mr Clegg to come and be in too, and even his missis came and had a few. So that night we were all happy.

Then when I knocked off Boxing Day Terry was waiting to tell me I'd landed the double I had on with the taxi-driver. So that was a bit of real All Right. We decided to have another spree, which we did with the same crowd, and we were all happy a second time. Then the next morning I decided to turn in the job at the Dally's. What with my wages and winning the double, I had a fair bit of sugar in my pocket even though the two sprees had knocked me back considerably. And Terry said why not try my luck at the Races. Well, the weather was still staying good as gold, and I thought it would be great to have a day out at the Races with Terry. So I told the Dally a yarn about how I had to go and see my mother because she was sick, and he let me finish up that evening. And when the cook found out I could hardly stop him from sort of getting all over me, and you can believe it or not but he went out and bought me a bunch of flowers. I thought he must have heard the yarn about my mother, but when I said something so help me if he didn't begin to cry. He hadn't bought the flowers for anyone except me, he said.

It turned out a bosker day the day I went out to the Races with Terry. Though it hadn't rained for so long each day was just about as good as the one before if you didn't mind the heat. I paid Mrs Clegg some rent in advance just in case, then we went out in the tram and there was a tremendous crowd going, all flossied up for a day out and looking a lot different from what they looked like coming home. Though of course I wasn't thinking of that at the time. No, like everybody else Terry and me were out for the day, and you know the feeling. Terry looked good and didn't cough much, he was funny the way he piped off people he saw in the crowd, and I could have grabbed him round the waist and chucked him up in the air, I was that full of beans I was sort of feeling that way.

But once we were on the Course, which had all the grass burnt off by the sun and looked hard-going for the horses, it was easy to see that going to the Races wasn't exactly a holiday for Terry. He took it all very serious. And if I said anything when he was standing in front of the Tote trying to figure out what he'd back he'd go crook and tell me not to be a nark.

Well, I said, put on ten bob and we'll go down and see them at the barrier.

No, he said, you go.

No, I said, you come too.

No, he said.

So I said O.K. and gave him a couple of smackers. And after he'd
been up to a window we went and got a good possie, and it wasn't
long before the balloon came down and then they were off. And it was
certainly great to watch, you could see the colours on the jockeys
coming round the rail smooth as if they were birds flying, and I
wished Terry had said what we were on, but I felt that way I didn't
care. It was only ten bob anyhow, and I got all worked up just out of
the fun of the thing, though Terry didn't look any different, not even
when they were coming down the straight. Of course I thought he'd
say if we were in the money once they'd passed the post, but he
never said anything so I thought we must be stiff. He just waited until
the judge's placings went up, then we went down to the birdcage to
watch the horses coming in for the next race, and I forgot all about
being stiff because I was thinking what real good horses they looked.
There were a couple I thought I wouldn't have minded backing if I'd
been there on my own, but I thought no, Terry knows his stuff so I'll
just leave it to him. But when the prelims were over and we were
going back to the Tote, Christ, if Terry didn't pull out four tickets that
were duds.

Gee four, I said. But I knew I'd torn it soon as I spoke, because
Terry pretended he was too busy with his card to take any notice. So
I just said too bad, and I gave him a couple more smackers.

And so help me if this time it didn't turn out that Terry was on a
good thing. But gee, I felt sore I'd opened my trap, because it turned
out he'd gone easy with only ten bob and it was a pretty good divvy.
All the same we went and had a few beers on the strength of it, and
I was feeling that sore I had to make Terry let me shout. Then next
race he went in solid but he had no luck, and after that it didn't matter
what he did, he couldn't do anything right. And I was trying all the
time to laugh it off, but there were times when I'd be feeling bad at
the sight of people coming away from the pay-out windows. Because
they'd be sticking money in their pockets and looking that pleased
with themselves. I knew I'd have looked the same way myself, but I
couldn't help thinking it just showed what money does to you.

Then it came on to the last race and Terry hadn't had any luck so

I told him to take my last quid, though I didn't tell him it was the last. He didn't want to take it but I had to make him, because I was still feeling sore over not keeping my mouth shut.

We better quit, he said.

No, I said, give it one last pop.

No, Terry said, better not.

Go on, I said, you take the sugar.

Well, Terry put the quid on but we didn't go down to our usual possie. Terry said he was getting done-in, and you could go round the side of the Tote where the pay-out windows were, and see the finish of the race pretty good from there. So we stood on a seat under the trees and joked about how we'd be first to the pay-out windows anyhow.

But I never took much interest in the race because I was busy getting an eyeful of a joker that was already waiting over by the pay-out windows. He looked a weak sort of joker, just a little runt, though all turned out in his Sunday best. And to begin with I thought he was canned, because fast as he was eating a sandwich it came out his mouth again. I told Terry to look but just then they were coming down the straight, then when I turned round again the joker was coming over our way.

What won? he said, and he stood there with lumps of chewed bread coming out of his mouth.

Teatime won, Terry said, and I believe the joker would have fallen down if he hadn't grabbed us round the legs. So we got off the seat and sat him down, and for a while he looked real sick.

I knew he'd be tough, he said. I saw the way he lifted his feet up in the prelim, he said, and he had me and Terry staring at a handful of tickets.

I put a tenner on, he said, and he'll pay that.

Maybe, Terry said, and then the figures went up and Teatime had paid a tenner sure enough.

Twenty tickets, the joker said, it was all the money I had. I lost my job, he said, and I've got my mother to keep, but I did like the way he lifted his feet up.

Well, we got introduced all round and the joker said his name was

Reg, and Terry began to get sort of friendly with him, and maybe I began to get an uneasy sort of feeling. But I'd had enough experience of opening my mouth for one day so I didn't say anything.

Terry said we'd take Reg over to collect his dough, so we went over and got first at a window, and we all stood in the queue, this Reg in between the pair of us, and Terry talking nineteen to the dozen about racehorses. I'd never heard him say so much before, though I noticed he never said a word how Reg was going to collect a hundred quid.

Then after a bit the windows went up and Reg got his money and Terry took us out a gate where he said we'd get a taxi, and sure enough we were lucky enough to get one. And the first pub we came to Reg wanted to stop for a drink, but Terry said leave things to him, and we finally pulled up at the biggest pub in town. Reg paid for the taxi and inside there was a crowd, but Terry pushed up to the counter and Reg stood us drinks just as fast as we could get the barman to serve us, and although it wasn't far off closing time we all had a good few in by then.

But right until we were turned out I hadn't sparked up much. Because Terry was still doing all the talking, and he was getting that friendly with this Reg. He certainly had me thinking things, though I admit I couldn't properly get a line on what it was all about. But I didn't want to interfere, so when we were all standing outside in the street I said I was going home.

No, Terry said, you come and eat.

No, I said, I want to have a lie-down.

What you want is a bellyful of tucker, Terry said.

No, I said, and I said so long and shoved off, and I thought Terry would go crook but he just let me go.

I wasn't happy about shoving off, but I was in one of those moods you get in sometimes. Before I turned the corner I took a look round and Terry and Reg were still standing outside the pub, and it looked as if Terry was still doing all the talking. It made me feel sore, though I couldn't get things at all straight in my mind. Terry's after that boy's dough, I told myself, but I didn't believe it all the same. No, I thought,

Terry's a decent bloke and I don't reckon he'd do a thing like that. On the other hand what did I know about Terry? He wasn't the sort that ever lets you know much about himself, though you could tell he always had a lot going on in his mind, even if you had to guess what it was about. Terry wouldn't do a thing like that, I kept telling myself, but I sort of felt it was no good telling yourself that about anybody. Anybody is liable to do anything, I told myself, particularly where there's money concerned. And I remembered how out at the Races I'd been thinking what money does to you.

But what was I worrying about anyhow? Because Terry could do what he liked so far as I was concerned. He was up against it the same as I was, and when things are tough a man can't be worried. That's what I'd thought when I pinched the money out of the milk billies, so where was the difference? And then I thought maybe I was only feeling sore because I was jealous of this Reg. Because I'd thought Terry was the sort of joker who'd go solid with a cobber, and quite apart from the money business I didn't like the way he cottoned on to Reg.

But it was no good letting myself be worried, and I wasn't doing myself a bit of good standing there watching the pair of them. So I turned the corner thinking I'd go to the flicks, but then I remembered I only had a few odd bits of chicken feed in my pocket, and that made me start thinking all over again. Oh hell, I said to myself, I'll go and have a feed.

So up towards Mrs Clegg's place I turned into a quick-lunch eating joint, and so help me if I didn't run into Maggie.

Hello Maggie, I said. All on your pat, I said, and seeing she was eating a pie I asked for one myself.

Fancy meeting you without your boy-friend, Maggie said.

That's all right Maggie, I said. And who's my boy-friend anyhow?

As if you don't know, she said, and she started doing the blinking doll stunt.

No Maggie, I said, I don't know.

Go on, she said.

So I told her not to talk like a blinking idiot and that sort of shut her up, though it was a blinking doll I should have said. And I started to kid her a bit and you could see she was in the mood for a bit of kidding too. I put my hand on her leg underneath the table, and instead of carrying on and acting silly she just let it stay there, so when we'd finished eating I asked her what she was doing to put in the evening.

I got nothing on, she said.

Then let's go somewhere, I said.

No, she said, I better not. My husband's ship comes home any day now, so I better be a good girl.

Sort of save up, I said.

That's right, she said. Matelots have got to save up so I ought to too.

Do they save up? I said.

Well, she said, you're asking me.

And what about you? I said.

Well, she said, sometimes. It all depends. Anyhow, she said, what about yourself?

You can save up too damn long Maggie, I said.

I know, she said. My God, she said.

Come on Maggie, I said.

So I paid for the pair of us which left me practically a skinner, but what with the way things were I was too far gone to care about almost anything, except maybe whether I could do a line with Maggie.

Do you want to go to the pictures? she said.

No, I said, let's walk, and we just walked and Maggie was sort of serious, I'd never struck her in the same mood before. She didn't seem to be taking notice of anything I said, and we just kept on walking and turning corners. But she was the one who sort of decided which corners to turn, and seeing I hadn't taken much notice where we were going I got a surprise when I discovered we'd parked nearly outside Mrs Clegg's. But I hadn't time to say anything before Maggie said no, let's keep on walking. So we kept walking, but now I was a wake-up to what was in Maggie's mind. I was sitting up and taking notice so to speak while we went on turning the corners, and I wasn't surprised when we pulled up outside Mrs Clegg's a second time.

And this time Maggie said come on up, and she went up the stairs pretty fast with me following. And upstairs I followed her straight into her room and she shut the door. Then when I looked at her and saw the way she was breathing I knew she wouldn't be able to stop herself, so I naturally felt my heart begin to beat a bit.

Take it easy Maggie, I said, and we sat on the edge of the bed and she was shivering, but I told her to take it easy, and I put my arm round her and she cuddled up until I got my hand on her bubs. But so help me if she wasn't that flat-chested I couldn't even feel anything. And seeing I didn't know what to say I said something about that. But it made her go crook as anything.

You needn't be personal, she said, and she jumped up and stood there looking at me, and she looked properly hot and bothered.

Don't be silly Maggie, I said. Come over here, I said.

But she went on standing there and I was wondering what I did next, though as it turned out she didn't waste much time deciding things for me.

Take it easy Maggie, I said. Struth, I said, but she was too keen. So I just lay back, I thought I'd let her work off steam a bit. And it was just as well I did back-pedal, because the pair of us were wake-ups when we heard somebody coming up the stairs, and when the door opened we were just sitting on the edge of the bed, though I suppose a man has to admit we must have both looked considerably hot and bothered.

Anyhow it was Maggie's bloke Bert. And he was a big matelot, though not a Pom, it was easy to tell he was a Pig Islander.

Hello, he said, but he didn't look at all pleased to see me there, though of course Maggie jumped up and began to make a fuss of him.

You're looking good Bert, she said, and Bert said he was a box of birds, and until Maggie chipped in he began telling her how his ship had got in late that afternoon and he'd got leave.

Bert, Maggie said, this is Bill.

How are you Bill, he said, and I got up off the bed but he didn't shake hands or anything, he just went on talking to Maggie, and I could tell she was worried over the way he was taking it.

Things didn't look any too good to me so I thought I'd best clear out. I said I was going and Maggie said hooray Bill, and I went over to my room. And there wasn't any sign of Terry so I sat down for a bit. I felt I needed to pull myself together, because what with running into Reg at the Races, and now this Maggie business coming afterwards, everything seemed to have gone wrong. And the last few weeks things had been that good.

It wasn't a bit of good just sitting there though, I knew I'd have to get out in the streets. But I'd hardly made up my mind to go when I heard an argument start over in Maggie's room, and I opened the door a bit so I could listen. And to begin with I couldn't hear much, and later on when they'd got to arguing loud enough for me to hear I didn't want to hear. In a way I didn't anyhow, because my name was being brought in, and the way things were developing it sounded as though there was going to be a serious row. Things didn't ease off any either, they got a lot worse. It was you did and I didn't more and more and louder and louder, and when it developed into let me go and you're hurting me I knew things were getting serious. He's going to beat her up, I thought, and I thought it was about time I got off down the street. Because what could I do? Terry'd always reckoned Maggie wasn't married but who could say? No, I told myself, I'm not going in there. I felt sorry for Maggie naturally, but I thought it was no good trying to do anything if I was the cause of the trouble. So I went out, and in the street you could still hear the pair of them tearing into each other, and it only took a minute or two before Maggie began to yell. Christ, I thought. But I knew it was best to keep out of it, and I began walking the streets just the same as I'd done with Maggie.

And I didn't go home for a long time that night. I thought I'd wait until Terry was sure to be home, so I kicked around the streets until it was well after midnight, and it did me good because there's always plenty to see going on round the streets, and it takes your mind off things when they go wrong. There's lots of other people in the world you tell yourself, and you start wondering what they're like. And maybe you decide everybody must be pretty much the same in most ways if you could only find out. That's my idea anyhow, though I admit I may be wrong.

I walked about for quite a while, then I decided I'd go and sit on a seat on the waterfront. And down there I watched some white patches that you could just see rocking on the water, and I decided they must be seagulls. I wondered why you never see them sitting on wires like you do other birds, and I decided it must be because of their feet. And thinking of birds made me remember about the pigeons I used to shoot in the bush, and next minute I'd started calling myself a fool for wanting to come into town. Town's no good, I told myself, a man doesn't have any say, he just gets pushed about. And when I started to go the length of the main street just once more, I was thinking I'd go and try for a farm job first thing next morning. But next minute I was remembering how I'd nearly come a thud over Maggie, and then I forgot everything else because I was thinking about Terry again.

But I got a knock, because up at Mrs Clegg's there still wasn't any sign of Terry, and all the stuffing sort of went out of me so to speak. I certainly felt blue. But I thought chin up, a man can't be worried. I listened but there wasn't any sound from Maggie's room and it sort of cheered me up. I bet it all ended up in a good old kafuffle, I thought. Good luck to them anyhow, I thought. Then I turned in and I never thought I would, but I went right off to sleep without doing any more thinking.

But when I woke up late next morning Terry still wasn't there. It made me feel bad, but I thought never mind, he'll turn up. Yet I felt sort of jumpy. All sorts of things that might have happened kept coming into my head, and just because there wasn't any sign of life from Maggie's room I worried over that as well. Though I told myself I needn't, because they'd naturally be sleeping in, that was, if Bert hadn't had to go back to his ship.

Then when I'd had a cup of tea I didn't know what to do. I didn't want to go out and miss Terry, yet I knew it would give me the dingbats if I just stayed on there waiting. So I decided I'd leave a note and then go out. Which is what I did, and along the street I caught up to Mrs Clegg who'd gone out ahead of me and was pushing an old pram. And walking along I looked in the pram and it was filled with things out of the kitchen, including a few tools that must have belonged to her old man.

Gee, I said, selling up the home.

Not yet, she said. It's this weather, she said, it makes that man think he can take things easy.

It makes me lazy, I said. I wouldn't mind if it rained.

You know, she said, he never done that to her before.

Mr Popeye? I said.

If it wasn't for the money I'd turn her out, she said.

Yes? I said.

Then next minute she pulled up outside a pawnshop I'd noticed there before.

I go in here, she said, and she wheeled the pram inside. Things must be tough, I thought. And then I turned the corner and ran right into Terry.

Hello boy, he said, and I couldn't help it, I had to tell him I was that pleased to see him.

How are you feeling? I said.

Good, he said, but I thought he looked pretty crook on it.

Have you had your breakfast? I asked him.

No, he said, I haven't had anything.

Come on, I said, and when we passed the pawnshop I could see Mrs Clegg was still inside. Let's step on it, I said, and soon as we got in I let Terry go upstairs while I went into the kitchen. I couldn't find anything to eat though, there was nothing that would have fed even the budgie. But Terry said never mind, he couldn't eat anything anyhow. So I made him a cup of tea and he drank that, then he took off his coat for a lie-down, and I was all the time wanting to ask him if he had any money but I didn't like to.

It was good having him back though, but while I was wondering whether I couldn't think up another of my stunts for picking up a little ready cash he went off to sleep. So I thought I'd walk about in the streets for a bit and maybe I'd get an idea. But when I got downstairs there were two jokers knocking on the door. I picked them for what they were right away, and so help me if it wasn't me they were looking for, and when they said they wanted to ask me a few questions I told them to go ahead, but I admit I had the wind up considerably.

You'd better come along to the police station, they said.

All right, I said, but what's it all about? And they said I'd soon find out about that.

O.K. I said, but first I want to speak to my cobber upstairs.

Then I thought no, why worry Terry when he needed to get some sleep. And I wouldn't be away long, I thought. So I told them it didn't matter about my cobber.

Well, they walked one on each side of me, and I tried to talk to them now and then but they took no notice. Though sometimes they'd have some joke on of their own, they'd talk across me just as if I wasn't there, and it made me feel as if I was some sort of wild animal they were taking through the streets. And occasionally I'd see people we passed who'd pick them for dees, and I knew they'd be turning round for an eyeful. So all things considered I wasn't feeling so good by the time we got to the police station.

I didn't feel any better there either, because it was a big place, not at all the sort of place you feel you can make yourself at home in. We went up a lot of stairs and finally they took me in a room and we all sat down round a table.

You've been interfering with a woman, one of them said.

Go on, I said. Have I?

But you'd never have guessed the way I was feeling from what I said.

It won't do you any good telling lies, the same one said, and he looked at some papers and said it was a serious something or other. Anyhow, he said, all we want you to do is answer a few questions.

All right, I said, first you give me the works, then I'll tell you my story.

And it was Maggie who'd been putting it across me, which is what I'd guessed, though how it had all come about I don't know. You'd have thought they'd have told me that, but they never did. Instead they just sort of threw out hints, and the way they made out they knew everything that had happened just about had me thinking they must have had somebody there watching.

There's no question about what happened, one of them kept on saying, and they kept on at me until I said, All right, I'll tell you my story. Which is what I did, though I didn't say anything about Bert beating her up afterwards.

So then they sort of went over it all again.

You admit you put your hand on her, the one who did nearly all the talking said.

Yes, I said, but she didn't object.

She objected all right, he said.

Well, I said, maybe she did, but afterwards she didn't.

No? he said. Then why did her husband come in and find her fighting to save herself? And that was a new one on me because they certainly hadn't told me that part of Maggie's story.

That's just baloney, I said.

Well, he said, she can show the bruises.

So then I said how Bert had beaten her up. But they said I'd only just made that up, if I hadn't why hadn't I told them before? And they said it would make things a lot worse for me if I told lies.

Well, I tried to explain but it did no good, they just went on saying I'd admitted I put my hand on her and she'd objected. And I got that fed up of arguing I felt that way I didn't care much if they believed me or not, though I sort of woke up when they said they were sorry but they'd have to bring a case against me.

And it was certainly a knock because up till then I'd never realized I was properly in the cart, I certainly had no idea it was going to end up in a Court case. And it naturally made me begin to worry about Terry. I didn't know what to say, and they said I was lucky it wasn't a more serious charge, and seeing I'd admitted what I'd done and hadn't told any serious lies I'd probably get probation.

I still sort of had too much stuffing knocked out of me to say anything, but probation didn't sound so bad, and maybe I wouldn't have minded so much if I hadn't been thinking of Terry. All the same I didn't see how they could prove anything against me, but when I told them they said there wasn't any question about it because of what I'd admitted. And finally they said it would be best for me if they put it all in writing. And after we'd argued a bit more I got that fed up I thought writing it down wouldn't make any difference, so I went over it all again while one of them did the writing. And I admitted I put my hand on her, and I admitted she objected, and I admitted I let her go when I heard Bert coming, but I never admitted anything more, and besides other things I wanted them to put in about Bert beating her up, but they said it had nothing to do with it, and I couldn't say I'd actually seen him do it anyhow. Then when it was all finished they got me to sign, and I could sort of tell they were thinking they'd done quite a good stroke of work. But I was so fed up I was past caring about anything much.

They wouldn't let me go away then, no, they said they'd try to have the case brought up in the Police Court that afternoon, but it mightn't be until the next morning. So I asked them if I could send a message to my cobber, I wanted him to come and see me I said, and they said that would be O.K. they'd see Terry got the message. Then I asked them what the time was, and I'd no idea it had all taken hours and hours. The twelve o'clock whistles must have blown and I'd never even heard them.

I'll admit another thing, I said, I'm feeling empty.

We'll soon fix you up, one of them said, and they took me downstairs and turned me over to a john who wrote my name down in a book and told me to hand in all my money, but there was nothing doing because I didn't have any. Then when he'd taken my belt off me (it was so as I couldn't hang myself I suppose), he took me along a passage and locked me up. I sat down to save myself from holding my pants up, and I was sitting there thinking how it was the first time I'd ever been in one of those places, when the john came back with a tray that was loaded up with a big dinner. It was a real good dinner too, two courses and plenty to eat, and I could have eaten the lot and more, but I thought gee, so far as tucker goes I'm better off than poor old Terry is. I might be anyhow, I thought, because I remembered I didn't know whether he'd got any money out of Reg. All the same I didn't like to think of Terry going hungry, so I tore some pages out of a Western that was in the cell, and wrapped up half of both courses and put the parcel in my pocket. All in together it certainly looked an awful mess, but I thought Terry wouldn't mind if he was feeling empty.

Then when I'd got outside the tucker I felt a lot better. I stretched myself out on a sort of long seat that was the only bit of furniture in the cell, and I thought if only a man never had any cobbers or anything, getting picked up by the police would take away some of your worries anyhow.

I must have gone to sleep because it seemed no time before the john was unlocking the door and telling me to come along. And along at the end of the passage Terry was waiting for me. And if I wasn't pleased to see his wrinkled old Aussie's face! I certainly was. He grinned back at me too, and the john let us sit together on a seat there and I asked him how he was feeling now. And he said he was feeling good.

You don't look any too good, I said, but he said not to worry about him.

I'm in a jam, I said, and I gave him the works, and Christ if he didn't begin to laugh when I told him how I'd nearly had Maggie on.

How far did you get? he asked me.

This far, I said, and I showed him. But I never even felt anything, I said.

I bet you didn't, he said. But go ahead, he said, and I told him the rest and when I'd finished he said some pretty rude things about Maggie.

But don't you worry, he said, because there won't be any case.

They're going to bring one, I said.

Don't you worry, he said.

I'll need to get a lawyer, I said.

You won't need any lawyer, he said. Listen boy, he said, you don't need to worry, because I'm promising you there won't be any case.

All right Terry, I said, but are you sure?

Shake, he said.

All right, I said. And I certainly felt bucked, though I had no idea what he was going to do, yet I felt dead sure I could depend on him all the same, which was a peculiar feeling to have after the way I'd been feeling only the day before.

When does the case come on? Terry asked me. And he said there was just one thing. I've got to get hold of Maggie, he said, and he told me if he couldn't get hold of her by next morning the case might go as far as the Supreme Court, which meant they'd keep me in clink until the sittings came on unless somebody would go bail.

Do you know anyone? I said, and he said yes, maybe he might be able to fix things.

All right, I said, I'm leaving it to you. But Terry, I said, how are you off for sugar?

I'll be O.K. he said.

Have you got any? I said.

I've got a few bob, he said.

What about Reg? I said, and I couldn't help asking him but I bet I went red in the face.

I won't be seeing Reg, he said. He sounded a bit annoyed, and I didn't know whether I felt glad or sorry, because Reg might have been good for a loan.

I'll be worried about you Terry, I said.

You got no need to worry, he said, and I knew I'd better lay off, because I was getting him narked.

So I said O.K. and I told him not to move, and it was easy to put the parcel in his pocket without the john seeing. Then I couldn't think of anything more to say, so we just sat there, and I wouldn't have minded if it had lasted like that for hours. But the john said if we'd finished talking I'd better come along, so we shook again and Terry said he'd tell Mrs Clegg some yarn if she asked. Then we said cheers and I went along and was locked up thinking everything was going to be O.K.

Nothing happened that afternoon. I had a lie-down on the seat again and I must have gone to sleep, because I don't remember anything until the john brought me another feed. And it was just as good as the one before, and I thought it was no wonder there were such a lot of cases when they stood you good tucker inside.

Then when the john came for the tray he brought me the blankets to sleep in, so after I'd had a read of the Western I decided to turn in, and I'd have had quite a good night if I hadn't been waked up by somebody who started kicking up a row somewhere along the passage. And by the sound of the voice I thought it must be some old girl who'd been picked up for being tight. It kept me awake for hours anyhow, but when I woke up at daylight everything was quiet.

And I woke up still feeling that everything was going to be O.K. so I was sort of impatient for them to take me into Court and get it over. I had bacon and eggs for breakfast, then the doors all along the passage were unlocked and we all came out and they collected us along at the end where Terry and me had done our talking. There was a fair collection too, I'd had no idea, though only one woman, and if she was the one who'd kicked up the row you could hardly believe it, because she looked quite all right. I thought she might have been any man's own mother, but of course it's a fact that nobody's the same person once they've sobered up.

We all had to stand there with a crowd of jacks in plain clothes standing round, and one in uniform called out our names and said what we'd been picked up for. And I didn't know what it was all about, but I suppose it was so as they could get us taped and pick out anybody they had anything else on. It made me go red though when I heard what it was I was charged with. It didn't sound too nice I can tell you, and I thought damn it all, why give it that sort of name? Anyhow, I thought, I bet all those jacks have done plenty they wouldn't like anybody to know about, particularly when you can give it such a rotten name.

Still, there was nothing I could do about it, I just stood there with the rest, and when it was all over they put us back in our cells again. Then when I was beginning to get the dingbats through being there so long on my own I was taken out by the two demons who'd picked me up. It was time to go over to the Court they said, and they asked me if I'd got a lawyer.

No, I said, I don't want any lawyer.

All right, one of them said, but don't say we didn't ask you.

Then they told me to come along, and it wasn't far to the Police Court but I wished it could have been further. Because it was a fine summer's day (though no different to what it had been for weeks), and we cut across an open place where there were flowers and trees. The grass was all dried up by the sun yet it looked nice and cool there, just seeing a hose going made you feel cool. And it was nice to see some kids that were cutting across on their way to school, but I thought if a pair of dees hadn't been taking me to Court I might never have noticed these things.

But as I say the walk was over too soon, and when we got inside the Court we had to wait quite a time before my case came on. First there were traffic cases, then after a few drunks had been hauled up an old man that nobody could have much liked the look of was told off by his Nibs for trying to do himself in. The bandage round his neck didn't improve his looks either, he looked sick I can tell you, and you'd have thought no man would have treated him as rough as the Magistrate did. But I bet he thought he was treating him good by letting him off.

Then after the old man it was my turn, and I'd been sitting down with one of the dees while I kept my eyes open for Terry. And there wasn't much of a crowd that'd come to watch, so it was easy to tell he hadn't turned up. I had to stand there while they told the magistrate the case and then Maggie was brought in to say her piece. And she only took one look at me and never looked my way again. And you'd hardly believe anyone could tell a story that was all baloney as well as she did, and it certainly knocked me plenty. She was all flossied up and to begin with you sort of felt she was enjoying herself properly. But when she'd got nearly to the end something went wrong, because instead of answering a question she suddenly went white and hung on to the rail in front of her. And his Nibs said to let her take her time, and he looked at me as if he thought I needed to be watched or I'd be trying to swing another one across her. But it never worried me much because it was just then I spotted Terry. He was standing in front of the crowd with a grin a mile wide, and when he saw me looking at him he winked and jerked his head over towards Maggie. And it certainly gave me a nice feeling to know he was there, but things were sort of going round in my head so much I couldn't even wink back.

Maggie got going again and I fixed my attention on her, and when she'd finished one of the dees went into the box and read out what they'd written down. Then there was some talk about Bert, his ship was away, they said, but the magistrate said it didn't matter about

Bert because of what I'd admitted in my statement. And then he went on and said a whole rigmarole about what he was going to do, and what would happen if I said I was guilty or not guilty. But I never had much idea of what he was saying because I was suddenly a wake-up to what I'd let myself in for when I signed that statement. I understood things then I can tell you, and it made me feel hopping mad. Instead of listening to his Nibs I just couldn't take my eyes off the two demons. And Christ, I thought. And I couldn't think of anything except, Christ!

But I knew it was no good letting my feelings get the better of me. So I told myself to hang on. I said not guilty all right, and when he asked me something about bail I said I didn't want any bail, because I'd looked at Terry and he'd shaken his head. I remembered how he'd said the case might go as far as the Supreme Court anyhow, and way at the back of my mind I was still feeling dead sure of Terry even if things had got in a worse tangle than I'd expected.

All the same it was a hard job trying to stop my feelings from getting the better of me when I was walking back to the police station with the two dees. Because I thought they'd played me a rotten trick. But I didn't say anything except ask them what happened next.

You wait, one of them said, we'll look after you.

Yes, I said, I'm reckoning on that.

But I needn't have tried to be sarcastic, because a man needs a lot sharper tongue than I've got to get under any dee's skin.

It was all right being back though, because of the tucker. I asked the john who fetched the tray what happened next, and being quite a decent bloke as I'd thought he was right from the beginning, he stayed and talked and told me a lot.

They'll take you out there, he said, and he said it might be in a taxi or it might be in the Black Maria. And when I asked him what it was like out there he said he didn't know much about it, but he reckoned they'd treat me all right until I got convicted.

I'm not getting convicted, I said, but he only said, Good luck boy, and shook hands.

Well, it wasn't until late in the afternoon that the Black Maria came for me. It had blokes on it dressed more like soldiers than cops, and another joker was taken out and put inside as well as me, and there wasn't much room inside because it was chock full of stuff they were taking out to the gaol, and I had to sit right up behind the driver's seat where I could look out a little window and see what streets we were going through. And instead of going straight out to the gaol we went down the main street and pulled up outside a butcher's shop while they put some boxes of meat on board, and it looked more like dogs' meat to me. But while we were waiting I looked out the window, and so help me if Maggie didn't go past. She stopped to cross the road too, and watching out for the traffic it seemed as if she looked right at the window. I don't suppose she did really, and it was only for a second, but it made me feel very funny inside.

There were no more stops though, after that we kept right on to the gaol which was a long way out of town, and soon as we were out there we had to help unload the stuff. Then they took us inside and put our names down, and after they'd put black stuff on our fingers and got our fingerprints, they took us into a big sort of hall with iron doors along both sides, and locked the pair of us up on our own.

So there I was. And I'd only had time to look out through the bars and see there was nothing to see except a concrete wall and some sky above, when they brought me a hunk of bread and a pannikin of tea, which was certainly not so good after what I'd been getting. Then after a bit the light went on, and to stop myself from doing any thinking I had a read of a detective mag that was lying there. But the yarns were all about crooks and I reckoned they were a lot of baloney, nothing like the real thing at all. So I chucked the mag away and walked round a bit, and I may as well tell you that when you're in clink there's always a spyhole in your door. You can't see out, but if you keep your eyes skinned you can always tell when anybody has come along for an eyeful. And that first night I just happened to be watching when somebody came along and moved the slide, so I asked could I have a dab of vaseline to put on my piles. And mister peeping Tom said he'd have to see about that.

Of course it was mainly a gag just to have somebody to speak to, though as a matter of fact my piles were hurting pretty bad. And while I was waiting I thought I'd have a read of what was left of a Bible, and I'm blowed if I didn't strike the yarn about Joseph and his coat of all colours. It was a real good yarn too, I liked reading it a hell of a lot, but before I'd got through the light went out, and there I was in the dark and it didn't look as if the vaseline was going to turn up. So I thought I'd better turn in, and it sounded as if the jokers locked up alongside were doing the same thing because I could hear their beds creaking.

And maybe it was because of the way those beds creaked that I couldn't get to sleep. They didn't stop creaking, and I thought maybe they were jokers like me who'd been locked up for the first time. It made me start thinking about what makes a man get tough and land himself in clink. Because all those jokers must have been the same as I was once too, just kids. And I started to remember about when I was a kid. I remembered the times when I'd get a kick on the behind for pinching out of the bin where they threw the rotten fruit along at the auction mart in the town where I lived. And the times when the old man would come home tight, and us kids'd go out in the morning and find him lying in the onion bed without hardly a stitch on. And I remembered other times too, and I never thought about Terry or Maggie much. I just couldn't take my mind off the jokers that were locked up alongside me, because their beds never left off creaking all night.

I was glad when it was morning, because as I say it doesn't matter what sort of a night you have, things are always different in the morning. When I heard a noise of doors being unlocked I got up and put my pants on, and when the doors were all unlocked you had to stand outside while a sort of procession came round. First you had to empty your jerry into a can, then you got your tins of porridge and stew off a tray, and last you got your pannikin full of tea out of another can. Then you had to be locked in again while you ate your breakfast. But that first morning I couldn't eat much of it, because they might have called it porridge, but you couldn't tell by the taste. You could hardly tell the tea by the taste either, but I'm not going to tell all about what it's like in the clink. Most things you soon get used to, if you don't eat you feel empty, so it's best to eat and after a while you never leave any. And maybe the main reason why I couldn't eat my breakfast the first morning was because I was wondering whether they'd leave me locked up on my pat all day. Also I was beginning to worry about Terry again. I wondered how the hell he'd get on for chips, and I was hoping to God they'd give me his letter if he wrote one, though it turned out I needn't have worried about that.

It wasn't long before the doors were unlocked again and they took us out in a yard with concrete walls all round, and I thought it was all right because of the company, though a screw shouted out we were not to tell each other about our cases. Everybody had plenty to talk about without talking about their cases anyhow, and when it got too hot in the sun we all went under a little roofed-in part, and with everybody squatting down and taking it easy while they talked the usual sort of talk, it might have been any crowd of jokers that were cutting scrub or working on the roads on relief. Because they all had ordinary clothes on, and up till then I hadn't found out they were all jokers that were waiting to come up in court, though a few were dinkum lags who were all togged up to go into town in the van because they needed to go into hospital.

But as I say I'm not going to tell all about what it's like inside just because I was in for a few weeks. There'd be too much to tell anyhow.

I never got any letter from Terry the first day or the day after, and I felt if one didn't come soon I'd have the dingbats worse than I'd ever had them before. What with hardly getting any sleep and listening to the beds creaking all night I thought I'd go silly, and then maybe they'd have to take me away to the rat house. But a letter came all right. And was it a relief! Terry said chin up and cheers and I needn't worry because he'd fixed things, though he couldn't get anybody to go bail, he said, but he was still trying and maybe he'd have some luck. And he wound up that I was not to worry if he didn't write again because things were fixed for sure, (with a line under the word sure), and I needn't be worrying about him either because he'd be O.K.

So while I was feeling the relief I wrote back saying what a great cobber he was, and how he certainly had my thanks. And I put a letter inside for Fanny. I told her I'd gone away for a few weeks so I was leaving her to look after Terry. Get your mother to give him something to eat sometimes Fanny, I said. And I put a bit about the money tree, and how I know for certain it liked little girls that were kind to people. I didn't think it would do much good but maybe it was worth trying. And I asked her in a P.S. if she'd taught the budgie to do any new tricks.

And it wasn't until several days after I'd written the letters that I began to get the jitters again. Because Terry didn't write any more, and even though he'd told me he mightn't I couldn't make it out. And lying in bed at night when I couldn't sleep I'd start thinking he might only have pretended to help me, while all the time he hadn't done anything at all. I hadn't said anything about my case to anybody inside but quite a number had told me about theirs, and they all said you were a goner once you'd signed a statement admitting anything you'd done. There was no way of getting out of it then, they said, and they'd be that certain they knew the whole works I'd get the wind up considerably. So lying awake at night I'd start thinking rotten things about Terry. He wants me put away, I'd tell myself. Yes, I'd think, that's what he wants, because I'm the only bloke that knows he was with Reg after he collected the hundred quid. And once I'd got as far as thinking that way I'd sort of let myself go, and work out all the different ways he might have used to get the money out of Reg. And I'd tell myself I could bet he'd left Mrs Clegg's and I'd never see him again. Because say they put me away for five years? I'd think. And I couldn't help it, I'd break out in a sweat.

But of course it was mainly during the night time that I'd be thinking these things. When it was daylight I'd sort of feel maybe I'd gone off to sleep without knowing, and only dreamed all I'd been thinking. I'd go out into the yard thinking everything was going to be O.K. and I'd be all right unless any joker said something that was liable to start me worrying again. Some days they'd talk about their lawyers, and they'd all reckon they'd got good ones. If they didn't get off, they reckoned, they'd get only a light stretch. And I hadn't got a lawyer. I had the law dead against me, and instead of trying to do anything about it I was just relying on Terry. And I'd ask myself what could Terry do against the law all on his own any more than I could?

But then I'd think if I tried to do anything I might only spoil what it was that Terry had said he'd fixed. So there I was, sort of feeling I was liable to be caught which ever way I went, and some days I'd feel if things didn't stop going round in my head I'd end up in the rat house for sure.

I've never known time to drag like it did during those weeks. Some days were that long I thought they'd never finish, and the nights were worse. Yet it seemed no time when they started taking away a few jokers each morning to have their cases tried. And when I sort of woke up I found I'd got easy about things. I felt I didn't care what happened. When they asked me didn't I want a lawyer to defend me, because the country would pay if I couldn't, I still said I didn't want any lawyer. Because I'd worked myself into a state. Things couldn't be any worse than they were, I thought, and if Terry was going to let me down it was just too bad. Yet even though I'd got to the stage of thinking I didn't care what happened to me, I'd be liable to break out in a sweat at the thought of what might be happening to Terry. He might be no good, I thought, but he was sick anyhow, I'd liked having him for a cobber and we'd had some good times together. And the thought of him having nothing to eat was the one thing I could never make myself feel easy about.

You could feel the difference in the place once the van started going in each day with a few jokers to be tried. All the rest were wondering which day it was going to be their turn, and that's the sort of thing that would give any man the jitters. We'd always be keen to find out how things had gone yet we never got much chance. Because several got off and never came back, and those who'd got convicted would be wondering how long a stretch they'd get, and that's the sort of time when you don't feel like asking a man too many questions. Or if their cases hadn't finished they'd be in just as rotten a state, so it wasn't easy to find out anything much.

Then the morning came when it was my turn, and I was told to get myself shaved and make myself look respectable. And I was just a bundle of nerves waiting to be taken out of the yard, but once we were in the bus, three of us, each with our pannikin and a hunk of bread to eat at midday, I didn't feel so bad. I was lucky enough to be sitting up by the window again and it was good to look out and see the places we went past.

We didn't see much of the outside world though, because the bus backed right in at a door, and we were taken out and locked in a cell right away, all of us in together. And it was easy to tell the courtroom was somewhere upstairs because of the sound of feet moving. My two mates were going up for sentence and it wasn't long before they were taken out. I was left there on my pat so just to calm myself down I walked about the cell, and it was a terribly dirty place, nothing like what I'd been used to. All over the walls there were drawings that must have been done by jokers who'd had to wait there, and they were nearly all drawings of jokers being hanged or lying on their backs with knives stuck through them. And underneath it would say, NEVER MAKE A STATEMENT TO A DEE. Or, THIS IS A BLOODY DEE AND THIS IS WHAT HE'S GOING TO GET. And calling the dees for all the names you can think of.

But it wasn't long before one of my mates was put back in again, and I didn't know what he'd got but he took it pretty hard. He just sat there with his head in his hands and didn't say anything, and I would have liked him to talk because it was hard to bear the sight of him sitting there. I'd been told he had a missis and several kids too. But I didn't have to put up with it for long, because my other mate came back and then it was my turn. I said O.K. but before I got out the door the first joker jumped up and gave me his fist to shake. Good luck boy, he said, and I thought it mighty nice of him. It made me feel as if I was nearly going to cry.

Well, the screw took me along a passage to the bottom of a little stairway and I had to sit there and wait, and another joker was waiting there as well, and when he looked at me so help me if it wasn't Ted, the bloke who'd pinched my money that day on the beach.

Well I'm blowed, I said, and just for a second I thought he was going to pretend he didn't know me.

No talking about your cases, the screw said.

O.K. brother, I said, and I asked Ted how things were, though it was a stupid question to ask.

Not so good, he said.

I'm telling you in your own interests, the screw said.

That's O.K. brother, I said, and I told Ted I was pleased to see him anyhow. Though that was a stupid thing to say too, because before I could say any more another screw came down the stairway to fetch Ted, and I thought he might be going up thinking I was trying to rub it in over pinching my money. Which I hadn't intended to do at all, no, it was just that seeing somebody I knew I was only trying to be friendly.

And waiting there on my own I began wondering what had happened to his girl Mavis, but it seemed hardly more than just a few minutes before he came down again, and this time I didn't say anything because he looked well shaken up. He certainly looked white. The screw took him straight off down the passage and he said something as he passed me, but he seemed to be only talking to himself. And I was wondering why I'd never struck him out there, he'd been out on bail I supposed, when it was my turn to go up the stairway.

And it was a surprise to find I'd come out right inside the dock where I had to stand while my case was on. It wasn't so good standing up there with the court full of people that had come to watch, all sorts, besides men for the jury and all the officials and lawyers. But after a time I had a look round to see if Terry was there, though I soon turned round again, because there were too many that were looking me straight in the face and taking me in as if they'd never seen anyone like me before.

There was nobody on the jury I could have said I'd ever seen before and I had to wait a fair time while it was being called. I thought things would never get started, but they did at last when the charge was read out and I was asked if I pleaded guilty or not guilty. Then a lawyer got up and said what my case was about, and after the judge had said something, sort of saying it so nobody could get the guts of it at all, Maggie's name was called out and she came in looking all flossied up. She had to swear on the Bible and the lawyer asked her her name and other things about how we'd been living at Mrs Clegg's. Then he asked her to tell about the night of such and such a day, and he gave the date, and how anybody had remembered I don't know, because I hadn't. And Maggie said how I'd come into the quick lunch place and started talking to her, and afterwards we'd gone up to her room.

Did you invite him to go with you to your room? the lawyer said, and Maggie said she didn't remember.

I didn't mind him coming, she said, and the lawyer said oh. Then he blew his nose and looked at his papers before he said anything more.

Well, he said, what happened?

There wasn't anything happened, Maggie said.

You must tell the court what he did to you, he said.

He never did anything, Maggie said, and the lawyer said oh again.

Come along now, he said, we can all understand your feelings, and he sort of looked round at everybody. But you must tell the court, he said.

And Maggie began to go red but she still said I never did anything. And you could tell it was a surprise to everybody. They stayed that quiet listening you couldn't hear any sound except the sound of breathing, and when the lawyer blew his nose it sounded that loud everybody jumped, and after that it wasn't quiet any more. You could hear people talking and they had to be told to pipe down.

Maggie didn't go any redder than her lawyer did anyhow, he started to get in a temper I can tell you, but the judge chipped in and started to talk to Maggie, but she went on saying no and no. Then the judge said something to the lawyer and he went on asking Maggie questions. Hadn't I done this to her? he said, and hadn't I done that? And Maggie got a bit rattled but she still went on saying no.

So in the end the judge chipped in again, and I couldn't hear all he was saying, nobody could, but he said something about wasting time, and when the lawyer said something about what I'd admitted in my statement he said he wasn't going to let the case go to the jury just on that. And he went on and said a lot more that I couldn't get the guts of at all, but in the end he did say I'd have to be discharged.

And he'd hardly got finished before the screw that had been sitting on the stairs, where he was just out of sight of everybody, told me to come down, and while I was going down he grabbed me by the hand and said I was the luckiest bloke he'd ever known in his experience.

You mind your step in future boy, he said, and going along the passage I was in a sort of daze. All the screws came round to shake me by the hand and I had to sit down because my legs felt as if they wouldn't hold me up.

When I was outside I was still shaking, but I felt a lot better after I'd taken a few big lungfuls of air. And I reckon that's what anybody would feel the need of if they'd just walked out of court without getting a stretch.

But of course I was thinking of Terry, so I didn't waste any time getting round to the front of the court. There were people standing about talking and a few recognised me, and I noticed that now I wasn't standing in the dock they looked at me in quite a different way, but I couldn't be bothered because I had Terry on my mind. I looked inside but there was no sign of him, the place was empty, so just as fast as I could travel I made tracks for Mrs Clegg's place.

The budgie was out on the front of the house, but inside it was all quiet down below. I went up the stairs a good many at a time and Terry's and my room was empty, the bed was made up but the stretcher was gone and there was no sign of anybody's things, and I couldn't help noticing a smell of disinfectant. So without hardly knowing what I was doing I went over and opened Maggie's door, and there was an old man lying on the bed with only his shirt on.

Sorry, I said, Where's Terry? But instead of saying anything he just heaved a half-eaten apple at me. So I slammed the door and called out sorry again, then when I looked out the window of the other room I saw Mrs Clegg along the end of the clothes line, and I didn't waste any time in getting down to her.

Hello, I said, and straight off I said, Where's Terry?

But she bent down and put a clothes peg in her mouth, and I had to wait until she'd pegged it on the line before she answered.

He's in the hospital, she said.

Where've you been? she said, and I looked her straight in the eye even if I did pick on the glass one.

I've just been away, I said.

Look at that, she said, that's where he coughed up his blood, and she pointed to a sheet on the line.

How long ago? I said, and she said two days, and I turned round to go without saying anything more. But Mrs Clegg called out.

There's rent owing mister, she said.

O.K. I said, I'll come back.

And making fresh tracks for the hospital I felt in as bad a daze as I'd felt in only a short time before.

Up at the hospital they wanted to make a fuss about me seeing Terry.

Are you a relative? they said.

No, I said, just a cobber.

And the bloke on the other side of the counter looked at me as if he was down on anybody that was just a cobber.

Well, he said, don't you come here again out of visiting hours. And he told me the number of the ward and said to ask for the sister.

The sister wasn't a bad sort, she gave me a smile and took me out on the verandah, and there was old Aussie face sitting up and leaning on a heap of pillows. He grinned when he saw me too, but Christ, if he didn't look crook.

Hello Terry, I said, and he said Hello boy, and for a while we didn't seem to have anything else to say. I just sat there holding on to his hand, and after giving us a few looks the jokers in the other beds looked away, and I thought it was mighty nice of them.

You're not feeling too good, I said, but just as usual Terry said there was nothing wrong with him.

I want to get out of here, he said.

You better stay if you're crook, I said.

I'm not crook, he said. Listen boy, he said, tomorrow they're going to put me down in a shelter, and he sat up further to look over the verandah rail, and I could see the little shanties he was talking about. It'll be easy to walk out from there, he said.

But can you walk Terry? I said.

I can walk, he said. You come up tomorrow afternoon. They can't keep me, he said.

All right Terry, I said, but I knew I'd have to think it over.

You fix things, he said.

I'll have a try, I said, but have you got any chips?

No, he said.

Never mind, I said, I'll fix things.

So you got off all right, he said.

How did you work it Terry? I said.

I worked it, he said, and he wouldn't say anything more.

Forget it, he said.

Then the sister came back and said my time was up. So I said so long to Terry, and caught up to the sister and asked her a few questions. Terry was pretty bad, she said.

How bad? I said, but she said I'd better ask the doctor if I could find him.

And my luck was in, because going down the stairs I stopped a young joker in a white coat, and he just happened to be Terry's doctor.

That man's in a bad way, he said.

That's no good, I said, but will he get better?

No hope, he said.

Well, I said, how long will he last?

Too hard to say, he said. It's just like that, he said, and he ran on up the stairs.

And it's too hard to say just how I was feeling when I came out of the hospital. I got the feeling again that my legs wouldn't hold me up, so I went and sat on a seat in a bus-stop shelter shed, and I remember I was in such a daze I didn't seem to be thinking of anything at all, not even Terry. Nor noticing anything either. Because people would go past, or they'd come in and sit on the seat and talk, but I never moved or took the slightest bit of notice.

I sort of began to take notice when a dog came up and started sniffing me. Hello dog, I said, and he stood there in front of me with his tail going. And after a bit his mouth started dribbling. You're thinking of tucker are you? I said, and I remembered the piece of bread I had in my pocket, and when I took it out the dog's tail wagged faster. I didn't know the time, it must have been well on in the afternoon, but I hadn't felt hungry. The bread tasted good though, and I broke off small pieces and gave them to the dog, and when I had no more to give him he went down on his belly with his paws stretched out in front, and his tail swept a clean place on the floor of the shed.

But when I'd eaten I decided I'd have to do something, so after I'd kidded to the dog a bit I went down town and waited until I got a chance to use the phone in a pub. Then I looked in the book and rang up a parson that came visiting once while I was out there. I got him all right and he said he remembered me, and after he'd talked a lot of palaver I said I'd got no money and was in need of a job.

Well, he said, I know a gentleman who helps young fellows in your position. He's a very fine gentleman indeed, he said, and he told me the name and I waited while he looked up the phone number.

You ring that number, he said. And remember, he said, any one of us may stumble if we depend on our own strength alone.

That's right, I said.

Goodbye, he said. May you receive grace and strength, he said.

Yes goodoh, I said, and thanks very much.

Then I rang the other number but a girl said the joker wasn't there. She told me to ring his house number which I did, and got on to his missis. And she said he wasn't home but he would be in the evening, and instead of ringing again I'd better call and see him.

So I promised I would, and then I went into the bar but the counter-lunch hadn't come out. I went outside and waited and then I went back and picked on a pretty classy joker that was there on his own. I just went straight up to him and asked him if he'd stand me a half-handle.

Sure, he said. Have a large one, he said, and he called the barman and got the drink.

Things a bit tough? he said.

I'll say, I said, and he talked about the depression and I made the drink last until the tucker arrived. Then we both went over and I put away quite a lot in quite a short time, and when the joker saw the way I was eating he sort of turned the plates round so as the biggest pieces were next to me.

Eat up, he said.

But next minute some of his cobbers came in. They were all classy jokers too, and the first one didn't take much notice of me because he was too busy talking. I stood there finishing the drink, and so help me if I didn't hear them start talking about the Court cases. And by the way they talked I thought they must be lawyers. It made me feel a bit nervous because I thought they might say something about my case, so when they had more drinks all round, and my joker turned and asked me if I'd have another, I said no thanks and shoved off.

I thought I'd need somewhere to sleep that night, though I wouldn't have minded flopping in the park with the weather so good, but of course there was Terry to consider, so I thought it wouldn't do any good to put off trying to fix things with Mrs Clegg.

But soon as I got up there I ran right into Fanny, and it was a hard job getting her to put off paying a visit to the money-tree.

You promised Bill, she said.

Yes I know, I said, but did you look after Terry?

Yes, she said, because he was sick.

You're a good girl Fanny, I said. And seeing I was feeling glad that Terry had been looked after I said that later on I might buy her another budgie, though I told myself I oughtn't to be making any rash promises.

Then I went in and Mrs Clegg and her old man had finished dinner and were having a cup of tea. So I sat down and had a cup and we had quite a long talk, though Mr Clegg was all the time going on about politics and rocking it into the government. Off and on he was reading the paper too, and I had the jitters wondering if he might come across my name.

If things don't improve there's going to be hell to pay, he said.

You may be right, I said.

Yes, he said, when the winter comes there'll be trouble. And it was a fair dinkum prophecy, though I had no idea at the time.

But later on when he went off down the street I had Mrs Clegg on her own, and it was a hard job putting it up to her.

I have to think of the money, she said.

I know, I said. But listen, I said, you've got two rooms empty now, because when people can live in wash houses and sheds for a few bob they won't rent rooms. So why not take Terry and me?

You mightn't pay, she said.

I'll pay, I said. Look, I said, I've got hands, I can work. If I don't pay today I'll pay tomorrow.

And in the end I got her to say yes when I promised I'd let her have ten bob just to show her first thing in the morning.

Well, that was something off my mind, and when I looked at the clock I thought it was about time to go and see the joker the parson had put me on to.

I had to walk a long way to get there, and it was a posh house, one standing in a big garden. But I thought well, he can't eat me, and I rang the front doorbell. It was his missis that opened the door though, and she took me inside into a big room that was fitted up like a sort of gymnasium. Over in a corner there were parallel bars and all that sort of gear, and a heap of things like soccer balls, crash helmets and golf-sticks. And all round the walls were pictures out of the Bible with texts underneath.

She made me sit down and then she said she was sorry but her husband had gone out.

He's so busy, she said, and she asked me if I'd ever been there before.

No, I said.

Well, she said, my husband is such a busy man. I'm sure you wouldn't want to come and take up any more of his time, she said.

So I asked her how did she mean.

My husband is so good to all his boys, she said, but if he doesn't give it all up I think he'll have a breakdown. I do really, she said.

I said I was sorry to hear that, but I was only being polite because it was her I felt a bit sorry for. She looked pretty sick on it. I've never seen anyone look as black round the eyes, and besides everything else she looked a bit batty because her hair was all over the place.

I only wanted to know if he could get me a job, I said, and I told her how the parson had put me on to him.

Yes I know, she said, he sends so many, but she smiled and said of course it wasn't my fault.

Couldn't you go away and do farm work? she said.

Yes, I said, I'd like to, but just now I haven't got a penny to my name.

Then if I give you a pound, she said, will you promise you won't waste it or spend it on drink?

Yes, I said, I'll promise that.

And you'll try very hard to find a place on the farm? she said.

Yes, I said, I'll do that.

Very well, she said, here's more than a pound, and she got up and took thirty bob off the mantelpiece. Though she held on to it until we were out on the verandah, and before she handed it over she said there was just one more thing.

I want you to promise you won't ring my husband up any more, she said.

All right, I said, I'll promise that.

The poor man, she said, he's just wearing himself out.

You want to get him to take a holiday, I said.

She said it was nice of me to say that, and I went down the path thinking she must be a bit crazy. But I had the thirty bob in my hand.

Well, it was late by the time I got to bed, and when I woke up in the morning I felt done. Another day, I thought, and I sort of didn't want to face it, so I kept my eyes shut and turned over and tried to go off to sleep again. It wasn't any good though, I was only kidding myself and I knew I'd better get moving. I hopped out of bed, and while I was stretching I looked out the window at Mrs Clegg's washing which was hanging on the line just like it was on the first morning I stayed there. The weather didn't look any different either, it was just as hot, and I wasn't sure but I thought I could get the whiff from the heap of sawdust in the butcher's backyard. And just for a second it all gave me a sort of peculiar feeling. Because it seemed to be that first morning all over again, and as though I'd gone back and started again, and nothing had happened in between.

If only it hadn't all happened, I thought, but then I thought if one thing doesn't happen another one does, so what's the difference? But I couldn't help feeling there's always a difference all the same.

I went downstairs and collected my things and Terry's from Mrs Clegg and borrowed the teapot again, and she lent me a few teaspoonfuls of tea. And she looked bucked when I gave her half a quid. I fixed up with her about the stretcher and told her I'd be bringing my mate home later on. Though I didn't say anything about how I was going to manage about his tucker if he had to stay in bed. I thought it best to leave that over in the meantime.

Then when I'd had my tea and was out in the streets I felt life wasn't so bad, though I had a longing to go up and see Terry right away. But I'd looked in the phone book and found out the visiting hours, so I was putting it off until the afternoon.

I went and looked at the paper in the library but there didn't seem to be anything doing, so instead of trying the registry offices I decided I'd go and have a shot at getting on relief. And after a long wait in a queue down at the place I got to a window, and the joker there said right away that as a single man they wouldn't consider me unless I'd go to a camp in the country.

Yes, I said, but I've got a sick cobber.

That's nothing to do with us, he said.

No, I said, but I've been sick myself.

What's wrong with you? he said. And I didn't know what to say so I said I'd strained my heart.

Who's your doctor? he said.

Well, I said, I haven't been to one here, and I told him I'd had a job in the country which I'd had to give up because of my heart.

All right, he said, we'll see if you're fit. And after he'd written on a form he gave me a slip of paper and told me where to go.

If you go now, he said, he might put you through this morning.

So what was I to do? I'd told the yarn about my heart but I didn't think there was anything wrong with me. Yet I thought I might as well go and give it a pop, so I went round to the place, and it was a broken-down building in a back street, and when I looked inside there was a big dark room with rows of jokers sitting on wooden seats.

They didn't look any too cheerful either, no, most of them were old jokers, and they all looked as if they were properly up against it.

And while I was standing there a door opened up the far end, and an old joker came out buttoning up his strides. Then a young fellow came out and called a number, and another one of the crowd got up and went in, after which he called me up and changed my slip for a piece of cardboard with my number.

Sit down and wait your turn, he said.

So I went back and sat with the last row of jokers, and the one next to me started talking.

Wait your turn's right, he said. That's what I've been doing all my life.

It's no good, I said.

Yes wait, he said. You can wait here or you can go home and wait, it don't make no difference. It might as well be your funeral you're waiting for, he said.

It's certainly no good, I said.

Wait, he said, yes, wait till the guns go off. You wait boy, he said, you'll find out you were born just at the right time.

But knocking around I'd heard all that sort of talk, so I asked him how long you had to wait.

It depends, he said, you can never tell. We might have to come back tomorrow if the quack's not through by the time he feels like having a bite. I bet he has a good bite too, he said.

I bet he does, I said. Anyhow, I said, I'm going out for a breath of air, and he said I'd better be careful if I didn't want to miss. You can't ever tell, he said.

I went outside anyhow, and just across the road there was a parking place for cars, and up against the wall of a building I noticed a lot of bikes were parked. And so help me if I didn't get one of my notions.

I picked one of the bikes and rode off, and not far along there was a street that cut right up through the park. And I pedalled up that hill just as fast as I could make the bike go. When I got to the top I was done, and I turned round and let her run down again. I parked the bike outside the place and looked inside, but there was still nearly the same number of jokers, not counting a few more that had turned up. So I came out and repeated what I'd done, and kept on several times over. Then I reckoned I'd have time for just one more, and when I got back I was that done I could hardly stagger over and put the bike back where I'd got it from.

Well, I timed it pretty nicely. I just had time to cool off and get my breath under control when it was my turn, and once inside the room the quack asked me straight off what my trouble was.

I've got a bad heart, I said. And without saying anything he put the things in his ears and had a listen. He listened for quite a time too, then he stood back and looked at me.

Who's your family doctor? he said.

You are, I said.

You look all right, he said.

I don't feel too good, I said.

So then he had another listen.

Breathe naturally, he said.

I'm trying to, I said.

And after a bit he sat down and wrote, and before he'd finished writing he told me to go back to the office next morning.

Next, he said, and the young fellow shoved me out, and I came away without having any idea how things had gone.

It was over anyway, and next minute the whistles blew and I decided I'd go a bob dinner. It seemed a mean thing to do, considering the hole Terry and me might be going to be in, but I thought it might be as well if I kept my strength up. I risked going to the Dally's, and as usual at that time he was standing behind the peter, and he seemed as if he was quite pleased to see me.

Is your mother better? he said.

And I had to think because I'd forgotten that yarn.

She's fine, I said.

Good, he said. That is good for you. And it is good for me now you are back to eat here.

Yes, I said. And I sort of realized for the first time he must talk about it being good for somebody to just about all his customers. And

I thought that seeing he hadn't said anything, it was no good asking him about a job just then.

After I'd eaten I just slowly worked my way over to the hospital. Visiting time hadn't started when I got there but I risked going round the building, and I found Terry all right after I'd looked in a good few shelters. He had one all to himself, though there was another bed and he said he'd have a mate by tomorrow. But he started on right away about how he wasn't going to be there tomorrow.

There's nothing wrong with me, he said.

Did you walk down here? I said.

I can walk, he said.

Have you tried? I said.

Listen boy, he said, there's nothing wrong with me except I feel a bit done-in.

O.K. I said, because it wouldn't have done any good telling him he looked awful, and I knew if I kept on I'd only get him narked.

I never could stand being kept in at school when I was a kid, he said.

No, I said, no more could I.

How did Mrs Clegg take it? he said.

She took it good, I said. She's a real nice woman, I said.

She's all right, Terry said.

Listen, I said, I've got enough chips for a taxi, so why not come now?

No, he said, because I don't want any fuss. And you hang on to your chips, he said.

So I said O.K. again and he started talking horses, and all the time I was hearing about which ones would win the autumn meetings I was wishing he'd give me the works about Maggie instead, because I still couldn't get that business out of my mind. But Terry was still talking about the horses when a bell rang and a nurse came past and said visiting time was over. And Terry told me to come up again after nine o'clock when lights were out.

Nobody will see you if you come up from the bottom of the hill, he said.

And I thought that was a good idea, so I said so long and went straight over the grass and down the hill from where I was, just so as I'd have an idea of the way in the dark. And I knew it would be easy, because I could turn round and wave to Terry almost until I was down on the road.

It was lucky I went that way too, because some relief jokers that were working on the road had just finished up for the day. They were locking their shovels in a box and putting their barrows all together, and as I went past I couldn't help thinking that one of those barrows might come in handy.

Well, I kicked about the streets until it was time to pick up the usual bit of counter-lunch, then I went up to Mrs Clegg's and got her to lend me a piece of dripping, which I thought I might need just in case the barrow wheel started squeaking. And I took the blanket off my stretcher and carried it folded up over my arm, though I thought Terry wouldn't need it on such a warm night.

Then time began to drag pretty badly while I was waiting to bring off the stunt, but I went and had a cup of coffee in a coffee and sandwich place, and a hard-case old sheila in sandshoes came and sat next to me. She was the sort you see going into pubs carrying shopping bags with good wide mouths. She kept putting her hand on my arm so I bought her a cup of coffee, and she said wouldn't it be nice to go for a run in a taxi.

Sorry, I said, nothing doing. But with things as they were, I thought maybe I wouldn't have minded if I could have got her to pay *me*.

By nine o'clock though, I was up on the road below the hospital, where it was pretty quiet at that time of night. I tried the barrows until I got the one that ran easiest, and after I'd greased her up and left her by the fence, I climbed over, and Terry saw me coming up the hill and struck a match so I wouldn't mistake his shelter.

And everything went O.K. though all the time we were a bit windy in case some joker in one of the other shelters might ring his bell and give the show away. Terry had managed to hang on to his clothes and they were folded in his locker. He could hardly stand but I got him dressed, and before we shoved off he left a note he had written all ready. Then I got him on my back, and it was easy taking him down hill because he didn't seem to be any weight at all.

We've got our taxi waiting, I said, and he said oh yeah, but he thought it was a great stunt when he saw the barrow.

He didn't need the blanket but he sat on it folded up, and to begin with it was easy because it was still downhill. But then there was a long hill to go up and I had to keep stopping for rests, and Terry joked about how I needed more benzine, and said horsey keep your tail up. And a few people passed us, though no cops, and if we saw them coming I'd have a rest, and Terry'd get out and sit on the edge of the barrow just so as not to attract too much attention.

We had to get across the main street though, and that was worrying me considerably. But we took the barrow down pretty close and parked it on the edge of the footpath, then Terry got out, and with me hanging on to him he could walk, though only slowly, but I got him across, and propped him up against a railing where he could sort of half sit down while I went back for the barrow. And wheeling the empty barrow across didn't attract much attention, and we were lucky, because there weren't any cops.

And we got up to Mrs Clegg's all right, and I got Terry on my back again and carried him up the stairs, though when I'd put him on his bed I just had to flop myself, because I was nearly busted.

Maybe it was the joke of my weak heart that helped me to get my strength back, and I certainly needed it because Terry was lying there helpless just like I'd dumped him. And I thought I could bet he looked a long sight worse than I did, even though I'd been doing all the work. So I doubled his pillow up and used my own as well, then I got him undressed, and I'd never noticed it before but there was a string round his neck with a medal-thing at the end of the loop. I had a look and it said, I AM A CATHOLIC IN CASE OF ACCIDENT SEND FOR A PRIEST.

It was a new one on me, but I asked him if he wanted me to.

If you like, he said, and he closed his eyes again and I had to pull him about until I finished off trying to get him comfy.

Are you all right? I said.

I'm O.K. boy, he said, and I turned off the light and left him, because I knew I'd better go and put the barrow back, even though I was feeling more like leaving it until the morning.

Gee but I was tired the next morning. My head felt as if it was stuck to the bed, and my eyes felt as if they'd had some glue used on them as well. But there was Terry with his wide open, and that was always one thing about him, no matter how crook he was, his eyes always looked bright and lively as a bird's.

I just lay there trying to get over the tired feeling, and after a bit I started joking with Terry about how we only needed to ring a bell and we'd get our breakfast brought in, and in the end I hopped up feeling quite lively.

You won't be getting up today, I said.

Not today, tomorrow, he said.

So I mucked about and got two cups of tea, and then Terry said how about the paper? I went out and got him one, and bought a loaf of bread and a quarter of a pound of butter as well, and he said he didn't want any breakfast but he ate some. And while he was eating I got him to look at the jobs, but he said there didn't seem to be any going.

Then when I'd got myself looking tidy I told him I was going out but I'd be back to see him at midday, and I gave him the tobacco I had left, and he was sitting up reading the paper and looking as if he never had a worry in the world when I went out. Except that he looked so crook.

I went straight down to the unemployment office and waited in the queue, and when I got to the window the joker looked up my papers, and then I had to go round to a counter and wait to see another joker. And he said they wouldn't send me to camp, instead they'd give me about a day and a half's relief work a week, and I'd draw fourteen shillings. I thought that would be all right because it would pay the rent with quite a few bob over, but when I'd filled in the papers he said I'd have to wait a fortnight before I began. And I tried to argue it out with him but it did no good, he said I could take it or leave it. So there wasn't anything I could do, but I came away feeling sore over having to wait a fortnight.

Except for a ten bob note and some chicken feed I had hardly anything left in my pocket, so I went down on the waterfront for a sit-down while I tried to decide what I'd do next. Though what with the ships and the wharves there was so much going on down there, my mind would sort of shy away from trying to decide anything for me. And I was just beginning to think I'd better get off up the street again when a young joker came and sat next to me. We got talking and he said he was out of a job but he'd soon be going back on a farm again. He'd been working there before, he said, and the farmer bloke had sent him a letter to say he could come back if he liked to break in twenty five acres of rough land, and take it over on easy payments. He told me all about it, and if there wasn't any catch it sounded as if there might be something in it. So I told him the jobs I'd had on farms.

Well, he said, how about being mates and going together?

And I liked the look of him so I said O.K. right off, and the thought of being back working on the land again made me feel suddenly all worked up. But next minute I remembered, so I said wait on a bit, because I'd need longer time to decide.

Where can I see you tonight? I said.

Well, he said, it will have to be early, and he said how he was sleeping in a railway carriage, but you needed to be early if you wanted to get a decent possie. So we fixed a date for the afternoon.

Where do you eat? I said, and he said he went on the ships, there were some of them that stood you quite a good feed, he said.

I'm going on now, he said, so you come along.

Sure, I said, and we'd got a fair way along the wharf before I remembered again. I stopped and said I'd changed my mind, and I suppose he thought I was batty, because he went on without stopping. And I suppose he knew I'd never turn up at the place where we'd fixed the date.

But I put it all out of my mind and went up the street and spent my chicken feed on a couple of pies, and got the girl to put on tomato sauce just to give them a taste. Then coming out I ran right into Maggie, and she went red but she stopped and said she'd been wanting to see me.

How are you anyway? I said.

I'm feeling good, she said.

You didn't look as if you were feeling any too good in that witness box, I said.

And she looked away and said wasn't it a pity, and she'd been wanting to apologise.

He beat me up that bad, she said.

He certainly did, I said.

He was a brute, she said. I ran away right into a cop, and he stopped me and I said a man had tried to put one across me.

Too bad, I said.

I didn't know what I was saying Bill, she said. He wouldn't let me go, he made me go to the police station so he could give me to those awful men.

The two demons, I said.

Yes, she said, they kept on that long I had to say it was you.

You didn't have to Maggie, I said.

Yes I did, she said, and she went red again. I didn't want to get Bert into trouble. Bert's all right, she said, I like Bert, he's been good to me.

So I said I supposed that was why he beat her up.

I can't help liking him Bill, she said.

All right Maggie, I said, let's forget it. You put things right again anyhow.

But I had to, she said. Terry said he'd put me away if I didn't. I'd forgot about Terry, she said.

I don't get you Maggie, I said.

Yes you do, she said. You can't tell me you don't know.

Skip it Maggie, I said.

Of course you know, she said.

Cut it out Maggie, I said, and I was feeling pretty annoyed.

All right, she said, but you can't kid me.

Well, I didn't know what she was driving at, and I thought the pies would be getting cold. I said I'd have to go, and Maggie asked me how Terry was keeping and I told her the way things were.

Poor old Terry, she said. I might come up and see him sometime. I might bring Bert and some beer, she said.

Beer mightn't be good for him Maggie, I said.

Aw heck Bill, she said, beer's always good for everybody.

All right Maggie, I said, I might be seeing you.

I said so long and I hurried up to Mrs Clegg's and found Terry half asleep, though he was lying on the top of the bed. It was too hot under the blanket, he said. He certainly looked hot and I was worried, because I didn't think eating a pie would do him any good. But he didn't complain and he ate bread and butter as well, and drank two cups of tea afterwards.

I was worried about leaving him again and he didn't want me to go either. He got me to get a pack of cards out of his suit-case and I played him whisky poker for matches. But after a few games he said he felt like having another sleep, so he settled down and I got him to let me put his overcoat on top of him just in case he caught cold.

I didn't stay long down town anyhow, because kicking round the streets I couldn't think of a single thing to do. And in the end I began to feel reckless and decided to blow in nearly the whole of my last ten bob. I went to cheap places in back streets and bought mutton flap, and things from the grocer's, besides a few nice things for Terry. And when I got up to Mrs Clegg's with an armful she hummed and hahed, but I said everything was for her as well as Terry and me, and in the end she said she didn't mind putting on a bit extra, though she said she hoped Terry wasn't going to be in bed for long.

I thought I'd done a great stroke, I did the vegetables, then I went upstairs to lie on my stretcher and yarn to Terry. And while we were waiting for Mrs Clegg to call out we joked about how it was just as good as staying in a flash hotel.

But later on we'd hardly finished eating when there was a noise on the stairs, and a second later it sounded as if someone had fallen down. I went out and it was Bert and Maggie, and Bert had slipped on the stairs and was trying to get up, while at the same time he was hanging on to an armful of riggers. I went down and took the beer off him and with Maggie shoving behind we got him to the top. Then he was O.K. he had a good few in certainly, and so had Maggie, but they weren't all that tight. They'd brought a lot of riggers and I was worried, because I thought beer wouldn't do Terry any good, but I couldn't do anything, because he looked that bucked when he saw the pair of them. And he said straight off he was feeling dry.

It gave me a rotten feeling watching Terry put away the first few drinks, but once I had a few in myself I felt different. Way at the back of my mind I was remembering what the young hospital quack had said. And I asked myself who was I to be interfering with anyone's pleasure in a world like this? Though it wasn't too nice remembering what the quack had said, and I told myself the sooner I got lit up the better for my own peace of mind. And it wasn't long before I was telling myself it was nice to see a bit of colour in Terry's cheeks anyhow.

It turned out quite an evening, though the pair of them stayed on far too long for my liking. Among four of us the beer didn't last any too long, and when there wasn't any more Bert turned sort of sour, and the way he started picking on Maggie reminded me of Ted and Mavis, though with them it had been the other way about. Maggie was silly the way she took it too, she tried to throw everything back and that only made Bert worse.

I'll make a proper job of you if I start this time, he said.

You better not start, Maggie said, and Bert said wouldn't he start?

You do, Maggie said, I'll put you away.

And maybe Bert would have started on her right then if Terry hadn't managed to grab hold of his two arms.

No rough house, he said.

No, I said, because we don't want any more cot cases.

But Maggie was too far gone to hold her tongue.

Anyhow, she said, I'm sick of wearing these glad rags round my legs.

You shut up Maggie, Terry said, and he spoke mighty sharp.

I won't shut up, she said. What do I care? she said, I'll put the both of us away.

And Bert tried to go for her then, but with Terry and me holding on Maggie got quite a good start down the stairs before he could tear himself away.

Terry and me just lay back on our beds, and it was mighty nice to lie there listening to the quiet after all the row. And I didn't feel like saying anything, because all of a sudden I was a wake-up so far as Maggie was concerned. I lay there thinking back and trying to put two and two together. And I dozed off to sleep thinking unless you do it on paper, it's not always so easy to make two and two add up right.

I could go on and tell a lot more but I don't see the use. Terry never picked up after the night of the party, no, he just sort of went steadily downhill. And there was hardly a thing I could say or do, though he never went short of tucker if he felt like eating.

I'd look at him lying there.

Terry, I'd say.

What is it boy? he'd say.

Nothing, I'd say.

And then I'd say, Terry.

And instead of answering he'd just have a sort of faint grin on his face.

Terry, I'd say.

But I never could get any further than just saying Terry.

I wanted to say something but I didn't know what it was, and I couldn't say it.

Terry, I'd say.

And he'd sort of grin. And sometimes I'd take his hand and hold it tight, and he'd let it stay in my hand, and there'd be the faint grin on his face.

Terry, I'd say.

I'm all right boy, he'd say.

And sometimes I couldn't stand it, I'd have to just rush off and leave him there.

And one night when I came back again I looked at him and knew it was the finish.

Terry, I said, and he didn't answer.

Terry, I said, and I said I was going to get the priest.

Cheers boy, is what I think he said, and I rushed off without even saying goodbye.

I found the place and the priest said he'd come. So I waited and took him along and showed him Mrs Clegg's, and told him where to find the room upstairs. Then I went along the street and the taxi-driver I'd won the double with was on the stand.

Do you want to take one? he said.

No, I said, and I'd only got a few bob, but I asked him if he knew of any decent sheilas.

He grinned and put away the paper he was reading and told me to hop in.

You surprise me, he said.

And it was a fine warm night for a drive. Maybe if only it had rained, I remember I thought.

1938–41

maurice duggan
o'leary's orchard

AFTER all the sun was shining. And Miss Bernstein was due at four. Even so a wind of incredible bitterness was blowing from the south west, carrying from grinding ice floes or the circle about the pole perhaps, a few penguin feathers and, from regions less remote, autumnal and rural smells. O'Leary raked up leaves and prunings, working with his back to the icy blast, preparing with a strong anticipation of pleasure another of his seasonal pyres. His plan was not so much one of smoking out the district as of rewarding himself with dense and pungent billows — and only incidentally getting rid of the orchard trash. These great white clouds of smoke were one of O'Leary's addictions: another, at this time, was Miss Bernstein. He called her Isobel: she called him Mr O'Leary, or Gambo when they were alone.

It was as O'Leary, owner of the place, that he started the base fire of newspapers and dry stuff, waiting for the flames to take hold; but it was as Gambo, lively defector, that he began to pile on the debris of a fruitful year. He used a long-handled fork with curved tines. He took his time. Smoke began to rise in pleasing volume, white or dun.

The imminent visit of Miss Bernstein was a trouble at the back of his mind. Without it he would have been free to become totally absorbed in his present mania. Miss Bernstein was fixed in her expectation that he would seduce her: that was the trouble. But where she would limn simplicities or, worse, a casual unimportance, O'Leary's greater age and more diverse experience had him with his foot on the brake. There were questions of age, discrepancies of May and December. He loved the autumn: she, he fancied, would favour blossom and warmth and downright sun. There were other questions also, among which Mrs Bernstein was notable. She would figure as widow, matron and mother: a sternness could be expected, at the least.

Moodily O'Leary added to the smouldering heap.

Oh he liked her — most immensely he liked her — the lush and lovely Miss Bernstein or Isobel. Better men than O'Leary, or worse, for both were to be found, would sing her praises in their differing keys. He could all but hear the contrapuntal paean. And wiser men, or more foolish, for both again were somewhere about on the unterminating camber of the globe, might find themselves similarly discommoded by Miss Bernstein's headlong rush. She kept her foot down and took the sharpest bends at an undiminishing pace: the passenger seat and its occupant were a mere optional extra. So, at least, O'Leary saw it.

It was unsatisfactory. At first the smoke rose in languid volume and was comforting; but the wind began to gust and fan flames. Soon, where he'd hoped for billows and plumes, an obliteration of white, there was a trembling of fierce heat and no smoke at all. However much he heaped on damp leaves the flames burst through, sending blasts of heat between the fruit trees. The whole orchard trembled. O'Leary sensed danger: this was not his addiction. Even upwind the heat had him sweating. His face was hot while his back gathered a burden, as it felt, of wet snow. He stood back and let the fire burn.

It was three. The sun was only fitful now, but Miss Bernstein was due at four. It would take him that time to shower and shave and change.

He accepted the wind on his face and walked towards the barn.

* * *

Without benefit of hindsight no event could be described as a beginning. Every gesture required a future, looked back on, for significance. O'Leary, at least, could have thought as much.

Faced then with the event O'Leary was forced to remember his own past ambitions, even elements of his own past career.

Acquiescence came easily. Especially with Isobel Bernstein, as spokeswoman for the small group, so encouraging an affirmative, so offering the delightful assurance of gravity and, as far as he could make out in the half-light, charmingly exhibiting a very definite sort of expectation. She did not, that's to say, expect him to refuse; and how, given the circumstances, could he? He had trod for so long that road on which, with an eagerness he could not rebuke, they were now seeking to set foot. If on his side the door was marked 'Exit', on theirs the sign presumably read 'Entrance' in boldest letters. He could resent it as it swung between them, in less of an arc than would be required to reverse their roles or readings. But for her, he saw, he might have been less welcoming; but for her he might have been less accommodating; without Isobel he might have refused.

That, precisely, was what they wanted: accommodation. Room in his great barn to rehearse their play, at a distance from the adverse appraisal and vulgar interference they thought could only be expected from recourse to the usual premises, school or church halls. They knew him to have been, well, not unconnected with the theatre in his day; although they stumbled a little over the absurdity this represented. His day! O'Leary felt them gather about him, the illustrious dead, Garrick, Kemble, Kean — even the great bard himself — among whom he was held to have been contemporary.

Was he, he wondered, so antic a figure? Did he suggest, so directly, a lifetime of bit parts in provincial and amateur repertory? He supposed he did. The little group were so intimidating in their confidence, their dismissals: they so promised to put, in their very first words on stage, his meagre past to shame. He did not matter: the facilities he could offer did.

They stood before him like executioners, a firing squad: they had nothing against him personally. He could even, they pretended, shut the door in their faces. They watched him as Isobel spoke: O'Leary felt a small tremor of alarm. Equally, he thought, could she have ordered his extinction. The merest gesture would do it: her expression would not change. She would continue to look just so, charming and fresh and young, while he surrendered his last breath. Would it not, therefore, be better to be sensible? To step aside and ask them to come in? O'Leary thought it would. He invited them to enter, and apologized for the poor light. His apology was accepted.

O'Leary lingered at a distance, wanting to interfere. Lights blazed and the stage was set; but the play was incomprehensible to him. Part of the time the players were grotesquely masked. Miss Bernstein took the centre. O'Leary, working hard at his exegesis, supposed her to be representing either lust or carnal temptation — in body tights of sheerest black. He could scarcely as yet cry 'bravo'.

That she had her talents he could immediately concede: though her voice, he thought, rather failed to carry. 'Junoesque' was a word that came rather inevitably to O'Leary's mind: 'absurd' was another, as he tried to decipher the mask she carried before her face. A snout, he made out, pointed ears and a fangy sort of grin or leer. A hyena? He sighed for all dead playwrights spinning in their graves. He was resentful: there was no part for O'Leary here. The players did not welcome him. Yet he had helped them rig extra lights and had taken out extra insurance in the form of a public risk policy; and could expect to foot the bill for both. But there was Miss Bernstein, the only female in the cast.

After the first few nights of rehearsal O'Leary kept as much as possible to his quarters at the rear of the barn, regretting his acquiescence. It had not been explained to him that his accommodation could be required not for a few nights but for weeks or even months to come. The play was complex: the producer was a perfectionist — these were the reasons given. O'Leary tried to convince himself that it would be nothing, in retrospect. Probably it was sleep he was missing; it seemed a plausible explanation.

Normally he was in bed by ten thirty; but rehearsals continued most nights to a late hour and O'Leary stayed up to see the players out and bolt the door and switch off lights. He was afraid of fire and the producer scattered matches like a man broadcasting seed. Sometimes it was two in the morning before O'Leary got to bed. A routine was necessary to him: he had no routine, now. And it was absurd that he felt he could do no more about it than grumble to himself.

* * *

It was a night O'Leary would remember for reasons other than lack of sleep and the lateness of the hour.

Miss Bernstein fell and opened the flesh of her palm. It was a superficial if bloody wound and O'Leary, emerging to investigate the crash, had offered antiseptic and tape, and recommended a tetanus shot, although it was not on any of his gear she had cut herself. She followed him to his room.

At close quarters her skin-tight garment held its surprises. O'Leary insofar as conditions permitted, resolutely kept his eyes from undulations and declivities: the flesh was so flawless, the cloth clung so tight, and there was so much youthful hauteur in the extended hand. Miss Bernstein calmly watched trails of blood stain the hot water in the white bowl. O'Leary painted the wound and neatly taped it up. Her finger nails were silver.

He'd made it clear: his quarters were definitely out of bounds: he wanted none of them through here. Therefore the room intrigued Miss Bernstein just that much more. It was bright; it was snug; it was impeccable, if spare. O'Leary, a traveller in his time, watched her finger mementoes of many journeys, the curious objects littering dustless shelves. Her delight was unsimulated: she would never have bothered to pretend. She inspected the equally impeccable kitchen and bathroom. O'Leary, relieved to have her at a distance, wondered did she wear anything at all beneath her extraordinary costume. She was full of questions; but O'Leary was short on answers. She pressed, he felt, too fast; and the others were waiting.

Young she might be, resplendent animal, but the reaches between were great. He needed no looking glass to instruct him in what she saw. He did not pretend to be young, however far he was from the bath chair and the hot cocoa toddy. He watched Miss Bernstein run a fingernail along the spines of a shelf of books; it could have been a stick rattling along a slat fence. Her friends were calling.

Somehow he urged her out without actually touching her. The last thing he wanted was to have the whole troupe in his room. She took her time in going. Her eyes were quick and no more demure than her impossible garment which she would presumably slough before bedtime, like a snake its skin. O'Leary shuddered on that.

Later that same evening O'Leary put down his book and went out into the barn to close up. The players had gone but the lights still burned.

He enjoyed stalking here in the rich smells of fertilizer and packing straw and sawn timber. The stage and bright lights did not affect him now: he had grown used to them. The young people had commandeered so much of his gear — packing bench, boxes, crates, even a new tarpaulin — that he was sometimes forced to improvise as he worked in the orchard. They had lost his hammer: the space they occupied forced him to leave the tractor out in the weather: his routine was a joke.

O'Leary took his stand in the centre of the stage and looked on shadows and darkness. Mice or birds made small discontinuous noises above. He tried a phrase or two, softly: he spoke a line or two, loudly. The barn received his voice with a murmur of sound: the acoustics were of medium quality only. O'Leary sang at the top of his voice; it was the prize song from the Mastersingers, for which he invented words. He'd played Shakespeare in his time: Lear when he was too young and Hamlet when he was too old. Neither performance had inspired the critics: there were references to melodrama, he remembered: 'ham' was a word he winced over. O'Leary shook his fist.

> I'll tell thee. Life and death! I am ashamed
> That thou hast power to shake my manhood thus.

The sad bellow trembled among the small denizens of the roof. He was beginning to enjoy himself. A man could enjoy being ridiculous on his own: he could sing in a moony yell, skipping the high notes: he could spit and leer: he could swagger and strike out, bygod. He stopped, stood stock still, and let himself go upon the emptiness. He was rehearsed.

> You do me wrong to take me out o' the grave;
> Thou art a soul in bliss; but I am bound
> Upon a wheel of fire, that mine own tears
> Do scald like molten lead.

Listening for the dying echoes or the starlings' applause, O'Leary in some amazement heard:

Sir, do you know me?

Miss Bernstein expressing pity or heartbreak came close with clasped hands: Cordelia in black tights and a cardigan, all tenderness.

Sir, do you know me?

O'Leary's embarrassment operated as a mnemonic engram: he couldn't remember a bloody thing. He stood in silence, hunched forward and frowning; it was appropriate.

Sir, do you know me?

Miss Bernstein insisted, piteously: O'Leary gave a gusty groan.

You are a spirit I know . . .

Miss Bernstein prompted. O'Leary shifted up a gear and was off, as Miss Bernstein came near, vibrating with filial love. Shamelessly O'Leary quavered, looking with blankest puzzlement into Miss Bernstein's bluest eyes. He reached out a hand. Miss Bernstein was cold to his touch.

O! look upon me, sir . . .

O'Leary crouched further down and found an old man's falsetto.

. . . I think this lady
To be my child Cordelia.

O'Leary agedly peered: Miss Bernstein all but wept.

And so I am, I am.

Oh wonderful, gently wilting Miss Bernstein. O'Leary's heart was at flood. He leaned upon her as she led him from the stage. He retained his hold as in the dimmer light an active embarrassment grew in him again. He made pointless movements and small coughing sounds and patted Miss Bernstein unnecessarily.

'Naturally,' he said, 'I had supposed you gone. I shouldn't else have been so free, you understand?'

'I loved it.' Miss Bernstein was intense.

O'Leary supposed she didn't mean his caperings and skirls of purely experimental song. 'Lear?' O'Leary said.

'I played Cordelia, at school.' It was too recent to be forgotten. Miss Bernstein hugged her cardigan across her chest: the barn was cold.

O'Leary congratulated himself on a happy escape: he'd been toying with Romeo as the only other part he was up on. (It was at pruning time he practised, generally, from the top of the ladder.)

'Let's do it again.' Miss Bernstein meant it.

'Good grief,' O'Leary said. He stood full height and placed his palms at the small of his back in the region of his kidneys. 'You're frozen, as it is.'

'I'm not.' Miss Bernstein to prove it removed her cardigan; but it was not convincing to a close observer.

Old and stooped with more than orchard weather O'Leary moved on stage.

You do me wrong to take me out o' the grave . . .

Miss Bernstein waited with tender eyes, at a slight distance.

Lear wept; and Cordelia dried his eyes. Until it was two or three.

'How will you explain?' O'Leary switched off lights and was tired. 'Won't your family be worried?' Though rehearsals had gone on late before.

'Mummy doesn't worry.' Miss Bernstein had resumed her cardigan and was wearing in addition what appeared to be a short pelisse of animal skin. Her dark legs emerged beneath: she seemed warmer. 'I'm used to making excuses, anyway.'

O'Leary couldn't believe it. 'I'll see you to the wicket,' he said.

'The wicket?'

'The small door in the big door to save heaving at the vastness.'

It was drizzling at the exit. Miss Bernstein had accepted a shot of whisky and prepared now to brave it to her car. O'Leary felt it would be presumptuous to comment on the weather after what they had just been through. He was, even, masterful in his exhaustion.

'The barge she sat in was a Bentley, eh, or Rolls? You stole it?'

'It's Mummy's.'

'Goodnight, then, Miss Bernstein.'

'Isobel.'

'Goodnight, Isobel. Take the road, at least, with care.'

Isobel Bernstein revealed the tips of delicious teeth in a grateful smile. It was at this point that O'Leary found himself kissing Miss Bernstein in more than farewell, as she stood one step down in the light rain. He desisted, after a minute: Miss Bernstein lingered.

'I'd love to do it again,' Miss Bernstein said, and held her face at a charming cant.

O'Leary's mind had passed into a state of shock. He almost neglected to wave as the spinning wheels flung gravel and the too relaxed turning circle demolished part of his hedge and the car growled sexily out of the drive.

The emptiness of the barn was not its usual comfort as he locked the wicket and walked slowly past the unlighted stage. Miss Bernstein — he preferred to think of her, at the moment, as that — Miss Bernstein had accepted his kiss. Her mouth had been warm. Had he only imagined a return of pressure? Had Miss Bernstein been kissing him, too? Absurd. Consider the reaches between: May and December; Lear and Cordelia; autumn and spring. But on the whole he had enjoyed himself more than somewhat.

O'Leary's numbness began to pass; and sleep came instantly.

* * *

O'Leary's passion was sleep. He slept stark and hated to rise. For winter he would have chosen hibernation, had there been any way of working it without a programme of continuous sedation and intravenous sustenance. In the hour or two, before getting out of bed became an unavoidable action, under the twin dictates of time and his bladder, it was O'Leary's habit to curl himself as nearly as was possible into the foetal position and give his mind free play in that limbo between sleep and waking. It was not a process of thought: that was to be avoided as fatal to the reverie. First his fantasy; and only then, in the last despairing ten minutes, his plans for the day; only then. Although once up he did not find himself longing to be back in bed.

As O'Leary saw it, it was an experiment. You took someone like Miss Bernstein, like Isobel, and dropped her, a chemical of only partly known elements, into the bubbling alembic — where she might or might not prove to be the universal solvent or alkahest. You waited.

In fact O'Leary's fantasy life was thin and had for some years been unsatisfactory. It was repetitious; it was boring. The process of transmutation by acceleration or modification of the elements involved evaded him. Sex tended to disappear as money came to the fore. Miss Bernstein was an admixture of which much might be hoped; although he was not insensible, even in a torpid state, to the dangers attendant on his indulgence. Though he might conjure his wraith in so many moods, the danger, of course, would lie in the way this might affect his dealings with the Miss Bernstein of lovely flesh and blood. The important thing was not to infect fact with fantasy, not to follow her every mood so closely nor wear, while shaving, so bemused and soppy a look.

O'Leary began, therefore, to restrain his passion; even to set the clock an hour fast in the (vain) hope of deceiving himself. He began to be stern with himself. He made braver resolutions as he took his morning shower: he sang sadder songs. If his dreamy figurings prepared him to receive a benison of youth, to draw a sustenance and to bask, after all these years, in fresher light, here in the shower box the light was harsher and his very stance a reminder of other roles. Here, too, there was a tap to douse the sybarite cold.

O'Leary braced himself, held his breath, and accepted the discipline. Hadn't the great Jabir or Geber (Abu Musa Jabir ibn Hayyan) himself put it thus: A medicine of the third order, when projected upon an imperfect metal, takes away all corruption and brings the metal to perfection. Or was that Baden-Powell on the subject of self abuse? No matter. Distillation, sublimation, calcination, solution, crystallization and reduction — these were the steps. He could only do his best. What man could or would do more?

Victory over the baser passions being the anticipated outcome of the new regimen, O'Leary next devoted himself to making some provision for the opposite outcome — the untoward victory of the passions themselves. Both the history of military strategy and the conduct of international diplomacy provided precedent for negative preparedness. With a resolution of spirit and a power of will long supposed by O'Leary to be decrepit in him he embarked on a course of exercises originally developed for personnel of the Royal Canadian Air Force, including combatant units. He omitted neither Saturday nor Sunday and followed faithfully the rate of acceleration recommended for men in the age group just two places lower than his own. At the same time he began to swallow vitamin pills and bought himself a sun lamp.

More than this would have been too resounding an expression of hope, as he followed rehearsals from, as it were, the wings.

The play, to say the least, was bold and curious.

* * *

It was after four.

'Gold,' O'Leary said and lobbed the miniature nugget into her lap. It was the first time he had seen her in a dress and he smiled on what he saw. Blue was her colour and grace her attribute. And he was nervous in the warm room, which was his own.

Isobel gathered it up on its fine chain and cupped it into her palm where it gathered a dull glow: she shook her hand and the chain slithered into coils about the blob of gold.

'Variously described,' O'Leary said. 'A metallic body, citrine, ponderous, mute, fulgid, equally digested in the bowels of the earth and very long washed with mineral water; under the hammer extensible, fusible and sustaining the trial of the cupel and cement. In a word, gold.' He saw that she had not understood that it was a gift. 'Wear it,' he said. 'It may be lucky.'

'Do you mean I am to have it?' Well-spaced eyes she had, blue in a pretty face.

Isobel slipped the chain over her head and the weight drew it down. The nugget plummeted and was arrested at the base of the loop: O'Leary's token nestled and received a mild warmth. He was grateful for felicities: the day seemed to have drooped. Thoughtfully Isobel thanked him and fingered the unfamiliar chain, the golden thread.

While O'Leary lay back in his chair and wondered was it heart attack or cerebral haemorrhage — as exhaustion flooded him abruptly and darkness drew precipitately down. He tightened his forehead in a feline way and squinted and held on. Until, after a lapse of time whose duration he could not have told the measure of, the world reassembled its white walls and soiled coffee cups — and reality its usual discomforts — all to reinforce his sense of having just missed sinking the long putt, that time at least.

It could only have been a few seconds: Isobel had not moved. She sat sideways in the wicker chair and stared out on the orchard where light was dying.

Flesh, mused O'Leary, logically following up the fright he'd had. Grass. Dust. Isobel Bernstein just so many motes flickering in the barn. Himself, too, miraculously aloft, suspired, a wafting in orchard airs and bosky places, enchoired among angels.

He opened his eyes wide to find his sight wholly restored, with a blessing. From under an aery halo his Isobel was profiled upon the green environ, thinking him wrapt still, perhaps, in his meditations upon mortality. The low-cut armhole of her dress revealed the beginnings of the youthful camber of her breast. O'Leary gazed upon it as if upon sculptured perfection, a flawless and formal mounting of a mass, in pure appreciation. These were glimpses that undid the world. All was delicate. He lusted, surely? The armpit itself was naked, axillary fuzz having been, presumably, depilated.

'It must be the smoke I inhaled,' O'Leary said. 'Over the bonfire. I feel somewhat giddy. Should we have a drink? Would you mind?'

'I thought you had fallen asleep.'

'Isobel.' He could find power for that.

It was what enslaved him, he thought, this perfection of bodily beauty. He admired it for what it was, in a spirit of passive and slightly despairing tenderness. Here, indeed, were the reaches between — that perfection and these sore eyes. He could have been content to praise and depart if life, he managed to construe, were ever like that.

She brought him the bottle, and water in a jug. She knelt to pour. She seemed very young, just then. How long to the hours when he must rise?

'They say it's worse than dope,' O'Leary said. 'The psychopath is neither calmed by it nor incapacitated. Which must be hell, for someone.'

But it did the trick. He found his feet and held his young woman in blue: she leaned into his embrace without surprise. O'Leary headily inhaled hair spray and wisps of hair.

'Sir, do you know me?' Isobel was prepared to play; but it was not O'Leary's present mood.

'Do you mind?' O'Leary said. "Will you, I suppose I mean?'

'Oh Gambo. Of course I don't. Why should I?'

O'Leary could accept absolutes, even so softly delivered.

Geber had no description for these elements, no voice in this arena, no ear for this pounding of blood, as Isobel emerged white from blue in truly superb glissades, and then authentic rose.

'I am ashamed,' O'Leary murmured, 'that thou hast power to shake my manhood thus.'

'Ashamed?' It was a moment when Isobel could welcome for her shyness a lightening of the note.

'Enthralled,' said O'Leary, and raised his glass for her to sip.

'I must be careful,' Isobel said. 'I mustn't be too late.'

An appalling thought struck O'Leary.

'Isobel, you aren't by any chance . . .?'

'No. Of course not.' She was quick to soothe. 'Don't worry. Shall I leave the chain?'

'Ah,' O'Leary said. 'I think not. No, no chains.'

Briskly, noisily a starling was chattering at the apex of the barn. Light lay along dusty beams, remotely. A long way up hard light showed in piercing perforations through the iron. Then afternoon had deepened and rain was falling: falling.

The avidity could not have frightened her, it involved her too much; but the gloom and the lofty birds and the hard pinpricks of light were sources of unease as she resumed white, then blue — the rose Miss Bernstein.

'I'll be late. I must run.'

'Will you take the old brolly?' O'Leary was aware of rained-out fires and charred leaves.

Isobel in her bright rain-hood would have no need of it; it would be an embarrassment. Her face was calm and serious before the luminous mirror whose silvering had blackened.

'I'll see you to the wicket.'

'The little door in the big door to save heaving at the vastness?'

O'Leary allowed it: she was a good mimic. For another thing, she had memory; it would be a blessing or a curse.

'It sounds like popular theology,' O'Leary said. 'Like who will get God back into the re-entry system.'

The empty stage was merely empty.

Isobel took his arm, swinging the frail charm like a censer.

'It's only a bauble,' O'Leary said. 'Sentimental value, only.'

'I know.'

At the barn door she waited to be kissed, of right. O'Leary bent to her, his sight blackening. The delicate flanges of cheek bone, impatience pulling a tension into her upper lip, the regard that was simply unblinking and unevasive — this was too great a gift to return.

'Look. At any time. This place, whatever . . .' He could not face it out, and even wished it unsaid.

'Sunday,' Isobel said. 'At four.'

The refusal of coyness, the choice of the surest and smallest of smiles, remained with O'Leary long after Miss Bernstein had gone — or Isobel as he preferred, at the moment, to think of her — in red and blue and, as he knew, in white and rose; and gold sustaining trial of the cupel and cement.

It remained with him while he changed into gumboots and went down through the orchard: dark facets, bright cambers and peace of a kind. And blue for a colour, and rose. All animals are sad at such a time.

The gumtree towered and seemed to loom, wheeling across the empty sky. Dark was well and truly down. The fire was not completely extinguished and a few wisps of smoke trailed through branches. O'Leary was struck with a redolence that evaded, as the cold air smartened his flesh. He felt tired. He scattered grain before the hens in their long coop. Rain dribbled down the mesh of wires. The birds ate quickly with bright concentration, as the wind turned the ends of feathers in ruffs of gold.

Indoors again he righted his room and poured himself a drink. Objects took up their old positions with reluctance: things appeared to be different. The manual cautioned against undue haste: no steps should be omitted.

* * *

O'Leary resented the chill and the hard chairs. Having retained his topcoat he waited for the house lights to dim so that he might resume his gloves: he was delicate in company. There was nothing he could do for his ankles except cross them for companionship and in hope of warmth. The space required for this manoeuvre, however, was greater than the space provided: having crossed his ankles O'Leary found them locked in a position of extreme discomfort, jammed, in fact, through the back of the chair immediately in front of him.

'If you don't mind.' Lacking the warmth, her stare lacked nothing of the colour of burning acetylene.

'Forgive me. A thousand apologies, of course.' He had to use his hands to prise his shins and ankles apart: the attention this attracted was not kind. In a mood of some petulance O'Leary thrust his feet under the rungs of his chair.

The hall was not full but the vicar, from whom it had been rented, occupied a position of prominence before the stage curtain. His profession O'Leary identified from his collar: his role of custodian was blind surmise. Equally a surmise was O'Leary's identification of a small man with a pointed beard as representative of the fourth estate: a reporter if not a critic. The fellow was scribbling full pelt and the show hadn't even started.

O'Leary could not wait: he drew on his gloves and placed his hands in his armpits, the left in the right the right in the left, hugging himself without pleasure. The thought of Isobel in nothing more than a body-stocking froze his blood. He sucked a peppermint to disguise the whisky on his breath; it was all too easy to offend.

The programme spared no expense to be elegant; in the chastity of its typography it acknowledged the kindness of Mr G. O'Leary in making premises available for rehearsal and rendered, to Mrs Rebecca Bernstein, those thanks so fully due to one whose generous contribution alone made possible this et cetera and et cetera.

O'Leary deeply regretted it: the reference to himself, set down with such civility, was a disaster. Knowing what was to come he prepared his plea of not guilty, basing it on the argument that as the vicar had also made premises available he, the vicar, should also, in all logic, be charged as party to the commission of a public indecency. Justice demanded it. Mrs Bernstein, on the other hand, whatever she might think of being yoked with O'Leary as an active supporter of the players in this misguided venture, was truly in the gun: with sums great or little, with cash, including the copyright fee presumably, she had actually financed the bloody thing. Her daughter, this innocent girl your honour on my honour, actually played the vicious and debauched heroine of this wholly offensive play in total ignorance, could it be doubted?, of the blasphemy and filth she was taught to parrot and the obscene actions she was taught to mime. How do you plead, Mrs Bernstein, wherever you are? Remember, before you speak, that it is not denied that this play was translated from the French: any mother anxious for the welfare of her daughter and only child might well have taken that as warning enough.

The vicar, more of a stayer than O'Leary would have believed from knowing nothing about him, left soon after the rise of the curtain on the third act. His departure involved a decidedly noisy shuffle along half the length of one row: his progress up the aisle was magnetic. By the time he reached the door he had a good twenty people in tow. His look threatened action.

Half way through the third act a uniformed sergeant of police climbed up on the stage and stopped the play. The representative of the press approached the sergeant with pad and pencil. The players stood about. Isobel, who after all had not worn a body-stocking, was wrapped in a grubby rug. A fierce argument broke out among a group of young people and a florid gentleman who had been close to the vicar: the young people appeared not to condone the police action. The florid gentleman offered a number of opinions on the class and intellectual competence of the young people, disparaging their appearance as his choler brightened. Several police constables entered the hall and proceeded down the aisles: the audience began to disperse.

O'Leary, who was not sure just what was going on in his mind — it was just now, through some trick of light and difficulty of breathing, a tabula smaragdina — pushed away the empty chair in front of him and crossed his ankles. He placed his hands in his armpits, as before, and lay back as comfortably as the chair would allow. The police sergeant was speaking to the players. He was a burly man, perfectly cast for his role; and for a moment O'Leary wondered whether this was part of the play. A constable was taking notes, when told to. Of the reporter or critic there was now no sign. The question of refund of the price of admission, in whole or in part, had not been raised by the audience and seemed unlikely to be mentioned by the police.

O'Leary calculated that he had received seven-eighths the value of his complimentary ticket.

O'Leary soon became a conspicuous figure: he was the only one seated. Indeed he was the only occupant of the rows of seats. What portion of the audience had remained was gathered at the back of the hall near the door. O'Leary was thus in excellent position to be observed by Isobel — a consideration he had not overlooked. Pale but proud, he thought, she let her eyes rest on him. O'Leary met it with a simultaneous pursing of the mouth and a drawing together of the eyebrows: intended as a grimace or mime whose meaning she should read as reassurance and support, it gave him a vaguely simian look.

O'Leary then withdrew his hands from his armpits and the gloves from his hands. By vigorously opposing his palms he produced a fusillade of applause, a series of rapid and loud reports. He continued this for a full fifteen seconds, sensing the moment when he would pass over into anticlimax or bathos. The sound was arresting. Police and players froze in surprise and the silence to the rear of O'Leary was broken by a babble of distant geese. O'Leary resumed his gloves. The sergeant spoke to the constable: the stage emptied and the curtain came down.

'I'm afraid I must ask you to leave, sir. The performance has been discontinued.'

'You can say that again,' O'Leary said. 'I'm waiting for someone. The danger is surely past.'

'The danger, sir?'

'Of corruption, contamination, infestation; call it what you will. I am undebauched.'

'Orders are to clear the hall, sir. Now if you wouldn't mind moving.'

'Clear? It would be considered empty, by some.'

O'Leary shuffled sideways along the row, away from and not towards the constable. His passage up the aisle was noble, if less magnetic than that of the vicar: he walked alone. The persons in the porch, which he soon gained, evaded his eye. O'Leary stood among them easily: they were unremarkable: not one, he noted, was slavering with lust or outrage. Beyond the door, across the gravelled drive and the width of footpath, the police sergeant was holding the door of the Bentley as Isobel bundled in still wrapped in her rug. O'Leary thought he could reasonably assume it to be Mrs Bernstein at the wheel. He stepped clear of the porch and waved and, yes, Mrs Bernstein flashed him that acetylene blue stare with, perhaps, just the slightest diminution of confidence, the mildest increase in warmth. Isobel waved in reply; it was a semi-regal acknowledgement, really. She said something to her mother. Mrs Bernstein replied: her lips moved with energy: her plosives would be immense. The car hesitated in its slow forward movement while Mrs Bernstein leaned to look across to O'Leary. The police sergeant also looked. O'Leary continued to stand. It was at such moments that he wished he were a smoker: a cigarette or the action of lighting one could do so much to relieve situations such as this of their rigor. The car resumed its forward movement; its speed increased. O'Leary, in a style totally foreign to him, turned up his coat collar. He passed before the police sergeant and up the street, giving a curt nod which the sergeant did not return.

He hadn't covered fifty yards, his numb feet paining, when the little man with the pointed beard caught him up.

'Hot foot from the news room?' O'Leary was affable.

'You applauded? I didn't see it, but they said you did.'

'I clapped,' O'Leary said. 'Yes. The intervals between are vital to an assessment of my intention. Slow means one thing; fast, another: you checked on the timing?'

'You were the only one, you know. The consensus of opinion was definitely in the opposite direction.'

O'Leary recognized that his companion was composing his piece as he walked.

'I am not an official,' O'Leary said. 'I don't feel committed to the official view.' It was deeply said and it pleased him.

'Would you like to express an opinion, give your name?'

'For publication?' They had reached the bus stop. O'Leary entered the bleak niche, glancing at his watch.

'Well, I can't promise.'

'I'd hardly meant to elicit a promise,' O'Leary said. 'No I think not:

I'd miss my bus. Goodnight. Oh, by the way, it didn't occur to anyone that I might be applauding the action of the police?'

'No. Were you?'

'No. Fast clapping, though.'

O'Leary ascended the steps of the bus. He found his hands were trembling as he deposited coins.

'A cold night,' O'Leary said. 'The wind's bitter.'

The driver found nothing exceptionable in the remark: the bus pulled away.

* * *

The morning paper found a place for it, on the front page. O'Leary settled himself with toast and coffee.

POLICE CLOSE DOWN FIRST PERFORMANCE
OF 'THE WOMAN FROM OMSK'
UNPARALLELED DEPRAVITY, SAYS VICAR
Last night's opening performance of 'The Woman from Omsk' came to an unplanned climax when police closed down the play some time before the final curtain.

The Reverend Kindleysides, Vicar of St. Jerome's in whose hall the play was being presented, described the play as unparalleled in its depravity.

It was a shocking comment on the corruption of so many of today's youth, the Vicar said, that such filth, blasphemy and straight-out sexual perversion could be so casually accepted as subjects for dramatic exploitation.

Referring to a golden inheritance from our rich, dramatic past the Reverend Kindleysides said he had been blatantly hoodwinked into believing the play to be unexceptionable, even though cast in the modern idiom.

PLAY TOO OFFENSIVE

Detective Inspector Farrant, speaking for the police, said investigations were proceeding but it was not yet determined whether further action would be taken.

Inspector Farrant denied that the police had acted on a complaint by the vicar. Action had been initiated by a member of the Special Branch who had been a member of the audience. The officer concerned deemed the play too offensive on several grounds and for that reason the play had been stopped. Police monitoring of doubtful plays was common procedure in most countries, the Inspector remarked.

DRAMA HEAD SPEAKS

Dr Robert Love, Professor of Drama, said last night that although he had not read the text of the play, nor seen the performance in question, he believed the playwright, Vincent de Beauvais, enjoyed a considerable reputation. He was considered one of the foremost exponents of the so-called theatre of cruelty.

Professor Love pointed out that experiment was vital to the theatre. He thought the young people concerned were to be commended for their courage. Given the audience, however, the Professor said, and the venue of the performance, a less controversial play might have been a wiser choice. 'This is definitely not Paris or New York,' the Professor said, 'and we would do well to bear that in mind.'

The university library has no copy of the play.

A MODERN ALLEGORY, SAYS PRODUCER

Prime mover behind the Group, the company responsible for last night's interrupted performance of 'The Woman from Omsk' is Mr Robert Boyle.

Mr Boyle pointed out that the company had no university affiliations.

Miss Isobel Bernstein, who last night played the role of the infamous woman from whom the play takes its title, is a first-year drama student. This was her first appearance with a professional company, though she had previously acted in school plays.

Mr Boyle described the play as a modern allegory that has been acclaimed by critics in Paris and New York. The fact that the play had been banned in London was hardly relevant, Mr Boyle said.

We live in a century of cruelty and horror, said Mr Boyle, and he hoped the reverend gentleman was not being hoodwinked over that.

Regardless of the outcome of the present 'brouhaha' as he called it, Mr Boyle intends to commence rehearsal, immediately, of another play — *Sister Maybelle*. Our drama critic writes about last night's performance on page 9.

The critic could wait; but the producer's intention of rehearsing another play, under, doubtless, the same difficulties as to premises, had O'Leary hopping. He went out into the barn without clearing away his dishes: he was almost running.

By two in the afternoon the stage had been dismantled and the barn restored to a more usual state of practical disorder. The tractor, jacked up and with the front wheel removed, stood in the space previously occupied by the stage. The stage lights were dismantled and stacked by the door. O'Leary's system of graded exercises stood him in good stead: he panted but was not disqualified by fatigue from finishing the job.

* * *

Time: 4 p.m. Day: Sunday. Weather: south-westerly squalls with hail; thunderstorms intermittent. Temperature: 52 degrees Fahrenheit. Humidity: 70 degrees. Position of Miss Isobel Bernstein on O'Leary's bed: axis NNE SSW, as near as dammit. O'Leary's position: SSW

NNE, axis unstable and veering. Lighting up time: not given. Room temperature: 72 degrees Fahrenheit. Miss Bernstein's vital measurements: 34, 26, 36. For O'Leary: $7\frac{1}{8}$ $8\frac{1}{2}$ $10\frac{1}{2}$ $16\frac{1}{2}$; hat, gloves, shoes, shirt — none of which he was wearing.

Isobel Bernstein had been comforted: she felt herself also to have been befriended, to have been loved. She was pleased to be warm, as rain or hail rattled on the roof and the wood-fired stove pulsed. It was perfect weather for being indoors and naked in bed. Earth has no power without the moist.

O'Leary had moved off, to attend to the making of coffee.

Why in hell, it may be asked, was not O'Leary in bed and Isobel brewing up in whatever condition of dress or undress best suited her? O'Leary's answer: life was a calculated risk. He had given for the moment his all: the challenge of a persisting contiguity he knew to be sometimes excessive. It was also, though the relevance could be questioned, O'Leary's birthday: he kept it secret, as he also kept secret the fact that given a choice between water steam and earthly smoke he would have preferred an orchard blaze-up any day to standing around waiting for the bloody coffee to percolate. But, irritation apart, O'Leary enjoyed coffee as only he could make it; and Isobel Bernstein also. It was, in short, a Sunday like many others. Sometimes, some Sundays, the sun shone; at other times, on other Sundays, it rained; occasionally, on yet other Sundays, it was merely overcast. This was the weather of the orchard.

Isobel's distress, after last night's first-and-last-night fiasco, had not been great: her vanity had not been wounded. O'Leary admittedly had dried small tears and prescribed strong drink as a stimulant and, in its exact sense, a depressant. He had assuaged. Hand held and a flawless cheek smoothed — this had occupied a little time. Then with the liberty claimed and the comfort accepted he had bundled his miss into bed, where her eyes were soon dry.

Now they drank coffee together. Isobel sat up in bed and O'Leary, in only moderate comfort, perched on the edge. She was wearing O'Leary's gift, tenderly. The situation was wholly compromising to both, the moreso as the temperature of the room was not such as to require O'Leary's partner to cover herself for warmth.

They had reached, easily enough, just that stage of freedom in each other's company; throughout the protracted rehearsals and since. O'Leary suspected that he was the more enchanted, for the simple reason that Isobel offered enchantments he could scarcely match. As a gentle if somewhat dramatic lover he had done what he could to diminish the years between: he brought her forward while himself moving back. Isobel had developed: she offered the diagnosis herself. And this day O'Leary had felt free to read to youth a strong and silent lesson; free to revenge himself on a day of nativity. He was a little bored with his miss, although Isobel confessedly found the whole thing wonderful to the point of being fabulous.

O'Leary put down his cup and paid homage to splendours, not least his gift of gold on white. The supplicant was honoured and the woman from Omsk exorcised.

All animals are sad at such a time.

The acoustics of the barn, considered by O'Leary as being of medium quality only, tended to magnify all sound other than the human voice. Mice could be loud and starlings thunderous.

The knocking, therefore, separated them as abruptly as if shots had been fired — while they assured each other, in whispers, that all doors were bolted and curtains drawn. O'Leary supposed the plume of smoke might tell a tale but not, surely, of more than a general kind: he could have slipped out for a minute. Nevertheless they lay quiet. The knocking continued intermittently.

O'Leary, having recently discarded his few garments, crawled on hands and knees to the farthest corner of the room. From here, by bringing his eyes just above the level of the sill, he could see under the curtain. His position commanded a view of the corner of the barn and the driveway, though not of the door itself. He crouched there. The knocking ceased. O'Leary crept back to the bed where Isobel was huddled deep, more in amusement than fright. O'Leary could not see what there was to titter at.

'Didn't you say you came by taxi?'

'Yes, why?'

'There's a Bentley in the drive.'

'Mummy.' Isobel giggled into a wad of bedclothes.

'Could she suspect you were here?'

'No, of course not. It must be something to do with last night. She asked about you in the car.'

'She's probably setting fire to the barn right now.'

'Oh, Gambo. You don't know Mummy. She'd feel she had to talk to someone — someone who understood.'

'Understood?'

'About modern plays.'

'That lets me out. I don't understand a bloody thing.'

'Yes, but you wouldn't be stuffy.'

'Thank you. Would your mother, then, be liberal in her view?'

'She'd try to be, probably. But that's why she came.'

'Let's hope. Fervently.'

O'Leary went more boldly to the curtain. The Bentley was wheeling away. Isobel joined him. They stood there as naked as candles.

'It could be another Bentley,' O'Leary said. 'I believe they make more than one of a model.'

'There'll be a note,' Isobel said. 'Through the flap in the door. Mummy would always come prepared for everything.'

'You frighten me,' O'Leary said. 'I think of a loaded pistol in the glove box: I think of a limpet mine fixed to the wall: I think of canisters of poison gas. Comfort me quick.'

'Let me go and see.'

O'Leary let her go, with all her vital numbers. There seemed to him to be far too much bare flesh about. Comparison could sometimes be too vivid: he put on a robe. Isobel sprinted amazingly back and flung herself into bed.

'Look, I've got goose flesh. It's like an ice-chamber out there. I couldn't find my way: I forgot you'd changed everything back.'

'No time bomb ticking? No trace of poison gas? You should have taken a canary with you?'

Isobel opened the pale blue envelope and extracted the folded note. Her fingers were quick and predatory.

'She wants to see you.'

O'Leary accepted it. Mrs Bernstein wrote upon plain notepaper in a firm hand. She would welcome an opportunity to speak about last night's debacle (accent and circumflex). Isobel had spoken of him, O'Leary, as being a theatrical person. If he, O'Leary, could name a time.

'Will you?' Isobel toyed with the nugget of gold.

'I doubt if we'd see eye to eye,' O'Leary said.

'You could say a word for me. She's mad about the whole thing — about its being me. And all that publicity. She wants me to get right out of drama school altogether. Right out. Or go away, somewhere, to study.'

'Go away?' Did his heart heave and the firmament blacken? O'Leary considered it. 'The part, you know, was ambitious for a novice. It must be conceded. The critic, as I remember skimming, remarked that an ability to compass a role of that kind could only be actively deplored in an actress of such tender et cetera ceteras. He didn't, doubtless, put it so well.' O'Leary was preparing a speech for Mrs Bernstein.

'You're forgetting the physical presence,' Isobel crowed.

'Please,' O'Leary said. 'It was the topless drama bit that did it. Don't arouse the sleeping beast in me. Anyway, I can't speak for you. We have, remember, only the most remote of relationships. I do not, you will notice, smirk; but this would hardly be acceptable to your mum.'

His allusion, not at all obscure, was to intimacies; to a casual scatter of clothing and to distressing jubes of flesh; to obscured windows and locked doors; and to other things he could not entirely forget — discrepancies of the calendar, for one.

'I'm merely the proprietor,' O'Leary said, 'of this place and its chattels.'

He was pleased to have said that.

'You are absurd,' Isobel said.

O'Leary accepted the remark as obscure in its reference.

'Gambo, can we have a drink? Can we have a whole lot to drink?'

'Moderation,' O'Leary said. 'The consequences of an excessive ingestion are described in the literature. Many a young woman has been undone down that road. And besides, it would be poor policy, positively unwise, to arrive home loaded at such a time. The air is charged with emotion; and the stuff doesn't encourage reticence.'

Isobel's free laughter, surprisingly mature in its tone, charmed and perplexed him as always. If he thought her a girl or, at the farthest reach his mind could tolerate, a young woman, her laughter suggested that she had changed under his eyes. The processes of her thought, the way through to her bursts of amusement, were not always open to him: her mirth seemed at times to bear no relation to what he either said or implied. This occasion was not, however, an example of that: he knew what amused her.

O'Leary poured drinks: this was not a medicine of the third order and purification was not to be expected, now. Splendidly Isobel emerged and crossed to the stove to toast herself and turn deeper rose in its glow.

'Alcohol,' O'Leary said. 'A powder for painting the eyes, I believe.' He had found that a little pedantry could sometimes take the place of dangerous endearments; as Isobel simply showed him, in firelight, the perfection of her body and the pride of her youth. 'Junoesque' now seemed to O'Leary, seeing her like this, too solid a word. The gold gathered light. In the orchard it was dark. O'Leary toasted the toasting Isobel. Time: 6.10 p.m.

Superficially, he would have admitted, they seemed interchangeable. That is to say that often enough in his infrequent wanderings at the heart of the city he had picked from the file of flesh so tenderly observed many who matched and not a few who excelled his Isobel. Beauties were rare and Isobel was not such a one; but O'Leary could be bemused by less. In their wake O'Leary had wandered, having forgotten to strap himself to the mast. He had wished for that confidence, if not for that veneer — while their chatter appalled him.

Superficially interchangeable only, then. O'Leary fancied he saw Isobel's grace as glowing at greater depths — as now, when she was not boring him at all. She had for him so many advantages over all the others: simply expressed this meant that she was, however tenuously, his. Dark facets, bright cambers, rose declivities; and that regard that was simply the most open and calm of looks. Not a pore out of place, bygod.

For himself, as said, he needed no mirror: he wore his personality like a disguise.

'Gambo, what if I became pregnant?'

'Good God,' O'Leary tossed his drink straight off. 'But you told me you took them. Do you mean you don't?'

'It's all right. I do. But I was just thinking.'

'Abandon it,' O'Leary said. 'You have a frightening mind.' O'Leary poured a medium shot. 'Please don't indulge it. I'm old enough to be your father.' He could recognize vagueness, inconsequentiality, even obscurity — in himself. And he could wonder why she had raised the question, and be worried.

'You don't have to keep saying that,' Isobel said, turning the long scoop of her back to the warmth. 'What difference does it make?'

(How do you plead, O'Leary?)

'Some girls prefer older men, that's all.' She offered a pout.

'My dear girl, you do have your brevities. That's all, indeed.' He was distracted.

'Don't laugh at me.'

Could a woman be without guile, O'Leary wondered? 'Doesn't it occur to you,' he said, 'that my surely infrequent references to my age might have the purpose not of reminding you of differences but of eliciting your increased respect?'

'What? No.'

'I doesn't to me, either. Doesn't occur, I mean.' O'Leary put down his glass. 'I am a very foolish fond old man,' O'Leary trembled. 'And skipping the next bit, pray undo me this button.'

'What button?' Isobel said, but moved from the fire.

The great barn magnified all sounds except the human voice; mice were loud and starlings thunderous. A moon showed somewhere. And they laughed.

* * *

The Mappae Clavicula recorded it: On mixing a pure and very strong wine with a third part of salt (xkok cum 111 qbsuf tbmkt — decoded by Berthelot), and heating it in vessels suitable for the purpose, an inflammable water is obtained which on ignition burns away consuming only itself.

O'Leary drank his whisky without ignition.

'You must forgive my hands, Mrs Bernstein.'

O'Leary displayed them. Knuckles were variously abrased and a strip of plaster concealed a wound.

'It's the tractor,' O'Leary said. 'The time of year for overhaul. The sap you see is down.'

'I have remarked, Mr O'Leary, that you alone had opportunity to observe. You alone, therefore, could warn.'

'Another?'

'Thank you. In this weather, without the ice I think.'

'Warned the Reverend XYZ? Kindleysides, it was.'

'Warned me, Mr O'Leary. Thank you.'

'I am here, they are through there.' O'Leary pointed to a wall. 'In my life I have been rather more recipient than donor — of warnings. Have I drowned it?'

'I am enjoying it. But you are a person of the theatre, Mr O'Leary. Or so I am told. This is not true?'

'Of antiquity,' O'Leary said. 'See me as Lear: see me as Bottom; see me as Caliban.'

'A brute,' said Mrs Bernstein.

'Precisely.'

'But the very language, to begin with — you could assess that.'

'Anglo Saxon in places: a translation. A profound history of usage is required to establish an obscenity. Blasphemy, on the other hand, has been described as the obverse of veneration. It too requires a history — a couple of millennia in this case. Correct me if I'm wrong.'

'I do not expect to see, well, breasts bared on stage.'

'With drama, Mrs Bernstein, that is surely of the essence.'

'I am speaking, forgive me, of my daughter's breasts. It is not propriety I am concerned with, Mr O'Leary; it is notoriety. I do not wish to see Isobel confused with the woman from Omsk.'

'In O'Leary's barn . . .' O'Leary said. 'No, let me put it another way: in what I sometimes overlooked but did not supervise — I ask you to remember that — there was no exposure of the person, the upper torso.' O'Leary lowered his eyes, in reverence — or in concealment, should his eyes be shining with the glory of his reminiscence.

'Had Isobel been your daughter, you would have permitted all this?'

'I am old enough to be her father.'

'Are you intending to flatter me, Mr O'Leary? I am her mother.'

'Another?'

'A small one. I am driving.' Mrs Bernstein stood up. She was a tall woman. 'Through there?'

'Yes, to your right.'

'Drinking one night in O'Leary's barn . . .' O'Leary sang soft and poured big drinks. The guest towel she would find immaculate and the soap Imperial Leather.

'Dear Mrs Bernstein, I must warn you. The play in which your daughter intends to perform, publicly, is blasphemous, scurrilous, obscene and indecent. Furthermore it involves exposure of the person. Intimacy is suggested and acts are performed on stage which a decent intelligence could only describe as sadistic, masochistic and phlogistic. Signed, a friend.'

'Isobel has spoken of you, Mr O'Leary.'

'I beg your pardon?' Was he, he wondered, being warned?

'You could have put your signature to it. You could have spoken.'

'Alcohol,' O'Leary said. 'A powder for painting the eyes, I believe.' He considered his glass. 'I am merely the proprietor of this absurdity and its chattels.'

'Have you the time?'

'Early,' O'Leary said. 'Approaching ten. Coffee?'

'Please. Black without sugar.'

'I had no picture of you, Mrs Bernstein. A warning of whatever kind could well have been wholly unacceptable. And on what basis was I to warn? As guardian of the public morality and the tender innocence of the young? Black, without sugar.'

'Oh innocence.' Mrs Bernstein was impatient. 'Thank you, it smells delicious.'

'I pride myself on it,' O'Leary said. 'But two things are confused. If I could have predicted the unacceptability of the play, to that sort of audience, that is not to be read as a censuring of the play itself. I don't see how I could have spoken nor, reasonably, how you could expect it.'

'The theatre was your profession, Mr O'Leary?'

'Amateur,' O'Leary said. 'Whose derivation is love. Repertory, that was all.'

'Do you see Isobel, Mr O'Leary . . .' She paused. 'Do you see her as having a career in drama? An essential career? From what you know and have seen?'

What he had seen? Gold on white on rose: a nimbus of bright hair: an unction — that was the Isobel he had seen. He could concede the possibility of figmentation: sometimes Isobel looked quite plain.

'How could I comment?' O'Leary said. 'The part, you know, was an ambitious one for a novice to attempt. The critics allowed her a physical presence.'

'Oh I dare say she has that. But haven't a great many others, also? It's not so rare as to be a great distinction, surely?'

'She performed bravely, at best.'

'Boldly, at least. Thank you, only half a cup.'

'Mrs Bernstein, let me be frank. If you consider it an indiscretion, my having allowed the play to be rehearsed here, how am I to consider your having given financial assistance?'

'Call it ignorance, Mr O'Leary. Call it spoiling the child. There was no copy of the play in the library.'

'As financial backer you could have asked the producer to provide you with a copy.'

'It simply didn't occur to me, Mr O'Leary. I was unsuspecting.'

'Then the fact that there was no copy in the library is irrelevant.'

Mrs Bernstein chose to move about, circling O'Leary and the room. She moved with confidence. O'Leary poured whisky into his coffee and drank; the brew was tepid and distasteful.

'You are a reader, Mr O'Leary. Have you been here long?'

'I bought the place years ago as an investment and made it my hobby, at week-ends and odd times, to bring it back into shape. It was derelict. I moved in, permanently, a few years ago. Happily I have a green thumb: I enjoy it.' He sensed that he was rambling. 'Mrs Bernstein, may I ask what it was you expected from your visit that I am, apparently, unable to provide?'

'I was curious, Mr O'Leary. Isobel prattles, about this place. Perhaps I'd hoped we might put our heads together, to deplore the play and the performance — that sort of thing can be such a luxury. Perhaps I was looking for an ally, an expert to reinforce my opinion and back my argument.'

'Your argument?'

'For getting Isobel out of the whole thing. Mr Bernstein, who had views, died when Isobel was very young. I over-indulge her.'

'I grant you your grounds, as a mother. That the shut-down of the play, the circumstances of it, distressed you, I can believe. That you deplore your daughter's involvement, even her daring, I can understand. I can't however see where I can assist. We deplore different things. Anyway the play is finished.' O'Leary drew breath.

'There is to be another. I have found a text for this one. I am alarmed.'

'You fear that I will provide space, again?'

'Well . . .'

'I am involved with spring,' O'Leary said. 'There isn't an inch of space they could use. If they're determined, however, that won't deter them: they'll find somewhere. So you see I don't come into it, as one who could prohibit.'

Mrs Bernstein was examining the trinkets on the shelves, moving them slightly without displacing them. She appeared thoughtful, preparing to speak. O'Leary found himself under consideration for long seconds — there too a thin hauteur.

'If you should see Isobel again, Mr O'Leary, I take it you wouldn't support my view? You wouldn't, as a theatrical person, comment on the unsuitability of such parts for a girl of her years and inexperience — without condemning, that is, the plays themselves?'

'My place is not to be used, Mrs Bernstein: you've forgotten that.'

'No, I haven't forgotten.' Mrs Bernstein drew on black gloves. 'But I could suggest she talk it over with you. I could send her, for that.'

O'Leary, on that, could wonder whether he was being rather openly bribed? Impossible, surely?

'I hardly think my view would count,' O'Leary said. 'They see me as fearfully antique, a sort of relic of the splendid, stupid, conventional days. From what position would I speak?'

'You lent them space, Mr O'Leary. You helped them set up their stage. You stayed on, singly, to applaud.' Mrs Bernstein toured along the bookshelf. 'You bandaged Isobel's hand.'

'She wasn't quite bleeding to death.' O'Leary was jocular.

'And you are not a parent: you would speak with another voice.'

'It seems unlikely, Mrs Bernstein.'

'Have you read this play, Mr O'Leary? *Sister Maybelle*, the one they intend to rehearse?'

'I haven't; no.'

'I have. It concerns a rather pretentious strip-tease artist — I think that's the term. Apparently she is convinced that Christianity has staled or become too exclusive: I forget how she puts it. Anyway, she achieves a certain fame by stripping, as she says, for the Lord. Every garment discarded is a small prayer. She is also known as The Heavenly Body. Her G-string is called her God-string; it is composed of rosary beads. I gather that she is required, the actress portraying her is required, to do a strip-tease on stage. The beads are presumably to be shown. The taste is, at the least, questionable: the blasphemy I won't refer to.'

O'Leary laughed, tentatively. 'I'd like to read it. Is it in the library?'

'Oh, read it by all means. I will send you a copy. You'll find it, perhaps, amusing.'

'I take it you didn't?'

'That's not the point, Mr O'Leary. I am not a prude, in that sense.'

'The point is that you fear Isobel may consent to play Sister Maybelle?'

'A point hardly designed to further Mr Boyle's requests, as you may imagine. You still wouldn't be prepared to speak to Isobel?'

'Mrs Bernstein, there must be others better qualified — by family association, friendship and ties of that sort.'

'Those are rather disqualifications, in Isobel's mind, Mr O'Leary.'

'I see.' O'Leary considered it: did he in fact give a damn about Mrs Bernstein's feelings or Isobel's possible strip-tease? On the whole, yes; but he realized that Isobel could be stubborn.

'If I'm not to be put in the ridiculous position of approving every play she is to act in, I must appeal to her discretion. Or to yours. I realize I have no right to ask for that; but I do. When her mind is mature enough to appreciate the nature of the decisions she makes, the implications, she may act in what she likes. At her present age I feel I have to accept the responsibilities.'

'I can appreciate your feelings — though the danger may not be as great as you fear. The question is whether the notoriety you foresee will be as distasteful to her as to you. She may indeed positively enjoy it. Might not the producer be encouraged, in some way, to take another direction and choose plays less embarrassing? Less embarrassing to you, I mean. Or might not Isobel be encouraged to introduce herself to another producer? Financial backing, forgive me, would be quite a bait.'

'You think she could be encouraged?'

'I? Well of course, how could I possibly know?'

'Will you think it over? The possibility, I mean, of your speaking to her? It's late: I must go. Thank you for the coffee, and the drinks.'

The sky was brilliant and frost was forming. There was nothing Mrs Bernstein could do about that: she would have to accept it on her expensive car, on her, doubtless, barbered lawns. O'Leary held the door as Mrs Bernstein swung creditable legs. It had been an inconclusive evening: the undertones were absurd. Isobel in a G-string of rosary beads? How brilliant these modern playwrights were.

'I forgot to mention, Mr O'Leary, that I called last Sunday. Sometime around four. The place looked closed up, but there was smoke. I knocked. A discreet retirement seemed suggested.'

'My nap,' O'Leary said. Why was he mumbling? 'It's a routine, of a Sunday.'

'You must allow me to return your hospitality, Mr O'Leary.'

'Sometime, yes,' O'Leary said. 'It would be pleasant. Oh, by the way, I owe you an apology. For bruising you with my clumsy feet.'

'I didn't bruise, Mr O'Leary.' Amusement transfigured her — even her eyes joined in, acetylene blue. O'Leary reappraised the silken knees in the light of the dash lamp. It was natural that a pretty girl should have a handsome mother.

'Goodnight, Mr O'Leary.'

'Goodnight, Mrs Bernstein. Mind the road, it's appalling.'

O stars whose element is ether.

* * *

O'Leary was spraying the orchard. He wore protective clothing and an ugly mask. Great jets of spray sprang out behind the tractor and drifted slowly. The day was still and the hour was almost four. He was not quite finished.

Isobel, who had arrived early, was standing before a tall open cupboard in O'Leary's quarters. The key had been in the lock but the cupboard had not been open when Isobel entered the room. There was nothing furtive in her exploration of the contents.

'I know I'm an awful snoop, but you aren't Mr O'Leary at all, are you?'

'Come out of it, there's a girl.'

Impurely deluged by hazardous elements, O'Leary was hastening into the shower. Total ablution required this state of skin.

'G. A. M. O'Brien M.P.S.' Isobel read.

The day was warmer: the room received natural light, and sunlight on a sill. O'Leary stepped into the shower and meticulously scrubbed. He discouraged Isobel from joining him. Which one of the simple bodies or their natural elements would consume him, he naturally pondered? Would O'Leary stand trial of the cupel and cement.

In slacks and bare chest O'Leary said, 'I am O'Leary.'

'Then all this . . .?'

'I am O'Leary, by deed poll. Perfectly legal. As O'Brien, as you've fossicked, I was a sometime chemist, dispenser of unguents and pomades, elixirs and panaceas — antibiotics, mostly. Was. Shall we drink something? Gerald Aloysius Martin O'Brien which, with some inversion explains the nickname. My father in his pride had it engraved in gold letters on my first school bag: from then on it was unavoidable. I was not a clever student: O'Brien's pharmacy was a compromise: my father, a man of law, intended me for medicine and the Royal College. His patrimony, he would think, has been mis-spent here.'

'You never stop talking,' Isobel said. 'I don't mean I mind; but don't you ever think something and not say it?'

'My God,' O'Leary said. 'Of what are you accusing me?'

'I thought you were an actor.'

'Amateur,' O'Leary said. 'Whose derivation is love. Repertory, that was all: a passion.'

'Then why?' She showed among other things her confusion and headlong curiosity. 'I always thought there was something, some secret, I don't know why. Mummy said it was odd to find a man like you in a place like this.'

'And a girl like you, she'd doubtless think, too.'

Behind his eyes the years flooded their faded light. His chest tightened and the room was void for a moment. He refused the past his indulgence.

'It makes no difference,' O'Leary said. 'Close the cupboard on the skeleton. There's actually one in there, I think — disarticulated, of course. And as you're wondering, let me tell you it was a small thing; but large enough, too. I am O'Leary by legal enactment. This isn't a TV serial. I am not a man on the run. I keep a small orchard and a great bloody troublesome barn.' Where mice could be loud and starlings thunderous. 'O'Leary's barn: O'Leary's orchard.'

'Oh Gambo.'

Her eyes were brimming. He did not, could not, relish a superficial impression. These were the tediums of his miss.

'Come here,' O'Leary said. 'Let me tell you about your mother's visit. Or has she told you, already? Lock the cupboard and put the key over there; it was never a secret I worked hard to keep. But I'm not sure I shouldn't smack your bottom, miss, all the same.' He relished the vulgarity, seriously; it was so superb.

'But what did happen, Gambo?' She was close, as requested.

'Decently, my Isobel, a reticence is required. I was somewhat naughty and was magisterially rebuked. I retired amid greenery: there was little else I could do, having had my fill of travel. I regret nothing but would be obliged if you could observe a certain silence for my sake, merely, of convenience. I am happy.'

'I am happy,' Isobel said. 'Gambo, I don't care what you did, I love you.'

'What I did, as you put it, wasn't such as to disqualify me entirely from the world's affection, or your love.' O'Leary was amused, as both overplayed their parts. 'You are a most sweet and beautiful girl and I am an extremely favoured man. Now lie back and listen: I will tell you how the world is made. Once upon a time . . .'

* * *

The conditions vital to O'Leary's function were these: A knowledge of the reason for each operation. A full understanding of the instructions. Avoidance of the profitless and impossible. A careful choice of time and season. Seclusion. Trusty friends. Patience and reticence. Perseverance. A determination not to be deceived by appearances into bringing operations to too hasty a conclusion.

But could he run the place or the project on those lines? Doubtful.

Agricola having discovered bismuth, O'Leary took some, with water. The drinking years had given him catarrh of the stomach: he feared for other organs, deeply.

What is witnessed from behind the silverings? O'Leary speculated on this as he shaved, pulling on his life, as he thought of it, like an old Burberry, simply to go down upon the town and revenge himself.

'Before you came,' O'Leary said, 'I lived alone like a hermit in bosky places, philosophically regretting nothing except perhaps the absence of trusty friends, choosing time and season for my operations of, now, a merely vegetable kind. What have you brought me, tell me? Bluebirds? Would the court care to consider my defence?

Is it the overt nature of the flower — unfolded and tremulous — that rapes the bee?'

There was no answer: there was no one to answer. O'Leary was addressing his mottled reflection.

'That's my plea,' O'Leary said. 'Even my swan song. Hold still, you devil, you've got me into trouble enough already.'

He was shaving closely for his visit to Mrs Bernstein. His hand was trembling. He thought it natural.

O'Leary saw tumbling sward, pin-oak and pine, burning cannas and distant gleam of sea. He was spruce in grey flannel of lately unfashionable cut and downright elated on a generous tipple of fine scotch. He stood in the porch and composed himself before ringing the bell. The button was illuminated: he pressed. He was aware of having overdone the aftershave while Isobel, glancing only casually to see that the coast was clear, kissed him on the mouth. She held on like a suction cup, as O'Leary struggled.

O'Leary followed her cheeky haunches and dabbed at his lips. He determined to lave his face at the earliest opportunity. To ask to be shown immediately to the lavatory would be gross. Mrs Bernstein would suspect his prostate, or imagine him to be of a nervous disposition, a diuretic if not an acolyte of the divine sprite herself. What Isobel would think O'Leary could not imagine.

Barometer, yes, falling in polished brass solid and seaworthy. Was the dead husband and father a blue-water man? Did callipygian Isobel take for granted these fathoms of white pile? How happy he was in her wake over wall to wall floors.

'Mummy, Mr O'Leary is here.'

'Good evening, Mr O'Leary. I am pleased you could come.'

'It was kind of you to ask.'

They passed from white to blue, silently: there seemed no end.

'What will you drink, Mr O'Leary?'

'Scotch, if I may. I'd a little for Dutch courage before coming away.' O'Leary was aware that he had probably had enough. He wondered whether he would ever be Gambo to her or she Becky or Rebecca to him. It seemed remote, he to her Hecuba.

'Dutch courage? Mr O'Leary you make us sound a veritable nest of Gorgons.'

It wasn't bad: he must try to match it. The ball was in his court.

'The journey,' O'Leary said. 'I meant, of course, the journey. To tell the truth I go out so little that the operations of the public transport system are as great a mystery to me as the Dead Sea Scrolls.'

Did she get it? Yes. Another subscriber to the Readers' Digest.

'Yes, ice please,' O'Leary said. 'And water.' He was at ease now, accepting the weighty glass. 'Do you know, on a morning's venture recently, intending no further than the public library, I found myself wading waist deep in cows, in dairy country, and dark coming down.' He warned himself to drink slowly: he wasn't as much at ease as all that.

Mrs Bernstein put her head at an angle to receive his foolish banter. Considered décolletage, wide eyes neutral at present (he wasn't kicking), a large mouth painted a dark black-red. Time very properly at bay or riding the billow; and the pressure falling. Effluvium waning? O'Leary secretly sniffed.

'Isobel would happily have called for you, Mr O'Leary.'

'Right round the bay? It's miles.'

'If it's not too far for one purpose, it's not too far for another.'

Aghast, O'Leary struggled to organize a perplexed smile.

'I'm not sure I follow, Mrs Bernstein.'

'Why, if it wasn't too far for rehearsals it can't be too far to fetch a guest.'

O'Leary was not reassured: more than the low table and the tray of drinks lay between them.

'A pleasant room,' O'Leary said. 'There's distinction in the touch. And you've a prospect.' He just nodded to the windows.

Mrs Bernstein's look went out across the severely formal room. O'Leary, following, took in the dark loom of trees, heard shrill sparrows, saw the final declension of westward light — the prospect through another's eyes.

'Tell me, Mr O'Leary, you've kept to your resolve? Isobel, you may have sherry.'

'My resolve? I'm sorry . . .' Which one, bygod? This woman's ambiguities were unsettling to O'Leary.

'Are you a man of so many resolutions, Mr O'Leary? I meant your decision about rehearsals; about your barn.'

To O'Leary's ear, hypercritical at this time, it bore its suggestion that he lived in squalor and slept among manure and broken crates. Was he too hypercritical? Could he be?

'The seasons dictate,' he said with care. 'The place is increasingly cluttered as we advance into summer. There's simply no room, as I think I said.'

'You did,' Mrs Bernstein said. 'Did you read the play I sent?'

'Yes. Yes, I did. I'd meant to bring it with me: I'll post it back.'

'Don't bother. Isobel could pick it up, sometime when she's out that way. Help yourself, please. What was your opinion?'

'An excellent whisky,' O'Leary said.

Isobel passed the ice bucket: O'Leary kept his head down.

'I was, well, what . . .?' O'Leary was forcing himself hard upstream. 'Amused? No that's hardly the word. Let's say it was all a bit like the bishop slipping on a banana skin, dignity in absurdity, that sort of thing. Certainly it stones glasshouses; but I can't see it as important. Oh I chuckled, yes. It's brilliantly witty — like a fire in a fireworks factory. Too much so.'

It was tediously said: he had rehearsed it and was pleased to be done.

'Can you conceive of it as being actually playable? Can you see it on the stage?'

O'Leary raised his head then and looked once at the mother and once, more obliquely, at the daughter. He wrinkled the skin of his forehead: he was pondering his answer.

'No,' O'Leary said, and falsely laughed for his conceptions. 'I can't. Not in the ordinary sense. The costume, for one thing. Perhaps a private performance — I can't say.'

'What costume?' Isobel said. 'What play?' Although she knew.

O'Leary returned to the contemplation of his glass.

'A play,' Mrs Bernstein said, 'requiring total nudity on stage, except for a string of beads — rosary beads.'

'Oh, *Sister Maybelle*,' Isobel said.

O'Leary, aware that Isobel had read the play while stretched more nude than Maybelle in the sun of O'Leary's orchard, thought it dangerous ground. Nudity seemed to be all the play contained, for Mrs Bernstein; but he could understand that, given the possibilities.

'I wasn't aware you'd read the play,' Mrs Bernstein said.

'Oh, somewhere,' Isobel said. 'I forget who passed it on.'

'And you can see yourself as Sister Maybelle, on stage in nothing more than a string of beads?'

'What?' Isobel's surprise was explosive. 'Oh Mummy, what an idea.' She pealed merrily.

'Well, thank God for that.' Mrs Bernstein rose sheathed and serious. 'You'll admit there were recently reasons for thinking you might. Mr O'Leary, if you'll excuse me, I must go through to the kitchen for a moment. Isobel will entertain you.'

The door closed behind her. O'Leary sloshed whisky into his glass.

'Phew,' O'Leary said.

'Mummy doesn't like being teased, so I tease her.' Isobel filled and drained her sherry glass twice in quick succession. This left her with an empty glass which she filled and placed on the table. 'What do you think of Mummy?'

'Flabbergasting,' O'Leary said. 'Terrifying, on home ground. We mustn't underestimate her intelligence: she knows more than she's saying.'

'She likes that, to be severe. It's her sense of humour, she says.'

'Has she a sense of humour?' He remembered she had: she didn't bruise.

O'Leary considered a vase of great beauty placed to one side of the mantel: the white porcelain threw a soft bellying shadow on the wall. The belly of the vase itself was reflected in a muted mirror: the lighting was masterful.

'Nevertheless,' O'Leary said, 'sense of humour or no, I think we had better take a little more care.'

'Care, Mr O'Leary? Care of what? I missed it.'

O'Leary experienced the rictus of pure surprise. Mrs Bernstein's moments were precisely calculated.

'Care? Did I say care?' His muscles were slow to relax. 'Oh, care of the parts, of course,' O'Leary said. 'The parts that are chosen. For one, I mean, as an actress, a player. Or that one chooses. Notoriety not being the same thing as a solid reputation. You know the sort of thing I mean.' Was he blind drunk? Was he totally incapacitated by ethyl vapours? He summoned a smile, with God knows what result. Isobel was positively staring at him.

Mrs Bernstein let silence hang as she finished her drink.

'If you are ready, Mr O'Leary, we can go through to dinner. Finish your sherry Isobel.'

'Might I just brush up?' His legs, after all, supported him.

'Of course. Isobel will show you.' She turned to the mantel to make a minute adjustment to the white vase, as though aware his appreciation had sullied it. Her profile was mirrored, her back unrelenting.

In the bathroom another mirror revealed to O'Leary the traces of lipstick his handkerchief had missed. He stared upon it then laved his face. It was unlikely that Mrs Bernstein would assume that he had passionately embraced a woman on the public transport: such encounters were rare, and such assumptions moreso.

O'Leary let the cold tap run: he had decided on a quick snoop. It was what she smelled of, this soap; it was what her mouth sometimes tasted of, this toothpaste; with this she sprayed her hair.

For what was Mrs Bernstein taking tablets Evipot, Neonacex, Polaramine, Urolucosil, Mycostatin, Floraquin? The syndrome was vast in its inclusions. The packet of oral contraceptives bore no user's name. Mrs Bernstein, surely? Isobel would hardly be so bold. O'Leary continued his evaluation of the weapons for a war that would never be won. Arrid underarms and Murine eyes, a Selsun scalp, depilatory for legs and thighs. It appeared that both mother and daughter were addicts of every known uncertain cure for established comforts including conception, perception, the process of age and hormonal imbalance. The eye, the ear, the mouth, the nose — all orifices were catered for, a secular do-it-yourself extreme-unction kit. Irritation, inflammation, wakefulness and narcolepsy — all again were catered for: O'Leary searched wildly for the anti-mortality pill. He hoped he was not going to faint — not here of all places. Was this his simple world of gold and beauty? Oil of Ulan. Olé!

Mirrors were clouded and walls just perceptibly moist: someone had recently bathed or showered. It was so intimate a place O'Leary could excuse his slightly lewd curiosity. Who in the world was hooked on Xylocaine viscous?

A latent puritanism was outraged in O'Leary; and time was running short. These were things O'Leary wished not to acknowledge — the imperfections, even of Isobel. Beauty was hard won; and regularity. He felt cold and mournfully considered his broken capillaries. He switched off the merciless tube of light over the mirror (how could they?) and turned off the tap. The rose dimness was consoling. The price of beauty plus the price of the concept of beauty: he would think of that. He was exhausted by his ablutions: he used the towel with care. He emerged in panic.

Isobel was by the door. O'Leary laid his hand flat at the vertex of her belly, the mere hypogastrium, and summoned all his strength. His palm was lifeless, his mind engaged: he said a prayer for Dalton and all his band. He had forgotten too much of what little he knew.

Isobel walked free of his gentle, lifeless hand. She was as cool as paint.

'Why didn't you tell me I'd your precocious war-paint all over my face?' O'Leary whispered it violently. 'She can't have failed to notice.'

'No,' Isobel said. 'She can't, can she? The dining room is through here. Mummy is waiting. You smell nice.'

'I feel awful,' O'Leary said. 'Dying. Something I drank.'

They passed from blue to gold, silently: there seemed no end.

* * *

'What did you do when I went to bed? When I was sent to bed, I mean. I was so mad. Mummy treats me like a schoolgirl.'

'Well, it's only so very recently she's had occasion not to. Come here.'

Could he ask her, he wondered, to dress for him in school uniform?

It had been a fantastic wish; it would entrance him. But how suggest it? This wasn't the moment: she would think him strange.

'What did you talk about?' Being closer she could speak more softly.

'I drank a little brandy for my stomach's sake, and went home. Was driven home. Do you know how your mother drives? Of course, you must. Wrists like iron and no nerves at all, simply daring the poor devils not to give way. Racing changes, heel and toe, good Lord.' He would keep his fantasies in their proper place. 'Did you think we perhaps struggled together in mortal tussle on the blue Wilton or whatever?'

'That's not funny, Gambo. What did you talk about?'

'I was some way past the masterly coherence: I was not at ease, at first. Where, by the way, do you keep your supply of the pill?'

'In the medicine cabinet, in the bathroom. Did you look?'

'Good God,' O'Leary said. 'You can be that open?'

'Mummy doesn't mind. She says it's reassuring.'

'Pass that glass, do you mind? You're nearest. I feel weak. I'll never understand your mother — perhaps I'll never understand you, either. Do you mean she approves?'

'Of you?'

'God's mouth, I hope not. I mean I hope the question doesn't arise. You haven't by any chance confessed?'

'She might guess,' Isobel said.

'After your lipstick, she might indeed.'

'She knows there's someone. She expected there to be.'

'Behold,' O'Leary said, 'the bemused victim of a mother's expectations. What sort of world have we put on?'

'I can keep secrets,' Isobel said.

'Are you getting right into bed?' O'Leary was nervous.

'Do you mind?' Isobel was not nervous. 'What did you talk about?'

'The pure filth of modern drama. About which she displayed a tolerance, short of wanting to see you bare on stage. We spoke, too, of girls and their circumstances in this modern age. We touched on the fabric of life, if I remember, its flaws and perforations. Do you want something to drink?'

'All right.'

'We reached, I might say, a profound understanding — while drinking cognac one for one.'

'Thanks. You mean Mummy drank too much? Gambo, come and sit here.'

'Let me finish my paean, first. Your mother, to continue, drank an amount exactly consonant with her capacity to hold it like a grande dame. I, as is my habit, fairly wallowed.' O'Leary began to wander about the room. 'Then together, windblown and lapped in luxury, we belted through the starlight to O'Leary's O. Where she dumped me.'

O'Leary sat on the bed; it was never a comfortable position and often a distracting one.

'Didn't she come in?' Isobel's mind was quite capable of attending to more than one thing at a time.

'To this anticlimax? Sweet child, for what do you take me? I knelt by the roadside and licked the dust of the district off her tyres. Her condescension demanded it.'

'She isn't condescending.' Isobel was warm. 'She's just rather cold. She takes a long time to get to know people. That's what she says.'

'I may tell you I revolved here an hour in O'Leary's dark navel making my comparisons and my mea culpas. These humble quarters and the four-square castle of the merchant prince, if you follow.'

'This is all right, Gambo. What's wrong with it? You don't need those other things. I love it here. I always have: I always will.'

'Need was never the point. But no, you're right. I haven't really told you what we talked about, you know. She told me you were leaving: she told me you were booked. She's persuaded you to go.'

'Oh, Gambo.' It was a wail. 'Why? I was going to tell you: I just wanted to wait until the right time. I'm sorry. I wanted to tell you myself.'

O'Leary involuntarily yawned. There seemed to be too little air. He crossed to a window and flung it open upon a sweet profusion of blossom, upon the great cadence of the orchard. He felt saddened.

'A matter of weeks, or a month or two at most,' O'Leary said. 'Don't let's consider it now. Come and inspect the glory of my place, the reach of O'Leary's acres. Smell the air? God's mouth,' O'Leary said, 'you're bitter flesh, you young.'

Had fact and fantasy inextricably merged? Dark facets, bright cambers and peace of a kind — could these be enough? O'Leary picked at his watch-strap.

In the simplicity of her flesh Isobel came to the window to inhale the simple mystery. She could smell blossom and damp earth. There were crickets and a felicitous movement of fruitful branches: so much O'Leary knew.

'I'm sorry, Gambo.'

For both it was for more than themselves, this reach of O'Leary's orchard, this place, this melancholy.

'Don't let's consider it now,' O'Leary said. 'There is a time for everything, a time to embrace and a time to refrain from embracing. What time is it, anyway? Are you rushing?'

'No.'

Light thudded and facets brightened: birds came flying under the eaves.

'Then not another word,' O'Leary said, in humour again. 'The password is Rhazes, I imagine.'

'What password?'

'Nothing. I was thinking.'

But behind his smile, in deep self-pity, he sensed frozen tundras and cold northern lights. He would not consider it now. Autumn was behind him; and ahead spring and summer were upon him; then autumn again. It were better to inhale deeply and close the sash; it were better not to consider it now. There were weeks, even months perhaps. She would leave in summer if things went to plan.

There remained the reaches between them, corners which neither could invade, subjects not to be broached and silences to be kept: they were not many but they were there. She could move with more freedom in O'Leary's world than he in hers. Her life beyond the orchard was closed to him: questions elicited very little of it; she was not a talkative young woman (he had once been grateful), and how could the great belch of his memory serve her? If he talked more it was to say less: his ribald monologue excused them both from anything approaching a conversation. She tended to the monosyllabic: if she was truthful she didn't care for elucidations and refinements. Impatience, O'Leary wondered? Or a certain intellectual dullness? He wouldn't care to say.

O'Leary had said it once and he'd say it again: he detested sentimentality. He just couldn't handle it. He thought of himself as a man behind a shield. Because the shield was so small he had to be quick in his use of it. Sometimes he was too quick, too suspicious; but that was how it was. Sylphs, salamanders, gnomes and ondines might pray for him; but to whom? Gold was his colour — citrine, ponderous, mute, fulgid — his substance. He wished it were his gift. All the compound bodies are composed of all the simple bodies, he reminded himself. Seek ye knowledge even to China. Every simple body is found specially and most abundantly in its own place.

As a credo it did not help. Least of all with Miss Bernstein, who was calling.

'Gambo, leave the window. It's lovely. No one will come.'

Gambo left the window, after one long look. Time, season and seclusion commanded him. He knew the reason for this operation and appearances did not deceive. He would not be deceived into haste.

* * *

'What would it prove?' O'Leary said. 'That you are stronger? That your youthful vigour is superior to my elderly decrepitude? I concede it, without trial.'

'It would give me a bloody great satisfaction,' Robert Boyle said.

'I thought you'd already enjoyed that, in your conversation with her mother.'

'In blowing the gaff on you? Yes, I took pleasure in that.'

'I can understand it,' O'Leary said. 'But you mustn't be greedy for sensations of that order. How was I to know you'd been thrown over? And what would it have meant, had I known? Doesn't the stage satisfy your instinct for drama?'

'I'm asking you, will you lay off?'

'Discontinue a friendship under threat, do you mean? No, Mr Boyle, I most certainly will not.'

O'Leary found himself on the floor: his Canadian exercises and his vitamin pills had not helped: his reflexes had never been fast. Blood was issuing copiously from his nose. Presently the numbness passed and his nose and face began to pain him. Mr Robert Boyle had gone, taking his satisfaction with him: the open door supported the assumption.

O'Leary, in this position, was succoured by Mrs Bernstein. She entered and bent over him. She had tried the barn door and had come round the path to the back of the barn. Her fashionable shoes were muddy: he was placed to observe it.

'Are you hurt?'

'Not,' O'Leary said, 'as badly as you are perhaps hoping. My nose is bloodied, the claret flows; a lip feels split. Did you, by any chance, order the execution?'

'What would be the reason, Mr O'Leary? Even if I had the power?'

'I think you know,' O'Leary said, keeping his face averted.

'Isobel?'

'In a word, Isobel.'

'Mr O'Leary, if I had been going to act on that I would hardly have waited until now. I have known about it for a long time. Since the night you came to dinner, you might have supposed. In fact, much earlier.'

'Excuse me,' O'Leary said. 'If you would wait a moment.'

Trails of blood stained the water in the white handbasin. Once again he held his face down and held his breath. The bleeding had stopped and the damage to his lip was not great: his nose was swollen or swelling. O'Leary bathed his face and tidied himself.

'It isn't possible,' Mrs Bernstein said, examining the damage, 'it isn't possible, in a place like this, to keep things secret for long. Not, least of all, when the young woman comes in daylight in a rather identifiable car. There were, after all, so many motives the world might have for letting me know; and so many motives I might have, for enquiring. One motive has just been displayed, Mr O'Leary.'

'Oh, vigorously,' O'Leary could look at her now. 'By Mr Robert

Boyle who felt jilted. Not an effeminate man: I feel he was vindicating his profession as much as displaying a blunt jealousy.'

'I met him in the driveway,' Mrs Bernstein said. 'It was pure coincidence. He was running. It did cross my mind that he might have murdered you: though that would have been excessive. I knew his interest in Isobel: I also knew yours. I thought it best to see if I could find another entrance. As it turns out, my fears were groundless: you will sting, Mr O'Leary, but you will live.'

'Don't go,' O'Leary said. 'Unless you must. I could use a drink. Have you time to join me?'

'Thank you, yes. I'm in no immediate hurry.'

'You were coming here, anyway, it would seem.'

Remembering his visit to Mrs Bernstein, O'Leary took pains in setting out glasses and ice and water; he did not own a decanter.

'I was coming here, yes. But not, I suggest, for the reason you have in mind, Mr O'Leary. Yes, ice please, in this weather. It's charming among your trees at this time.'

'The best is over,' O'Leary said. 'I've never known a more superb blossoming.'

'I don't doubt it, Mr O'Leary.' Mrs Bernstein drew it out: she could be dry.

A toast would have been vulgar: they drank.

'I came, Mr O'Leary, because Isobel's departure is getting close. Specifically I wanted to be sure that you had not been working to discourage that; to be reassured that you will not. With things rather in the open now, I felt it was a question I might ask. Is it?'

'Yes,' O'Leary said. 'All things considered, it is. I have not discouraged: I shall not. Her going is accepted; it isn't thought plans should be, or could be, changed.'

'By her, or by you?'

'If I can speak for her, then by both.'

'I am sure you can speak for her, Mr O'Leary. It was, if you remember, my reason for asking you, earlier, to discourage her from unsuitable parts. I accept the reassurance.' Mrs Bernstein looked out upon the orchard and seemed prepared to be silent.

O'Leary palped the swollen flesh of his nose: the septum felt torn.

The whisky stung his lip and he welcomed it for the asepsis that was in it.

'You don't wish to say more?' O'Leary said.

'Do you, Mr O'Leary?'

'If you've suspected, Mrs Bernstein — if you've known all this time . . .? I wonder would it have been different had I known you knew?'

'Oh, doubtless, Mr O'Leary. It may even have been essential that you should think I didn't. Secrecy contributes its portion, I believe.'

'Then why . . .?'

'Why consent to, why condone, such an unusual relationship? Except that it isn't all that unusual, surely? For one thing, Mr O'Leary, Isobel is of an age for agreement or consent. However barely. There was no case I could bring, however undesirable I might have thought the whole affair.' She let him see that she could make her own distinctions. 'Not quite so much whisky please. Thank you.'

O'Leary moved to the window but kept his back to the light. Mrs Bernstein swung to face him. He felt no sense of intimidation, no awe. She was a pleasant-looking woman with a generous mouth.

'You thought,' Mrs Bernstein said, 'you even perhaps hoped, at first, that she was under age. When it began, I mean. You know she is not; but it may amuse you to continue the fiction. There are men like that: we live in the world.' She waited but O'Leary did not answer. 'Isobel was a precocious child: she is a precocious young woman. There are reasons, the usual ones, and there's no point in going into them. She will have told you.'

'Something,' O'Leary said. 'Yes, she has told me.' It was a story that did not honour the dead: he could, in such cases, find a tact.

'So I simply saw a choice between the young and possibly irresponsible, and an older man for whom she appeared to have, forgive me, a strange, even a wayward affection. I did not go so far as to encourage, nor to prohibit. It did occur to me that the choice might not in fact be made — she could have, that's to say, chosen both. But I thought not. My illusions about Isobel are nil: my objectivity might be thought monstrous, by some.'

'I was to be used,' O'Leary said. 'A responsible safety-valve, until you could pack her off. You inferred impermanence, and trusted to a probable discretion?' O'Leary was enjoying it; it was something he missed — conversation.

'Mr O'Leary, I'm going to shock you. At the beginning I had Isobel watched — oh, very discreetly and privately. The hours of rehearsal were extending; and there were other signs. I am a woman as well as a mother. As soon as I had my confirmations, the watching ceased.'

'You had your proof,' O'Leary said. 'And then?'

'Then it was either act, or do not act. There were precedents to assist me: I could consult those. Although I confess I most actively resented your being smeared with her lipstick, in my house.'

'I owe you an apology, Mrs Bernstein. Another?'

'Perhaps not. I am, after all, driving.'

'Nonsense. Your driving that night was impeccable.'

'You are reminding me that I drank more on that occasion? That's not gracious of you, Mr O'Leary. Thank you, then.'

'You spoke of precedents, Mrs Bernstein. I don't follow.'

Their positions were reversed. Mrs Bernstein received sunlight on head and shoulders. O'Leary sat at the table.

'It was my intention simply to ask for your reassurance, and leave. I didn't anticipate this.'

'Nevertheless,' O'Leary said. 'Since you are here . . .'

'The point is a simple one: I sometimes see myself as mirrored in my daughter. Not in appearance, or not absolutely. I didn't quite have — what shall we call it? — the physical confidence.'

O'Leary murmured: they were sounds, not words.

'I don't wish to embarrass you.' Mrs Bernstein turned away, looking over the orchard. 'I even, you see, at her age had the same problems, if they are problems. Yes, they are. Perhaps we inherit them: perhaps they are passed down, from mother to daughter — especially if there's only one.'

'One mother; or one of each; or one problem for each one?' O'Leary felt need of light relief. If Mrs Bernstein smiled he could not see it: she kept her face from him.

'At least if they are common problems, I couldn't know. I felt mine to be intense. Then I met an older man.'

'Ah,' O'Leary drew it out. 'I begin, at least, to see the boldness.'

'I wonder,' Mrs Bernstein said.

O'Leary wished she would face into the room: he was having difficulty in following her. His hearing, like his reflexes, was not perfect.

'I was just the age Isobel is now.' She granted him his wish. 'I was infatuated: I was flattered.' Mrs Bernstein made a gesture that, given her composure, was almost theatrical. 'Oh, I can't pretend to look back on it with any sort of yearning, please believe that.'

'Surely from where I sit I should prefer that you could.'

'Be reassured, Mr O'Leary: I don't see him as the evil seducer, either. To tell the truth he wasn't at all attractive or even especially intelligent. But he was kind, and tender. And he did care for me without hurting me, without asking for or expecting things in return that I couldn't have given — things I couldn't have possessed at that age.'

'What things are these then?' O'Leary was alert.

'I'm not sure. Not love, anyway. I was no more ready for that, capable of that, than Isobel is now. I suppose I'm thinking of unselfishness, a sort of tenderness to match his. I didn't posses that. I was a selfish little bitch, really; and I suppose I used him in the most selfish way.'

'I am following the lesson,' O'Leary said. 'And?'

'It ran its course, and that was that. I wasn't heart-broken. I didn't even particularly mind: there were other things to take its place. I imagine I had regrets of some kind: I can't remember. I missed the flattery, I know.'

'I wonder,' O'Leary said, 'are you discovering similarities or imposing them? The experience was such that you now feel no young girl should be without it? But it depends on the man, surely? Or doesn't that matter?'

'I didn't send her to you, Mr O'Leary. I didn't invent you or the circumstances. The situation had reached a point before I moved to find out just what it was. I even had the poor taste, as you may think it, to find out a little about you.'

'Not quite wanting to deliver your child into the hands of an actual or potential sexual psychopath?'

'From "O'Brien" to "O'Leary" — you didn't change far. Is one to detect a national loyalty?'

'A national disease. You do indeed take precautions. Isobel, of course, knows this. I didn't tell her; she discovered. I thought my past might have been a burden — all except the amateur dramatics.' O'Leary opened his palms. 'I have my role, then: you've cast me.'

'If it were that simple, Mr O'Leary, I wouldn't be saying all this; it isn't necessary that you know so much. I simply feel that she has experienced something: she is changed. At least I fancy I can see it.'

'You've a sophisticated approach, Mrs Bernstein. I hadn't seen O'Leary's orchard as a finishing school for precocious beauties. Will you mind if I get out of step and have another?' Something was paining O'Leary. His face? His lip? He gently explored.

'You haven't enjoyed it, Mr O'Leary?' The stare was that blue, the mouth sardonic.

'Do you know,' O'Leary said, 'you have shocked me.'

'Ah then . . .'

'And I'm wondering, in purest vanity, how at your age she'll see me? Not particularly attractive or intelligent? Or rather, I'm refusing to wonder. That would be the final irrelevance, for me.'

'He wasn't Mr O'Leary.' An open statement, a droll one.

'And neither will I be, sneaking back from the shadows all those years hence.'

'Regret is a simple thing, Mr O'Leary; it only requires that you indulge it.'

'Suppose she hadn't been willing? Willing to go, I mean?'

Mrs Bernstein shook her head, pleasantly confident.

'You've missed the point, Mr O'Leary. I didn't dictate the move: I merely provided the money. She is genuinely excited at the prospect: she was from the very first. She loves spending money on herself: she loves expensive things, expensive clothes.'

'May and December.' It was O'Leary's turn to be droll. 'An old man's fondness, a young girl's infatuation. We move to the novelette, of course. You wish me not to write?'

Mrs Bernstein shrugged; it was a sufficient movement.

'Love and kisses,' O'Leary said. 'X marks my room.'

'I must go,' Mrs Bernstein said. 'What time is it?'

'After four; indeed well after perhaps. My watch has stopped.'

O'Leary walked with Mrs Bernstein to her car: the distance was not great. He held the door: the metal handle was hot.

'You've had your plans,' O'Leary said. 'And your fulfilments.'

'One last thing, Mr O'Leary. I know I shouldn't say it — I've already said far too much — but tell me, what do you see in her? Is it because I am her mother that there are qualities hidden from me? Oh, she's a pretty thing, but well . . . I can't for the life of me see it.'

It would be the wrong moment to reply: a body, an appetite, a charmed and uncritical audience, a mind that could take an impression, a passion.

'Youth and beauty,' O'Leary said. 'Both barrels; it never misses. But I'm pleased for her: I mean that in various ways. You might tell her that.'

'I, Mr O'Leary? Oh I shall tell her nothing. You are the one to speak. Oh no. You see I haven't interfered: I've indulged her. That's all the point. I shan't mention my visit; and Mr Boyle can no doubt be persuaded to be discreet. It's all entirely over to you, Mr O'Leary.'

'To make as pleasant an ending as possible?'

'Mr O'Leary, from what I know, from what I have found out, an ending is the only possibility. I give you credit for having enough intelligence to see that: you would hardly wish to make the same mistake, twice.'

'The cases are different, at least.'

'The girl is older. I don't wish to say any more.'

'I hope we will not completely lose touch, after Isobel is gone.'

'Tell me, Mr O'Leary, shall you mind so much?'

'No,' O'Leary said. 'A little more than she will because I won't have that immediate distraction — a clever stroke on your part — but not so much. I think I'm not of a deeply emotional nature, not sentimental I mean. Though, like yourself, I fancy I'm capable of certain regrets.'

'I should hope so,' Mrs Bernstein said. She was laughing. 'Goodbye then, Mr O'Leary.'

'Might I phone, sometime?'

'Of course. You'll find me in the phone book.' She paused. 'The woman from Omsk: the real one.' She enjoyed her joke immensely, as she eased away.

O'Leary was not pleased. He had meant to get her opinion on a question that was troubling him.

'Is it, Mrs Bernstein . . .?' he questioned the air. 'Is it the overt nature of the flower — open, tremulous — that rapes the bee? Would you care to comment? Is that your answer, Mrs Bernstein, this sexy growling and this rattling gravel? Very well, I will say no more.'

O'Leary was tipsy on something: he also felt he was cheating someone. His memory went back a long way — further than Mrs Bernstein's research, by a long way.

* * *

Summer among gravenstein and grannysmith; summer among golden queens and nectarines; avenues of gold, lanes of light, a benediction of leaves.

Isobel was sunbathing naked on a bright towel. The towel itself was spread on the square of mown grass behind the barn: the grass was still green. The gate that gave entry through the board fence enclosing the area was rarely closed; it was locked, now. This privacy O'Leary thought proper for Isobel. For himself he sunbathed in bathing trunks and a barrel chest: he was in equipoise between Canada and Scotland, between exercise and whisky just holding his own.

The equipoise of Isobel was of a different order: she sunned her front, she sunned her back — a golden spool winding golden light, languidly. Oh doze of hours. O'Leary teased spring of buttock with blade of grass.

'Don't Gambo; it tickles.'

'A metallic body,' O'Leary said. 'Citrine, ponderous, mute, fulgid et cetera.' He reached under her propped arm to weigh the particle as it swung at her throat. At the cost of considerable embarrassment to O'Leary, at the jewellers, the nugget now bore in minute letters the inscription: O'Leary's O. The apostrophe was indiscoverable except with a hand glass; but it was there. Isobel's breasts were squashed against the towel: O'Leary feared for them. He drained the last drops from his glass.

'Gambo, you drink too much. You do.'

'An excess of what's pleasurable is always subject to unfavourable comment: an excess of unpleasantness, say work for instance, is praiseworthy. Why? Don't go out into the world with your mind in that disorder. For what do you think old maids are vulgarly supposed to search under their beds? Their fears are ambiguous. Lost doves, they don't know it. I feel sorry for the world, at times.' There was a thought in it, somewhere.

'What about me?'

'Given the necessary perspective it were even possible to feel sorry for you, my dove.'

'Gambo, don't get drunk on our last day, please.'

'I shan't, don't fear. Stay to supper, our last. My nerves are shot. Don't go, stay. No, I don't mean it; but I'd like to mean it. Are you burning?'

Her upper lip, O'Leary saw, was beaded: along the nodes of her spine, a heartbreaking down. Isobel rolled over, putting her hands under her head with consequent flexion of the pectorals et cetera. It was intolerable. The air was not reaching them in this sheltered, private place. O'Leary was sweating. What did he see in her? In a matter of hours she would cease to be his. It was a day to perform wonders, magic rites. Intolerable cambers, then; impossible light. Ice-floes ground deafeningly in the bright lanes of summer. Then hermetical silence descended. He didn't have Mrs Bernstein's monstrous objectivity.

Isobel sat up. O'Leary was defeated by vibrant bronze. She put her hands upon his chest and pushed. They fell back on the prickling grass.

'Not here, my dove. In case . . .' O'Leary, preferring autumn and its pyres and palls, embraced summer: her flesh was almost too hot to hold.

So time flowed, in sunlight and a movement of leaves, until returning to pluck up the bright towel she gathered in innocence all light to herself upon bosses of flesh, as she stooped then ran.

'Going, going,' O'Leary said, with Isobel under the gavel. 'How soon to be gone?'

'Don't keep reminding me, Gambo.' She could be petulant.

'Or remembering? You're coming in one end and I'm going out the other; it's the cosmic chute.'

There was an artificiality in her mood of sadness: she would confront the unexpected with what was expected of her. But could he match soft words with softer? Could he, he wondered? The grey bleating was not so easily stilled. He lay beside her, summoning strength; it was an exhausting invocation. The last thing he wanted was to be himself — this day, this night, of all days and nights.

'Change,' O'Leary said in mimic bitterness. 'I see you sigh for it.' Heaving up on one elbow he looked down fathoms to find her, determined if possible to be gay, as she lay graced with dappled light. Nature was against him. 'One more kiss is all it would take, perhaps, to change me into the handsome prince, silver Alvis at the door and a million banknotes crisp in the boot.'

He wasn't managing. Would he miss her so much? Was she asleep? He traced his fingers down her side. 'Jump in my dove,' O'Leary said, 'and off to faery with never a puncture, pleasure without end, amen.'

Most definitely he was not managing. He was surprised to discover that he was, abruptly, bored.

'Don't Gambo. I hate you when you're like this. Please.' She opened her eyes. 'Mummy says your vulgarity is only an act.' Drowsily said, in a voice without expression.

'Mummy does, eh? Bygod, I can hear her saying it, too. And what did you say? Are there any in the world left to defend me?'

'I didn't say anything. I never do. It doesn't matter now.'

Two days running, he remembered, he'd forgotten to feed his fowls; it was a measure of his distress.

'Gambo, will you miss me? Will you write?'

Eyes plainly open and blue; as if she were thinking of something. Chiaroscuro: on the dark bed cover white flesh and the darker brand, the delta. Why if they dyed their hair was this never subject of that cosmetic attention? Purple would be amazing. Tremors of broken light.

'I solemnly promise never to give you another thought.' He teased her: he had better be smiling. 'Never another.'

'Gambo, be serious. Oh, I love it here.'

To him who would not dare seriousness she said it; at a moment when he was bored with the inevitability of himself, wishing this were done. His end of the see-saw was excessively weighted: why else this elevation of his dove, blond against the light? Never another . . . as he eased himself into the background, mere proprietor of this absurdity and its chattels. Is it the overt nature? A lovely thought, mute but ponderous: summer temperature 79 degrees Fahrenheit. Could he let her down gently? He'd long wondered it and now there seemed no need. Oh the see-saw of bee and flower. Fathoms thudded sturdily on O'Leary's heart: he registered certain depths: the blasphemy of beauty, the cost and concept. How do you plead, O'Leary? Unsentimental man?

He was capable of simple regrets over present simplicities on a day where wonders worked. He considered her tears which would not quite come.

'I'm sorry I'm sad,' Isobel said.

'It's heartening to observe a natural phenomenon in this naughty world.'

'No don't, don't Gambo. If I move too close, that's what you say, that's how you say it, in that voice. It's like touching something, something that goes into its shell when you touch.'

Bygod they matured fast — too fast. Or was she infected by her mother? O'Leary, who could treasure girlish nonsense of a kind, fled abruptly from the voice of Mrs Bernstein speaking through her daughter's lips. Had they discussed him, in cold blood?

'A carapace,' O'Leary said in miserable consideration, 'is sometimes necessary.'

'Come here,' Isobel said. 'Come here.' She had found authority.

Predictably O'Leary's vision darkened, his chest heaved.

'Gambo, say you love me.'

'I do, my love.'

'No, say it. Say it this once, please.'

He had never been able to: he never would be. O'Leary, who was immensely fond of Isobel Bernstein, bent over her. There was a great deal to Isobel, really. This much he could keep for a minute or two: this much she could endure, or eagerly accept.

'Please, Gambo.'

She was no longer asking him to speak: he supposed he should compliment himself.

O'LEARY stood on the road verge. Isobel sat at the wheel of her mother's car.

'Goodbye, Gambo.'

'I shan't come to the airport, you know.'

'I know. It doesn't matter. Goodbye.'

'Goodbye, Isobel.'

'Gambo, I'll write.'

'Love and kisses. X marks my room.'

They laughed. O'Leary put a hand on her shoulder gaily. He was squinting into the light, the westward haze.

'Take the road slowly,' O'Leary said. 'All roads you travel.'

She put her head out the window and O'Leary bussed her on the cheek — a resounding avuncular farewell as he would have remembered it had she not turned her head and found his mouth. O'Leary gave himself a smart blow on the head as he stepped clear.

'Gambo, look after yourself.'

'Go,' O'Leary said. 'Go now. Goodbye.'

He had to stand clear as she turned, waving with her free hand. It was a perfect evening: she was crying at last, and smiling.

He had lied. He would miss her more than that. His life had been a preparation for a sense of loss. He had missed her often enough already, over the years. It would continue, an indulgence of himself, O'Leary's O of regret, unvoiced. It was what his life was fashioned to contain, this gentle fabrication, this bright figment.

* * *

O'Leary re-entered his oasis slowly, closing the wicket behind him and standing in the dark of the barn. Oasis flooded with smells —

lingering, acrid, inexpungeable smells: rotted fruit long dried, sawn boxwood, packing straw, oil, petrol, fertilizer. And over-riding all, the natural full-bodied smell of blood and bone, dominant, pervasive, as pungent as loving.

patricia grace

valley

Summer

THE sun-filled sky wraps the morning in warmth. Already the asphalt has begun to shimmer with light and heat, and the children are arriving.

They spill out of the first bus with sandwiches and cordial, in twos and threes, heads together, strangely quiet. Uncertain they stand with bare feet warming on asphalt, clutching belongings, wondering. They are wondering what I will be like.

It is half past eight. I am watching from my kitchen window and see them glance this way, wondering. In a minute or two I will be ready to go over for them to look at me, but now they are moving away slowly, slapping feet on the warmed playground.

They are wondering what he will be like too. He is in his classroom already, sorting out names, chalking up reminders, and cleaning dead starlings from the grate of the chip heater in the corner. They stand back from the glass doors and stare, and he comes out with the dead birds on a shovel and gives them to a big boy to take away and bury. They all stare, and the younger ones wonder if he killed the birds, but the older ones know that starlings get trapped in the chimneys every summer and have to be cleaned out always on the first day of school.

I pick up the baby and my bag and walk across. Their eyes are on me.

'Hullo,' I say, but no one speaks, and they hurry away to the middle room, which is Tahi's, because they know her. Some of them call her Mrs Kaa because they have been told to; others call her Auntie because she is their aunt; and others call her Hey Tahi because they are little and don't know so much.

At nine he rings the bell and makes a come-here sign with his arm. They see, and know what he wants, and walk slowly to stand on the square of concrete by the staffroom steps. They stand close together, touching, and he tells them his name and mine. Then he reads their names from a list and Tahi tells each where to stand. Soon we have three groups: one for the little room which is mine, one for the middle room which is hers, and one for the big room which is his.

We find a place for the sandwiches and cordial and then they sit looking at me and not speaking, wondering what I am like.

I put the baby on a rug with his toys. I put my bag by the table, then write my name on the board to show them how it looks. And I read it for them so they know its sound. I write the baby's name as well and read it too, but they remain silent.

And when I say good morning they look at one another and at the floor, so I tell them what to say. But although some open their mouths and show a certain willingness no sound comes out. Some of them are new and haven't been to school before, and all of them are shy.

The silence frightens me, beating strongly into the room like sun through glass.

But suddenly one of them speaks. He jumps up and points excitedly. Necks swivel. 'Hey! You fullas' little brother, he done a mimi. Na!'

And there is little Eru with a puddle at his feet. And there we are, they and I, with a sentence hanging in the sun-filled room waiting for another to dovetail its ending.

I thank him and ask his name but his mouth is shut again. The little girl in shirt and rompers says, 'He's Samuel.'

'Mop?' Samuel asks, and means shall I get the wet mop from the broom cupboard and clean up the puddle. Which is friendly of him.

'Yes please,' I say, but again he stands confused.

Shirt and rompers shoves him towards the door. 'Go,' she says.

He mops up the water and washes the mop at the outside tap. Then he stands on the soggy mop-strings with his warmed feet, and the water squeezes out and runs in little rivers, then steams dry. Samuel wears large serge shorts belted with a man's necktie and there is one button on his shirt. His large dark eyes bulge from a wide flat face like two spuds. His head is flat too, and his hair has been clipped round in a straight line above his ears. The hair that is left sticks straight up as though he is wearing a kina.

Shirt and rompers tells me all the names and I write them on the board. Her name is Margaret.

> Samuel
> Margaret
> Kopu, Hiriwa
> Cowboy
> Lillian, Roimata
> Glen
> Wiki, Steven
> Marama, Evelyn
> Michael, Edie
> Hippy
> Stan.

We have made a poem. The last two are twins; I don't know how I'll ever tell them apart.

We find a place for everyone at the tables and a locker for each one's belongings, but although they talk in whispers and nudge one another they do not offer me any words. And when I speak to them they nod or shake their heads. Their eyes take the floor.

The play bell rings and I let them go. They eat briefly, swig at the cordial or go to the drinking taps. Then they pad across the hot asphalt to the big field where the grass is long and dry. Then they begin to run and shout through the long grass as though suddenly they have been given legs and arms, as though the voices have at that moment been put into them.

Ahead of them the grasshoppers flick up and out into the ever-heating day.

Hiriwa sits every morning at the clay table modelling clay. He is a small boy with a thin face and the fingers that press into the clay are long and careful about what they do.

This morning he makes a cricket — female by the pointed egg-laying mechanism on its tail. He has managed the correct angles of the sets of legs, and shows the fine rasps on the hind set by lifting little specks of clay with his pencil. Soon he will tell me a story so I can write it for him; then later he will show the children what he has made and read the story for them.

We collected the crickets yesterday because we are learning about insects and small animals in summer. The crickets are housed in a large jar containing damp earth and stones and a wine biscuit. The book tells me that this is the way to keep crickets, and they seem content enough to live like this as they begin their ringing in the warmth of mid-morning.

Two weeks ago we walked down past the incinerator to where nasturtiums flood a hollow of ground at the edge of bush, covering long grass and fern beginnings with round dollar leaves and orange and gold honey flowers blowing trumpets at the sky.

The first thing was to sit among the leaves and suck nectar from the flowers, which wasn't why we had come but had to be done first. And it gave us a poem for the poem book too. Roimata, who finds a secret language inside herself, gave us the poem:

> I squeeze the tail off the nasturtium flower
> And suck the honey,
> The honey runs all round inside me,
> Making me sweet
> Like sugar,,
> And treacle,
> And lollies,
> And chocolate fish.
> And all the children lick my skin

And say, 'Sweet, sweet,
Roimata is a sweet, sweet girl.'

The next thing was to turn each flat nasturtium leaf carefully and look on the soft green underside for the pinprick-sized butterfly eggs. We found them there, little ovals of yellow, like tiny turned-on light bulbs, and found the mint-green caterpillars too, chewing holes in their umbrellas.

The next thing was to put down the leaves they had picked and to begin rolling down the bank in the long grass, laughing and shouting, which wasn't why we had come but had to be done as well:

I rolled busting down the bank
On cold seagrass,
And I thought I was a wave of the sea,
But I am only a skinny girl
With sticking out eyes,
And two pigtails
That my nanny plaits every morning
With spider fingers.

Now all the eggs have hatched, and every afternoon they pick fresh leaves for the caterpillars. Every morning we find the leaves eaten to the stems, and the table and floor littered with black droppings like scattered crumbs or burnt toast.

The caterpillars are at several stages of growth. Some are little threads of green cotton, and difficult to see, camouflaged by the leaf and its markings. Others are half grown and working at the business of growing by eating steadily all day and night. The largest ones are becoming sluggish with growth, and have gone away from food and attached themselves to the back of the room to pupate:

The caterpillar,
Up on the classroom wall,
Spins a magic house around itself
To hide from all the boys and girls.

Then yesterday on coming in from lunch we found the first of the butterflies, wing-beating the sun-filled room in convoy. We kept them for the afternoon, then let them out the window and watched them fly away:

> Butterfly out in the sun,
> Flying high by the roof,
> 'Look up there,' Kopu said.
> 'Butterfly. Na.
> The best butterfly.
> I want to be a butterfly flying.'

I said that he would tell me a story to write about his cricket. And that later he would show the children what he had made and read the story for them. But I turned and saw his arm raised and his fist clenched. His thin arm, with the small fingers curled, like a daisy stem with its flower closed after sundown. The fist came down three times on the carefully modelled insect. Head, thorax, abdomen. He looked at what he'd done and walked away.

'Why?' I asked but he had no words for me.

'That's why, he don't like it,' Samuel told me.

'That's why, his cricket is too dumb,' Kopu said.

Those two have made a bird's nest out of clay and are filling it with little round eggs, heaping the eggs up as high as they will go.

'I made a nest.'

'I made some eggs.'

I made a cricket as best I could with my careful fingers. Then my flower hand thumped three times down on the cricket. Abdomen, thorax, head. And my cricket is nothing but clay.

Autumn

Autumn bends the lights of summer and spreads evening skies with reds and golds. These colours are taken up by falling leaves which jiggle at the fingertips of small-handed winds.

Trees give off crowds of starlings which shoot the valley with scarcely a wing beat, flocking together to replace warmth stolen by diminishing sun.

Feet that were soft and supple in summer are hardening now and, although it is warm yet, cardigans and jerseys are turning up in the lost-property box. And John, our neighbour, looks into his vat one morning and sees a single sheet of milk lining the bottom. He puts his herd out and goes on holiday.

Each day we have been visiting the trees — the silver poplar, the liquid amber, and the plum, peach, and the apple. And, on looking up through the branches, each day a greater patch of sky is visible. Yet, despite the preoccupation with leaves and colours and change, the greater part of what we see has not changed at all. The gum tree as ever leaves its shed bark, shed twigs, shed branches untidily on its floor, and the pohutukawa remains dull and lifeless after its December spree and has nothing new for this season.

About us are the same green paddocks where cows undulate, rosetting the grass with soft pancake plops; and further on in the valley the variegated greens of the bush begin, then give way to the black-green of distant hills.

They have all gone home. I tidy my table, which is really a dumping ground for insects in matchboxes, leftover lunches and lost property. Then I go out to look for Eru. The boys are pushing him round in the wood cart and he is grinning at the sky with his four teeth, two top and two bottom, biting against each other in ecstasy.

Tahi is in the staffroom peeling an apple. She points the knife into the dimple of apple where the stem is and works the knife carefully in a circle. A thin wisp of skin curls out from the blade. She peels slowly round and down the apple, keeping the skin paper-thin so that there is neither a speck of skin on the apple nor a speck of apple flesh left on the skin. Nor is there a ridge of a bump on the fruit when she has finished peeling. A perfect apple. Skinless. As though it has grown that way on the tree.

Then she stands the apple on a plate and slashes it down the middle with a knife as though it is nothing special and gives me half.

'Gala Day in five days' time,' she says.

'Yes,' I say. 'They'll want to practise for the races.'

'We always have a three-legged and a sack.'

Then Ed comes in and picks up the phone. 'I've got to order a whole lot of stuff for the gala. Gala in five days' time.'

We wake this morning to the scented burning of manuka and, looking out, see the bell-shaped figure of Turei Mathews outlined by the fire's light against the half-lit morning. He stands with his feet apart and his hands bunched on his short legs, he looks like a pear man in a fruit advertisement, except that he has a woman's sunhat pulled down over his ears.

Beside him Ron and Skippy Anderson are tossing branches into the flames and turning the burning sticks with shovels. We hear the snap, snap of burning tea-tree and see the flames spread and diminish, spread, diminish — watch the ash flakes spill upwards and outwards into lighting day.

Yesterday afternoon Turei, Ron, and Skippy brought the truckload of wood and the hangi stones and collected the two wire baskets from the hall. They spat on their hands, took up the shovels, and dug the hole, then threw their tools on the back of the truck and went.

Yesterday Ed and the boys put up the tents, moved tables and chairs, and set up trestles. The girls tidied the grounds, covered tables with newspaper, and wrote numbers in books for raffles.

We were worried by the clouds yesterday. But now on waking we watch the day lighting clear; we pack our cakes and pickles into a carton and are ready to leave.

By eight o'clock the cars and trucks are arriving and heaving out of their doors bags of corn, kumara, potatoes, pumpkin, and hunks of meat. Women establish themselves under the gum tree with buckets of water, peelers, and vegetable knives. Turei and his helpers begin zipping their knives up and down steel in preparation for slicing into the pork. Tahi is organising the cakes and pickles and other goods for sale, Eru is riding in the wood cart, and Ed is giving out tins for raffle money. I take up my peeler and go towards the gum tree.

Roimata's grandmother is there.

'It's a good day,' she says.

'Yes,' I say. 'We are lucky.'

'I open these eyes this morning and I say to my mokopuna, "The day it is good." She flies all around tidying her room, making her bed, no trouble. Every smile she has is on her face. I look at her and I say, "We got the sun outside in the sky, and we got the sun inside dancing around." I try to do her hair for her. "Hurry, Nanny, hurry," she says. "Anyhow will do." "Anyhow? Anyhow?" I say. "Be patient, Roimata, or they all think it's Turei's dog coming to the gala." '

Opposite me Taupeke smokes a skinny fag, and every now and again takes time off from peeling for a session of coughing. Her face is as old as the hills, but her eyes are young and birdlike and watchful. Her coughing has all the sounds of a stone quarry in full swing, and almost sends her toppling from the small primer chair on which she sits.

'Too much this,' she explains to me, pointing to her tobacco tin. 'Too much cigarette, too much cough.'

And Connie next to her says, 'Yes, Auntie. You take off into space one of these days with your cough.'

She nods. 'Old Taupeke be a sputnik then. Never mind. I take my old tin with me. No trouble.'

Hiriwa's mother is there too. She is pale and serious-looking and very young. Every now and again Hiriwa comes and stands beside her and watches her working; his small hands rest lightly on her arm, his wrist bones protrude like two white marbles. I notice a white scar curving from her temple to her chin.

Tahi comes and says, 'Right, give us a spud,' then spreads her bulk on a primer chair and begins her reverent peeling. A tissue-thin paring downward downward from her knife.

'How are you, Auntie? How are you, Connie? How are you, Rita? Gee Elsie, you want to put your peel in the hangi and throw your kumara away.'

'Never mind,' says Elsie. 'That's the quick way. Leave plenty on for the pigs.'

'Hullo, Auntie, hullo, ladies. How are all these potato and kumara getting on?' asks Turei. He takes off his sunhat and wipes the sweat from his neck and head.

'Never mind our potato and kumara,' Tahi says. 'What about your stones? Have you cooks got the stones hot? We don't want our pork jumping off our plates and taking off for the hills.'

'No trouble,' Turei says. 'The meal will be superb. Extra delicious.'

'Wii! Listen to him talk.'

'You got a mouthful there, Turei!'

'Plenty of kai in the head, that's why,' he says.

'And plenty in the puku too. Na. Plenty of hinu there, Turei.'

'Ah well. I'm going. You women slinging off at my figure, I better go.'

He puts his hat on and pats his paunch. 'Hurry up with those vegies. Not too much of the yakkety-yak.' He ambles away followed by a bunch of kids and a large scruffy dog.

The sacks are empty. We have peeled the kumara and potatoes, stripped and washed the corn, and cut and skinned the pumpkin. The prepared vegetables are in buckets of water and we stand to go and wash our hands.

But suddenly we are showered with water. We are ankle-deep in water and potatoes, kumara, pumpkin, and corn. Connie, who hasn't yet stood, has a red bucket upside down on her lap and she is decorated with peelings. Turei's dog is running round and round and looks as though he has been caught in a storm.

'Turei, look what your mutt did,' Tahi yells, and Turei hurries over to look, while the rest of us stand speechless. Taupeke's cigarette is hanging down her chin like an anaemic worm.

'That mutt of mine, he can't wait for hangi. He has to come and get it now. Hey, you kids. Come and pick up all this. Come on, you kids.'

The kids like Turei and they hang around. They enjoy watching him get the hangi ready and listening to him talk.

'They're the best stones,' he tells them. 'These old ones that have been used before. From the river these stones.'

The boys take their shirts off because Turei wears only a singlet over his big drum chest.

'How's that, Turei?' they ask, showing off their arm muscles.

'What's that?' he says.

'What do you think?'

'I seen pipis in the sand bigger than that.'

'You got too much muscles, Turei.'

'Show us, Turei.'

'Better not. Might be you'll get your eyes sore.'

'Go on,' they shout.

So he puts the shovel down, and they all watch the big fist shut and the thick forearm pull up while the great pumpkin swells and shivers at the top of his arm.

'Wii na, Turei! Some more, Turei.'

'You kids don't want any kai? You want full eyes and empty pukus?'

'Some more, Turei. Some more.'

But Turei is shovelling the white-hot stones into the hangi hole. 'You kids better move. Might be I'll get you on the end of this shovel and stick you all in the hole.'

He makes towards them and they scatter.

The prepared food is covered with cloths and the baskets are lowered over the stones. Steam rises as the men turn on the hose. They begin shovelling earth on to the covered food.

'Ready by twelve,' one of them says.

'Better be sweet.'

'Superb. Extra delicious.'

'Na. Listen to that cook talk.'

Over at the chopping arena the men finish setting up the blocks and get ready to stand to. The crowd moves there to watch as the names and handicaps are called. Hiriwa stands opposite his father's block, watching.

Different, the father. Unsmiling. Heavy in build and mood. Blunt-fingered hands gripping the slim-handled axe.

Hiriwa watches for a while, then walks away.

The choppers stand to and the starter calls 'Go' and begins the count. The lowest handicapped hit into their blocks, and as the count rises, the other axemen join in. The morning is filled with sound as voices rise, as axes strike and wood splits. White chips fly.

By three o'clock the stalls have done their selling. The last bottle of drink has been sold, many of the smaller children are asleep in the cars and trucks, and the older ones have gone down to the big field to play. Some of the tents are down already and the remains of the hangi have been cleared away. At the chopping arena the men are wrenching off the bottom halves of the blocks from the final chop and throwing split wood and chips on to the trucks.

Turei's dog is asleep under a tree. Finally the raffles are drawn.

Joe Blow wins a bag of kumara which he gives to Ed. Ed wins a carton of cigarettes which he gives to Taupeke. And Tahi wins a live sheep which she tries to put in the boot of her car but which finds its feet and runs out the gate and down the road, chased by all the kids and Turei's dog.

The kids come back and later the dog, but the sheep is never seen again.

> I said to Nanny,
> 'Do my hair anyhow,
> Anyhow,
> Anyhow,
> Today the gala is on.'
> But she said, 'Be patient, Roimata,
> They'll think it's Turei's dog.'

Winter

> It rains.
> The skies weep.
> As do we.

Earth stands open to receive her and beside the opened earth we stand to give her our farewell.

'Our auntie, she fell down.' They stood by the glass doors touching each other, eyes filling. Afraid.

'Our auntie, she fell.'

And I went with them to the next room and found her lying on the floor, Ed bending over her, and the other children standing, frightened. Not knowing.

'Mrs Kaa, she has fallen on the floor.'

Rain.

It has rained for a fortnight, the water topped the river banks then flowed over. The flats are flooded. Water stirred itself into soil and formed a dark oozing mud causing bare feet to become chapped and sore and hard.

> Like sky people crying,
> Because the sun is too lazy
> And won't get up,
> And won't shine,
> He is too lazy.
> I shout and shout,
> 'Get up, get up, you lazy,
> You make the sky people cry,'
> But the sun is fast asleep.

The trees we have visited daily are bare now, clawing grey-fingered at cold winds. Birds have left the trees and gone elsewhere to find shelter, and the insects that in other seasons walk the trunks and branches and hurry about root formations have tucked themselves into split bark and wood holes to winter over.

Birds have come closer to the buildings, crowding under ledges and spoutings. We have erected a bird table and every morning put out crumbs of bread, wheat, bacon rind, honey, apple cores, and lumps of fat. And every day the birds come in their winter feathers, pecking at crumbs, haggling over fruit, fat, and honey. Moving from table to ground to rooftop, then back to table.

On John's paddock, the pied stilts have arrived, also in search of food, standing on frail red legs, their long thin beaks like straws, dripping into the swampy ground.

'Our auntie she has fallen.'

I took them out on to the verandah, where they stood back out of the rain, looking at the ground, not speaking. I went to the phone. Disbelief as I went to the phone.

An emptiness and an unbelieving.

Because they had all been singing an hour before, and she had been strumming the guitar. And now there was a half-sentence printed on the board with a long chalk mark trailing, and a smashed stick of chalk on the floor beside her.

Because at morning break she'd made the tea and he'd said, 'Where's the chocolate cake?' Joking.

'I'll run one up tonight,' she said. 'But you'll have to chase the hens around and get me a couple of eggs. My old chooks have gone off the lay.'

'Never mind the eggs,' he said. 'Substitute something, like water.'

'Water?' It had put a grin on her face.

'Water?' It had brought a laugh from deep inside her and soon she'd had the little room rocking with sound, which is a way of hers.

Or was. But she lay silent on the schoolroom floor and he came out and spoke to them.

'Mrs Kaa is very sick. Soon the bus will come to take you home. Don't be frightened.' And there was nothing else he could say.

'Our auntie, she fell down.'

Standing by the glass doors, the pot-bellied heater in the corner rumbling with burning pine and the room steaming. She had laughed about my washing too, that morning. My classroom with the naps strung across it steaming in the fire's heat.

'I'm coming in for a sauna this afternoon. And a feed. I'm coming in for a feed too.'

Each morning the children had been finding a feast in the split logs that the big boys bring in for the fire. Kopu and Samuel busy themselves with safety pins, digging into the holes in the wood and finding the dormant white larvae of the huhu beetle.

'Us, we like these.'

And they hook the fat concertina grubs out on the pins and put them on the chip heater to cook.

Soon there is a bacon and roasted peanut smell in the room and the others leave what they are doing and go to look. And wait, hoping there will be enough to go round.

Like two figures in the mist they stood by the doors behind the veil of steam, rain beating behind them. Large drops hitting the asphalt, splintering and running together again.

Eyes filling.

'Mrs Kaa, she fell down.'

Gently they lower her into earth's darkness, into the deep earth. Into earth salved by the touch of sky, the benediction of tears. And sad the cries come from those dearest to her. Welling up, filling the void between earth and sky and filling the beings of those who watch and weep.

'Look what your mutt did, Turei.'

'We always have a three-legged and a sack.'

'Water?' the room rocking with sound, the bright apple skinless on a plate, smashed chalk beside her on the floor.

'A sauna and a feed.'

'Our auntie.'

'Mrs Kaa . . .'

It is right that it should rain today, that earth and sky should meet and touch, mingle. That the soil pouring into the opened ground should be newly blessed by sky, and that our tears should mingle with those of sky and then with earth that receives her.

And it is right too that threading through our final song we should hear the sound of children's voices, laughter, a bright guitar strumming.

Spring

The children know about spring.

> Grass grows.
> Flowers come up.
> Lambs drop out.
> Cows have big bags swinging.

And fat tits.
And new calves.
Trees have blossoms.
And boy calves go away to the works on the trucks
and get their heads chopped off.

The remainder of the pine has been taken back to the shed, and the chips and wood scraps and ash have been cleaned away from the corner. The big boys make bonfires by the incinerator, heaping on them the winter's debris. Old leaves and sticks and strips of bark from under the pohutukawa and gum, dry brown heads of hydrangea, dead wood from plum, peach, and apple.

Pipiwharauroa has arrived.

'Time for planting,' he calls from places high in the trees.

'Take up spade and hoe, turn the soil, it's planting time.'

So we all go out and plant a memorial garden. A garden that when it matures will be full of colour and fragrance.

Children spend many of their out-of-school hours training and tending pets which they will parade at the pet show on auction day. They rise early each morning to feed their lambs and calves, and after school brush the animals, walk them, and feed them again.

Hippy and Stan have adopted Michael, who hangs between them like an odd-looking triplet. The twins have four large eyes the colour of coal, four sets of false eye lashes and no front teeth. They are a noisy pair. Both like to talk at once and shout at each other, neither likes to listen. They send their words at each other across the top of Michael's head, and land punches on one another that way too.

Bang!

'Na, Hippy.'

Bang!

'Na, Stan.'

Bang!

'Serve yourself right, Hippy.'

Bang!

'Serve yourself right, Stan.'

Bang!

'Sweet ay?'

Bang!

'Sweet ay?'

Until they both cry.

Michael is the opposite in appearance, having two surprised blue eyes high on his face, and no room to put a pin head between one freckle and the next. His long skinny limbs are the colour of boiled snapper and his hair is bright pink. Without his shirt he looks as though the skin on his chest and the skin on his back is being kept apart by mini tent poles. His neck swings from side to side as Hippy punches Stan, and Stan punches Hippy. And Michael joins in the chorus. 'Na, Hippy! Sweet? Sweet, Stan ay? Serve yourself right.' And when they both cry he joins in that as well.

New books have come, vivid with new ink and sweet with the smell of print and glue and stiff bright paper.

We find a table on which to display the books, and where they can sit and turn the pages and read. Or where I can sit and read for them and talk about all the newly discovered ideas.

'Hundreds of cats, thousands of cats, millions and billions and trillions of cats.'

'Who goes trip trap, trip trap, trip trap over my bridge?'

'Our brother is lost and I am lost too.'

'Run, run, as fast as you can, you can't catch me, I'm the gingerbread man.'

Hiriwa makes a gingerbread man with clay, and Kopu and Samuel make one too.

Out of the ovens jump the gingerbread men, outrunning the old woman, the old man, the cat, the bear. 'That's why, the gingerbread man is too fast.' Then is gone in three snaps of the fox's jaws. Snip, Snap, Snap. Which is sad, they think.

'Wii, the fox.'

'Us, we don't like the fox.'

'That's why, the fox is too tough.'

'Cunning that fox.'

Then again the closed hand comes down on clay. Snip. Snap. Snap.

He writes in his diary, 'The gingerbread man is lost and I am lost too.' One side of his face is heavy with bruising.

On the day of the pet show and auction his mother says to me, 'We are going away, Hiriwa and me. We need to go, there is nothing left for us to do. By tomorrow we will be gone.' I go into the classroom to get his things together.

The cars and trucks are here again. The children give the pets a drink of water and a last brush. Then they lead the animals in the ring for the judges to look over, discuss, award prizes to. Some of the pets are well behaved and some are not. Patsy's calf has dug its toes in and refuses to budge, and Patsy looks as though she is almost ready to take Kopu's advice. Kopu is standing on the sideline yelling, 'Boot it in the puku, Patsy. Boot it in the puku.' And when the judges tell him to go away he looks put out for a moment. But then he sees Samuel and they run off together, hanging on to each other's shirts calling, 'Boot it in the puku. Boot it in the puku,' until they see somebody's goat standing on the bonnet of a truck, and begin rescue operations.

Inside the building, women from WDFF are judging cakes and sweets and arrangements of flowers. I go and help Connie and the others prepare lunch.

'Pity we can't have another hangi,' Connie says.

'Too bad, no kumara and corn this time of year,' Elsie says. 'After Christmas, no trouble.'

Joe Blow stands on a box with all the goods about him. He is a tall man with a broad face. He has a mouth like a letter box, containing a few stained stumps of teeth which grow out of his gums at several angles. His large nose is round and pitted like a golf ball, and his little eyes are set deep under thick grey eyebrows which are knotted and tangled like escape-proof barbed wire. Above his eyebrows is a ribbon width of corrugated brow, and his hair sits close on top of his head like a small, tight-fitting, stocking-stitch beanie. His ears are hand-sized and bright red.

'What am I bid, ladies and gentlemen, for this lovely chocolate cake? Who'll open the bidding?

'Made it myself this morning, all the best ingredients.

'What do I get, do I hear twenty-five?

'Twenty I've got. Thirty I've got.

'Forty cents.

'Forty-five.

'Forty-five. Forty-five. Gone at forty-five to my old pal Charlie, stingy bugger. You'll have to do better than that mates. Put your hands in your pockets now and what do I get for the coffee cake? Made it and iced it myself this morning. Walnuts on top. Thirty.

'I have thirty. Thirty-five here.

'Forty-five. Advance on forty-five; come on, all you cockies, take it home for afternoon tea.

'Fifty I have; keep it up, friends.

'Fifty-five. Sixty; now you're talking.

'Sixty-five, sixty-five, seventy.

'Seventy again. Seventy for the third time. Sold at seventy and an extra bob for the walnuts, Skippy my boy.

'Now this kit of potatoes. What am I bid?'

'Do we keep the kit?' someone calls.

'Did I hear fifty? Fifty? Fifty I've got. Any advance on fifty?'

'Do we keep the kit too?'

'Seventy-five I've got. Come on now, grew them myself this morning. Make it a dollar. A dollar I've got.'

'What about the kit?'

'One dollar fifty I've got. One seventy-five. Make it two. Two we've got. Two once, two twice, two sold. Sorry about the kit, darling, we need it for the next lot.' He tips the potatoes into her lap and gives the kit to one of his helpers to refill.

'Two geranium plants for the garden. Two good plants. What do I get? Come on, Billy Boy, take them home for the wife. Make her sweet.'

'I already got something for that.'

'That's had it, man, say it with flowers.'

'I got much better.'

'Skiting bugger, twenty-five I've got. Thirty, I've got. Advance on thirty? Forty. Forty. Forty again. Forty, sold!

'Now here's one especially for Turei. Filled sponge decorated with peaches and cream. Come on, cook, I'll start you off at forty.

'Forty cents, ladies, gents, and Charlie, from our friend Turei at the back. And forty-five at the front here, come on, Turei. Sixty?

'Sixty. And seventy up front.

'Eighty. Ninety.

'One dollar from the district's most outstanding hangi maker and a dollar twenty from the opposition.

'One dollar fifty. Two? Two up front. Two fifty from the back.

'Two fifty, two fifty . . . Three.

'Three we have, come on, friend.

'Three fifty. What do you say, Turei?

'Five. Five from the back there.

'Five once, five twice, five sold. One cream sponge to Turei the best cook in the district. Thank you boys.

'Time's getting on, friends. What do you say to a leg a mutton, a bunch a silver beet, a jar a pickle, a bag a spuds, there's your dinner. A dollar? Two? Two ten, twenty, fifty, seventy. Two seventy, two seventy, two seventy; no mucking around, sold.

'Another kit of potatoes. I'll take them myself for fifty. Will you let me take them home for fifty? Seventy. Seventy to you, eighty to me. Ninety to you, a dollar to me. Dollar twenty, okay, one fifty. Let me have them for one fifty? One fifty to me, ladies and gents and Charlie. One seventy-five? Okay, one ninety. Two?

'Two we have once, two we have twice, two for the third time, sold. All yours, boy, I've got two acres of my own at home.

'Here we are, friends, another of these lovely home-made sponges. What do you say, Turei . . .?'

But Turei is away under the gum tree sharing his cake with a lot of children and his dog.

And back again to summer, with all the children talking about Christmas and holidays, their pockets bulging with ripe plums.

The branches of the pohutukawa are flagged in brilliant red, and three pairs of tuis have arrived with their old incongruous talking, 'See-saw, Crack, Burr, Ding. See-saw, See-saw, Ding.' By the time they have been there a week they are almost too heavy to fly, their wings beat desperately in flight in order to keep their bodies airborne.

On the last day of school we wait under the pohutukawa for the bus to arrive, and a light wind sends down a shower of nectar which dries on our arms and legs and faces in small white spots.

They scramble into the bus talking and pushing, licking their skins. They heave their belongings under the seats and turn to the windows to wave. Kopu and Samuel, who are last in line, stand on the bus step and turn.

'Goodbye,' Kopu says, and cracks Sam in the ribs with his elbow.

'Goodbye,' Samuel says, and slams his hands down on top of his kina and blushes.

As the bus pulls away we hear singing. Waving hands protrude from the windows on either side. Hippy, Michael, and Stan have their heads together at the back window, and Roimata is there too, waving, chewing a pigtail —

> I am a tui bird,
> Up in the pohutukawa tree,
> And a teacher and some children came out
> And stood under my tree,
> And honey rained all over them,
> But I am a tui bird,
> And when I fly
> It sounds like ripping rags.

albert wendt

flying-fox in a freedom tree

THERE is a buzzing fly in my hospital room. It is hitting against the wire screen all the time, killing itself slowly. Ten o'clock in the morning. A hot sun is coming through the windows onto the foot of my bed. Through the window I see the plain on which this hospital stands, dropping down to the ravine, and on the other side the land rises up through taro and banana patches and mango and tamaligi trees to palms at the top of the range. Further up the range, Robert Louis Stevenson is buried there. (If my novel is as good as Stevenson's *Treasure Island*, I will be satisfied.) I had breakfast. A cup of tea, a piece of toast. They tasted like a stale horse or something. On the ravine edge stands a shed surrounded by mounds of dry coconut husks. The shed has no walls and I can see (as I have seen for the last three months) the two old men stoking the fire in the big urn in that shed. Now and then they throw white parcels into the fire. Stink of burning meat, guts, bits and pieces of people from the surgery department. (At least the sun is not ever going to change, it is for ever, I hope.) On the platform outside the shed, which is what the nurses call the crematorium, I think, are kerosene drums full of rubbish and flies and stink. One of the old men, the one with the billiardbald head and the bad limp, is foraging in one of the drums. He takes out scraps and puts them into a basket. Food for his pigs, I think. He eats some of the scraps himself. Some nights a pack of dogs hangs around the urn and rubbish tins and they yelp and howl and fight over the scraps both of food and people, and I wake up in a sweat and remember the two old men and the urn and the fire and get scared. The fly now lies on the window sill, legs up, still. I could have saved it but what the hell. A fly is a fly. I must not get scared watching the two old bastards stoking their fire with the white bundles. I have no regrets. None.

There is an old woman in the next room. She is dying — so the nurse tells me — from three husbands, eighteen children and too much money. She groans and moans all night long. She begs God for her life. A pastor comes to see her every afternoon, and she weeps and he prays. But she is still going to die. No miracle to save her. Nothing. Just a scared old woman dying in a white disinfected room. I have not seen her. Perhaps, like Jesus, I can command her to get up, grab her bed and go home, maggot-proof. But if the pastor cannot perform the miracle, I cannot either.

My room is getting hot, the heat is buzzing in my ears. There is a rosary hanging above my head. My wife Susana put it there last week. Now and then I get it down and count the beads and look at the silver Jesus on the silver cross, and I think the artist who made the rosary is very good. I do not understand why Susana brought it. I suppose she is still trying to save me because when I die she will not have a steady source of money. I was her source of money. God, she told me, is her source of 'moral and spiritual food'. Her poor faafafine halfman-halfwoman father is her main source of gossip. Her poor nearly-all-male mother is her main source of thrilling punishment. The rest of mankind, so she will tell you, is her source of 'love'. (Love for what, I do not know.) Susana by the way was and is and always will be crazy on the Roman religion. But more of that later. I have to get ready for the doctor's visit this morning.

I am a poet who is three months old. Ever since I got the Tb worm (is it a worm?) I have tried to put pen to paper to make some poetry. Before I got Tb I never had the worm for poetry. Who knows, maybe the two go together. You get Tb and you want to be a verse-maker. I grew old as a poet in three months, and I am now a poet failure. Two days ago I could not finish a three-line masterpiece, one line for every month in hospital, and so decided to become the second Robert Louis Stevenson, a tusitala or teller of tales, but with a big difference. I want to write a novel about me. By the way, here are the two lines of verse I wrote:

> *I am a man*
> *Got a plan.*

A novelist, so a palagi tourist once told me, has got to be honest (with whom, he did not say). So before I continue my novel let me tell you that I am, so my friends know well, a tall teller of tales. (Or is it a teller of tall tales?) So please read this humble testament with 15 grains of epsom salts, and please excuse the very poor grammar. You see I didn't have much formal education. (Unlike many of the present generation who went away overseas and returned with degrees in such things as education, drinking, revolutions, themselves and more themselves etc. and who wave before you the rounded 'r' and the long 'e' and the short 't' in just about everything, especially their own importance.) Pepe is local-born, local-bred, local-educated, so please do not expect too much scholarship, grammar, and etc. in this weak novel about his (my) life.

The young palagi doctor came this morning as usual, and as usual I pretended I did not know any English and he pretended I was fit as a ten-ton horse. He smiled as usual, he listened to my cough as usual, and told the nurse to give me the usual pills, as usual. While he did the usual I looked at the juicy nurse by his side. (Me, I am no longer interested in making fire.) I look at her because every time she looks at the doctor she has the clinging octopus eyes on him, but he does not know it.

Before he goes out he tells the nurse to tell me I am getting better, as usual. He smiles and winks at me as usual, then out the usual door. I pinch the nurse's juicy backside and she giggles and runs out after the doctor. 'Get him!' I call to her.

The doctor, who is a freckle-faced, blond-haired, false-toothed, rabbit-eared, woman-scared fellow of my age and who knows the female biology from books only, knows I am a goner; but because he wants to be kind to me he tells me I am recovering. He thinks like this: let him die without knowing he is a hopeless case and was always a hopeless case from the day he shot out of mamma to the day he shoots back into the six-foot womb. I like this doctor, he is a gentle kid. If the nurse seduces him he will be a better man at biology and everything else. Nothing like a succulent, warm, hot-blooded woman to cure shyness and a nervous condition and stutters, and this doctor is a nervous condition.

I have only a few days to write this novel about the self. I was/am no hero. So if you do not like stories without heroes, you better stop reading right here. Sex, violence, plenty-action, love any style there will be in my novel. God there will not be. No saints either. And no sermons. So straight into it without any pissing around (is that the phrase?). I cannot keep the maggots waiting.

Here we go English-style, Vaipe-style. My style.

The Pink House in the Town

My mother Lupe is dead. My father Tauilopepe is alive. He is now one of the richest in these little islands, which the big god Tagoloaalagi threw down from the heavens into the Pacific Ocean to be used by him as stepping stones across the water, but which are now used by people, like my honourable father, as shithouses, battlefields, altars of sacrifice and so on.

Like all the Tauilopepe men before me, I was born in Sapepe, and my aiga is one of the main branches of the Sapepe family who founded the village and district of Sapepe in long ago times. Sapepe is a long way from Apia, toward the west and, so legend tells, only a short way from the edge of the world. It is one of the biggest villages in Samoa, and it is cut off from other districts by low mountains to the east and west and the main mountain range behind it. Because of these mountains, Sapepe was separated from the rest of Samoa for hundreds of years and so Sapepe had its own history and titles and customs different in many ways from the other districts. Things did not change very much. Life was slow until the papalagi came and changed many things, including people like my father . . .

I get into the bus in my best clothes and sit beside Tauilopepe (Tauilo for short). I look out the bus window. Lupe, my mother, and my sisters are watching me. I look away from Lupe because I do not want to see her pain. The bus roars and off we go. I wave. My sisters call goodbye, waving to me. Lupe just stands there. I look back at her till the bus goes round the bend and I do not see her no more. Soon we pass the last fale in Sapepe and we are heading for the range eastwards to the morning sun.

The bus is full of people who laugh and talk like they are going to burn the town with their laughter. I feel hot and uncomfortable in my best clothes. Tauilo is talking with a man who has rotten teeth. Tauilo tells the man that he is going to Apia to take his son (me) to school there. The man says he wishes he had the money to send his son to a town school. Tauilo gives the man an American cigarette. They talk about the Bible and how God is good to men who work hard, and all that. It is Tauilo's usual talk. I fall asleep as we come over the range, thinking of my mother.

We get off the bus beside the Apia market and Tauilo smoothes down his clothes and leads me toward my Uncle Tautala's home just behind the picture theatre. The picture theatre looks like a big tin coffin.

'Now, you behave like a man,' Tauilo tells me. 'Tautala is a god-fearing man who does not want any silly nonsense. You understand?' I nod the head. 'You work hard at school. You only going to stay with Tautala until I get enough money to buy us a house here. You understand?' I nod the head again.

I have met Tautala many times before. He used to visit Sapepe to see Lupe, who is his sister, but it was only an excuse to get from us some loads of taro and bananas. Tautala is a short man who is nearly as fat as he is tall. Some of my aiga call him 'Piggy' because that is what he looks like. He looks all the time like he is looking for a toilet or bit of bush to shit in. He always talks of palagi like they are his best friends. He works in a government office where he gets $12 a month. Because he is a government worker with the white shirt and shorts and long socks and shoes, just like a palagi, most of the Sapepe people, including my father, are very impressed by him. Especially when he speaks English, which the Sapepe people do not understand. He is an educated man, Tauilo tells everyone. He is a palagi who does not know how to read, some of my aiga say. A nobody who is small between the fat legs, some of them laugh.

I look at the neighbourhood as we walk to Tautala's house. The fale look like old men who are waiting to die. Some of them are made of banana boxes and rusty iron and the area smells like a dead horse because of the toilets on the black stream flowing through it. The stream is called the Vaipe, my father tells me. (In English that means 'dead water'.)

We go over the small wooden bridge over the stream and I see some children playing under the breadfruit trees, and on the steps of a dirty-looking house there sit two women who have on the lipstick and coloured dresses. Tauilo sees them and he holds my hand and pulls me quickly through the neighbourhood, and I wonder why. Then we go through a high hibiscus hedge.

And there it is. Tautala's house. The pink house. It has two storeys and many windows of real glass. Next to the house is a fale with a sugarcane patch behind it. All around the house and fale stands a high hibiscus hedge, just like a wall to protect something from thieves. At the far side, over the hedge and stream, is the police station and prison. Two boys and a girl are playing marbles in front of the house. They come running when they see us. One boy takes my suitcase. He is about my age but smaller. He leads us to the door.

I have never been in a palagi home before, so when I stand on the steps I feel like I am going to enter a temple or something. The smell of the house and the way it is so shiny scares me. Tauilo looks afraid too. Faafetai, Tautala's wife, comes and welcomes us inside. (My mother told me once that Faafetai runs Tautala's life. No wonder all the time he looks like he is going to shit his clothes.)

'Sit down,' Faafetai says, pointing at two wooden chairs.

'It is all right down here,' says Tauilo, sitting on the shiny floor. I sit down beside him. Faafetai sits on the chair facing us; she smiles.

Then Tauilo and her go through the Samoan oratory of welcome.

'How is your family?' she asks later.

Tauilo is lost for words. He is in a nervous condition. 'They are well, thank you,' he says finally.

'Tautala will be home soon,' she says. She tries to smile as she looks at me and my suitcase.

'That is good. And how is he?'

'Working hard, very hard. Overtime all the time,' she says. I wonder what overtime is. 'He is so tired when he comes home that all he does is sleep.'

'Is he working on important government business?'

'Yes, all the time.'

'Did you hear that, Pepe?' Tauilo asks me. I nod the head.

'You get a good education and you will be like Tautala.'

I nod again.

While they talk, I look around and sigh in wonder. There are photos of hundreds of people maybe, on the walls; smiling people, sad people, old people, ugly people, and one dead man covered with ietoga with Faafetai weeping beside him. On one wall I see certificates like the ones on our Sapepe pastor's house. All the certificates belong to Tautala. I read one. It says that Tautala passed the standard four examinations.

'. . . I will take good care of Pepe,' I hear Faafetai say.

'Thank you. He is a good boy,' says Tauilo.

At the back of the room stands a table with chairs round it. I have never eaten on a table before so I look forward to it. On the other side is the biggest radio I have ever seen. It is so shiny I want to go and touch it. Faafetai's children giggle. The girl pokes her tongue at me. I hit her. She cries. Faafetai laughs but I know she doesn't mean it. Tauilo tells me not to do it again or else.

'I am sorry,' he says to Faafetai.

'It is all right,' she replies.

The boy, the one who took my suitcase, comes over and sits by me. 'What is your name, boy?' he asks. I do not answer. 'Have you got a palagi house like ours?' he asks. 'Bet you do not because you are poor.' He is the most childish kid I have ever met.

'Why you come to stay here?' his sister asks ''Cause you are poor, that is why!' She is ugly bad.

My aiga in Sapepe teach me never to let common people insult me so I say to the children, 'Who you think you are?' They sit up. I repeat what I said but they are too stupid to know what I am talking about.

'You know how to play marbles?' the boy asks.

'That game is for kids,' I reply. 'You know how to spear fish?' I ask. The children get up, poke their tongues at me and leave, and I feel good because I am alone again.

I try to remember Sapepe and how if I were there now I would be out fishing with my friends, but here I am in the pink house with only the self for company.

Then Tautala enters, panting like he is drowning, with the starched palagi clothes and long white socks and brown shoes, with pencils and pens in his shirt pocket.

'Do not get up!' he greets Tauilo. They shake hands. 'Very hot day. And how is our family?' Tauilo makes the usual reply. Tautala sinks into the soft chair next to Faafetai and is wiping his face with a red handkerchief. 'Hot day. Oh!' He gets up and nearly runs out of the room to the back. I have the feeling he is going to the toilet.

'Hot, is it not? Hungry too,' he says when he returns, wiping his hands. Faafetai goes out to get the food ready. 'Been working all day adding up government money,' he says. Then he tells Tauilo, who is sitting like a lost boy on the floor, how Dave, his palagi boss, likes him because he can add up difficult sums of money and how Dave is going to promote him soon. He takes out a silver fountain pen and shows it to Tauilo. 'Dave gave that to me last week!' Tauilo looks at the pen and sighs in envy.

I get bored. I get up and leave the house. I sit on the bank of the stream and look at the jail on the other side. Smoke is rising from the prison umu and two prisoners, in striped lavalava, are fixing the food. A fat policeman comes and talks with them. They laugh behind the barbed-wire fence. The stream is narrow at this point, and it has a steel pipe for a bridge across it to the prison. The stream is loaded with rubbish, shit, and it stinks, as I have said before. I pick up a rock and break my face in the water with it. The prisoners and the policeman are talking still. I try to hear what they are saying but they are too far away. I bend my head into my hands on my knees and cry. Even when I think of all my friends in Sapepe I am still alone. There is only the black water and the stink.

'Boy!' someone calls. I look up scared. He is a giant prisoner with a bird tattoo on his chest. 'Why you cry?' he asks. 'You got no reason to cry, you not a prisoner!' he laughs. Then he is gone into the prison.

I return to the pink house.

The next morning Tauilo takes me to enrol in the government primary school. (Tautala is a graduate of this school.) In the afternoon my father gives me $2 before he leaves on the bus for Sapepe. I stand and hold the money. He waves at me from the bus window. Then the bus is off and I am alone in the market where there are so many people buying and selling. I start to shake. It is the first time I have been alone in the town. But when I see some kids eating icecreams I run to the shop and buy one.

I whistle and run home past the police station, eating my icecream.

That night my icecream courage leaves me as I lie in the mosquito net. I pray to God, tell Him to look after me. I fall asleep saying I am going to be all right.

First Day School

There is no one in the classroom. A prayer comes to my mouth. I pray. Giggling behind me. I jump and look around. The two girls look queerly at me. They run away yelling, 'The new boy is a fool!'

I walk into the classroom and stand by the windows and look out at the playground. Many kids are playing out there, but they do not look real behind the dirty glass. I turn and survey the classroom.

It is a big box of cement with five windows facing the playground and rows of desks and a blackboard in front. There are pictures on the walls, and diagrams too with English sentences. I try to read a few sentences and get scared because I cannot read them very well. The classroom is so different from the one in Sapepe. There, it is an open fale and we sit on the pebble floor and it is not hot like this one.

The slap-slap of sandals. I turn. The afakasi woman looks at me. I at her. Then she comes in to her desk at the front and does not look at me any more. She is severe-looking, like Faafetai maybe. About forty years old and going grey in the hair already. She slaps down her satchel, papers spill out on the desk. Her fingernails are long and red with paint.

'You are the new boy?' She does not look at me.

'Yes,' I reply.

'You take the empty desk at the back.' She points to the corner desk. She still does not look at me as she puts her papers back into the satchel. I go and put my satchel on the back desk. She is looking at me when I turn. 'I hear you were in standard two?' she says in quick English. I do not understand. 'I . . . hear . . . you . . . were . . . in . . . standard . . . two?' she repeats slowly. I nod the head. 'I am Mrs Brown,' she adds. I nod the head. She picks up a chalk and starts printing on the blackboard.

'My name is Pepe,' I introduce the self. She continues to write like she does not care whether I have a name or not. She is skin and bone in the white shirt and black lavalava.

I look at the window because I do not know what else to do. I see the other children playing under the tamaligi trees, but they are so far away.

Three boys enter talking all the time and they do not see Mrs Brown. She turns. 'You know the rule. NO NOISE. Understand?' she says to them. The kids nod. I make up my mind fast that I am never going to offend Mrs Brown. Never. I sit down.

Children come in and go out. They just look at me. I at them. But we do not say anything.

Clang-clang-clang! dongs the school bell. All the children leave quickly. I wonder why but I sit there like a fool. She looks at me. I at her.

'Leave. It is assembly time,' she says. I get up fast and out to the playground.

The other children are standing in lines in front of the tamaligi trees, which have a platform under them in the shade. I go and join the end of the line of the children who came into my classroom that morning. I stand at ease. Everyone is looking ahead, arms back, chests out. I do the same even though I have never been a soldier before.

'Boy, she in a bad mood today,' someone next to me says. I look round but there is no one. I look down to my left and there he is — the dwarf, the first I have ever seen. He has a shaved head and sores on it and he is only as tall as up to my biceps. Like me he wears no shirt but only a red lavalava with two white stripes on it.

'My name is Pepe,' I introduce the self.

'Mine is Tagata,' he introduces his self. He does not look at me. His eyes are looking up at the rooftops of the school.

'My father owns the market.' Then he picks his nose.

'She is going to kill someone today,' the boy next to him whispers. The speaker, who is not a dwarf, is black like midnight. He looks at me and his eyes shine like white coral in all his blackness.

'My name is Pepe,' I say to him.

He nods the head and says, 'Mrs Brown is . . . a . . . a . . .' But he cannot finish.

'A bitch?' I suggest. Tagata giggles but the black boy looks ahead.

'Simi's father is a pastor, that is why he does not swear,' Tagata tells me. I want to ask Tagata if Simi's parents are Solomon Islanders but I do not because it is impolite. Clang-clang-clang! the bell rings again. Everyone is still, like dead soldiers maybe. No talk. Crunch-crunch-crunch-crunch! the shoes of the teachers march from the building toward the platform in the tamaligi shade. The sun is very hot now, it is hanging over the school like a fat boil. Crunch-crunch! the shoes stop and the teachers get onto the platform. Women in front, men behind. All in white like Sunday. I count six palagi teachers and only two Samoan. Out in front, in long socks nearly to his knees to cover his cowboy legs, is the palagi headmaster.

'That is Mr Croft,' whispers Tagata. Mr Croft has short hair the colour of the sun and white skin like cooked pork. He holds his chest out and his head up.

'Mr Croft,' Simi says, 'he used to be a captain in the army.'

'Ahh . . . ahh . . . ten-shun!' Mr Croft commands. Bang! everyone is at attention, even the teachers. 'Let us pray!' Everyone obeys. My English is not good enough to follow his fast prayer. The sun is burning my neck. Tagata is rubbing his bald head.

'*Now!*' says Mr Croft, then he is off and his English is too fast for me. All I know is that he is very angry about something.

'What is he saying?' I ask Tagata.

'He is yelling that no one is allowed to go down the road at playtime because some boys stoned his house last night. He says if he catches the culprits he is going to murder them . . . But he is never going to catch them.'

'Why not?' I ask him.

'Because I am the one who did it,' he says. That dwarf, he is not afraid of anyone, not even palagi.

'Why you tell him?' whispers Simi, looking at me. 'He may tell Croft.'

'You going to tell him?' Tagata asks me. I shake the head.

'Why did you do it?' I ask.

'Because he beat me last week for something I did not do,' replies Tagata.

I am astounded by his bravery. 'You and Simi be my friends?' I ask. But they do not say anything.

Mr Croft finishes. He wipes his mouth with the hanky. Two boys beat drums. 'Left turn!' shouts Mr Croft. We turn. 'Left-right, left-right, left-right!'

We march into the school building.

No one says anything as Mrs Brown takes out her books.

'Stand up!' she calls. I do not know she is calling me because she is not looking at anyone, or at me. 'Stand up!' she says again. She looks at me. I jump up. The girls giggle. 'This boy is the new boy. He is from the *back*,' she tells the others. I look at the floor at my dirty feet. 'Now he is going to give us a morning talk about his village.' She smiles for the first time. 'What is your name?' she asks.

'Pe . . . Pepe,' I stutter.

'Louder!'

'Pepe.'

'Very good. Now tell the others about your village.' She speaks slowly. I continue to look at my dirty feet. 'Come to the front!' I do not move. 'Hear me?'

My two dirty feet begin to follow each other to the front of the class. I turn. They are all looking at me.

'Well?' says Mrs Brown. I swallow tears in my throat. 'Well, go on!'

'My . . . my village . . .'

'Louder!'

'Mine village it is called Sapepe,' I begin. Everyone laughs at my English, including Mrs Brown. I look at Simi and Tagata at the back; they are not laughing. I stop the tears and look down.

'Please, Mrs Brown,' a boy's voice saves me. I look up. It is Tagata. He has his hand up.

'Yes?' Mrs Brown asks him.

'I want to talk this morning,' says Tagata. He gets up before Mrs Brown says all right and is coming to the front to save me.

'Sit down,' she says to me. I nearly run to my desk.

Tagata stands alone. He looks everyone full in the face. No one laughs at his ugliness.

'This morning I am going to talk about the barracuda that my father bought for my mother yesterday at our market,' he begins. His English is the best I have ever heard from any dwarf or from any Samoan for that matter. I understand what he is saying because he speaks slowly, clearly. 'As we all know, the barracuda is a killer. It looks like a torpedo and it can torpedo through the water faster than any torpedo. And, as we all should know, torpedoes kill people!' Simi's hand is up.

'Yes?' asks Tagata.

'What is the torpedo?' Simi asks.

'Well, as we all should know, a torpedo is a bomb fired by a submarine, and when it hits something, like another ship or a whale, it goes *bang* and that something is blown to bits,' he explains. But Simi's hand is up again.

'What is the whale?' Simi asks. I realise that they are playing a game like we do in Sapepe. You take a small joke and build it up till you get a deadly joke.

'Well, the whale is a mammal, the biggest mammal on earth, which lives in the sea.'

'What is the mammal?'

'A mammal,' replies Tagata, 'is a big fish with a tail and a nostril and blubber and the fish which swallowed Jonah in the Bible.'

'I understand,' says Simi. I nearly burst with laughter, but no one else is laughing, they are too dumb, including Mrs Brown.

'That is my talk,' Tagata says to Mrs Brown. He comes and sits down, and Mrs Brown asks a girl to give a talk.

'Excuse me, Mrs Brown,' Tagata says. 'I want to talk about our horse.'

'What has your horse done now?' she tries to joke.

'Well, Midnight, our horse, had a child horse last night.'

'Go on,' says Mrs Brown.

'Well, Midnight never had children before,' says Tagata. Simi is laughing behind his hand. (I find out at interval from Tagata and Simi that they call Mrs Brown 'Horse' and Mrs Brown has no children either.) 'Not long ago, my father gets a stallion . . .'

'That is enough!' says Mrs Brown. 'Sit down!' Simi's hand is up. 'Yes?' she asks him.

'What is the stallion?' Simi asks her.

'Take out your spelling books, children. Time for spelling,' she orders.

For the rest of that day she leaves Tagata and Simi and me alone.

That first day at school I also learn ten new English words: HORSE, BROWN, STALLION (Tagata teaches me what this means), BRIGHT, TOWN, SHIT (I see this on the toilet wall and Simi tells me what it means), SUNLIGHT, SPEECH, FEMALE and TOILET.

During the two years at primary school, I progress until I am nearly top of the class. I master the English quickly and I am always obedient to Mrs Brown, Tautala and Faafetai. Tagata and Simi and me are like brothers. Every fourth weekend and school holidays I spend at Sapepe. But every time I return to Sapepe, it seems like I am returning to something less important, like a step back, and I cannot help feeling this way.

At the end of these two years, Tauilo has built a large palagi house for us next to our fale in Sapepe. The house has many glass windows, five bedrooms, a big sitting room with photos on the walls, and a radio and furniture, a flush toilet, which is the first and only flush toilet in Sapepe, and a room which Tauilo calls his 'office' in which he spends most of his time when he is at home, writing and writing. He buys books on book keeping and shorthand, and three Bibles, all in English. And a typewriter which he teaches himself to use. Tauilo also buys a safe of iron in which he locks most of his money, the rest he puts in the town bank. My father, the failed theological student who was treated as a disgrace to the aiga because he had been expelled from Malua College, becomes the most powerful and successful son Sapepe has begotten.

In this time the Leaves of the Banyan Tree, my father's plantation, covers most of the valley behind Sapepe village and is reaching out to the foothills and range. Many of the people of Sapepe now work on this plantation for wages. The money has come to stay in Sapepe.

A Haunted House in the Town

Reader, stop here for a moment for I have to stop because the coughing is killing me. It hurts like hell. I had a short sleep this morning. When I woke up I found the self with an erection, something which surprised me because I have had no such thing for the past few weeks. I think it is because I am nearly dead. I read somewhere that when a man is hanged by the neck until dead, you find that he is hanging up there with his weapon erect like a flag waving goodbye to the hangman. I hope that when I kick the air finally they will come into my room and find my weapon laughing at them. Got to have a rest now. Am finding it hard to write longer than two hours per day.

In my fourth year at high school, Tauilo buys us a large house in Apia. The house is opposite the primary school I used to go to and it belonged to a palagi plantation owner from Germany who died at the age of eighty. He came to Samoa sixty years before. And from what I hear, he died because aitu scared him to death. He did not have a wife or children. He retired from his plantation and settled in this house all by himself. Some people will tell you that he drank himself to the grave and he used to spend his time with faafafine.

The house has many rooms and it is on stilts. It has beautiful gardens round it. Orchids, hydrangeas, bougainvillaea, ferns, hibiscus, frangipani, flamboyant trees, tamaligi, cactus, flower of the night, puataunofo (I do not know the English for this), lilies, tiger orchids, beautiful creepers and lianas whose names I do not know. In fact just about any tropical flower you can think of.

Tauilo is not satisfied with the house. He hires carpenters and they renew it all, change it into a house like our house in Sapepe. He fills it with expensive furniture which he buys cheaply from his business friends, and he has a new toilet built. This toilet is so big you can fit maybe ten people in it. The sitting room, which takes up the whole middle and front of the house facing the road across a veranda, has a blood-coloured wall on which hang all the family photos. There is a big glass cabinet in it too. This is full of crystal glasses and bottles of whisky. (When we were poor my father was against liquor. Now he is rich he loves it, despite his deacon's position in our church; and our church preaches against alcohol, called the 'Devil's Water' by the Sapepe people.) Beside the cabinet is a long three-shelf bookcase where Tauilo keeps books he buys but does not read. Behind the house Tauilo builds a fale in which some of my Sapepe aiga come to stay to serve us, the people in this house.

Tauilo comes to spend nearly all his weekends in this house. He puts on parties for his town friends. I never once see a Samoan at these parties. Only palagi and rich afakasi etc. Even my aiga are not allowed to attend as guests. He is ashamed of his relatives, they are good only as servants to his guests. When I shift into this house away from the Tautalas I am barman at these parties, but I am not allowed to touch a drop of the Devil's Water. Lupe, my mother, shifts here too. Tauilo says that the town climate will be good for her failing health.

Lupe is very interested in the old German who owned the house before us. When anybody in Apia visits her she always asks them if they knew the German and how he died, whether he died of aitu or not. Everyone tells her that he died because of loneliness and drink, but she does not believe them. When she is alone in the house she goes through it looking into every corner, but she does not find any trace of the man who lived there before. Tauilo tries to get members of our aiga to change the flower gardens into taro patches but Lupe will not allow it. It is in these gardens that she spends her evenings before the sun sets completely. She wanders through them like a bird looking for a nest which it can never find. If it is dark, she never goes near the garden because she believes that when it is darkness the gardens belong again to the German whose aitu she thinks is wandering the world because he was not accepted into heaven.

Into the Dead Water

And so I begin my journey into the Vaipe neighbourhood, into what churchgoers call the dark world of sin and allthings that they believe is against religion and good living. For some years I still live with Lupe and never visit Sapepe because Tauilo does not allow me. (He says I am a disgrace to the aiga because I got expelled from school.) And because Sapepe holds little for me now. During this time I do not need to work because Lupe gives me all the money I need. Anyway, I only sleep and eat at home, the rest of the time I journey out into Apia and the Vaipe.

Tagata, who left high school three years before me, hears that I have been expelled and he laughs like it is the funniest joke he ever heard. I laugh with him. For months Tagata and me form our own team.

The market, which is owned by Tagata's parents, sprawls over a big area. It smells of rotting food and people and is loud all the time with people's conversation and buying and cheating, but I soon get used to it. Tagata and me go to the movies about every night. The cowboy movies are the best because they have the action and blood and quick justice. Tagata and me wear jeans like the cowboy. We smoke the American cigarettes, drink the yankee coca-cola, and talk smooth like the gangsters of Chicago. We can smooth-talk any stranger to make the easy dollar and laughter . . .

Late Sunday night. Apia is quiet like the graveyard. I suddenly feel we are aitu that are going to haunt Apia for a long time. And I feel invisible and powerful. Tagata and me are in command of the operation, so the movies say. There are twelve of us behind the store. Twelve disciples. In the dark. Just like in the movies, but this is not make-believe, and I shake like the breeze blowing through Apia. The town clock strikes the midnight hour when Sapepe people believe the aitu come out of their graves to haunt the living. There is nobody in the streets. Only a few street lights are on. Now.

'Got the kerosene?' I whisper to the boy who is in charge of the fire.

'What building?' he asks.

'Any one on the other side of town,' I reply, without thinking smart enough. 'Start the fire in one half-hour. Make sure it is big.' The five boys move off into the streets. There are seven of us left. I instruct two to go and hide on the other side of the store and watch out for the police just in case they come too early. There are five left, and Tagata is breathing heavy beside me. The silence is dead as we wait for the sound of the fire engine and siren. My throat is dry sand. There are stars in the sky. Tomorrow will be fine. The fire siren wails like madness. One boy runs and tells me that the fire is in full swing. It is the Protestant church hall that is being eaten by the flames. I do not care. We smash open the glass doors and rush in with torches. The others fill their baskets with food and clothes and other goods. Tagata and me run upstairs and smash into the office.

I break open the drawers and small safe. We fill the bag with money, then move down and out the front door.

The police car lights hit us for a moment as we dive over the road and then sprint along the waterfront in the shadows.

'Stop!' they shout. We keep running past the wharf. Tagata is too slow, they will catch us. I stop.

'Some bastard told the cops!' he says to me. I give him the bag of money.

'You go on ahead!' I tell him. He does not want to. I push him forward. He disappears. I rip off my shirt and dive behind the wooden fence.

I hear one cop coming past fast. I whip behind him, smash down on his neck with the open hand like the detective in the movies, and he goes down without a sound. I turn and run off towards Mulinuu to lead them away from Tagata. The shadows hide me.

I hear them behind me. I dive behind the tree in front of the Crown Estates building. The footsteps come. I step out. He is too slow. I kick up and get him in the balls. He groans and goes down. I kick him again in the gut to make sure he stays down.

They are still coming. The street-light catches me. I break through the hibiscus hedge in front of the Casino Hotel. I duck too late. The night watchman sees me plain as sunlight. I leave him alone even though he is sure to recognise me.

I look back. The police are in front of the Crown Estates. I run along behind the hedge and into the dark again, cross back over the road and jump onto the beach and into the sea. The cold hits me, gives me back my breath. I swim quietly towards the buoy in the middle of the harbour. Well out, I float and look back at the shore. The police lights go past the Casino, heading for Mulinuu. I am safe.

The buoy bobs up and down under me. My teeth chatter. The lights of the town are all on. At one end the church hall is burning quickly to the ground, with a large crowd and helpless firemen watching it. The wind hits me with the cold, and the stars are laughing in the sky. Fear freezes me when I remember the night watchman.

I wait until the Protestant hall collapses and the flames start to die out. My bones are stiff and hurting. I dive into the sea and start for the market.

Tagata opens the door of his home when I knock. I fall into his arms. He sits me down and gets me a towel. 'They catch no one,' he says. 'But the police will be coming here for sure. They always do.'

He supports me as we hurry to my home. We keep in the shadows. 'Just like in the movies,' he says to cheer me up. I nod the head.

'We beat them,' I whisper.

The next morning I do not leave our house. That afternoon, Tauilo storms into the house. I hear him cursing the people who robbed his store. I get dressed and go to him in the sitting room. He is reading his account books. He looks up at me and then back into his accounts.

'What you grinning at?' he asks me. I say nothing, just watch him. He is flabby now, and has grey in his hair. We are the same height and I am catching up to him in strength. He has five stores in Sapepe and other villages, twelve buses, also shares in many town businesses. Also two palagi houses, six trucks, about 600 acres of the best cocoa plantation, plenty in the bank, a lawyer, and the whole of Sapepe under his command. I nearly laugh when the thought comes to me that I am his only heir now. Me, the worthless and only son. He looks ridiculous with his spectacles halfway down his nose. He does not need glasses really. He looks like he is preparing a sermon.

Lupe enters and sits down. I look at her from across the room where I am sitting and notice that life seems to be returning to her as she watches Tauilo, knowing he has been robbed. And I believe then that she hates him in some ways.

'About $5000 in damage and goods and money!' he says and stands up.

'What happened?' Lupe asks him, as if she does not know already.

'Get me a whisky,' he says to her. She does not move. I get one for him.

Lupe leaves and goes into the gardens outside. I watch her from the window. She starts planting flowers. It is the first time I have seen her doing this. I get Tauilo another whisky and then leave for the market.

Three policemen are talking with Tauilo when I return home in the evening. I feel no fear. I sit down. I know all the policemen. One of them is Galo, the sergeant I knew from the time I stayed with Tautala. Tauilo is very angry with the police about something. I wait for it. The police do not look at me.

'You do it, boy?' Tauilo asks me. I look puzzled. 'Did you rob our store?' I shake the head. 'See, my son says he did not do it,' Tauilo says to the police. 'And my son does not tell me lies!' The police look at each other, they are afraid of Tauilo.

'The night watchman at the Casino tells us that it was your son who did it, sir,' Galo says softly to Tauilo.

'You believe him or me?' Tauilo warns. Galo looks at the floor. 'Pepe is not a liar. He is my flesh and blood!'

'They have to do their job,' I tell Tauilo. 'Ask me any question,' I tell Galo.

'Go on,' Tauilo says to him. 'Ask him anything. He will tell you he did not do it.'

Galo clears his throat and asks me, 'Where were you last night?'

'Sleeping in my room,' I say.

'You prove that?'

I look at Tauilo and suddenly want him to lie for me. 'Ask my father,' I tell Galo. There is silence.

'Yes, he was sleeping here,' Tauilo says.

'Did you see him, sir?' Galo asks.

'Of course I saw him. You do not take my word for it?'

And immediately the police are lost. Tauilo tries not to look at me. I burst out laughing and the police are puzzled.

'I did it,' I tell them. They look scared. Tauilo has his back to me. 'I did it alone.'

'You sure?' Galo asks.

'I am sure,' I reply. I stand up. 'We go now?' I walk to the front door.

'He tells you a lie!' Tauilo shouts to the police.

I stop and face him. 'My father is the liar,' I say and then walk out. The police follow me.

Tauilo slams the door behind us.

Trial of the Native Son

Galo brings to my cell a breakfast of butter and jam and bread and tea. He sits down opposite me while I eat.

'You know something?' he says.

'What?' The bread and tea tastes good for I have not eaten for a day.

He looks away from me and says, 'You can be free.'

'Can I have some more tea?' I ask. He pours me another.

'They are calling it the "Big Robbery" already.'

'Who?'

'Everyone, even my sons. You are a hero. They are going to make songs and stories about you. But me, I am going to be the villain in them. I do not mind though because I am doing my job.'

'How long you been a police?' I ask.

'Twenty years.'

'Long time. Good job?'

'It is a job someone has to do,' he says.

We do not say anything for a while.

'You can be free,' he says.

'How?' I extend the empty cup. He fills it.

'The night watchman has no proof you are guilty. It is only his word.'

'But he tells the truth.'

'It is his word against yours,' he says.

I hand him the empty cup and plate. 'Who you afraid of?' I ask. 'Is it my father?'

He gives me a cigarette. 'Pepe, I have known you for a long time. You got everything. Money, brains, a future. Me, I got nine children and a big aiga. I struggled to get where I am.'

'Galo, I am not changing my mind.'

'You sure?' he asks. I nod my head. 'Anything else you need?' I shake the head. 'Do not blame me, Pepe.'

'For what?'

'For what I will have to do against you.'

'It is your job,' I reply.

'Yes, it is my job,' he says. Then he leaves.

After noontime, when my cell is hot, they come and take me to the office for questioning. 'Who you taking the blame for? Who else did it with you?' they keep asking. But I stick to my story. They keep on for hours until they are sweating and their uniforms are soaked. Galo leads all the questions, he does the job well.

'I also hit those police and I burned the hall down,' I add. I notice they are not writing anything down for evidence.

'If we charge you with robbery, arson and assault,' says Galo, 'the judge is going to send you to prison for a long time.'

But I do not budge.

The palagi Commissioner enters and sits down beside Galo. He smokes and watches me, the others continue their questioning. The Commissioner, so the Vaipe people have told me, is a cruel man. There are stories of Mr Towers (that is his name), about how he likes to watch people suffer. (His wife, after one year in Samoa, leaves him and returns to New Zealand.)

Towers goes with many women, especially after he watches somebody suffering. A few years before, three men escape from Tafaigata Prison and one of them puts a rifle bullet in Towers's lung. They say the bullet is still there and is poisoning him slowly.

'Why you telling all these lies, boy?' Towers suddenly asks me in English. 'You never did it alone.' Galo starts to interpret into Samoan.

'You scared of my father too?' I ask him in English. Towers jumps up.

'Boy, your father is a good man. I do not know how he comes to have so bad a son like you,' he says. I do not reply, I stare back at him. 'You believe in religion, boy?'

'It does not interest me,' I say.

'You love your mother, boy?' He is smiling now. I am suspicious about his questions because they have nothing to do with my crimes. 'You love her?' he repeats.

'Yes,' I say.

'You lie: you are never home, you do not look after her. You are destroying her slowly. Am I right?'

I do not reply.

I notice Galo is now writing down everything. I am puzzled by this.

'If you are a Christian, why you burn down the church hall?' Towers asks next.

'Because God does not live in it, and I do not want to burn places in which people live,' I reply.

'You an atheist?' Towers is like the preacher on the pulpit, like Tauilo.

'What is atheist?' I ask.

'He is an atheist,' Towers says to Galo. 'Put that down.' Galo writes it in the book. The other police look at me in a strange way as if I have an aitu inside me. 'Bring the Bible,' Towers instructs them.

When the Black Book comes, Towers holds it out to me and says, 'Take it.' I smile and take it. 'You ready to swear you alone committed the robbery, arson and assault, boy?' I nod the head. It is all ridiculous. The other police look afraid: perhaps they are waiting for their God to strike me dead if I lie on the Black Book.

'Say it!' Towers says.

'I swear by your almighty God and your almighty book that I robbed your store and bashed your police. All right?' While I say it, Galo is looking up like he is expecting the holy thunderbolt to burn me to cinders like the church hall.

'And you burned God's hall,' Towers adds.

'And I burned your hall to ashes,' I say.

'Put that all down. Every word of it,' Towers instructs Galo.

'What does all that prove?' I ask.

Towers smiles. 'You will find out. Wait till you appear before him.'

'Him?'

'The judge. He is going to put you away for a very long time of hard labour!' He laughs for the first time. Some of the police join him as if the joke is on me now. It has something to do with the judge, but I do not understand as yet.

That evening before the sun is fully set Galo brings Lupe to my cell. I turn away from her who is no longer the Lupe I once knew. She stands and cries.

'Stop crying,' I tell her.

'Pepe, you tell them you did not do it, please!' she pleads.

I sit her down on the cell bed. I stand looking out the window at the blood-red west where Sapepe is and always will be, at where the alive Lupe I loved is buried. And I can never forgive Tauilo for that. 'Pepe, please tell them what they want. You the only thing I have left!'

'It is too late,' I tell her. I do not know what else to say.

'It is not. They told me that if you confess they will set you free!'

'You do not understand,' I say. 'Not any more.'

'But I do, Pepe!'

'We are both different people now.'

'Tell them everything, Pepe. I understand, you just do not want to tell on your friends. That is what Tauilo told me!'

And I know then that they and Tauilo are using her again. 'So it is for Tauilo you are doing this?' I turn to face her.

'No, Pepe. It is for me, your mother!'

'You do not remember any more what he did to you and what he is doing to you now!'

'He loves me, Pepe. He loves you too still,' she cries. And I have to look away from the death and suffering I see in the woman who gave me birth and life.

'You better leave. It is late, too late,' I tell her. She is weeping again and I want to shut my ears and heart to her, to the beautiful memory of her back there in Sapepe in the years of my childhood before Tauilo destroyed it all. 'Galo!' I call.

He enters and looks at her and then at me and I see dislike in his eyes for me. 'Take her out,' I tell him. I turn to the window. The sun has drowned in Sapepe, the edge of the world.

Her footsteps fade away from my life.

The courtroom is like the inside of the Sapepe church. On my left is the high pulpit in which the judge will sit on his throne. On the wall behind him is a picture of the New Zealand and Samoan flags. I am sitting in front of the pulpit with my back to the windows that look out onto the main street and harbour. Opposite me at a desk sits the prosecutor in his police uniform. To his right is a wooden cage with a bench inside it. This is where the accused usually sits but seeing I am defending myself I do not have to sit in it. The congregation has been coming in all the time and sitting on the rows of benches that extend right to the back, all facing the pulpit. Soon the court is full and the congregation is looking at me. The judge is late. Two reporters come in and sit near the prosecutor; they look at me, their eyes say nothing, all they want is news. Some of the congregation are talking, and I know they are talking about me, making up stories they will return with to the villages and tell the others. Most of my Vaipe friends are in the congregation.

'Stand!' commands the policeman who enters and stands in front of the pulpit. The police behind me tell me to stand. Silence. No one moves.

The door behind the pulpit to the right opens. The judge enters. He looks like a priest in his black silk dress and white wig and shiny black shoes and steel spectacles. My judge, my priest, my confessor. He looks at no one. The sound of his shoes taps across my heart and up into the pulpit and throne.

The congregation bow their heads. The Black-dress, my judge, is praying. I begin to understand with fear why the Commissioner and police asked me about religion and God.

They tell me to stand up again.

One police in a loud voice reads out the crimes I committed. The congregation sighs in wonder.

'You plead guilty, or not?' the police asks.

'Guilty,' I reply. The congregation talks in surprise because I am not fighting. The reporters are writing.

The Black-dress wants to speak. It wants to know. 'Bring him forward,' It orders. The police take me up to stand in front of the pulpit.

My fear begins but I want to know who the Black-dress is. I look up at the face. It is pale behind glass, and the mouth is thin, the eyes are deep under the forehead and they show nothing — like the eyes of the owl that was the Tauilopepe family god in ancient times. The head is covered with a wig. The rest is black like wet river stone. It is a face you can see everywhere but you do not take much notice of it because it is the face of everybody you do not really remember. It is not important whether the face is white or black or brown or yellow.

The Black-dress is going to speak.

'What is your name?' It asks in English of me. The interpreter starts to interpret. I silence him. The eyes of the Black-dress burn for a moment, then go dead. I will play my joke.

'My name is Pepesa, son of Sapepe and the gods of Sapepe,' I declare in Samoan. The congregation talk in surprise. They know I am fighting at last, putting on a good show like in the movies.

'Pepesa? Why Pepesa?' It asks in Samoan.

'After the Sapepe hero who challenged all the gods and won,' I reply. But It does not smile or look amused.

'Good. But why "son of the gods"?' It asks.

'Because it is my genealogy.' I am feeling relaxed and want to tell It everything because It is taking my joke seriously.

'To the gods?' It asks.

'Yes, to the gods.'

'In our century as well?'

'Yes, in our century,' I extend the joke. It thinks for a moment.

'This is the twentieth century. There is one God.' It looks at me dead-on down. It is not a joke to him and he does not know who I am yet. 'You know who the missionaries were?'

'Yes, I know.'

'Who?'

'They break through the skies of our world and bring guns and the new religion and the new God and drive my gods into the bush and mountains where they live today,' I declare, nearly laughing. Some of the congregation talk loudly. The Black-dress raps the hammer down.

'The missionaries brought you the Light!' The voice is hard like the steel of Its spectacles. I hear the silence round me and in me.

'It is not for me to say whether the missionary brought the Light as you call it,' I reply. The right arm of the Black-dress rises up like the wing of a black bird. It starts to recognise who I am.

'Why not?' It demands.

'Because they are dead and gone and I am still here. We are still here,' I say. Some of the congregation talk again. The hammer goes Bang-bang-bang! Silence again. It coughs, picks up the glass and drinks the medicine.

'I cannot believe you,' It says after It wipes the mouth. 'Are you a Christian?' And now I understand why the police asked me all those questions and my courage to joke begins to go. 'Are you a Christian?' It repeats.

I remember a trial scene in one American gangster movie, and reply, 'I do not want to answer that in case I will incriminate myself!' Some of the people laugh. It silences them with the hammer.

'Now, boy, if you are not serious, I will punish you severely. Understand?' It says. The Black-dress has no sense of humour — like all other preachers and gods, the modern type. But I cannot go back on my challenge. I am committed to Pepesa. 'I repeat, boy, ARE YOU A CHRISTIAN?' Everyone waits for my answer.

'I do not know because I do not know what a Christian is,' I hear the self saying aloud.

'You go to church?'

'One time I did,' I reply. It says nothing to that.

'Why you burn down the Hall of God?' It asks me slowly.

'To take the police away from the store I was robbing.'

'Do not lie, boy. You have said already you are a pagan, a heathen!' It stops, then says, 'I ask you again: do you believe in Jehovah?' I shake the head. 'Speak up!'

'No!' I reply. The congregation is in an uproar — most of them are against me now. The Black-dress makes them quiet.

'Why you not believe in our God?' It asks next.

'You will not understand,' I say.

'Answer now!' It commands. Suddenly I get the feeling It is afraid of me.

'Because I know there is none.'

'How?' It says quickly.

'Because of who and what I am.'

'And what is that?' It looks amused.

'You were the one who told me who I am,' I reply, looking straight into the steel spectacles.

'A pagan?' It is smiling. I bow the head. 'Then you live in darkness and have nothing.'

I look up and say, 'I have the darkness and my self.'

It sighs for me and what It is going to do to me. 'No wonder you took to crime. You are evil. You are sick.' It stops for a moment. 'Do you think there is something or someone like God?' It asks. It is still not satisfied.

I nod the head slowly. I know what Its next question will be and I feel I no longer have the courage to answer it honestly because they do not understand and never will.

'What is it then? It leans forward. I hear It breathing. 'Go on.'

'I have only my darkness and my self living in my world, therefore . . .' I stop.

'Therefore what?'

I look straight into Its face. 'Therefore I am my god.' It blinks; the congregation is stunned. The criminal is mad, they now think. A few people laugh.

'Now I know why you committed all those evil things. You are a victim of your own madness. The devil has led you astray.' It stops. 'That is why I am going to be lenient — yes, lenient — on you. Your father is a good man. Perhaps you will become like him after we train you in jail to join us again. You were the ideal son who fell by the wayside, a prodigal son. No human being can be God, boy. There is only one God . . .' As It talks on and on I think I am listening again to my father, Tauilo, to all preachers on their wooden thrones who do not listen to their own message because their hearts are stone. 'We will pray for your repentance, for the healing of your madness by our Loving Father,' It ends Its sermon. 'You got anything to say, Pepe?' It asks. It is the first time It has called me by my name.

What is the use? The world now is their world and they will not understand anything I say. So I shake the head. I turn and face the congregation. Apart from my friends, they all look at me with their silence as if I am the aitu the missionaries banished. There is a world between us, I feel. A sky of stone, a river of stone, a silence as deep as the grave door between them and me and people like me. I can do nothing to change that. Nothing.

The police make me take my seat.

The Black-dress stands up. We stand and wait for It to leave the throne. Down the steps It comes. It suddenly stumbles to Its knees, the wig falls off Its head. Black human hair. The Black-dress is human after all, naked without his wig of power. He looks at me, grabs his wig, puts it on, and hurries out the door with my smile chasing him.

I get four years' hard labour.

Lava

'. . . This world that people believe they want so much is only true in the movies because people make the movies. You get me?' says

Tagata. I shake the head. 'Okay, well, let me explain it this way,' he continues. 'Have you seen the lava fields in Savai'i?' I shake the head again. 'Two years ago I went there with some friends. You travel for miles through forest and so many villages where the people have ruined the beauty, and then . . . And then it is there. You feel you are right in it at last. Get me? Like you are there where the peace lies, where all the dirty little places and lies and monuments we make to ourselves mean nothing because lava can be nothing else but lava. You get me?' He stops for a while and looks at me. 'The lava spreads for miles right into the sea. Nothing else. Just black silence, like the moon maybe. You remember that movie us guys saw years ago? Well, it looks like that, like the moon surface in that movie. A flood of lava everywhere. But in some places you see small plants growing through the cracks in the lava, like funny stories breaking through your stony mind. Get me? I felt like I have been searching for that all my miserable life. Boy, it made me see things so clear for once. That being a dwarf or a giant or a saint does not mean anything.' Tagata's eyes glow brightly. 'That we are all equal in silence, in the nothing, in lava. I did not want to leave the lava fields, but . . . but then you cannot stay there forever because you will die of thirst and hunger if you stay. There is no water, no food, just lava. All is lava.'

Wife and Son

As I am drinking faamafu with Tagata and other friends in the fale on the other side of the picture theatre, Susana enters. She is the daughter of the man who owns the fale and the faamafu that costs 20 sene a bottle. She is younger than me but she is the best-looker I have ever seen. She has graduated from the Sisters' school and is a typist for the government. As she goes behind the curtains on the opposite side of the fale, she stops and looks quickly at me before she disappears. All my friends are after her, but her parents make sure no one gets near her.

We drink some more. Some of the men start talking sexy about

Susana. I am getting angry about that. 'Bet you she be terrific in bed!' laughs someone.

All around the lights of the other fale and shacks are on and there are people moving about preparing the food and bathing and getting ready for sleep. Susana comes out of the curtains. The other men stop talking and look at her. She is frightened and walks quickly out to the back fale where her family are having their evening meal.

I drink until the head turns round and round and I cannot sit properly. Tagata and others hold me up and take me home and put me to bed. All the time, I am mumbling to Tagata that I sure want to be with Susana. He says he will fix it for me. Before this, after I leave our home for good, I am never attracted like this to any female. For me there is no shortage of women at the market. They come from everywhere. Village women, nurses, wives, fun women, unsatisfied women, women who go willing for money, plain women, pretty women, cat women, old women, cold women, ugly women, tourist women who look for the Polynesian noble savage with the mighty club, but no one like Susana.

The next night Tagata disappears from our home. He returns laughing and tells me what happened.

He walks right into the fale and sees Susana's father. Tagata sits on the floor and faces him. Tagata buys some faamafu and they drink and talk about religion and everything. Now Tagata, as you know, is a professional gunfighter at conversation. He can talk on the Bible and dazzle anyone, which is what he did to Susana's father. In the middle of their talk Susana enters and irons clothes not far from Tagata, who knows she is listening to everything he is saying. Before Tagata ends his talk he asks the man (and Susana) that they, because they are devout Christians, should pray to Jehovah to forgive him because he has been a sinner all his life. The man, who wants favours from Tagata because he owns the market, prays for Tagata, who bows his head but from the corner of his eyes he sees Susana praying too. After the long prayer, Tagata asks Susana questions about her religion. He tells her he is interested because he wants to join the 'true church'. Susana, with her father's permission, at once goes into a long talk about her faith. Her father starts to fall asleep. Tagata tells him politely to go to bed. Because he still does not trust Tagata the man goes to sleep behind the curtains. From there he can hear if Tagata tries anything with Susana. Tagata soon hears him snoring so he tells Susana that he has a best friend who is keen on joining her faith too. Susana asks who it is. He tells her that it is Pepe who told the judge that there is no God. She falls for that. When you going to talk to Pepe? he asks her. It has to be soon, he tells her, because Pepe is low in sin and there is nobody to help him see the Light. She says very soon. But what about her father? he asks. She will fix that, she says.

Tagata ends his story and we are laughing. As I said before, Tagata is a great storyteller and I do not know whether the whole story is all true or not, but I believe him.

The next night I dress up respectable and go to the fale. They sit me down. Susana's mother is there too. I get the feeling they do not only want me to be a Roman follower but also a husband for Susana. (They know that Tauilo is a rich man and I am his only son.) They talk all the time about religion. Susana's parents, I mean. Susana sits and looks everywhere but at me. I get bored with their talk but I look interested in it.

Near midnight I leave.

For four nights or so the same thing happens when I visit them. I get angry because the plan is not working. It is soon Vaipe talk that I am after Susana as my permanent wife. Susana's father spreads this rumour. Her mother, who is more male than female, starts to visit the market, which I am helping Tagata's parents run, and act there like she owns me already. My friends laugh at me. I want to give up this stupid courting, but every time I try to I remember Susana more alive than before. It is like the attraction of some people to religion, the sinner to his confessor and forgiver, the miser to his money. She is like the Hollywood dream. It is a new madness for me.

On the seventh night I run through the rain to her home and am surprised because she is by herself. Her parents are ready for sleep behind the curtains and the rest of their aiga are in the back fale. She does not look at me. She watches the rain.

She starts talking the usual about religion but her voice is unsure.

I watch her closely. I let her talk on. I find myself moving over slowly till my knee is against her knee. She jumps away a bit, but she remains next to me. Her lips quiver and, even though it is chilly, she looks hot.

Now as you know, fale are open on all sides and everyone can see inside when the light is on. People run by in the rain. It is impossible for me to win her right there where every shadow can see us. As she talks my right hand falls to lie on her knee. She pretends my hand is not there. 'Now, Pepe, God is good to all men,' she is saying. My hand slides down to her thigh. She talks faster. Her parents will not hear because of the rain. 'He will be good to you if you repent . . .' My hand slides down her lap. She is shivering a bit. 'God is everyone's Father, and He loves you and me . . .' The hand caresses down there and discovers soft hair, and the fingers are alive and they play slowly. 'Now, if you are a sinner and you want to be with God you got to be good and repent now . . .' Her legs move apart a little bit and her lavalava opens more and I see the black down there which is a small forest where the fingers are searching for the stream, and my heart beats in my ears and eyes and head. Her voice chatters like she is cold but she keeps talking. I find the stream. The fingers caress. The stream flows. 'Pepe . . . God . . . God is love . . . God, ohhh!' Her eyes are shut tight.

'Susana!' her mother calls. Susana pushes my hand away and jumps to her feet. 'Go to bed!' her mother says. She moves to leave. I whisper to her that I will come and see her when the light is out. She says nothing. She goes over and switches out the light and I hear her running down the back steps into the rain and then into the back fale which has no light on now. I creep after her.

I stand outside and can see little into the back fale. My eyes get used to the darkness. I am nearly soaking wet. I now see figures of people sleeping, but not Susana. However, I soon see someone waving to me from the far side. It is her. I enter. All the people are asleep, some are snoring. One step, two steps. Someone in front of me moves. I stop dead. If they catch me they will kill me alive. The person is still again. I step over him. One step, two steps and over the next person. It is the longest walk I ever made. I step over the fourth person. And then Susana is there lying under the sheet.

I lie down beside her. She lies still and does nothing. I move close to her till I am against her warm side. All the while my ears are wide open. They will kill me for sure. I caress her hair and slowly pull down the sheet off her. My hand falls to her breasts, she draws the deep breath. I pull up her shirt till it is round her shoulders and my fingers play tunes on her breasts and belly. Her skin is smooth like sleep.

'No, Pepe. It is a sin!' she whispers. But she does not stop my cheeky fingers, which have reached the top of her lavalava and are undoing it. 'Please, Pepe. It is a sin!' The lavalava is now down by her sides, the fingers are caressing her thighs and soon find the forest again. She does not move at all and she has her arm across her face. I kiss her face and body and then lie on her and she moves her legs apart. 'It is a sin, sin!' she whispers. I kneel between her legs. I shed my human clothes.

And then kneel down on she. The barrier is there in her sea. She starts to cry. I try slow. No show. All the while her sound is complaining it is a sin.

Hard. Success at last. She folds up in pain. I embrace her and move slowly in her sea, and she is responding like a woman should. Every trick I try to make her come but I find the self too eager and I am giving her the seed and the fire explodes in my eyes.

She flings her arms round me. 'Pepe, I love you,' she says. That hits me in the gut. I know she does not feel that about me. 'It is a sin what we did,' she says, 'but it is not a sin if we get married in the church. That is what my mother said.'

I put on my clothes and creep out of the fale. The whole dream is a fake, hollow. They planned it all.

For a few months Tagata's parents go to American Samoa for holidays and Tagata and me are left to manage the market. I slowly notice that something is happening to Tagata. He looks sick but he never tells me the trouble, he does not do his job properly so I do all the work and the market makes more money than before. I introduce new methods and keep account books. Some people tell that my success is because I am Tauilo's son and business runs in my aiga's blood.

Tagata starts to stay in his room most of the time and he grows his hair long. Sometimes he does weightlifting and goes for long runs to get fit. To cheer him up I join his exercises. He is escaping, I think, and it is like a new madness. He is like the flying-fox, his nickname, which has no nest with other birds because they laugh at him and treat him different because he is not what a bird should be. Now he, my brother, is trying to grow and be like other men, that is my understanding of his problem. Why he suddenly starts to do this, I never find out.

Because of the hard work at the market and my worries about Tagata, I forget Susana.

Tagata suddenly takes up the L.M.S. religion. I am really worried because it is against what he believed before. Every Sunday he puts on his white clothes and goes to church. However, when he returns and I see he is happy, my worry goes away. It is at this time that Susana comes into my life again.

In the small market office, I am working on the books. There is a knock on the door. I open it. It is Susana's father.

'Have you come?' I greet him.

He stands looking at the floor and says, 'Yes, sir.' When he calls me sir I get suspicious at once. Most people in the market when they want something for free start to flatter you.

'Sit down.' I give him a chair.

'No thank you, sir.' He stands there. I know him very well, he has a reputation for making the last penny off his starving mother.

'What you want?' I ask him straight.

Then his wife fills the doorway. Susana does not look like both of them put together. The mother is like a cow, and the father is small like a sick pig.

She sits in the chair without asking me and says, 'Hot day, is it not?' I stare straight at her. 'How is the business, Pepe?' Then she laughs. I do not reply. She scratches the armpits. Her husband is still looking at the floor. 'You not been for a long time to see us,' she says. 'We still have the best faamafu. For you, it is free!' She roars the laughter again.

'I have much work to do,' I tell them.

'You go ahead,' she says, winking at me. 'Boy, you really educated and brainy as your father. Look at all those figures and books you are adding up. You wrote all those?' I do not answer. She picks up one book and looks at it. 'Pepe is bright,' she says to her husband. 'Look at all this English and figures. He is as bright as any palagi. You making much money these days?' she asks. 'Business is bad for us. We find it hard to feed all our big aiga.'

'What you want?' I ask. She looks at her husband, he is still looking at the floor. She coughs but he still does not do anything. 'What is it?' I ask him.

He blinks and whispers, 'It . . . it is our Susana, sir.'

'Louder!' she commands him.

'It is about Susana, sir,' he repeats. She nods.

'What about her?' I ask. She is looking at me like I am the fly and she is the spider.

'She is . . . she is with child, sir,' he says, and he looks at me for the first time that day.

'What that got to do with me?' I demand. He does not say anything.

'Tell him,' she orders him.

He blinks again and says, 'Susana says . . .' And stops. Blinks and says, 'She says you are the father, sir.'

'Now we are not saying that you are the father, Pepe. Susana is saying it,' she says.

'You trying to blackmail me?' I ask.

'No, but Susana said . . .' she says.

'Said what?' I demand.

'Tell him!' she orders him. He shakes the head. 'Tell him what your daughter said. Go on!'

'She may be lying,' I say.

'Oh, Pepe, she does not lie to me. Oh, no. She is a religious girl,' she says.

'Yes, Susana is a good girl,' he says. 'She is not like the other girls in the Vaipe.'

'If she is so good,' I say, 'why she got the fat belly now?' I have them. She sits and he stands. They are both looking at the floor.

I sit and look out at the people passing by and I remember Sapepe and my mother Lupe and my anger goes. The desire for someone of my own flesh to care for and give meaning to me fills me as I watch the market people. My own child growing in Susana's womb, the meaning perhaps to all the gone years. A son or a daughter.

Tagata bursts into the room. 'It is all a lie!' he laughs. 'I am sick of religion!' It is the old Tagata again and I am full of joy. He stops his dancing when he sees Susana's parents. He looks at them and then at me. 'What is the matter?' he asks me.

'Susana is going to have my child,' I tell him. He jumps up and down, then he runs out into the market. I hear him telling our friends that he is going to be an uncle.

'I will take her as my wife, but I do not want you to come near me and my family, understand?' I threaten Susana's parents.

'Yes, sir,' he says. She gets up angrily and leaves.

So it passes that Susana comes to stay with me in Tagata's house which is now my home too. She insists we get married in church. I refuse absolutely.

Last Will and Testament of the Flying-fox

. . . One morning I wake to find Tagata gone. I send friends to look for him. They cannot find him anywhere. Even the police and the hospital do not know where he is.

I wait for him for six days. On the seventh, he returns. His hair and beard are long and uncombed and his clothes are torn and dirty and his eyes glow like those of the prophets in the desert.

'I went back, Pepe. Back to the lava fields, and it has brought me up from hell again. Lava is the only true thing left. It cannot change. The rock from whom we came, and it is with us at the back of our souls. You get me?' he says. 'It is there I found the self again. And the courage to accept all that has happened!' He laughs then and he seems his usual self again and I believe he is going to be okay. So I leave for work in the market.

That evening, when the sun sets over the sea and the birds fly back to the mountains and the forests, and the market is empty and shut down, I return home.

I find him hanging down from the mango tree behind the house.

I cut him down and take him into the house.

I bathe him.

I dress him.

I find this letter in English on my table:

> *The Vaipe,*
> *Judgement Day.*
>
> *To His Excellency,*
> *Pepesa Tauilopepe,*
> *Illegitimate Son of the Gods.*
>
> *My Beloved Brother Condemned,*
>
> *I know you will understand because you understand this dwarf and brother condemned really well. As I before said to you, I am the free man who got the right to dispose of his self. This life is the only life, and it is a good life because it is the only one we have. I was born a small man with a big man inside, the flying-fox with an eagle in the gut. All my life I tried for to free this eagle so he can fly high and dazzle the world. Anyway, on this my last day and hour, you will find the eagle flying on the mango tree with his one wing of rope. Life, as I said and always wanted to preach to you, is good. It is good because it is ridiculous like a dwarf is ridiculous, an accident caused when parents makefire too much. Because life is ridiculous it has to end the most ridiculous way, in*

suicide like Christ. Laugh, Pepesa, because I am right there inside the death-goddess which no one believes in any more, and her sacred channel is all lava. Laugh, Pepesa, because her lava machine is grinding me, the flying-fox, to dust. Laugh, Pepesa, because there is nothing else to do.

The papalagi and his world have turned us, and people like your rich but unhappy father and all the modern Samoans, into cartoons of themselves, funny crying ridiculous shadows on the picture screen. Never mind, we tried to be true to our selves. That is all I think any man with a club can do.

To you, your godly Excellency, I apologise because the flying-fox has nothing to leave in this my will but 1001 laughs, as the movies say, which I desire you, your Excellency, to laugh one laugh every night from now on until you die. One laugh laughed loud will keep away sorrow and your father and the Romans and the L.M.S. and the modernaitu and the police and the judge and bad breath. One laugh will turn everything to lava and joy and forgiveness.

For all this wealth I am leaving you, your most intelligent Excellency, I ask one last tiny favour. It is this — Dig a small hole on the bank of the Vaipe and into this hole dump this dwarf carcass of mine. Then fill it fast with Vaipe mud before it stinks our most excellent Vaipe neighbourhood. Plant on it taro and I swear on the lava that the taro will grow like nobody's business because I am excellent manure. When the taro is ready, give it to the market people. I am sure, as I am sure I am dead, that they will all die from greedy diarrhoea.

So long, Pepesa, I am moving down and out, as the cowboy says.

All is well in Lava. Tell your son and my nephew that.

I remain forever dead,
Your humble self,

Tagata, the Flying-fox in the Mango.

I bury him on the banks of the Vaipe.

Exit

It is hot in my hospital room, so hot it is hard to breathe, especially when I have rotten lungs. This morning the nurse tells me my father came again to try and see me; he comes every day but I refuse to see him. I look out the window, the two old men are stoking their fire as usual. The pain is getting too hard to bear. As usual the nurses are fixing the beds in the next ward. The old woman patient next door is dead, she died last night, her family collected her corpse this morning, there was much weeping and wailing. But hospital life goes on as usual.

I got out of bed this morning after the nurse bathed me and I carried my skeleton to the mirror. When I look at the man in the glass I find him a stranger and an ugly one at that. The skin hangs off his bones like old clothes. The eyes have no laughter in the hollow sockets. The skull is rising to the surface of his face; soon the skull will have no skin-face. Only white bone. I staggered back to bed and coughed out the blood. I lay there as usual and waited for the doctor's visit.

They enter, the nurse and the red-haired doctor. I hide my pain and is the usual gay self. The doctor smiles and examines the patient on the bed. I watch his hands as they go over the body, the skin and bone, and pronounce it living still. He tells the nurse in English to give me the usual medicine. The nurse writes it down.

'Is it alive?' I ask him in English. He is surprised because it is the first time I have spoken in English to him. I laugh and repeat the question.

'Is what alive?' he asks.

'This body,' I reply.

He laughs and says, 'Yes, it will rise and go home soon.'

'That is what you think,' I joke.

'You will be all right.' He does not laugh now. The nurse leaves.

'Have you makefire with her yet?' I ask. He does not know what I am referring to. 'With the nurse? She is mad on you.'

He stands up and his face is red like his hair. 'I am married,' he says.

'That does not matter,' I reply.

'My wife would not understand.'

'A pity. That nurse could teach you much,' I laugh. He is smiling, this palagi who has become my first palagi friend.

I have forgotten my novel on the table near my bed. He sees it and says, 'What are you writing?'

'A letter.'

'A long letter, is it not? Who is it to?'

'To my self,' I say. There is an amazed stare on his face.

'It is in English?' he asks. I nod the head. 'Well, happy writing!' He walks to the door.

'I am going to die, am I not?' I call. He stops but does not turn to face me. 'Am I not? I want you to admit it to me.'

'Yes,' he says. He turns to look at me.

'Think of that nurse,' I tell him.

He leaves the room.

I continue to write this for the last time.

From the world of Sapepe, which my father destroyed by changing it, I came. From the world of Lupe and my aiga to the world of the Vaipe and Tagata and all my other friends, only to find them steps toward my self and my end. From the dark of Lupe's womb to the other dark of the death-goddess, I, Pepesa, has travelled and has seen what there is to be seen and felt and done what there is to do, and I found laughter.

Last night as I lay in my bed after the pain left me and sleep came, I dreamed I saw the lava field, black like sea, flow in to cover Sapepe, the Vaipe, Apia, the marketplace and all the mistakes and monuments we make to our selves. And I found my self above the lava sea as it flowed in deep and forever. And like the sun in the sky I saw Tagata laughing as he hanged from the freedom tree.

A few more sentences and I am done with this novel about my life. A few more and I am done. Outside the hospital window the baldheaded men are feeding their fire.

The maggots are impatient. Soon they will break out from my flesh like bubbles as beautiful as diamonds.

All is well in Lava, so spake the flying-fox.

peter wells

of memory and desire

Part I

1

SHE was a short, slightly bow-legged woman who looked older than her 28 years; though this may have been the clothes she chose which were drab, poorly made on the whole and looked as if they had come from a factory shop. In fact she was one of those rare people who look better without any clothes: naked she was a smooth ivory shade all over, with pleasantly shaped breasts which were neither large nor small. Naked she was unselfconscious, most herself. She was a computer keyboard operator for the Suseychi Corporation, she was newly married and her name was Sayo.

They were an odd couple, everyone on the tour remarked on it. He was so handsome in an almost cinematic way, with perfect cheekbones to catch the light, a full sensuous mouth chiselled, it seemed, into his face. He was tall, particularly for a Japanese, as if he were part of the new Japanese race that, with better food and living conditions, was growing to outpace the Americans, the Germans, the Australians. But if Keiji were tall, he moved a little diffidently. In fact he was most at ease in a most peculiar position: standing on his hands. This was his party trick and even, stranger to relate, a form of relaxation.

Keiji was a tense young man, as perhaps befitted someone who was doing well in the same Suseychi Corporation as his wife: aged exactly 24 on his wedding day, he was within several years of being made a junior executive. Whether his marriage would help or hinder this, no one was quite sure. Sayo was not the usual kind of woman an executive's wife should be: she was no beauty; she came from a poorer class than Keiji, whose father had served in the Imperial Army and whose mother, a proud and somewhat overbearing woman, laid claim to descending from a noble, if impoverished, lineage. Keiji came to his marriage a virgin.

Sayo and Keiji had decided to get married in New Zealand, on a package tour, because it seemed easier. Keiji's mother had only grudgingly accepted the match, and then only because her son, her only son, had uncharacteristically refused to budge. In fact it was the first time in their intense life that his widowed mother had found her son obdurate. Perhaps it was this that had made her accept Sayo, whom she saw as common, ordinary in every way: incapable, indeed, of sustaining an intelligent conversation, uncertain about important matters of etiquette, and altogether what she expressed to herself as 'tarnished', 'second-rate', 'possibly even Korean'.

With a woman's intuition she saw that her son's bride was already sexually experienced. There was something in Sayo's level gaze which told her this, the somewhat indecorous way she sat; even, indeed, the way Sayo touched her son, which Mrs Nakajima, the mother, regarded as inappropriate, casual, too confident. Living with her son in their tiny Tokyo apartment, Mrs Nakajima felt sure he was a virgin. She saw Sayo as a kind of temptress, a perception which sat at odds with Sayo's ugly clothes, lack of refinement, even her rather ordinary face with widely spaced eyes and clichéd haircut.

Yet Mrs Nakajima sensed that the two young people were intensely in love: it was one of those accidents which happen. Privately she would have preferred Keiji to educate himself sexually with this young woman then move on to the kind of woman who would be useful to his career, provide handsome children and look after her in her dotage. But Keiji would not budge: in her view he was foolish and naive to propose to Sayo. She was a mere computer operator in a room so full of them that Mrs Nakajima, who had seen the room once, visualised it as a paddyfield viewed from a train, with the bent backs of workers intent upon their labour. Naturally Sayo had accepted. Mrs Nakajima had received her, done honour to her in a way which was calculated to make her feel miserable and uncomfortable: for example she unconsciously held her fingers under her nose, as if she perceived an unpleasant odour emanating from Sayo, a thing unforgivable on such an important occasion.

It was perhaps for this reason that Keiji decided, with Sayo's collaboration Mrs Nakajima was certain, to go to New Zealand, get wed alone and experience at least one week on their own before they returned to take up their residence in Mrs Nakajima's tiny apartment.

2

They were married on the front lawn of a colonial New Zealand church which had been shifted to a transport museum as an exhibit. It was a common place for Japanese weddings, and in fact, that day, there had already been two others. Confetti speckled the lawn like lightly trampled daisies, yellow, pink, pale blue.

Sayo wore a hired bridal gown, all white, while Keiji was handsome in his own dinner suit. Sayo thought of the brides before who had worn the dress, wondering to herself what had happened to them, whether they were happy or sad. But she cast these ideas out of her mind and decided, according to the European custom the dress itself was her something 'old'. Keiji, in her eyes, had never looked more handsome, pale beneath his taut skin, his eyes gazing at her with what seemed an almost fanatical intensity of desire.

They had had to ask a passer-by to take their photo.

Standing together, against a lake which had once been a reservoir, they posed, smiled into the bright, almost iridescent New Zealand sunlight, arms around each other's waists, tense with the happiness which was about to descend upon them like a storm, leaving them, hopefully, happily drowned.

3

They began their honeymoon tour that afternoon, right after a celebratory lunch in the most expensive hotel in Auckland. They had each had Chivas Regal whisky, which went straight to their heads, and Keiji, who liked to talk, entertained Sayo with a vision of their future, when they might have their own flat and perhaps go on foreign visits and Sayo could even stop working. Sayo did not feel comfortable talking when Keiji was outlining their future. For one thing, he was so much better spoken than her: indeed, in public with him, she often saw people turning to gaze at her speculatively, as if seeking to diagnose her relationship with a man so handsome, so well-dressed, so suited to success.

Besides, Sayo hardly talked much at all: she had learnt when she came to Tokyo from the provinces — her father was a railway worker till he had an accident and was forced to retire — that the less she said, the less people could learn about her and, hence, look down on her. It was true that her mother had died in Sayo's infancy and her father, who was too fond of pachinko parlours and sake, had found another woman to take her place. This woman was not unkind, but she never regarded Sayo as anything other than an impediment in her relationship with Sayo's father. Her father and the woman liked to get drunk, and laugh a lot, and play cards late into the night.

Sayo had escaped by working in two jobs and training herself to be a keyboard operator. Unlike Keiji's mother, to whom it was menial, Sayo saw her job as something which had removed her from an unhappy situation in which she was always in excess, and she even felt uncomfortable when Keiji mentioned, as a matter of course, that when he became more successful in the Suseychi Corporation, she would certainly give up work.

This was the only small cloud on their horizon as they went towards the hotel where the bus tour began. It would take them, in six hurried days, around the small islands that people back in Japan talked about as so green so clean so empty. Together they had agreed they would tell no one they were newly-weds. It would give them more privacy.

4

The tour was made up of 23 people, all Japanese: Keiji and Sayo were allotted seats which they would keep for the duration of the trip. In front of them were two younger women who already, as they looked from Keiji to Sayo and back to Keiji again, more lingeringly, broke out into giggles as if Keiji and Sayo had written all over them the almost guilty fact of their wedding.

Behind them sat an elderly couple who rose, bowed to them pleasantly, indeed courteously, the elderly man, who was deaf, offering to help Sayo put her luggage into the rack.

Across from them sat a rather beautiful young woman whose hand was held possessively by a powerfully built man who did not shift his gaze once as Keiji and Sayo came and sat down, preferring to look ahead and say to his companion, they were already running, by his watch, 4 minutes 30 seconds late. He then said things were not done that way where he came from, mentioning a small provincial city which Sayo could remember seeing from a train and thinking how ugly it was and how her spirit would die if she had to live there.

The bus slid away as Sayo and Keiji settled back in their lambswool seats. Sayo let her leg bump softly against Keiji as they turned a corner. Keiji turned his face to her for a moment and Sayo felt for the first time a misgiving that he could direct such a passionately driven glance at her, so powerful with love. She smiled at him softly, as if to intimate the pleasures of the night ahead. He let his leg rest against hers and so, bumping each other with each accidental motion of the landliner, they caressed each other's bodies, exchanging a duet of silent glances, each of which was full of answering affirmation and promises that the night to come would be a memorable one for them both.

Sayo hardly noticed what was outside the window. When she did so she gazed at it almost without comprehension, seeing it through the reflection of the man whom she was amazed she had met and whom, in a few short hours, she would divest, like a spirit which would be freed, of his virginity.

To everyone about them, apart from the man opposite, to whom nothing was apparent apart from the young woman to whom he was explaining the relative merits of the other bus tours, it was clear that Keiji and Sayo were newly-weds.

5

They could hardly wait to be alone. The last-minute arrangements took an eternity, during which they had stood apart, as if, almost decorously, they chose to be separate so that they could better enjoy that moment when they were alone behind the door.

Unfortunately there was a mess-up with the rooms and the elderly couple who had sat behind them ended up in a room with two single beds which, to the amusement of everyone on the bus, they indignantly refused. Sayo and Keiji had to wait around while the rooms were reallocated. They spent their time taking a short walk out into the crisp clear air, looking at the rough graded soil around the motel, marvelling at the unnatural greenness of the pasture all around them. For them the landscape had an eerie prescience, unsoftened by human form. There were hardly any animal forms either apart from a few distant, almost cosmetically placed, sheep. Neither talked as they returned to the motel. They were given their key and made their way down anonymous corridors towards their bridal suite. They were almost numb with desire and apprehension.

6

'Go slower, go slower', she had to beg him as she began to realise that he was, indeed, a virgin and, in a common mistake, was trying to roughly impress her with his love-making skills which she imagined he had picked up off pornographic films he had watched with his male friends in a bar. She had wanted to gaze upon his body which she longed to see naked: she wanted to take his cock into her mouth and tell him how much she loved every part of him. But he would not allow her to move much, he was intent on lavishing upon her a somewhat brutal passion which did little for her: though she realised, through love for him, she could not hurt his pride by not showing desire.

Everything went as he seemed to want it until the crucial moment when, murmuring with a rapture which to Sayo herself seemed completely false, Keiji attempted to penetrate her. Sayo had had an experienced lover before — just one — a kind elderly man, somewhat like her father to look at, she felt ashamed to admit to herself when she thought of him in hindsight. But this elderly man had been a knowledgeable lover, educating her in pleasure, the ways to seek and maximise pleasure between two humans.

The elderly man had travelled the East during the war: he had even spent time in the pleasure houses of Shanghai. Sayo, though no promiscuous woman, had gained the knowledge of the many actors in love whom her elderly lover had known: thus, in her one lover, she had as it were experienced many others. This gave to her love-making a sense of greater experience, just as it gave to Sayo that undeniable thing in a human being who has experienced early pleasure and who knows how to obtain it: the sense of being centred in oneself as a healthy animal being.

He who could talk so well, knew so such, now rolled off her, panting, sweating. He lay with his eyes closed and Sayo, raising herself slightly to touch him tentatively, heard a groan escape from him, almost a sob. He had lost his erection, and she looked down at it for the first time in the relative calmness and objectivity she knew she would come to in relation to this most vital part of his being.

Keiji's cock was slightly smaller than her elderly lover's, but her elderly lover had given her to understand he was well-endowed. Her husband's cock, though, was sweetly shaped, almost cherubic within its glans, lying there on his stomach as the de-escalation of his breathing continued.

He turned his face away from her, deeply shamed.

She slowly began to kiss Keiji, beginning first at his hairline, which, as was natural in a young man, was strong and marked, down to his brow, fierce and frowning, across the two rigid lines on his forehead: she kissed his eyelids which he kept shut, tight with shame, no matter how she tried to caress them, with light bird-like kisses, to open: she kissed down his nose to his lips which she touched with the very lightest of caresses: and so, down his body she adventured, touching him, kissing him, accustoming herself to his form with her lips till finally she reached the instep of his foot, which made him suddenly curl upwards, begin laughing involuntarily, even as he called out angrily for her to stop. Suddenly they were fighting, naked, and she was almost stronger than him until he suddenly pushed her aside and they kissed long, long and deep, their first really intense kiss, a promise almost of the pleasures they would eventually find: a kind of pact.

Later in the night, Keiji again tried to penetrate her. She woke from her light sleep to find him astride her. This was not pleasant — he had, as it were, penetrated her dreamworld — but she relaxed under him, seeking to offer him every assistance, through unguent movements, small cries in his ear, caresses on the inside of his thighs. But again, at the climactic moment, he did not remain hard. Instead they kept kissing as if nothing much had happened, or rather, as if they both expected this to be the outcome, which, for their mutual survival, they agreed to accept for the moment. So they fell into a slightly uneasy sleep, both aware they were revealed to each other in a particularly vulnerable state: she did not want to intervene on such vulnerable territory, but she knew enough to let him know he could relax: things would find their own course, it would be worked out.

She did not say this in words: rather, her kisses and caresses, and the way she held him as he slipped into the darkness of sleep, told him. And thus he was saved from being enormously unhappy.

7

Daylight brought them their faces almost as if the sun were a servant who had sneaked into their room and, on a tray, carefully laid out two dishes to welcome them back onto Earth. Yet they were tousled, sleeptorn: both seeing each other for the first time as they knew they would see each other again, time after time. Oddly enough, the night had made Sayo appear beautiful, tousling her rather prim hairstyle, loosening her body, while Sayo, gazing silently at Keiji as he gazed back at her, saw there were small lines on his face which would manifest themselves as he got older: it was as if, for a moment she saw what Keiji would be like as an old man. This oddly comforted her. That morning, together, they simply kissed, as if it were agreed, and each obtained great pleasure from it.

They showered, dressed and presented themselves to the others, who all gazed at them significantly, as if testing how their night of love had been. Most people concluded that they were drugged on a surfeit of love. Yet the elderly couple, to anyone looking closely, seemed the more happy.

8

That day Sayo took more interest in the scenery. They had been taken to the sulphurous district and Keiji talked to her knowledgeably about vapours, gases, energy, power. It was his opinion that the people of the country did not know how to harness the riches which were so evident about them. Indeed, the small town in which they found themselves had a certain dispirited air, as if, through its century of tourism, all that was genuine had been worn away, replaced by a gimcrack unreality of 'authentic' tourist experiences.

They went to look at a sheepshearing exhibition, gazed at charmingly naive and low-tech displays of how New Zealand gained its agricultural wealth. They walked over a small plastic wooden bridge where a recording played bellbird tunes and papier-mâché trees imitated a forest. Sayo was fascinated by a mechanical cow which illustrated how a cow eating grass turned out milk.

Keiji looked at all this with an uninterested air. He took out his video-camera and, while pretending to be filming the exhibits, turned it instead onto his new wife, observing her obsessively, possessing her through the camera. She pretended not to notice this, not out of conceit but because it was only by appearing not to be conscious of her husband's intense regard that she could relax with it. Thus she played to the camera at certain times, directing a coquettish gaze at it as they took in another sight. At other times she simply gazed back at him hungrily, as if she wanted to possess him then and there. She observed Keiji did not seem noticeably upset by what had happened the previous night: though whether this was simply keeping up 'face' she could not tell, she felt she did not know him well enough yet.

Keiji certainly seemed to be less obsessive about touching her all day. In fact she observed him, during lunch, flirting with a small group of schoolgirls from the bus who, unanimously, burst into thrilled laughter at his somewhat feeble humorisms. He did not look at her while he was doing this and Sayo assumed that Keiji was used to women finding him sexually exciting and that it was part of his personality, almost, to flirt and flatter these people's expectations. She did not feel jealous.

After lunch they went to a place called Hell's Gate where, in blinding white light, they walked over what seemed like a miniature desert, made up of boiling water and mud. There was a strong smell of sulphur in the air. As the guide explained the different names of the pools, 'Sodom and Gomorroh', 'Hell's Fury', 'Hate and Revenge', Sayo played hide and seek with Keiji's camera lens as he found and lost her again in drifting veils of white smoke.

9

That night, alone in their motel room, they were each struck by an attack of shyness. It was as if they knew each other both less and more than ever before. Yet Sayo recognised she had to take charge, to a certain extent: besides, she was driven mad by a desire for his body, his strong thighs, his sweet small nipples so cherrybrown on his pale pillowy chest. She went up to him and kissed him deep, on the mouth. He tried to pull his head away but soon he was kissing her as passionately and Sayo heard, as if from a long way away, Keiji making small supplicating sounds, almost subconsciously, like a small animal begging and calling and crying out for her to continue.

Their love-making now was both brutal and affectionate. They made love on the floor, right by the door, with footsteps coming and going beside them. This time she took his cock into her mouth and made love to him long and elaborately. Yet no matter how much he enjoyed this and their other mutual caresses he did not stay hard enough for penetration. Yet this fact, so baldly stated here, had become a mere incident on a longer journey, like something they had passed, fleetingly, outside the bus window: quickly seen, then gone. She encouraged him, then, to bring himself to orgasm, revelling in seeing his body stiffen, his thighs tauten, his toes even digging into the soles of her feet as his breathing grew faster and more hurried until finally, quickly, his eyelids fluttered closed and he jetted against her stomach warm and sticky.

He fell immediately into a deep sleep, in her arms, which lasted for a few minutes, possibly ten: then he awoke and kissed her with an almost dazzling degree of passion and love. Although she still had not achieved orgasmic satisfaction herself, or indeed even been penetrated, she felt a deep tenderness for Keiji, a profundity of feeling which was greater than any she had had with her older lover, or indeed any feeling she had known since her mother died. In fact, as she slipped off to sleep, in bed with Keiji, she dreamt of her mother for the first time in over 10 years. In her dream, her mother was washing her.

She woke up feeling blessed.

10

They went to some hot pools, the whole busload. There was much merriment looking at the body-shapes. Sayo and Keiji, playing together in the hot pool like a pair of languorous fishes, laughed at the elderly couple as they padded, very carefully, over the tiled floor and then slowly lowered themselves into the warmth. The old woman had a body made slack by child-bearing and age, skinny legs and soft, loose flesh. The old man had once had a fine physique, you could see that, but over-indulgence had weakened him till his body looked like jelly-white baked flounder.

Sayo and Keiji, lying in each other's arms in the water as delicately as possible so that, on the surface, it suggested that they were not even touching, exchanged whispered sentences about the old couple and rather unkindly laughed at them.

Later in the dressing-room, the man who sat opposite Sayo and him on the bus was changing beside Keiji. Keiji could see him comparing their bodies, the size of their penises. While they both dried themselves, the man — standing in ostentatious nakedness, displaying himself so all could see — talked about virgins, boasting about his sexual prowess with his new wife, making various indelicate puns and innuendos. The man, called Tatsuro, then ran his hand with mocking pleasure down to Keiji's buttock, which he squeezed appreciatively, all the while telling him how the women on the bus couldn't keep their eyes off him and all Keiji had to do was slip out of his room, late at night, and he would find any number of other — and here he used a crude word to describe women's private parts.

Keiji felt deeply uncomfortable but, being used to male chatter and the necessity for boastfulness, and the homoerotic voyeurism it signified, laughed but said he and Sayo were happy with each other. Whereupon Tatsuro, now fully dressed, said as a man he could never get enough. Keiji left the dressing room feeling oddly sad.

11

They went to a huge and powerful waterfall after this. The gush of water was so exhilarating that everyone rushed off the bus, chattering and holding their cameras, pushing into one another in their eagerness to get outside where they could hear the young schoolgirls already screaming in excitement as they ran down to the narrow bridge.

Keiji and Sayo walked together, silently, holding hands. It was as if they were unwilling to lose, for a moment, bodily contact. To the elderly couple behind them, they were touchingly in love, offering them a kind of memory of their own passion, from a time when they themselves had waited almost dumbly for all the company to leave so that they could be where they desired most: alone together, naked.

Keiji and Sayo walked towards the deafening roar: a fine mist rose around them. There was an almost erotic power in the drone of the water. Holding hands tightly now, because the sheer volume of the water frightened Sayo, who came from an inland area and could not swim, Keiji and Sayo walked across the narrow swinging bridge, then started back again. Halfway across Keiji forced Sayo to halt in the very middle of the suspension and pressed his body hard against hers, forcing her, half-crazy with fear, to turn to him, her lips trembling, dewed with water while he smiled into her face, cruel with love.

Miming because of the roar, Keiji got the deaf elderly man to take their photo. Standing in the mist, they posed, bodies hugging each other, Sayo's face white, her hand gripped tight as death around Keiji who, at that moment, looked paradisically happy.

When they reached land on the other side of the bridge, Sayo felt faint. She had a sudden longing for food. Abruptly removing her hand from Keiji, she walked alone to the bus and quickly went and sat down. Keiji came and sat beside her and in silence they travelled along till Sayo fell into sleep, her head coming to a natural rest against Keiji's shoulder while he sat there, looking beyond the somewhat brutal profile of Tatsuro, who was talking to the man in front of them. Keiji was unaware that the young woman opposite was stealing glances at him, as if she was wondering what it would be like to make love with a man as handsome and tender as Keiji.

12

They looked down at the plate in front of them, the round shelled peas the same unreal green as the pasture, the potatoes the same white as the mountains, the thick slice upon slice of beast, still bloody in parts, lying in a pool of gravy the colour of their mud pools.

Keiji turned to Sayo, and Sayo turned to Keiji as all around them the buzz of conversation took up, about what the food was, how to eat it correctly, what its taste might be. Already their guide and translator, Kaoru, was telling them it was 'New Zealand's national dish': this did not exactly recommend it. Keiji was beginning to see the islands as unevenly civilised, with the small cities which closed too early at night, and the large pink people looking at them with an unreal too-smiling courtesy and, beyond that, an outer ring of people looking at them with cool dislike. He did not know exactly what these hairy, uncouth people were saying but it was implicit in their eyes, in the way their mouths moved, that they were not saying complimentary things about them. Keiji, whose father had been in the Imperial Army and was in fact in Singapore when the British Army was forced into ignominious defeat, realised that history was full of hidden clauses: they were all existing in an uneasy juxtaposition, full of ironies: he a person from the land of Hiroshima, they a newly poor country dependent on the largesse of strangers.

Keiji and Sayo ate their meal, or as much as they could bear to, when the tastes were so unvaried and mild: only the meat, of which there was an unreal superabundance, had the necessary quality of fresh kill. Politely they ate, made appreciative sounds: but their plates were half-full when a rather surly waiter whisked them away from their table. Then they had watched a Maori dance group during which both Keiji and Sayo were aware of only one thing: how close their bodies were to each other, and how long it would be before they were freed from the seemingly interminable stretch of time which separated them from falling onto each other's bodies and beginning, afresh, that exciting voyage of discovery in which each could exchange personality with the other and so assume the transubstantiation which is the basis, and strength, of all love.

At last they were alone. The succession of bedrooms in which they met provided them with new scenery each night for the theatre of their passion. That night it gave them an oblong woody room, a large flat double-bed impersonal as to the conquests and defeats which had earlier happened there.

Alone, Sayo and Keiji began to undress each other, fumbling and furious in their passion to reveal each other, as if to test whether, during the infinite duration of the day which had kept their bodies muffled in clothes, the other had changed. Now they were naked, it was almost frightening the power they had over each other's bodies, the intimacy. Keiji led Sayo quickly to the bed and, not even pulling down the covers, kissed her so passionately that they both fell, in a slow delayed topple, back onto the bed, where lip found lip then broke apart, after a certain period of violent pleasure, both gasping as if for celestial air, then each mouth began to travel, frolicsome and flirtatious, about the body of the other.

Sayo found that the smooth stretch of Keiji's body, between his nipple and his thigh, was so tender that she only had to lick it, delicately, with her tongue, for him to crease down into helpless silent laughter. Keiji, to whom the business of a woman's body was new and hence full of marvel, found that gentleness was as persuasive as vigour, and that Sayo's hands, placed gently on his, educated him as to what gave her pleasure. Thus he ravaged her with tongue and fingertip till she was equally yielding and wanting, as if he were the most masterful and penetrating of lovers. This continued for an almost unbearable amount of time till Keiji, finding this so erotically charging that, gazing down at his lover, looking at her flushed face below his, the beads of sweat moistening her upper lip, the way her head tossed and turned from left to right, he pulled her arms crudely apart so that he might enjoy, unhindered, the full theatre of her passion. He pushed his stiff penis towards her and she now, as if a curtain had swiftly gone up, revealing before his eyes a fabulously gilded light, arched her body back and began raining a storm of kisses across his face, his chest, his nipples, all the while issuing sharp cries of desire, want, need.

Yet a terrible thing happened: just at that moment when he should penetrate her, his cock would not obey him. So it was that, suddenly retiring, but still kissing her so she did not understand his signals and, for a fatal moment, continued on her full theatrical performance of enticement, while he continued to make love to her with his tongue and fingers, he abruptly dropped away from her onto his back. He lay there silent, as if he dropped back down a deep dark well into sleep — so far, indeed, that there was no way she could reach him.

Humiliation, shame for her performance, disappointment meant that for long moments they both just lay there, in the now profoundly silent room, listening to the diminishing duet of their panting breath, Sayo alone keeping contact by placing her hand on that part of Keiji's belly which she knew to be most susceptible to touch: and she let her fingers lie there, hot, sweaty, still.

When she kissed him, he returned her kisses, but they were lacking the full depth of passion. They were automatic kisses, instantly full of regret. They broke off and Keiji said to her, after they lay for a while in silence, Sayo playing with his pubic hair, matting it thoughtfully with her fingers, that he would have a sauna in another part of the hotel. She did not ask him if he wanted her to be with him.

When she was alone, she lay there and thought of her old lover. Instantly she recalled images of their love-making, which occasionally had been quite bestial. This aroused her and alone, quickly, even crudely she drew herself to orgasm. Then she rose, showered, gazed at herself in the mirror wondering who that stranger was and how she had come to be in that strange room, on her honeymoon, alone. She crept under the cool covers and slept.

Coming back to their room much later, his skin tissue-thin from all the vapour, Keiji made the mistake of going to the wrong door, so identical were they all. For one moment he had had a terrible presentiment, for, behind the door, he could hear quite plainly the panting of a man rising up into orgasm, accompanied by the relentless shoving of a bed against a wall: a lower diminuendo was a woman's voice begging him to hurry, to finish, it was painful, too painful. Yet this seemed only to increase the fury of the man's actions for, as the woman began to issue a strange cry, pleasure inseparable from pain, Keiji realised it was not his own door but that of Tatsuro and his new bride. Keiji stood there, slowly losing the exact jab of his pain. Yet as he drew away a silence had fallen in the room, followed by the ugly snore of Tatsuro, clearly already in deep sleep, and the softer sound, almost plaintive, of a tap being turned on, ablutions made. Was he imagining it, or could he hear the sound of a woman crying?

When he found his own room, Sayo was already lost in sleep. He crept in beside her, not touching her, alone, bruised. Yet Sayo soon, as if the magnetic proximity of their bodies was too much, rolled towards him and fitted her body neatly to his side. Keiji felt a pure and hard erection. Alone he masturbated, then fell into profound sleep.

13

The following day they walked, as if in a trance, around a vast and echoing museum full of artefacts of a culture which appeared to them both, in the state they were in, as threateningly dark, primitive: signals of chaos. The schoolgirls asked Keiji to take their photo on the steps and for the rest of the tour Keiji hid his face behind his video-camera, filming indiscriminately every room, as if he did not possess the power to take away his eye from the lens.

Sayo looked down at some cruel combs, blunt pounders, filagreed spears of unusual refinement: she felt a moment of pure misery sweep over her. From behind the museum glass case, she saw the elderly couple looking down at the exhibits. Their cheerfulness lifted her spirits. Yet she followed around silently behind Keiji, almost like an unnecessary attaché, ignored. She saw the young wife of Tatsuro looking at her: she did not understand it was with complicity. She too was ignored; Tatsuro was in the middle of the flock of schoolgirls, making an embarrassment of himself by ostentatiously examining the penises on certain Maori carvings.

14

They sat on the bus as it travelled ever southwards. Keiji had fallen into a deep sleep, his face whitened and strained. Even in his sleep, he carefully did not allow his head to fall upon her shoulder. He removed his leg when it accidentally touched her own. Thus reprimanded, deeply unhappy, Sayo sat there, gazing at him with a saddened erotic intensity, allowing her eyes to caress his body, memorising, as she looked at him minutely, every detail of his flesh and hair and hands: as if she might one day lose him.

So she sat there, gazing, erotically moved into a state not unlike a trance, absorbing into her brain the whirl of his hair at the back of his neck, the way several strands of hair fell down across his forehead; the way his hands lay together and his perfectly manicured nails rested so lightly on the palm of the other hand. The bus rocked and lulled and shook their bodies and she longed, oh longed so much to simply disappear down onto the seat and worship his body with her face, her lips. Yet when she carefully placed her thigh against his, his leg, even in sleep, swerved away, as if her flesh burnt him, and not too soon after he woke up, glanced at her resentfully, turned to look out the window.

They were passing along a coastal road bordered by an ocean beach. Small rudimentary houses faced the sea. Turning his back on her, he stared out at the sea in silence.

15

They had had to pretend a certain modicum of tenderness towards each other in order that the others on the bus might not notice, and hence feel free to enter into their personal drama. Both Keiji and Sayo felt themselves observed, however, and it was singularly unfortunate that the very first time it was clear everyone knew they were newly-weds came now. Kaoru, a male busybody who enjoyed putting people into queues and telling them details they never wanted to know about the strange country they were in, called out loudly, 'Make way for the newly-weds,' as Keiji and Sayo filed off the bus.

The mortification Sayo felt for Keiji was profound.

They separated in their room, Sayo going to the bathroom, carefully closing the door behind her. The door had bevelled glass, which soon steamed up with the vapour from the shower. She stayed under the shower quite a long time, singing to herself, trying to lose her feeling of misery. Quickly she made her mind up: she stepped from the shower, aware Keiji was standing near the door, looking at her reflection through the glass. She moved back and forth in the range of the glass, giving him a small, almost geisha act, full of reluctance, displaying her nakedness. He had drawn closer. He was fully clothed still.

Now she came closer to the glass, pressed herself against it so the full outline and shape of her body was clear. She pretended that he was the glass and she made love, for a few pleasurable moments of sheer theatre, against it. After some moments' hesitation — he had less imagination than her — he moved closer to his side of the glass, his breath misting it, then his lips kissed it through the steam: for several moments they sent *billets-doux* to each other, safely separated by the strength of the glass between them.

This artificial barrier acted as an almost physical statement of what had occurred between them the night before. She waited, willing him to open the door. She would not open it. He opened the door, on his knees. She entered, still moist from the shower, steam rushing into the bedroom. He buried his face in her cunt, kissing her with a fierce, even angry passion. She cried out with the pain, he caught her round the hips, pulled her down onto the carpet. His face was white with passion or anger or strain. He cut her vision out by kissing her eyes shut, he smothered her with kisses so harsh and terrible that she was forced to fight him back so that, purely animal for several long minutes, they wrestled and attacked each other on the carpet, combatting each other with all the delayed passion of the hours they had been forcefully kept apart, Keiji moaning and crying out as, in successive waves, his passion attacked her body while Sayo banged her body into his and clawed his back, his thighs, his neck.

Erect, he would not penetrate her. Aware of the night before, she did not perform a choreography of desire for penetration. Achingly now, they kissed long and luxuriantly, as if the decision not to penetrate yet were a pact between them which would only escalate their love. Almost drugged with passion for him, Sayo lay on top of him and possessed his body, every inch of it, with her lips, turning him over, licking down between his buttocks, burrowing even into his arse with her tongue. He tried to resist but eventually played along with her passion so that finally he was pliant, erect, sensate over every inch of himself. Sweating and panting she lay beside him and began to masturbate.

This took him by surprise until, after several moments, he began to realise what she was doing. He turned on his side, then placed himself fully above her, not touching her, yet arched, his muscles straining while he looked into her face and every so often, gently, gently as the lap of purest water edging in across a beach, dipped a flick of his tongue between her lips. As she rose into orgasm, he began showering a storm of kisses over her face, encouraging, easing, affirming her passion. After she had come, he kissed her very tenderly, then, going to the bathroom and bringing back a soft, warmly wet towel, he bathed her all over, turning her over and around, lifting her legs, her arms, under her breasts, her chin, cleaning her.

That night they fell asleep in each other's arms.

16

They sat on board the ferry which took the tour party down towards the south. All around them ranged an enormity of sea. It was as if they had been cast off, into ocean. Because the boat was so large, Keiji and Sayo could be away from the tour party. They sat together on the upper deck, on a chair, looking out at the sea. Under their coats they held hands. Occasionally wind whipped spray onto their faces. Either Keiji or Sayo, laughing, would wipe it away. Keiji told Sayo, between kisses, they were at the bottom of the world, a place where humans could go hardly any further, 'not without dropping off the globe'.

Sayo laughed at this, then held tighter onto Keiji's arm as the boat suddenly went into a deep moaning fall. But, as if in a dream, the boat rose upwards again, bearing them up towards the sky: gulls cried, departed and everyone, sensing the couple's great happiness and peace, left them alone.

17

They had seen cities, farms, valleys, glaciers, motorways, tourist shops. As they went further and further south there appeared to be even fewer humans, so that for long hours they passed through a landscape which seemed miraculously devoid of any human or animal habitation, even though there were fences, lamp-posts, powerlines and the occasional letterbox. Kaoru, the busybody, talked a lot about Antarctica while Sayo and Keiji waited to be alone and gazed through glass at spectacular mountain ranges which lacked all meaning.

Occasionally Keiji got out his video and filmed the passing landscape: he also filmed Sayo, who had now lost all camera-consciousness. She no longer wondered what Keiji's mother would think of so much video being devoted to a portrait of her: Sayo had a feeling Keiji's mother might never see this video. She felt so safely alone with Keiji, further from Japan than she had ever been before. Behind it all, of course, like a vast dark curtain lay their return to Japan, and their taking up residence in Mrs Nakajima's apartment. There they would have no privacy. This frightened Sayo, because she and Keiji were still so much like illegal lovers, not newly-weds.

18

That night they came to rest at a coastal beach near the far south of the South Island. It had a spectacular coastline, almost Japanese in its calligraphy of cliff and cutting mist, of swifting birdfleet, crashing wave. They had a day of rest at the beach: those who wished to shop could go by landliner into a small town nearby, specially set up for the avarice of tourists; the others could spend the day as they pleased.

Thus it was that the people left behind formed almost a complicity among themselves: the elderly couple, one of the schoolgirls, the wife of Tatsuro who pleaded a stomach ache, Sayo and Keiji. The busybody, Tatsuro and most of the others had cheerfully gone off to conquer new artefacts.

Sayo and Keiji had stayed in their room, made rather languorous love after their own fashion. Now penetration had been forgotten and both Keiji and Sayo brought themselves, then each other, to orgasm in a way which was mutually satisfactory. Sayo, who looked forward to having a child some day, was willing to allow the mechanical act of fertilisation to happen whenever it would. She was confident it would follow naturally. The experience she had with her elderly lover had prepared her for some of the odd demands that humans make, in order to find a parallel between emotional and sexual satisfaction.

Exhausted, Keiji had begun an almost cruel form of lovemaking, one not inseparable from a delicate and pure pain, in which he inflicted on Sayo an extremity of pleasure, rising at times into an almost intolerable ecstasy. Sayo, at first, had been taken aback. Keiji's vigour, his passion, was almost terrifying. Then she answered his angst with her own. At its end, both felt — not shame, because they had done nothing to be ashamed of — but a kind of animal weariness, both pleasant and soporific, rather as an animal must feel after it has successfully attacked, killed and devoured another.

So, blitzed a little with each other's satisfaction, even glutted by their appetite for each other's flesh, they closed their motel door behind them and wandered out, dazed and amazed at finding themselves, not within the cave of a thigh, not under the bowl of a breast, but before an endless aura of sea, beneath an infinite sky.

Nearby, Hitomi, the schoolgirl, was sitting hunched, writing cards to home which she had neatly piled beside her, working through them methodically. Others from the tour party were sitting around, or making the first tentative moves across the sand which seemed, after the confinement of the bus, dauntingly empty and large. The surf itself emitted a harsh but satisfying growl.

As soon as they reached the sand, Keiji flipped up onto his hands and began to walk across the beach. He did this expertly for quite a few steps, causing everyone to stop and look at him, cheering when he managed a long stretch upside down, clapping sardonically when he folded down, very neatly, like a diver into water leaving hardly a ripple. He seemed full of animal spirits, like a small boy, an adolescent, showing off his muscular power. Several of the tour party took photos of him, the click of their cameras acting like a soothing murmur of approval.

On the beach itself surfers in wetsuits were sliding along the waves, wavering and waiting for a major roar of surf then rising unsteadily onto their feet, coasting along majestically with each opening sash of wave.

Keiji walked on his hands, upside-down.

The sun bore down. It was as if Sayo and Keiji had found paradise, at the end of the world there, where humans could go no further.

Sayo and Keiji walked along the beach further, investigating its wonders. They found an immense cave, which they entered and did not emerge from for a long time. Then they found a stream of clear water. The elderly deaf man was already minutely inspecting its marine life, putting some vegetation in his pocket. When he caught sight of Keiji and Sayo he inclined his head in a bow. Keiji bowed back. The old man's wife sat on her own, on a sandbank: she waved at Sayo, who waved back. Everyone seemed to agree: this was paradise.

After this, Sayo had to reconstruct for herself what happened.

She did this in the many months which followed, prompted not least by police, family, friends — even onlookers who felt they had a right to know the details from her.

She had separated from Keiji for a moment, they had walked apart with the happy satisfaction of those who know they are together: they could trust each other. He, it seemed, had wanted to look at the rocks at the end of the beach; she was more interested in the cliffs behind, in getting an overview of the beach. It was she who had made the decision to separate.

Once she had begun climbing she had kept going, seeing always a better viewing point, a more distant platform. At each point they had connected, waved at each other across the growing expanse of space. This space in itself had an erotic quality, as all their actions did, signifying the distance they were apart from each other yet telepathically connected. Then there was a long stretch of cliff for her to climb: there was a track of sorts and as she went on she fell into a reverie in which she reviewed their love-making and imagined their future, when they might live alone, away from Keiji's mother and able to make love whenever they felt like it. Perhaps an hour went by, she did not know.

She reached a plateau, she was breathless. She sank down, sat for a while, waited for her sight to equalise itself. Gradually the line of ocean, curl of beach settled into a fixed form and she began to search for Keiji.

Her first sight was a curious one: from all over the beach people were running towards one spot. For a second it reminded her of ants when they suddenly find a delicious piece of sweet food. Yet while most people ran towards the water's edge, one person ran away, faster than the others: this person was racing straight towards the motel, calling out, it seemed, as the people had come out of the motel, were standing stiff with alarm, hands shading their faces.

She looked now with more intensity at the small, distant scene down on the shore. There was a boat there, a sort of surfboat, people were carrying in a body, laying it on the sand, face up. She watched as someone crouched beside it, and began to lay the limbs out. She stood up now, searching among the onlookers for the familiar bodyshape of Keiji. She could not see him. It was this moment, more than any other, that she would recall later: the moment in which she grasped that he might no longer exist.

She could remember nothing of coming down the cliff except, in separate images, like stills in a film from which the remains had been cut away, flashes of their love-making that morning, igniting, flaring, fusing. Then, abruptly, she saw in the distance the action of a man trying to resuscitate a body. At this stage she did not know whose body it was: yet the very fact of a death happening on the beach filled her with foreboding. As she came nearer and nearer to the scene the actions of the person resuscitating grew increasingly desperate, almost flagellatory.

Now she was running towards the small crowd, people were turning to look at her. The lifesaver was pounding the body, as if it were a piece of obdurate machinery which, if only it would respond to the blows, might be reanimated. Then she was looking down at the body of Keiji: he was fully clothed, drenched, his neck at an odd angle as if it had been broken. Seaweed was wrapped around his body, like a funeral wreath.

She could remember nothing more: not the way she let out a scream so profound it had chilled the spines of everyone there: not how they had to drag her away from his body which she tried to hold and warm and bring back to life by kissing by calling by touching: not how she was lifted away, still calling out to him, and carried back to the motel where she had fought whoever was trying to hold her, and abused them and used language they did not know she possessed. None of this would she remember because a doctor came and, as she was held down by men and women who had suddenly grown much older, gave her an injection. The next she knew she opened her eyes and looked at a ceiling, wondered why Keiji was not there, then lowered her gaze and found the elderly woman sitting very quietly dozing in a chair beside her. For one moment she thought she had refound her mother.

Perhaps the abrupt arpeggio of her breath awoke the elderly woman. But while Sayo looked at this stranger who had come to share in her grief she suddenly recalled Keiji lying on the beach so cold and dead and her first thought was to get out of bed, to go to him: she was convinced he still lay there. Then she thought to herself that it was all an ugly dream; it was impossible. But it was there, written on the face of the old woman opposite who had begun to weep very softly, as if she were weeping for all the losses and deaths which had occurred in her own long life; from before the war, then through the war, then at the end of the war, at Hiroshima. Yet Sayo hated her briefly and unreasonably, she could not see what these other, more vague tragedies had to do with her own intolerable pain.

Everything from here became blank.

19

Now began the time of questions. The bus tour had moved on, speeding away as if it couldn't wait to remove itself from Sayo's ill luck. The other passengers had come forward individually and pressed her hand and murmured condolences. Sayo had gone to the nearest city, where she found herself completely alone, in a place she hardly knew the name of, in a foreign country whose language she did not speak. Sayo unpacked only what was strictly necessary, and awaited the strangers who came with an interpreter hurriedly obtained from the nearest university, a small earnest man from a different part of Japan from herself.

She had never felt so alone. The strangers were all gravely courteous, but this made it more unreal. She said what she knew had happened. After all, she did not know much. She turned it over and over in her mind, what had happened? It began to attack her that perhaps she had been a cause of his death: had she, perhaps, pursued him with her own unreasonable sexual demands? His drowning was without explanation. Why would a young man perfectly capable of swimming end up mysteriously drowning? Were there reasons for him to be unhappy? the interpreter had asked, carefully keeping his eyes lowered so as not to offend her. Was her silence too elongated, was the pause before she replied criminality itself? In the end the interpreter had had to repeat the question. She had whispered, so people had to strain their ears to hear, 'No.' Yet she felt she lied, for all humans have cause to be unhappy.

Then the strangers gave the interpreter their explanations of the tragedy. Keiji had gone for a walk along the rocks and, unfamiliar with the way waves could suddenly surge in, had been swept out to sea by an errant wave. (It was simply bad luck.) One of the surfers had seen him. Sayo could not bring herself to ask: was he calling for help? It was death by misadventure, the interpreter told her, pleased as if he himself had arranged what was, in the circumstances, a satisfactory solution to what was, after all, without solution, without resolution. Sayo could go back to Japan now. It was all over. Keiji's body would follow. His funeral obsequies would happen in the homeland.

PART II

20

The door had fallen open at Mrs Nakajima's apartment and the two women, widow and mother, looked into each other's faces as if to see, written there, some explanation, some final confidence. But Sayo was very tired by the long flight, then the trip in from the airport: she also felt acutely uncomfortable coming to the apartment of a woman who, after all, she hardly knew. Yet she was Keiji's mother. For this reason, Sayo decided, she would try to love her and find what in her was of Keiji, the man who had disappeared.

Yet as soon as the door slid open she knew in her heart she could never love this woman: there was some chemistry between the two which would never cohere. Besides the anger Mrs Nakajima felt about her only son's untimely death was all directed at his bride: without her, there would have been no honeymoon, no walk on the beach, no death. Nevertheless Mrs Nakajima was sufficiently of the old school to know how to dissemble her true feelings: she returned the profound obeisances the new widow made before her and their greeting of each other was an acceptable expression of mutual grief to everyone apart from themselves. For Sayo's discomfort was increased by the presence of Mrs Nakajima's sister, her sons-in-law and daughters who were all sitting in the room, as if a jury waiting for a prosecution witness to take the stand.

Sayo felt intensely watched. She wondered if she was not expressing enough grief: she to whom grief had quickly become, as it were, a mode of breathing. Mrs Nakajima's relatives, however, had begun to talk about Keiji, reviewing his life in intimate detail, talking of his father, his noble forefathers of which Mrs Nakajima was inordinately proud. Mrs Nakajima's sister, a stout fiercely respectable hotel proprietor, told a story about Keiji as a boy fishing at the beach, and how he had astonished everyone with his love of swimming.

Other stories quickly followed. Gradually Sayo began to feel she knew very little of Keiji: she had known only the complete intimacy of those six days and nights in motel rooms in New Zealand. This other Keiji, she did not know: except perhaps, conversely, in that one act of his he could not bring himself to complete.

So Sayo had sat there, a terrible headache clouding her mind, frightened even to put her bags away in a corner because it might not be where she was properly meant to go: Mrs Nakajima was a stickler for order and the tiny apartment, eerily clear and arranged as if for a piece of arcane, even vaguely cruel theatre, was like an obstacle course for anyone unfamiliar with the territory. Keiji had already told her that his mother was also extraordinarily 'economical', which Sayo translated into a wary, obstinate meanness.

Eventually the relatives departed and the two women were left alone. Almost immediately it became clear they had nothing to say to each other; nothing, that is, apart from the directions a person who controls a confined space needs to give to someone who is staying as a visitor. As Sayo fell into sleep that night, the sounds of Tokyo all around her, she thought she heard waves calling, calling and she strained her ears to listen. Then all was black.

21

Sayo took up her old life. There was in this, if not pleasure, at least relief. She took up a job in another corporation, doing the same kind of work. The work was so numbing that it stopped her thinking of the beach, that day, Keiji lying in the sand wreathed around with seaweed. She tried to accommodate herself to the patterns of the old widow's life, which were mercilessly cut-and-dried, running like clockwork, terminating always in an early night during which Sayo would lie awake listening to the older woman's breathing, its slow rise and fall. At times like this Sayo would listen for the waves which would come and retrieve her, and caress her and soothe her as they pulled her back like a tide to those few days and nights she had spent with the man she loved.

Life never goes according to an easy pattern, however. Sayo was deeply disturbed one day when the widow served her a bowl of miso: as she stared down into it, deeply depressed, she suddenly saw in the whirls of vegetable configurations an horrific vision of Keiji in the tide, his body rotting, unclaimed, a living mass of sea organisms, tossing and flopping with each lull and pull of the waves. This vision was so complete that she dropped her chopsticks and cried out. When the older widow enquired what was the matter (she did not like waste), the younger widow simply said that the soup was a little hotter than she had expected. Then, feeling she had been rude to her host, who was quick to take offence, she explained that day she had had some noodles which had scalded her tongue. The elder widow bowed slightly.

This horrific vision awoke in Sayo a further stage of grief. She now began to sleep badly, tortured by visions of their love-making intertwined with hideous visions of decay and putrefaction. She found at last she could not bear the silence of the apartment any longer and quietly, like a thief, she dressed and went out into the night and, lacking anything better to do, simply got on a train and began to ride the subway.

Thus began the time in her life when she constantly sat on the trains at quiet hours, soothed by the travel which, in its way, was not unlike those moments on the bus when, tired and hardly thinking, she had lowered her head onto Keiji's shoulder and gone into blissful sleep. She found she was not doing her job so well, she could not concentrate. And the sympathy which her workmates had initially had for her evaporated, as people cannot continue to feel sorry for someone over a great length of time.

One afternoon Sayo took the video Keiji had taken of their holiday and, because she was too embarrassed to show it to Mrs Nakajima, who, after all, knew so little of their passion, she went to a love hotel.

There, alone in a room decorated like a Memphis brothel, complete with a shell-shaped vibrating bed, she watched the video alone, obsessively returning, in slow motion, to the one small moment when she had taken up the camera and trained it on Keiji.

This was when he was standing on his hands, in the hotel room at Rotorua. She watched over and over again as he evaded gravity, walked, toppled, fell, then righted himself, laughing directly at her. Then he walked towards the camera, his hand out. The camera fled across the ceiling, down a wall, quickly, quickly, in a fleeting vision, across their bed which was unmade and had all the pleasant squalor of their love-making: then the camera showed her, pleading with him to turn it off. A television was on in the room, showing a news item about a flood. When she slowed the image down to almost frame-by-frame point she saw, on the television, animals floating along in dirty torrents, people standing on roofs, water rushing through living rooms. She looked again and again at this footage of Keiji, and felt at once soothed by his presence, the evidence that he had lived. Yet when she packed away the video and walked out of the love hotel, the receptionist staring with banal curiosity at what she had in her bag, she felt more bereft than ever: as if in the very act of locating Keiji she had only experienced, again, the completeness of his loss.

By now the two widows had, without any particular incident inspiring it, reached a tacit understanding whereby neither spoke to the other more than was strictly necessary. When Mrs Nakajima had her family around, which she did more often now that Keiji was dead — as if Keiji's death gave them all a common bond which, before, had been lacking, or was divided in rivalry over material success, a very strong motive with both sisters — Sayo felt a complete outsider, incapable of joining in their stories of other days before she was in Keiji's life. Subtly they negated her, even while they continued to treat her with an almost extravagantly uncomfortable degree of politeness. This only highlighted her provincial origins and made her feel inferior.

Sayo knew she must leave.

Mrs Nakajima had, anyway, confided in her sister that Sayo, whom she never called by her name but referred to as 'the young madame' — as if Sayo alone, with female sorcery, had enticed Keiji to his death — had another lover already. She mistook the long hours Sayo spent riding the subway for lurid hours spent in unspeakable acts. Sayo did not dispel these rumours, for she often looked both vacant and exhausted; she seemed to be listening to another sound, more distant, deeper, as if emanating from inside the hollow globe of the world — which she was: she could not get the sound of waves out of her head.

So, dazed, suffering from lack of sleep, pursued by the siren-call of the sea, Sayo went to her bank, took out whatever money she had saved, went to a travel agent, walked past the door twice before going in. Then, suddenly and exhilaratingly turning into an actor, so for the first time since returning to Tokyo she felt absolutely alive, she booked a return ticket to New Zealand on the nearest available flight. It left in three days.

She went home to the widow and broke their silence. She was returning to her home village, she lied. Her father had become ill, asked for her. She regretted leaving but that was that. She went into her room and began packing.

The widow Nakajima felt a fierce exhilaration. Her every fear had been confirmed: the young madame, the little slut, 'our friend from Korea', was going to live with whatever male it was who would have her. It meant that she, Mrs Nakajima, was freed from the burden of a woman who served only to remind her that her one son was dead.

She went into the tiny corner Sayo used as a room. She would make a celebratory feast for Sayo, asking all Keiji's family and Sayo could ask whoever she might like. It was not to farewell her, she hastened to add, but to do honour to Keiji's widow. Sayo tried to say she did not want this, indeed, she hinted it was in poor taste since her father was ill. Yet Mrs Nakajima would not be stopped.

Sayo said, in confusion, she did not know anyone to ask. Mrs Nakajima understood that her acquaintances might be of a type that could not be introduced into a family celebration. She went away, superbly confident that she would splurge out, make a feast such as she had not made before, certainly better and more extravagant than the one which greeted the news of Sayo and Keiji's wedding.

This meal was a form of torture for Sayo. Keiji's relatives all condemned her in their own minds for her lack of feeling, her seeming absence of grief. Indeed, she hardly seemed to partake of the meal at all, having barely anything to eat, explaining she was undergoing a fast, which they all considered was, in the circumstances, in extremely poor taste. Nevertheless, gorging themselves to excess — in particular the widow Nakajima who suffered acute indigestion for days afterwards — they took little notice of the curious mood Sayo was in, attributing it to her 'flightiness', her 'moodiness'. So, ignored at her own celebration, Sayo was left alone to concentrate on the sound of waves which in her own head sounded celebratory, welcoming, dancing with a lightness of relief: it was as if they were welcoming her home.

PART III

22

Her return to New Zealand was almost joyful to her: here, in this foreign country which now meant everything to her, she saw sights familiar from her honeymoon in an entirely new light. Whereas before they had been essentially meaningless, novelties of landscape or city, now they were invested with the sacred integrity of memory: they fitted within her own interior landscape. And as she took her seat on a landliner, with entirely different people aboard, another driver (only the explanations were the same), she felt a kind of solace overtake her, a serenity, peace.

She loved in particular looking at the water which, in these islands, was always in abundance, insisting on changing sides on the bus when they travelled along the coast, following the same route as the landliner had taken before. Only occasionally did she risk recognition, as they stayed in all the same hotels, motels, hostelries. She was protected by the fact that all Asians appear the same to undiscerning Europeans: besides, she had lost weight already with her fast, and she had cut her hair differently, more severely, in preparation for her forthcoming life.

All the time sitting on the bus she was poised, prepared, like a young novice about to undergo some sublime experience: every moment on the bus was spent in appreciation of the world outside the windows, the activity on the bus. Only at night would she find the proximity of the rooms where she had made love with Keiji almost overpowering in their magnetism: she would walk by in the corridors outside, hoping that by chance the door would open and she might refresh her memory, already indelible, of their honeymoon rooms.

One morning she had crept into such a room, vacated by some other passengers. The bed was unmade, it still looked exactly the same. This was the room, she remembered, where she and Keiji had made love by the door. She saw this vividly before her, on the carpet. When one of the passengers had come back into the room, unexpectedly, having left something behind in the bathroom, Sayo had not been confused, and had explained with serenity she, too, was looking for something she had lost.

By this time the other passengers on the bus left a small cordon around the young widow. They knew nothing of her story, yet her strict dietary habits, her seeming dislocation from the intense mood of people insistent upon having six days' holiday-and-fun, meant she was always a little to the side, unattached, almost untouched.

Finally the bus drew near the motel and the beach at which Keiji had died. As they came closer Sayo's mood underwent a subtle change. She became painfully upset by the thought that the owners of the motel, possessors of memory of the incident — possessors, even more so, of memories about her own responses, which were only now occurring to her — might still be there. This would complicate things considerably. Yet, when the bus pulled in, there was no sign of the old owners: there was a bright young couple determined to succeed in their new job. Sayo overheard the bus driver talking to them, and understood the original owners were having a much-deserved holiday in Queensland. A recent spate of drownings had cast a slight pall over their business.

Her plan had been prepared all along: during her tour of New Zealand she had been collecting matches, noodles, a grill. The following morning, before breakfast, she told the driver that she must return to Dunedin as soon as possible. It was nothing bad, she hastened to add: it was a monetary transaction in Tokyo which required her personal supervision. The day before she had, with considerable difficulty, arranged for a message to be sent. So it all seemed convincing: besides, nobody was directly concerned with her. And it was only as the bus took off, leaving her behind, that a general lightness of spirits overcame the entire bus, as if an invisible weight had been dropped off. But because nobody was really aware the widow had been left behind, it was attributed to nothing more than a general excess of good spirits.

23

The beach that day was peaceful, still. The enormous waves disgorged themselves onto the sand, ran in on great glassy floors, only to re-spume in another torrent. Further out on the horizon fishermen in boats plied their trade.

Sayo took her single bag, and suitcase, and appeared to head off to the bus-stop where another landliner, travelling in the opposite direction, came by within an hour. Certain countryfolk, travelling into the local town, noticed the rather odd sight of an Asian woman standing alone at the bus-stop. Some commented darkly on the penetration of 'the Asian invasion', while others, with heavily mortgaged farms to sell, were thoughtfully silent. Nobody noticed that, when the bus came by, she was no longer there. Thinking back on it later, the wife of the motel proprietor (who liked to think it was one of her professional qualifications that nothing escaped her eyes) noticed the bus roar by, unstopping. But she simply assumed some good-natured passer-by had offered the visitor to New Zealand a lift. The hospitality of the local district was famous.

Sayo cut along the beach with her bag, so light that anyone seeing her might have easily mistaken her for a day-tripper, part of a package tour, simply having a rather adventurous walk on her own. She had carefully stowed her suitcase behind a flaxbush. In her daybag were the necessities to get her through the night. She was heading towards the big airy cave she had noticed on her first trip to the beach. She and Keiji had walked into it together, wondering at its height, its suggestion of a majestic Gothic cathedral: indeed, they had taken advantage of its darkness and obscurity to make quick and pleasurably illicit love. Throughout their kisses Sayo had heard the boom and roar of waves: the very sound which had echoed in her head in Tokyo, drawn her back.

Now it was, as if for the first time, the sound of the waves fell into focus: it was as if, at last, the echo she had heard so troublingly in her head met with the actual, soothing roar, fell into rhythm, found peace. She felt both determined and happy as she made her campsite in the cave. She waited till dusk, then retraced her path back to the flaxbush and under a hugely refulgent moon walked with her case back along the beach. She felt deeply happy for the first time since Keiji had died. She was at home.

PART IV

24

She had been living in the cave for over two weeks now. Her food supply had almost gone and though her fast was continuing as much as was humanly possible, she needed to eat. In fact her fasting had changed her consciousness of time, place, reality. The waves still lulled and soothed her, though occasionally their call was harsh, and strong. She had taken to going down to the water's edge and standing, looking out to sea, at the particular point where Keiji had drowned. This was dangerous as she went into such a trance that she failed, one day, to notice some fishermen walking along the beach towards her. Their voices, carried on the wind, reached her and she listened acutely, like an animal raising its nose into the air, scenting danger. But she was used to hearing voices by this time: in fact she sought the sound of the waves to drown out the voices and relocate her silence.

Suddenly the men were quite close to her. She turned quickly, hurried back directly towards her cave. The men walked by, talking among themselves, laughing: yet one turned over his shoulder and looked quizzically in the direction she had taken. She told herself they were so distant they would not pick that she was Japanese. After an hour she returned to her cave and was henceforth much more careful.

She had a particular ritual she followed, where she went down to the sea and paid homage to the man she had loved so intensely, then lost. At these ceremonies, of both abasement and atonement, Keiji would appear to her out of the sea, at times refulgent with love, at other times, depending on his mood, angry as a kabuki demon, terrifying. The weather, too, was deteriorating. One night there was such a strong wind that the very heavens seemed to be screaming with agony. Dust whipped along the beach, obscuring the sun in the sky so that the day, when it dawned, had an odd, ominous white glow to it, the waves broken, sharded with seaweed, tossing out of the ocean as if driven by torment.

Sayo had walked out into this storm, driven by hunger. She tried to find on the beach anything, a bird which had been blown down from the sky, a fish washed up. She returned to her cave with her treasure, a small fish, some pippies, a gull. With shaking fingers she lit a fire made out of driftwood and slowly, oh slowly, the tiny flame fluttered and she waited for the wood to catch fire and burn. But the wind changed direction suddenly, flung sharp and bitter sand into her face. She could only retreat to her mat, cover herself with a few sacks she had found on the beach, and wait for the morning.

When it came she was awoken by Keiji kissing her so tenderly on her lips, running his soft hot tongue lightly along her lower lip, then trailing it across her top lip before, softly, gently, he probed into her mouth, cradling her head in his hands so his tongue might enter her mouth more fully. He kissed her then luxuriantly, his hands so warm and gentle passing down her body, animating her breasts, her stomach which he lingered over, softly caressing, massaging so that she stretched out flat and peaceful, issuing a long deep sigh as he entered her. It was as she knew it would always be: he whispered in her ear, delicately biting on her lobe as his other hand slid to her breast, softly, again and again, stroking her nipple while his cock smoothly slid within her, her insides parting, almost with relief, completely relaxed so that, once inside her, it was as if he fitted perfectly and so, locked together in a timeless configuration, they made sweetly rhythmical love, both their cries simultaneously rising up. At which point she awoke and found herself almost covered in sand, and the dark crease of the cave cut into an inverted V of light, down which the sound of the waves poured towards her, streaming their sound now slightly mocking in their presence, their insistence on reality: almost, too, as if they had been witnesses to the act of love and mocked it with their laughter.

Yet she had no doubt, as she rose and went and washed in the sea, which was more peaceful now, as if replete from its night of fury, that Keiji had come to her and made love. Indeed, as she bent over and washed between her legs there were unmistakable signs of his presence, a sort of rash where his legs had rubbed most urgently against her own. There was even a lovebite.

She returned to the cave, preparing for the daily advent of the fishermen who, each day, now walked past her cave in the early morning, then returned at night with their catch.

But that day something different occurred. After she emerged from the cave, in the evening, she found a single fresh fish laid out very carefully on the rock, cradled on a large leaf of some unknown vegetation. In the distance she saw the fishermen walking away, lost almost in sand, in mist. She looked again at the fish. Its mouth was open, a small slash of blood bubbled from its gill. The fishermen were now lost from sight. But she did not touch the fish.

The following evening, however, she waited in the flax for the fishermen to walk by. It was a beautiful evening in which the winter sun, the softest possible pink, had infused the entire sky with light vapours of pearl, aquamarine, with bruises of amethyst falling away, in the far far distance, to a few charcoal strokes of bruised black: far out at sea, leaving the islands untouched, a storm was moving by.

The fishermen walked along, their rods frail in the light. As they came nearer to her cave, she watched as one of them covered head to foot in wet-weather gear, which gave him an oddly martial appearance, separated from the others. He was an old man, by his gait, and he went towards the rock where the other fish lay untouched.

He stood there for a moment, thoughtfully, then, removing the stale fish, substituted for it a magnificent fish so fresh it curved in his grasp, even giving a last flick of its tail as it lay there, sacrificial on the rock.

Sayo stared at the old man, taken aback by the sudden knowledge that it was Keiji, now an old man, Keiji as he might have been if he had lived. His eyes connected with her own: he smiled at her, a smile of perfect serenity, even good-humoured charm: there was a twinkle in his eye. For the first time since coming to the cave, Sayo looked down at herself: she was aware her clothes had become like rags, stiff with salt, her hair was matted, her face bloated. She felt deep shame and buried her face in her hands till he went.

When the fishermen were gone she emerged, took the fish back to her cave and there lit a beautiful, crackling fire and cooked the fish and with her bare fingers devoured the flesh, whiter than the most beautiful skin in the world, stuffing the food into her mouth as she realised how deeply hungry she was. It was as if her whole soul was crying out for food. She finished the meal, lay there, then was sick.

She waited now for Keiji to return to her. Yet it was as if, in her very act of waiting, she had frightened him away: as if, in her hunger for him, she was again doing what she had done on her honeymoon, forcing on him, as she saw it now, her own appetites and desires. Another old man — not Keiji — was it perhaps her old lover? — now came and left her fish: she ate it more sensibly, in small delicate meals, more like rituals of remembrance than a placating of hunger. She would go down to the sea and sing songs to Keiji, chorusing along with the waves, joining in their eternally restful song: yet he would not appear.

These were her hardest days. She forced herself to review, in her mind, every day and night she had spent with him on their honeymoon, going into every act, providing in her mind alternative endings, more elaborate scenarios. She left her most precious possession, the video, down on the beach one morning, before high tide, hoping this would placate him. And sometimes, late at night, he would come to her: but at these times of loss, his love-making was cruel, vengeful, humiliating. Yet she still longed for him, because she knew that this form of love-making was an expression of his anger and that, if only she could have more time with him, she could cure him of this sadness and they could return to their more peaceful style of love-making.

One day she was observed by a youth on a land windsurfer, one of the many conveyances which, with the changing weather, had begun to make miraculous, slightly eerie appearances on the vast beach. Sayo was standing, looking out to sea; the windsurfer had tacked towards her, veered away.

Later in the pub the surfer, after a few drinks announced he'd seen an 'abominable yeti' down on the beach. He did not know that the fishermen had seen her for over a month now, and since one of them was in fact the man who had pulled in Keiji drowned, they both knew who she was and had decided amongst themselves, since she was doing no harm — except possibly to herself — to leave her there. This surfer, however, could not allow such a good opportunity for self promotion to pass. Later that evening, made brave by many drinks and having told themselves innumerable stories about ghosts, curious coincidences, actual murders, three young braves crept along the beach, heading towards the cave from which an eerie light issued.

They were ready for unearthly apparitions and indeed, inside the cave, they observed a young Asian woman dancing by herself, to her own odd tune, reminiscent of Chinese operas. The shadows cast on the walls were so strange, her tune so weird, that the youths, hitherto brave and feckless, fell silent and gazed upon her, then crept away, chastened by what they had seen. Later that night they got completely drunk and their actual vision merged into tales from movies, pulp novels, hearsay. The following morning the wind changed direction, the surfers all packed up their boards, took off to the other side of the island. Yet over breakfast, the least hungover, most garrulous of the three found time to raise a deliciously erotic frisson (in his view) in the breast of the young Maori woman serving sausages and baked beans from a huge stainless steel bin in the kitchen.

To this young woman, ghosts and spiritual presences were not the subject of jest. But a co-worker beside her, more attuned to television, overheard the conversation and thus word quickly spread around the small community that there was a weird Asian living in a cave on the beach.

Surreptitiously at first, Sayo was spied upon, to verify these reports. So little happened in that hospitable district that things like accidental deaths, traffic accidents, unplanned pregnancies took on the scale of international events, talked over, discussed, looked at from this angle and that till finally, every aspect of the subject exhausted, it either entered into folklore, to be inaccurately recalled at communal events, or it simply dropped from view, overtaken by a new, more pressing sensation.

People soon realised the young woman was the widow of the 'Jap' who had drowned there the previous winter. One of the men called in to restrain her, in her grief, verified that the woman was her. This gave her presence a sort of poetic symmetry which even the most hard-hearted could not fail to recognise. People uniformly felt pity for her, the more banal imagining she had gone crazy. Some people felt she had entered under the aegis of the district and, as such, they were all duty-bound to keep her anonymity protected. Others felt that her discovery might give the tourist image of the area a bad name, already under a cloud after the spate of recent drownings. This later group, who talked on the subject more tirelessly than the others, insisted their point of view was activated by concern. 'It just can't go on': 'she's doing herself a serious injury': 'it just isn't right'. The implication of possible death was even talked about, in terms of injurious headlines.

Yet, oddly enough, the possibility of a community response was made slower by a recognition of the very depth of grief of this thin, determined woman, speaking another language, coming from another country entirely, who had chosen their district to come and mourn her husband in. It was unavoidable, this figment of intense love, this calligraphy of human tragedy happening on their doorstep. Yet it was also this very intensity which frightened some. Grief occurs in everyone's life, it is inseparable from our being human: if someone grieves to an excessive degree, is this not a comment on the absence of tears in those men and women whose mothers, fathers, children, lovers have all died? She could not be left alone, it was not right. Something had to be done.

So finally, a few phone calls were made to the nearest city police, a surveillance discreetly took place. And because the woman was known to be Japanese, and Japan was a powerful, even feared, client of New Zealand, it was felt correct that an interpreter accompany a policeman when they made their now inevitable visit.

25

Sayo was now so habituated to her life in the cave, it was as if she had no other. Keiji came and went in her life, much as he might have in his real life: sometimes moody, at other times affectionate, occasionally staying out the whole night, returning in the morning to make groggy, slightly soiled love. She had even begun to wonder whether she was pregnant, a subject which worried her as a cave was not suitable for a child to grow up in. All the time through this the waves kept up their continuous and powerful music, playing in rhapsody, as it were, an accompaniment to the emotional states of her husband.

A sole policeman, who had cut down hanged men from beams, pulled sad housewives out of gas ovens — a man who took grieving relatives in to view corpses — now walked along the beach feeling a deep discomfort for the task ahead of him. It was fortunate, in a way, he had as a companion the same small earnest man who had earlier translated for Sayo. The two figures walked through the salt mist, one large, tall, ungainly and distinctly weird in his blue suburban uniform; the other slight, his glasses constantly fogged by salt, slipping slightly on the sand, hurrying to keep up with the taller man. Because the policeman was embarrassed he talked about fishing, a subject about which the small man from the university knew nothing, so that subject dried up. The sergeant fell back on his conversational backstop: travel and the respective merits of overseas countries compared with New Zealand.

Sayo saw the thin shape of the interpreter outlined against the sky in her cave. She was startled, as she was cleaning the cave, making it as tidy as possible for her husband who was returning that night. Yet she welcomed him courteously, as a housewife might welcome a fellow employee of her husband, bowing to him ceremoniously and enquiring after his wife. The shadow of the policeman now hovered at the cave entrance.

The interpreter then said to Sayo that she could not stay here; it was a contravention of passport laws. She looked at him as if he were quite mad. He took in another breath and explained to her, in Japanese, that she had entered the country on a visitor's permit and she was already over the limit by two months. It was a criminal offence, he added. She looked at him without expression: as if, indeed, he were talking a language entirely incomprehensible to her. Her eyes only moved slightly, to take in the sergeant who now bent over and entered the cave. She made a small, courteous movement with her hands, indicating he should make himself at home. The sergeant later embarrassed himself by recalling, as he went over the event in detail before falling into sleep, how he had responded in as courtly a way as he knew how, indicating he preferred to stand.

This was the odd thing, he recalled later, because the entire event disturbed a widower like himself: the way she, a gaunt woman, dressed practically in rags, with hair matted, had stood so straight, intimating that she was interviewing them as much as they were talking with her. She had a kind of dignity, he told himself, which was troubling. Standing there he did not immediately see how the situation would resolve itself. He hoped it would not have to be resolved by force. An immense weariness had overcome him at this thought.

The small interpreter had then raised his voice slightly and was speaking to her very quickly. He told her it was a serious criminal offence, she could go to jail: she must return to Tokyo immediately. It was causing problems between New Zealand and Japan.

She lifted her eyes from the interpreter then, and looked at the sergeant to whom she smiled, quite graciously.

I have no wish to cause problems between New Zealand and

Japan, she said, bowing slightly to the sergeant who could not help his head, of its own accord, jerking slightly. Then she shifted her eyes away from them and was silent. It was as if she were suddenly listening to something else entirely, another music, another sound. She did not look at them again.

So, taking her silence as agreement, first the sergeant, then the interpreter began gathering up the few items among her possessions they could see were worth saving: her carrybag, an empty video case, an overcoat. While they were doing this, Sayo had silently, as if magnetically drawn, moved out of the cave, walking very slowly towards the water. It was a shock for the sergeant; he turned around, she was not there. Then he saw her, a diminishing figure against the brilliantly lit sea. It was one of those days when everything appears white. It seemed for a moment that she were moving into the sea. He quickly dropped what he was carrying and hurried down to the beach. But the woman had just stopped by the sea. As he approached her, she, with her back towards him, performed a complete and deep bow before the waves. He stopped still behind, silent.

The interpreter now came out of the cave, carrying her few possessions. It was as if she was now waiting on them.

And together now, the three of them began their slow walk back towards the settlement, the young woman walking slowly because she was weak, the other two following yet accompanying her, almost like courtiers beside some rare captive princess.

In the mist on the beach, figures stood, watching this apparition move by. Nobody spoke.

PART V

26

Rush-hour Tokyo: there are people everywhere, hundreds, thousands, millions of humans rushing and pushing from one side of the immense city, trying to get to the other. Noise, dirt, pollution. One train is full, the doors are pushed shut, everyone within is squashed so tight that faces, limbs, bodies, briefcases all form a wall, pressing against the glass, like fish in an aquarium, threatening to burst out.

One of these faces pushed against the glass is a woman. It is Sayo. She looks much the same as she did before her marriage, her widowing, except she has a slightly different haircut, is older. And as the train disappears from view we see her face, and in her face is embedded all the haunted hidden richness of memory, written in lines which can never be replaced: yet there is also something else in her face, a blankness, a deep and utter silence. *Nothing.*

elizabeth knox

pomare

1

THE children found a stand of poisonous berries beside the metal footbridge that spanned the Hutt line. 'King Edward berries,' Hayley Moynihan told her friends, Jo and Lex Keene. 'Daddy says they'll kill you.'

To ten-year-old Jo she seemed to be offering death as a delicacy. Here was an opportunity for a more extravagant 'crime' than her latest plan — saving or stealing Hori's new litter before Mr Moynihan made good his threat to put the kittens in a sack and throw them in the river. Jo stripped a branch from the bush and held it to the seven-year-olds' faces. She asked, 'Shall we eat one?' It was a grey day, and chilly; as Hayley considered the proposition she buttoned her cardigan. The cardigan had belonged to an older cousin, its cuffs were turned up twice, it was pink and didn't suit Hayley. Very little did. Jo and Lex's mother sometimes thought *she* could make a better job of dressing the freckled redhead. Every other mother would put her girls in fashionable flounces, taffetas and gauzes, and Hayley's best dress was of turquoise crepe with white lace — very modish — but Hayley needed crisp green or blue cotton, plain, because her complexion was patterned. Hester Keene dressed her own girls in simple linen, or brown and white seersucker, or tartan skirts and jerseys in winter. And she cut their hair short.

Lex thought Hayley beautiful. At fifteen, twenty, thirty, Lex would say, 'I have a thing about red hair,' her 'thing' the result of how carefully she would watch her friend deliberate on her suggestions, to accept smiling, or reject with a quick cloudburst of blood and temper.

'Suicide is a crime,' Jo said dreamily. A crime that would put an end to all Jo's other experiments.

Hayley said, 'I don't want to be dead. Or even sick.'

'Aren't we going to feed Mercy and Playtime?' Lex asked.

Jo picked a berry and pinched it, she spread the pulp on her fingertips, seeds in their wet cauls of flesh. She put her hand to her nose — smelled poison, pungent and unappetising. This was a crime she wouldn't acquire: trespass, wagging, theft, rudies (better not to think of that), torture — but not suicide.

'And there's the election next Saturday,' Lex said, still presenting arguments.

'What's a lection?' Hayley asked.

'Grown-ups vote who's going to be Prime Minister,' Jo explained. 'There's National and Labour — that's the best — and Social Credit. Naomi Arapa says her mother and father vote Social Credit. It happens at the school next Saturday.'

Jo threw the stem of nightshade, which struck up a spicy scent from the hedge. The three children walked on. As if responding to the tardy pull-starter of a motor mower on the far side of the hedge, the sun came out and idled weakly behind a screen of high cloud.

When they stepped onto the metal stairway of the bridge it rang and trembled. Hayley stopped. 'I'm not allowed to cross the tracks.'

'That's what the bridge is for, silly.'

Hayley rattled back down. 'See you later.' She ran along the hedge-lined path. They saw her stop at the head of the right-of-way to shake the crab apple tree, shake down several red-skinned shells, scooped hollow by birds.

In the centre of the bridge Lex and Jo stopped to check the lines in either direction. They liked to wait and look down on the ferrous, blistered tops of the units. The stretch of line to Taita, and the one to the rail bridge, river and Silverstream, were both empty — four bright channels and a tributary of sidings by a ditch of dusty blackberry.

The horses were kept in a wedge-shaped paddock by the rail line.

The girls bent to pull the grass on their side of the fence and the mare, Mercy, ambled over. She thudded to a stop, huffed and scratched her chin on the top wire before lipping the grass from Jo's flat palm. Jo laughed as the whiskery lips tickled her. Playtime, the yearling, was slower to take his cue and put on a performance of fear — high-stepped over with his head swung side on, neck arched and eye rolling. Lex offered a brush of grass; he forgot his act and bit at her hand, his teeth a sprung trap. Lex flinched. Playtime lost half the grass and his mother lipped up the few strands draped over the wire. Then both animals turned their heads and stilled their jaws to sniff and listen. Lex stroked Playtime's neck, hair smooth over a wave of muscle.

Lex would say she loved horses. Her mother had taught her that song: 'Horses, horses, I love horses, white and dapple-grey . . . '

In the first term she made a horse in her weekly sewing class, a stuffed horse, in silhouette, two-legged, his nose oddly rounded. She had sketched her pattern on newspaper and pinned it to a doubled-over swatch of gingham — green and white chequered cotton poplin. She cut her horse out, tacked his outline, then carefully restitched in close, neat blanket-stitch. But when she turned him right way out Lex forgot to poke the stuffing — strips of her mother's old stockings — deep into his snout. In consequence he had, at first, a pouch mouth she could fasten to her nose or fingers. She gave her horse a bright pink wool mane and tail, black eyes and no saddle. 'It's a brumby, a mustang,' she told her sewing teacher. She had just earned library privileges and had slipped a shelf over into the nine to twelve-year-old section. This was a wild Walter Farley, Mary O'Hara horse. She named him Sweetpea, but he became Horsey.

Horsey was her sole toy talisman. A loved and grubby toy, the kind most children acquire in infancy, to cherish and grieve for when absent for even one night. Lex did that. Horsey was ill-advisedly washed on a day when clouds stood at the lip of the hills and the wind changed. Lex checked the warming cupboard every half hour to see whether Horsey was dry and they could both go to bed. She couldn't sleep without him wedged into her left palm. Yet Lex had made Horsey, and had no particular loyalty to a toy before that time. She slept with Horsey for ten years. Perhaps it was at seven that she began banking on dreams, on things she had made; from then was condemned to stand outside the gates of the Holy City, when the world has ended, with dogs and sorcerers, and whoremongers, and murderers, and idolaters, and *those who make and love lies.* At thirty she had Horsey still. He was coated with acidic grime; her ancient sleep-sweat had corroded his skin in brittle-edged holes, like cigarette burns. Skin? Skins. The first, green and white gingham; then, at ten, a smaller check in blue and white; then brown and white plaid at twelve; and at sixteen a final cover, very colourful, a white wool mane and cursory black cotton eye (a blurred black star that the writer brightens with ink).

Jo didn't take to sewing. Early in the year Mr Heron, an energetic teacher, a man with a shelf of books on educational theory, became worried about Jo Keene. Jo's mind wandered, she was slow in responding to questions, wouldn't do some things, took no pleasure in reciting her ninetimes table. The infant mistress had always called Jo 'dreamboat', she thought Jo fey, but the conscientious Mr Heron, trying to do well by his entire class of forty-two, booked Jo in for a psychological appraisal. Jo took a letter home to her parents. Frank Keene combed his black hair up into a swollen wattle. 'Who do they think they are? *Psychology!* I don't believe in it. Mumbo-jumbo as a tool of the State. Anyway, who *wants* a normal child?' Jo was frightened by this reaction; they — the school — must think she was nuts.

She was interviewed in the staffroom. It proved fun. Teachers ducked in and out, fetching things and apologising to both her interviewer and to *her.* Pretty, perfumed young women teachers saying 'sorry' to *Jo.* Her chair was comfortable and she enjoyed the psychologist's puzzles, his patter, his clock with a second hand. She took his searching questions about her family as permission to interrogate him about his wife and children. As the infant mistress said later to Hester Keene, 'When I popped in Jo was *grilling* the poor man.'

Jo had no learning disorder, Mr Heron reported to Hester, in fact she was possibly the brightest child in the school. Perhaps she would rather take model-making with the boys than sewing with the girls? Jo made a papier-mâché dinosaur, a balsa wood aeroplane, and a cardboard speedboat painted with high-gloss enamel and varnish, so that she could float it in the paddling pool at home. Lex, at seven, her first year of sewing, made Horsey.

Thomas Sand stood at the fence, waiting to waylay any children who passed along the right-of-way to Taita Drive. Under his arm he held an enamel basin full of fresh peas his mother had given him to pod for tea. His classmate Jo Keene and her little sister Lex stopped and leaned on the fence; the wire squawked and gave. They took some of his peas, popping and splitting the pods, prising out the odds and evens with their tongues. Thomas listened to all they had to say — about the bridge and Hayley turning tail, the King Edward berries, Mercy and Playtime. He told his own news: another gift, Mother's sponge cake, a phone call from an aunt in England to whom he'd been allowed to speak — all the things he had done during today's period of house arrest.

Thomas noticed everything, and reported in a soft, unhurried voice. His eyes were sleepy, his hair fair and sparse and his skin, like Hester's camellias, milky and prone to rusty bruises. He had been sick for some time. In the spring his hair fell out and he wore a knitted hat, like a tea cosy; it covered his scalp and conserved his heat. Thomas had two older sisters, one already at High. His father was a chauffeur and had driven the Daimler the Queen rode in on her last visit. Mr and Mrs Sand were from England.

Thomas's oldest sister, Glenda, came over. She took the basin from him. 'Mum will need the remainder of these.' Jo and Lex hid their pea pods behind their backs.

'Did you eat many?' Glenda asked her brother. When Thomas said he had she looked pleased.

It was lunchtime, so Jo ran on up Taita Drive while Lex took time to tuck her dress into her panties and execute a forward roll over the bars at the head of the right-of-way.

Hester asked, 'Why don't you eat the rest of your egg?'

'The remainder of my egg?' Lex asked, seeing how Glenda's word worked.

'Yes. What's left.'

Lex thoughtfully scooped the scrambled egg to the left side of her plate and was told not to play with her food. Her mother negotiated three more mouthfuls in exchange for Lex's drink. Lex renegotiated two if she had to put on her pinafore.

Jo, Lex and four-year-old Steph went down to the shed in the back garden, sucking their lemon and barley-water out of Cerebos sauce bottles. Jo's and Steph's had been soy bottles and had only a single hole in their lids. Jo could tip hers out in a stream onto her tongue — the way Spaniards drink wine from goatskins, she told her sisters. She had seen a film at school. Lex's bottle had five holes in its lid and drizzled. She liked to stopper the liquid with her tongue, feel five discrete, cool dimples, then a flood like the spit of hunger.

The shed was covered in honeysuckle and stood right up against the boundary fence of a house on Molesworth Street. Jo and Lex used to climb from the fence onto the shed roof and then jump off; Jo because it was a challenge, safe without any audience but her little sisters. At school Jo always ducked the softball and trailed in last in races. Yet only she and Naomi Arapa, of all the neighbourhood, would scale the parapets of old blackberry that grew over the felled willows on the river bank. If she did choose to catch the softball it wouldn't be to please Miss Patterson, who went on about sportsmanship and team spirit but abused any child who flinched, lagged, or lost. Jo *never* felt inept under the gaze of the dark compound eyes of inaccessible berries.

Whenever Lex jumped off the shed roof she thought she would fly, not fall. She dreamed of flying, of picking up her feet to bob at the corner of the kitchen, against the ceiling. Or she soared, dodging pylons and high tension wires, under the shadows of zeppelins or over seas of whales — long eerie shadows, like the swarms of wardrobe monsters that had kept her awake and watchful in her infancy. Or perhaps the shadows were like Jo's smelly, nebulous, ballooning 'pardies' — as the girls were taught to say when they farted, 'Pardon me' childishly commuted. Jo had described how a fart would look and behave, and Lex would still swear sometimes she could see them, like several of Jo's other inventions, invisible by daylight. Lex dreamed of flying, so after breakfast would climb onto the shed roof and leap off, looking out and up, rather than down, sure that *this time* she would be snatched upward.

Jo checked her tadpoles, in their plastic bucket filled with stones and duckweed. Little John's and Mayflower's legs had emerged from the buds by their tails; Big John's were longer and his eyes seemed to be moving towards the top of his head.

Steph found an old peach stone in the garden. She had Lex split it open for her on the path to the clothesline and then ate its shrivelled kernel. Like her sisters Steph was a keen forager. She didn't have their discernment, however, and sometimes ate things that made her sick.

Her younger sister's grubbing reminded Lex to disinter the dolls. She fetched her spade from the apple box in the back porch and first dug up the papier-mâché doll Jo had made and they had buried, in a shoebox coffin and with due ceremony, some weeks before. It was the second time he'd been dug up and he was becoming quite corpse-like — a faded, pale pulp. His mouth and moustache had become indistinguishable and the damp had scalped him, parted his rabbit fur crew-cut and paper cranium.

Tuppence was buried in a plastic lunch box, a survival capsule, equipped with a bed, water, food stores and reading matter — one of Hester's miniature books, the suede-bound *Thoughts from Tolstoy*. This project was inspired by a newspaper headline: FRENCH SCIENTIST SPENDS 52 DAYS UNDERGROUND. The final frontier had retreated beyond the means of lone explorers, but endurance feats were all the rage: land speed records on the dry salt lakes of Utah, papyrus boats on the Pacific waves. Lex told Tuppence she had spent twenty-three days underground and had some distance yet to go. She brushed the mildew out of Tuppence's hair and resealed the lunch box.

'The girls said they saw Thomas Sand today,' said Hester.

Frank Keene had his typewriter on the kitchen table; he was knocking off an article he hadn't been able to finish at work on Friday. He had paused to think and was, as always, rubbing his palms back and forth along his thighs. His suit pants grew shiny and corded velvet bald by these deliberations. 'Do the girls understand about Thomas?' Frank asked.

'I don't know. I mean, I can't say *I* understand it.' Hester felt grave, but found herself smiling at the cat, who came into the kitchen, looked warily at Frank and found him acceptable seated and with slippered feet — Brindle had no objection to Frank himself but Frank's dress or heavier work shoes appalled him.

Hester poured the cat a little milk and watched with pleasure as he sat and draped his front feet with his tail. She had always loved cats. There had been several batches in her childhood. When her father was alive the cats would wait for him on the front walk of the house on Maori Hill. The family would hear him in conversation with them: 'What have you been up to? What have you got there? You rogue. Lovely puss. Lizards again? What a spot for a cat. Ah. Don't snatch, mate!' To his family he would say just, 'Hello,' and shake the paper open.

Frank was saying, 'Do you mean you don't understand because Thomas is only a child? That's a little sentimental.'

'*Everybody* feels that way. And it's worse if you have children of your own.'

'Ours are healthy.'

'Look. I was as frightened by Steph's bronchitis as by your rushed appendix job. Poor Mrs Sand, it's like lightning striking.'

Frank finished his sentence and lit another cigarette. He wondered if he'd ever told Hester his lightning story.

'And Jo says he's the nicest boy. It's true. Possibly the illness has made him gentler and more thoughtful. He's a little girlish. His mother taught him French knitting so he'd have something else to do in bed. When he's up he walks about trailing his knitting.' Hester picked up the cat, who gave an alarming wet belch. She said, 'Sometimes it does seem true — that the good die young. Or the sweet, anyway.'

Frank remembered the dim front room of his childhood home, the white gloom of lace curtains, women in rusty black wool, taffeta, velvet, jet — and that supposed comforting commonplace: Suffer the little children.

'Think of Paul,' Hester said.

Paul, son of Hester's landlady, Frank's friend, was sweet-natured, not just friendly or pleasant, but good. Frank and Paul had gone walking on the lower slopes of Egmont in the spring, several months before Paul's nephritis finally killed him. Frank couldn't recall their conversation. He did remember a deer trail, the punctured, crusty snow, then a yellow trench of urine, steaming, a flurry on the bank above them and the stag looking back across its flank, red hide softened through a haze of its own breath, and frost in its eyelashes. And Frank remembered how he took the wheel on the way home, while Paul slept in the back seat. Paul was spent and pale. On the Himatangi straight the wind buffeted the little Austin. Frank fought to hold it steady. Dark night, deep sleep, rough ride — Paul might have been one of Frank's children, the way he felt.

Frank said, 'Have I ever told you about the lightning?'

Frank and another alpine guide had set out to carry supplies to a party of climbers stranded at Ball Hut. The road was snowed in and there was no getting a tractor through. Frank's partner carried a pack of food; Frank had a six-gallon drum of kerosene strapped to his back, which gurgled in a distinctly spiritous way at his every step.

The ceiling of cloud was low, snow on the slope to the left of the road loose and threatening. Mist moved now and then between the men and their view below and behind of that white and preposterously wide road, the Tasman glacier.

They heard the storm coming up the far side of Sefton, closer, sharp concussions of thunder then the bass chorus of an avalanche shaken loose in the opposite valley. The men stopped. The tin on Frank's back boomed. A small snowfall skidded down the slope above the road just in front of the guides. Frank's partner went ahead to take a look, first shrugging off the pack so that, if he must, he could make a quick retreat. His ice axe was still fastened to the top of his pack. Frank thrust the spike on his axe-handle into the snow, and used the head to rest on, like a hacking-cane. For a moment it was quiet, but for the creak of their feet in the snow. Then, beneath Frank's hand, his ice axe began to hum. He raised it, broke contact with the ground, but it went on vibrating like a tuning fork. Something was on its way, something unlike anything he knew — the jolts he'd heard when he put his ear to a railway line in a quiet landscape, or, his head underwater, the sound of the prop of a big ship coming into the bay. Frank flung the ice axe from him. It sailed out over the glacier and was struck by lightning. Only a thin capillary of electricity, but around the two men the air was instantly solid, deafening, and as brassy as small change.

They went on, with supplies to deliver. But on the way back the following morning, in finer weather, they climbed down from the road onto the glacier to look for the axe. And found a comma-shaped hole milled from the ice where the axe-head had melted its way down into the glacier, too deep for sight.

Lex met Hayley riding her trike along the footpath by the Keenes'. Hayley wore a blue brocade dress of her mother's — a discarded ballroom-dancing dress, eight years out of date, with a spangly train that trailed behind her along the concrete, catching. Its glitter fidgeted. Hayley showed Lex a small gilt box that held her mother's lipstick. She'd pinched it. The lipstick was sweating, a waxy red. The girls scooped some out with their fingers and rubbed it in, lip to lip, as they had seen their mothers do. It made Lex's throat catch, as if she'd been sucking on a crayon. Hayley bundled her train into the tray of her trike. Lex got in and Hayley dubbed her up the street.

On top of the stopbank some big boys were sky-lining like television Apaches. They had found the corpse of a large dead rat and took turns swinging it about by its tail. One saw Lex and Hayley, and spun in a circle to hammertoss the rat at them. It landed with a smack on the path behind the girls. Hayley pedalled quickly into the Sands' front yard. The boys stood watching them for a moment then dropped out of sight on the far side of the bank. Two of the boys were Hayley's brothers, twins, high-school boys and members of the gang that by report had built a pit fort over the stopbank. A deep pit, round (it was said) as an octopus's head with eight tunnels for tentacles, it was roofed with corrugated iron and camouflaged with cut willow branches and broom.

'Shall we follow them?' Hayley asked, then bent over to prise at the pennies Mr Sand had set into the drive. Every child tried in passing, but the pennies had withstood all assaults, even those of mad David Hough with his father's best screwdriver.

'Not today.' Lex could hear her older sister's voice behind the Sands' house. She got off the tray of the trike and waved to Hayley who pedalled on.

The Sand girls and Jo were playing darts. Thomas watched from the back steps. He was wearing plaid slippers and a duffel coat over his summer shirt and shorts. He was keeping score.

They let Lex join, then scoffed as her darts rebounded from the wire web on the board's face or sank themselves into the lawn behind the rotary clothesline — the board hung from the hook for the peg basket. Even Glenda, the sixteen-year-old, failed to say, 'Give her a chance, she's only young,' but, 'You little clot! It's just a flick of the wrist!' Jo was no good at it either, but was improving — besides, she'd been invited. Glenda threw wide once, her younger sister jeered and Thomas called out not to run around behind the board while Lex was taking her turn, then, 'Not yet, Lex!'

Lex threw very wide — or her eyes strayed from the board and she was looking down the shaft of plastic-fletched brass at Glenda beyond the clothesline stooping to retrieve her dart. Lex threw and her dart sank into Glenda's ankle. Glenda sat down, the dart drooped and a line of blood trickled down into Glenda's shoe. Lex dropped her other darts and ran.

She was sure she had aimed at Glenda, but never believed she would hit her mark. Anyway, the injury would look like an accident. She had made an impact; with Glenda's cry of pain, wilt, huddle, Lex had solidified. She was a big clot, a choking clot of thrombosis, a lethal, considerable clot.

The villain and fugitive ran across Taita Drive and scrambled up the stopbank. Last winter the council had built the bank up a little along that stretch of the river and the top was still furrowed and cross-hatched by bulldozer tracks. When the bulldozers had done, the council sprayed the bank with some substance that formed a gritty white scab then sprouted clover. Lex lay stomach down in the thick clover on the far slope. Across the summit of the bank she watched Jo leave Sands', look both ways along the road, then walk home.

It was Thomas who pulled the spike from Glenda's ankle. His other sister, Jenny, ran indoors to fetch their mum. Jo Keene said, 'I'd better be going.' She held her arms as if it were cold and her cardie out at its elbows. Glenda's eyes watered, but she wouldn't shed tears over an injury inflicted by a little kid. Mrs Sand hurried out and Jo Keene backed away around the corner of the house.

Thomas's mum said he was a good boy and not to linger outside and catch a chill. She helped Glenda to her feet and supported her up the back steps.

Thomas wasn't tough, like the boys who kept on fighting, even with bloodied noses; he just wasn't squeamish. When his sisters' budgie escaped its cage and got its leg entangled in the fishing line of a home-made mobile, and the Sand children found it, upside down, fluttering and shrieking, the girls pressed their hands to their cheeks and cried. But Thomas cut it down and held it quiet while he unwound turn after turn of the nylon thread sunk into the swollen flesh of its leg.

For Thomas was patient, and his patience gave him the substance to stay upright in the pressure waves of others' pain. It was easy if you could see the cause — steel spike or constricting thread — to do something to kick the wedges out from the wheels of *that* life, to get it rolling again. Blood would flow freely, then the wound close.

Thomas had thought that way of his own suffering and spells in bed. They were an interruption, static, a break in transmission. But then — there was something he saw on TV, when his headache hadn't let him sleep and Dad had bundled him up in candlewick and sat him between them on the settee. Mum and Dad. They were there, so he dozed. They were watching some drama, a grown-up programme, and Thomas heard the wise-old-woman character say that someone was 'young and unfinished'. He stored the phrase away. It was an illumination as vivid as his dreams of being younger and running, running not yet breathless along a colonnade of trees, in his strength, under sunlit leaves, great thunderclaps of green.

Jo Keene, who was his age — but his birthday was earlier in the year — was the cleverest girl Thomas knew. Jo had showed him a book she'd been writing: *Honey and John on Windy Hill.* She knew about Beethoven's deafness, and that Zeus and Jupiter were the same gods by different names. But Jo was unfinished. Nobody stared at her the way they would stare at Thomas (the way he'd peer into his own reflection) to see the thing that would one day leap out from behind his image and engulf it, like the scorched then fire-holed map of the Ponderosa at the beginning of *Bonanza*.

At dusk, when the sun had skipped along the top of the hills, touched three crests, then finally gone down, Frank came along Taita Drive from his Saturday evening walk to the dairy. Every Saturday, while the roast was cooking, he went for ice-cream cones and Hester's weekly bar of white chocolate.

As Frank turned in at his letterbox he saw his middle daughter, further along the road, sitting with her feet in the gutter. The lower half of Lex's face was red. Wind-chapped, Frank assumed; a rare November southerly had set in. Lex had found a sea shell and was holding it up to her ear. Where had she acquired that bit of whimsy? He must explain acoustics to her some time.

Lex had found the shell in the gutter by Arapas', bulky and brown among the empty halves of flat, white tuatua. It was warm in her hand, had a rim like a helmet and a spiral dome. She held it to her ear to hear the sea and it kissed her, a warm wet kiss. She touched her ear. Stickiness. It spilled from the shell onto her fingers, a curdled, olive-green slime that stank and seethed. Lex dropped the shell. She retched, but caught the bile in her mouth and swallowed.

She washed at the outside tap under the lounge windows, where Hester had planted pinks and carnations between the brown topknots of exhausted iris leaves. Both the rot and remains of lipstick were greasy and stubborn; grease sealed her skin like Vaseline so the water formed blisters on it. She went indoors to try soap.

In the lounge Steph and Jo were watching *The NZBC Report*, footage of the Gemini Twelve splash-down. It had been in the newspaper three days before, without pictures; Naomi had brought the item to school for current events. Mr Heron put 'gravity' and 'vacuum' on Standard Four's spelling list. James Lovell and 'Buzz' Aldrin stood on the foredeck of a battleship, waving, and smiling through their beards. 'Buzz' had the new record, a five-and-a-half hour space walk. More pictures. Jo was fascinated by this puffy figure spinning on the end of its umbilicus, without inertia, making big movements from small gestures, like a god tossing in its sleep. Steph sat in her TV chair, one of the cane dining chairs. Her parents wanted to encourage her to keep her back straight. All the girls were round-shouldered. Hester would nag the older two: 'Your torso should sit on your hips like an egg in an egg-cup.'

When Lex had washed her face thoroughly she joined her sisters. Jo hadn't told on her, had reported neither her 'mistake' nor her absence. Lex wondered how long she had hidden, skulking along the far side of the stopbank, almost to the rail bridge (but she never went there alone). Perhaps no time had passed, she had dawdled there and back in the time it takes the one who is 'he' at hide-and-seek to count to twenty — an age, eyes blind and ears pinned back to follow footfalls on cement or grass and the loose slat in the fence creaking as it tilted; no time for those scrambling to hide, their blood measuring and selling seconds by the yard, hearts' meters ticking over.

Frank joined the girls to watch the first item on *Town and Around*, then Hester called them all up to the table.

Frank waited till only Lex had meat on her plate; she always saved the best for last. He wasn't sure where to begin, then Hester helped him along. She asked Jo, 'Did you go along to Sands' this afternoon?'

Lex hunched over her plate as Jo stored her last mouthful in one cheek and said, 'Thomas was still outdoors. He kept score when we played darts.'

'Do you know,' Frank asked his eldest, 'what will happen to Thomas?'

'Will he die?'

Jo was too abrupt, even for her father, but he rallied. 'He will. Unless his cancer goes into remission. Or someone invents a cure.' The sparsely worded premises of Hamlet's proposition ran in Frank's head: *If it be now, 'tis not to come; if it be not to come, it will be now; if it be not now, yet it will come; the readiness is all.* But the boy's death was beside the point — or — there was *more to it.*

Frank had permitted Jo and Lex to go to Sunday school, because they insisted, because every other kid in the neighbourhood went. Lex had quit when an unChristian Christian classmate waylaid her at the edge of the school field and tore up her colouring-book (the golden calf in three shades of yellow, Moses's wrathful face scarlet crayon under white, blood beneath skin).

'It's always sad when a child dies,' Frank said.

'Partly because it's very rare,' Hester added, watching her daughters' faces for signs of fright. Jo's mouth was prim, her gaze level. She would try to please her father, favour him with her full attention, composed before the sentence of his rationality. Jo knew that to agree with him on these matters — religious matters — meant they were *better* than other people. People with legless arguments about God and Heaven, intoxicated by superstition, who couldn't see straight.

Lex, Hester saw, had wilted when her sister said that Thomas would die, but then, as if watered by the discussion, she unfolded quietly to look up at her father. Steph, sensing a distraction, helped herself to the last potato and gravy and ate quickly while they all talked.

Jo cued her father. 'Glenda says they pray for Thomas.'

'That may help them *feel* better. And, in Thomas's case, as far as I know, his parents have done everything the doctors have recommended. They've tried all treatments known to medical science — radiation therapy and so forth.'

Jo nodded.

'When I was a boy we had neighbours who were Christian Scientists. Their daughter, a pretty girl with blond plaits, was diagnosed as having a brain tumour. Christian Scientists don't believe in modern medicine, only in prayer. The girl's parents wouldn't give the doctors permission to operate on her — not even when she had fits and one eye began to poke out of her head. It was so primitive! They put their faith in God and she died. Her death was terrible, she was young and it was preventable. Their religious beliefs killed her.'

'What's a brain tumour?' Lex asked, horrified by the endless variations of death.

'A cancer that grows in some people's brains. It's *very rare*,' Hester told her.

Frank caught on. He was addressing his remarks mainly to Jo, who had done so well in that Education Department IQ test; but this meat was too gamy for Lex's palate, she was younger, a less robust mind and very impressionable. He said to Lex, 'It won't happen to you.'

Lex couldn't see why not, but chose to trust her father since he obviously knew so much more about death, this villain, this 'man of many guises'. Although brain tumours were patently not in that class of things that could be discounted because they didn't happen *these days* or *in New Zealand* — like the Black Plague or snakebite.

At least Frank stopped short of his litany — how we all, ultimately, go into the ground and rot. Hester wouldn't dispute this, nor was it something that greatly troubled her, but the children shouldn't have to think about it yet. Frank wanted to fortify his children against superstition — and sentimentality. He seemed to object to Christianity as much for what he saw as its sentimentality as for its falsehood. Hester had tried to explain to him that children are naturally sentimental. They would happily hearken to the sad, come-away strains of *Lassie*. (Frank hated the programme, and the girls kept their mouths shut, secret *Lassie* fans.) Besides, what were the girls supposed to make of going into the ground to rot? Did they even believe it? Earlier that year Jo had written a lovely story about a tram trip to heaven, and given her mother a refreshing glimpse of a glossy twenty-four carat sky through peach blossom clouds. What kind of story would Jo make of going into the ground? Frank was ready with his answers before his daughters had been troubled by the questions. They were wholly, roundly ignorant, without an itch, a suspicion of their deficiencies, souls' shortcomings or bodies' built-in obsolescence.

Frank got up from the table to fetch the brown paper bag of ice-cream cones from the fridge-freezer. He put the bag in the centre of the table and tore it open. The bag exhaled, mist cleared and there were the cones nestled in frost.

Lex found a hole in her ice-cream, an air bubble, sculpturally smooth inside, like a snow cave. She grizzled and was told to 'eat around the hole'. Lex sat and looked at the hole, trying to work out how to move her mouth around an absence. She puzzled, she sulked, finally she burst into tears and her father swapped his cone for hers.

2

It was nine-thirty and Lex had her eyes turned to the window. Current Affairs wound up with a talk about the fight between Cassius Clay and Cleveland 'Big Cat' Williams. Behind the speaker's head Miss Patterson drew down a rolled chart on which was written the eleven-times table. Eleven sevens are seventy-seven. The rhyme of it held Lex's attention for a moment, then she was done with school for the day and wanted, suddenly and acutely, to be at home. She put her hand to the front of her frock and caught hold of the cloth and a small fillet of flesh, twisted her stomach and tried to moan, but couldn't make a sound. That would be to remind everyone of last week's disgrace.

She had had some bug, a gripe in her guts, and had put up her hand to be excused. She left the room with her friend Avril Arapa, doubled over, her mouth running spit. It was too late. In the toilet she lifted her dress and peered into her pants — they were full of brown faecal mucus. No one offered to help her clean up, instead she was sent home under Avril's escort, walking gingerly with this squelching store of filth between her legs. Her mother hosed her down, dug a hole in the back yard and pursued her panties into it with the hose on hard jet. Then Lex was sent to sit on the toilet till her mother could be sure there was nothing more forthcoming.

Lex knew Avril had told anyone who was interested how she had pooed her pants, and knew they would all stare if she did manage to push a solid sound — a moan — through the hard valve of her mouth. But she wanted to *go*, didn't want to chant the tables, revise her spelling, or stick felt labels by felt figures on a felt backboard, which was supposed to be fun, an *activity* with *equipment*; a shallowly determined world where things and names, colourful and neat — so surely appealing to all little girls — would keep curling up and dropping off.

Lex groaned and everyone looked at her.

'What is it, Lex?'

'It's my stomach.'

Miss Patterson glanced at Avril, who jumped up, her face radiant.

They went together to the toilets, where Lex watched herself in the mirror and tightened her facial muscles in a way that whitened the flesh around her mouth.

Avril took Lex by the arm and led her to the school office. The secretary phoned Hester, who was out. Lex was sent to lie down in the sick-room. Its bed was as bowed as a hammock and the blanket had a label picturing a thistle — and it felt as much. It was quiet in the sick-room, apart from an occasional snore in the long throat of the sink.

Hester and Steph had taken the bus to Lower Hutt. Having only one child at home made Hester feel liberated; that, and this hopping on buses. With Jo she'd stuck to trains and trams and had shopped either at Taita or in town. Jo had motion sickness on motor transport. After the city council began to cut back on trams, even that last stretch to the Zoo, the straight run up Riddiford Street, had Jo white-faced and vomiting. Every trip was an expedition. Hester had carried nappies for the baby and wet cloths to wash Jo's face. Steph was the least obliging of all Hester's children, but she'd sit comfortably on the bus, especially if sweetened by an Eskimo baby or a handful of musky pink smokers. They would go to Woolworths, where Hester could take her time browsing in Haberdashery. If Steph strayed, she could always be found in the toy department parked, covetous, before the toy guns. Hester had already purchased her youngest's Christmas gifts: two six-guns with pearly plastic handles, holsters, a roll of caps, vinyl chaps and waistcoat, a pink ten-gallon hat and tin star.

Latterly, it was only in the school holidays that Hester shopped in town. She would wheel Steph one-handed in her pushchair, and hold Jo's hand. Jo kept hold of Lex, who would stumble across Bowen Street, from the station, her face lifted, staring at the 'man on a horsey', the statue on top of the cenotaph, which she had delighted in since it was first pointed out to her. For once, apparently, it wasn't the horse but the man who thrilled her; his bare torso, straining arm, the yearning supplication that had drawn the marble up under him, like pulled toffee, into a streamlined crag. Poor Hester, a pushchair, one child timid of traffic and another who tripped or dithered, her attention always caught on snags of novelty or drama or sentiment. With her children in tow Hester felt not like an animal with four free limbs but a clump of something complicated, bulky, like tide-borne kelp. Still, town was worth the trouble, the shops were so much more interesting and she could leave the girls to play on the escalators at Wright Stephenson's and rely on them to be there half an hour later. They could lunch at Kirks or meet Frank for a picnic in Bolton Street Cemetery — spread a rug by the Sexton's Cottage where Jo could keep the younger two entertained by collecting gum nuts and 'helicopters' from the sycamore. Town was less practical but more attractive than shopping in the Hutt, or — as Hester called it — 'the great metropolis of Naenae'.

In another six months Steph would be at school and Hester could walk about on her own — step out, swing her arms — except that she couldn't quite remember how to. Her adult life before she had children was with her still, quite clear and whole. She remembered old acquaintances, places, pastimes, herself among it all, but disembodied — she'd lost her memory of all the sensations that would *place* her in her past: of being a different size, smaller; of luxurious late-night wakefulness, a good book and a single bed; of the steel rims of her typewriter keys cupping her fingertips, rings, promissory riches; or the taste of an omelette from Sans Souci, an end-of-the-week lunch treat; and the taste of the cigarette she smoked afterward, the smoke of which had in it somehow the papery flavour of all those neatly typed letters; and the brass of Saturday morning sunlight and Saturday night beer. But this was memory. When Hester became *nostalgic* about being less encumbered it wasn't her single life she remembered, or even the first year of her married life in the mountain guides' quarters at the Hermitage — no, it was her and Frank's flat on Raroa Road. A one-bedroom flat up a flight of wooden steps. Hester had parked Jo's pram under the steps, made it up with sheets and blankets before each trip, and carried both baby and bedding up the stairs every time she came in. They had no washing machine so Hester hand-washed nappies in the bath. The flat was cold and close and steamy, but Jo was good and beautiful, a small baby with fair hair and black eyes. And in the fine weather Hester would get out every afternoon, would wheel Jo along Upland Road and down the Glen, through the Gardens to Tinakori Road and Frank's mother's house. Frank would meet them there and push the pram uphill home. They played 'Whee!', tilting the pram on its two back wheels. 'Whee!' Jo would laugh, her little wallet mouth fat with happiness. Hester's time and tasks were in pieces, but there were moments — like this — when all her feelings and expectations totalled. It wasn't an easy time, but Hester looked back and missed it all — the concentration and intimacy, the good new bread of a first baby, the old trees of central Wellington, days when it rained and she stood with her face to a porthole wiped in the foggy front window, breathless with a loneliness that was like rage.

At smoko Mervyn Barrett issued a challenge. They — the *Listener*'s three subs — would each make out a list proposing a number of English language writers who must win the Nobel Prize within the next twenty years.

At five to one Mervyn came back from the pub, where he'd been propping up the bar with a couple of local poets. He had a poem for the editor and gave it to Frank to read in exchange for Frank's list. The other sub, Peter, pushed the door open with his back and came in, re-knotting his knitted tie. Everyone stared. He'd been seen walking in the cemetery with a pretty girl in sandals and op-art earrings — a student maybe. They were reported heading for the place where the trees were thick and the gravestones tilted every which way like boats on choppy water.

Frank flicked the sheet of foolscap. (The poet didn't like stray stanzas on a second page; for longer poems he used longer paper, or he wrote short poems.) 'This is a suicide poem. As a genre it's only slightly above those verses in the *Post*'s In Memoriam column. You know: "We all love our Arthur more, since he flew to a farther shore ...".'

'It isn't one of his best, but he's a major poet, and it has my vote.'

Frank said, 'You're not doing him any favours you know.'

'He's feeling low. He needs a boost,' Mervyn said, then, 'Christ, Keene! Patrick White?'

'Yes.' Frank put the poem down on Mervyn's desk. 'Boost?' he said. 'Boozed. And it isn't even fit for *The Quaffer's Gazette*.'

'White's absolutely bogus. He overwrites. And he has no ideas — social ideas.'

'Five pounds,' Frank challenged.

Pete passed Mervyn his list. After a moment Mervyn turned to him and asked, 'Durrell?'

'Yes. *The Alexandria Quartet*.'

'Maybe. By the way, what have you two got against Graham Greene? There are a number of very highly praised writers you've both given the go-by.'

'My list is based on my reading, not reputations,' Frank said, rather too haughtily. 'Who says today's taste-makers are backing winners? They could be making the same — same as the famous — mistakes. Like Joyce and Lawrence. And I know what you're going to say,' for Mervyn had drawn himself up. 'That was just prudery, and we are less stuffy.'

'More hip,' Peter said.

'I suspect it's more a matter of time — time for taste to settle — than hipness. Is "ness" the right ending? Or should it be "hipity" like "brevity" and "divinity"?' Frank had begun to wave his arms about. Debating ideas he was never enough at ease to be emphatic without comic exaggeration. Fatherless, he was often on the back foot with other men. By which end to pick them up? So he would brood, or play the clown and kidder.

Mervyn was saying something about what Marx, Freud, the death of Queen Victoria and two world wars had done to the twentieth-century mind. He thought it had fewer illusions.

'Of course. We are the great unbenighted generation,' said Frank. 'We know a genius when we see one. We would have backed *The Magic Flute*, and purchased the paintings of Van Gogh.'

'Well, I trust my judgement.' Mervyn put the lists into an envelope and stowed the envelope in a filing cabinet. 'And after all, these are only opinions.'

Frank sat behind his typewriter and peered at the *something wrong* with his last sentence. 'Shallowly' — worse — 'only shallowly'. He pushed the carriage back and used the X to excise. Often, still, when his good judgement was, to his own mind, proven — in opposition to someone else's poor taste — and pumped up like yeasty dough left to 'prove', then, irritated and scornful and sitting as he was, approximate to a desk, typewriter, blank page, Frank felt he could one day *write that novel*. The one that would conclude with its hero hiding in a cave in the bush. Frank had so much *material*: great, untrammelled nature, the mountains' sudden weather and immense enduring architecture. And his hero, making his way through it all, alone and overawed and speechless — so Frank wouldn't have to 'do' too many people. It felt sound — the solitary character, icy grit, wetas, falling water. It would be good, if he could write it.

But Frank knew that, by the time he was at leisure to sit down and write a novel, *that* novel, planned and nursed, would have dried up — its people and forests desiccated and airy as ash. For in the balance was a savings book for the house in Wadestown, each month's purple ink stamp a fading bruise. And there was his job, last year's fully paid trip to Europe and, every week, his name in print. Besides, Frank had nothing from which to launch himself into the high dive and submerged swim in the surf pool of his own work.

Frank remembered his journals and the fireplace of his bachelor flat in Rolleston Street.

In his search for kindling he took the bath mat of wooden slats, laid it across the door sill and broke it in two with one foot. You need a good hot fire to burn books, especially books that have travelled on ships, in cabins below the water-line, books full of thick inky definite words, dreams and declarations and covenants with Art. Hester had broken off their engagement. She said he was selfish. He placed the books on the fire, where they lay, for a time not even scorched, the flames sprouting, thin and indolent, like weeds around a paving stone. He put up the fireguard and left the room.

Now, when Frank wound a page into his typewriter to work up his notes or make a record of some odd thing one of the girls had said, he felt as though he had just got off the boat, an immigrant, dispossessed not so much of his language and customs as of orientation — familiar landmarks, steep and shallow grades, rough and smooth places, an old stamping ground. Even if he had the time it would be difficult to begin to write without those past writings; he would set out, but his feet would come down where no step was and he would come a cropper.

Lex woke when Jenny Sand came into the sick-room. The older girl passed her a thermometer. 'The secretary says to put that in your mouth and she'll be in in a tick.' Jenny sat on the floor under the sink. She fiddled with the bloody plug of cotton wool in her left nostril. 'She'll be in in a tick to put a flea in your ear,' she said, then, 'Dad says the Nats are bloated ticks. National,' she explained.

'Jo's interested in all that,' Lex said.

'You're too young.'

'But we're going to watch the election.'

'Can you? How?'

'I don't know. Jo says.'

'Hadn't you better put that thing under your tongue? Otherwise it'll read room temperature and they'll decide you're dead.'

Lex tucked the bulb of the thermometer in one cheek.

'I might say you don't look sick.'

'That's because you're used to looking at your brother.'

'I suppose so.' Jenny pulled out the bloody plug, inspected it, snuffled experimentally and quickly replaced it. 'But we didn't realise Thomas was sick for ages. Till the day Mum saw him coming home up the right-of-way, and he was dragging his feet, like he was exhausted. Then when he was in the tub she noticed all these bruises on his legs. He said Glenda had kicked him — she had, but not hard enough to bruise like that. Mum and Dad took him to the Doctor and we found out how sick he was.'

'Didn't he know?' Lex asked around the thermometer.

'He was used to it.'

That anyone could be sick like that and not know. Lex shifted the glass stick, swizzling her spit; it pressed against the hinge of her tongue. She knew that to take a pulse meant counting the small flicks in her wrist but didn't know what amounted to good health. Sometimes her heartbeat troubled her, echoing out of her pillow. But to sicken, to die, seemed something the whole world was more apt to do, in dull weather or at the day's end when it cooled away from a girl, from her eyes and ears and skin.

Jenny said, thoughtfully, 'Jo must mean to hang around a polling booth. Funny girl.'

Lex tried to figure this out, but only came up with the title of a book Jo had read: *The Phantom Tollbooth*. It sounded even more frightening than standing under the rail bridge when the trains went over. Hayley wouldn't want to come.

'You're all funny girls,' Jenny said.

Lex didn't like to be baffled. Particularly when she needed to know she was well and would live. The mercury in the glass wand had stopped at the red line, which seemed good, but Lex could feel her blood, only temporarily coherent, like a trail of ants. The lunch bell rang and Lex got off the bed. She thrust the thermometer at Jenny and bolted from the room.

Lunch monitors, big kids, would see if she broke cover and ran for the end of the field — out-of-bounds — the long grass under the birches and the stand of fennel. Every child in the school sat on forms outside the classrooms to eat lunch and swing their legs. Lex hid under the hydrangea bush beside the incinerator. And collected herself. Gathered in —

The lights of Mount Victoria from the deck of an overnight ferry. Daddy buttoned her into his overcoat. He said words and warm nonsense: Lex. Look. Cold. Snuggle down, Lex. At Christchurch the girl cousin had a Wendy house. She was daddy, Jo was mummy, but Lex didn't want to be baby. Lex was a big girl, one and a half. The boy cousin chased Lex with his mother's shears, then threatened to sever his mother's stuffed draught-stopper. Sausage dog. Puffing Billy. The black engine they were taken to see.

And, earlier yet, Lex could remember her play-pen: the smeary bars, the sun, a sward — lawn — a horizon of vegies; Daddy, digging, framed in the frill of her bonnet. Jo came to the bars and shook Poochy-pup. The warm swooned and the lawn frowned. Poochy cocked his knitted ears at the cloud. Lex made Jo show her back and undone sash by throwing Poochy over the top rail of the playpen. Mummy came down the back steps with boiled water for the ants' nest. She stooped and poured; Lex smelled steamed dust, formic acid, the mint by the drain.

Lex brushed chaff out of a hollow in the hard-packed earth. The hydrangeas had grown over an old marbles patch. Marbles were banned — the commerce of swapsies had led to theft, it was said. Teachers hated fads; fads organised the children, and fired them up far too much. After all, schools are models of society — mass movements and fervour are only sanctioned when they come down from above.

Lex got up and shook the leaf-litter from her dress. She felt not so much soothed as hungry. Her ability to concentrate wasn't equal to the dread she felt considering Thomas's illness. Like a bubble trapped under her hand in the bath Lex's attention would wander, buoyant and ticklish, then float free, lose its boundaries and melt into the general air. She had forgotten her heartbeat and remembered the brown paper bag in her desk — sandwiches, an apple, Sun Maid raisins, and Hayley's shop-bought custard square that was always a little too much for one.

After school Jo explained the universe to Hayley and Lex. Jo stood at the bathroom sink cleaning a skeleton, all that remained of the corpse of a bird she and Lex had spoken rites over some months before. The younger girls sat on the edge of the bath while Jo soaped the bones and scrubbed them with her toothbrush. Steph came in to tell them Lampchop was on, but was arrested by Jo's inventory.

'We live on a planet in orbit around the sun, in the Solar System — which means us and all the other planets. Then there are other suns — all the stars are suns — which make up the galaxy, the Milky Way. Then there are other galaxies, thousands, which make up the universe. So the universe is bigger than — ' Jo, boggled, stretched out both her arms, her toothbrush dripping brown and white foam onto the bathroom lino. 'Bigger than the whole world.' She stamped her foot. 'Damn!' Damn the primers and their illustrated 'big' list: house, tree, car, elephant, bulldozer.

Lex wanted to know was the universe the same as out-of-space?

'*Outer* space. Yes. Except the universe means here too.'

Hayley asked, 'Here?' And Jo told her about the globe they had in Room Five, how they had 'looked up' New Zealand, how much better a globe was than a map for seeing how the land lay.

Steph wanted to know what New Zealand was.

Hayley was proud to explain. 'Here. The country we live in.'

Steph asked, aggrieved, 'Don't we live in America?'

The others laughed.

Lex wanted to know if the universe included made-up places, like Bedrock, Sherwood Forest, Heaven and the Wild West.

'Only everywhere real,' Jo said, and that the Wild West *was* real. She rinsed her toothbrush, put it back in the rack and placed the gleaming, foamy handful of bones on the windowsill. Then she began to list the nine planets.

But Steph had gone off to see Fergie Fang, Hayley was reaching for the bird skull, and Lex was saying, '*Was* is real,' not like someone starting an argument but like a smaller child playing a private game.

'Hayley! Put that down! Let's go watch *Shari Lewis*. Hurry, last weeks!' Jo said, like the cinema ads. She herded the girls out of the bathroom.

After *Travellers' Tales*, Lex walked Hayley back home then went up onto the stopbank to see if she could spot the big boys' fort. Among the willows she saw raised dust, and heard the sound of a sheet of tin shaken. It was warmer today and seed-pods popped in the last of the sunlight, a sound like someone stirring on a woven cane chair. As Lex walked along the top of the stopbank the sun was snuffed out by the hills above the river, its rays swept upward then flattened into feverish whiteness over half the sky. The scrub ticked like a cooling engine. Then Lex could hear wind in gorse prickles and the boys talking about mines and booby-traps.

Some day soon Lex would keep a watch for the boys to leave, count them all out, then go and see. For Lex feats of engineering were about the creation of new perspectives. She had wondered about the view from excavations, bridges, tall buildings, ever since the day she and Jo had ventured into a drainpipe.

Its outfall was the river bank, where the two girls stood on a welcome mat of smooth silt and looked at the perfect black circle of the drain mouth. Jo climbed inside. It was dry, she reported, and there were a few stones at the bottom, but it wasn't too close or uncomfortable. *Come in Lex.* They crawled a short way. The curve of the pipe bent Lex's hands at painful angles, grit chafed her palms. It was cold, and a cold hush pushed at her eardrums. Jo had to bargain with Lex to make her go on. 'If you follow me you can smack my bottom.' For a younger sister this was a privilege not to be turned down. They went on with giggles and thwacks. 'Ouch, ouch,' Jo said, her voice a sonar echo.

They crawled seventy feet and came out in a culvert beneath Taita Drive. Light shone through the bars of a drain on wet green walls and — in a few inches of water — a comb, a rusted bolt, a pearly bottle and plastic rain hat. The girls could hear traffic and children playing: the tinkle and slap of a musical skipping rope; shouts, and deep-voiced sobbing from David Hough, the boy in callipers who everyone teased. It sounded different, distinct — the girls listened more attentively — and innocent, or uninformed, because the skipper, shouter, sobber, were being overheard from an unguessable place.

On the return trip Lex was afraid. The novelty had worn off smacking Jo, and besides, Jo was in her way — the mouth of the drain appeared as a tiny white sun over Jo's back, then afterward a broken circle past her sister's slow, obstructive body.

Lex scrambled back down the home side of the stopbank. It was tea time and the street was quiet. The Keenes ate closer to — as Frank complained — society hours, so Lex knew she wasn't yet missed. As she passed Sands' she heard her name called and looked about. A window was open into the narrow gap between the side of the house and the neighbours' fence. Thomas was hooking his hand at her. She came on to the edge of the property then was barred by a low hedge.

'Push through it,' Thomas whispered.

The hedge grazed her legs, but she was quick and it scarcely stung. She stopped beneath his window and put her hand on the wall where the weatherboards were still warm from a glancing sun.

Thomas folded his arms on the sill. In this light his skin looked dark, congested with the colour behind him — not a dim room but the unlined purple curtains. 'I've been sent to bed; not for being bad but "too seedy", Dad says. What do you think of that?'

'Seedy is short for going to seed,' Lex said. This was what passed for an opinion with her. 'Are you in bed?'

'My feet are.'

Lex could recall being sent to bed, in the afternoon, sick with the English measles, and how she woke at evening to a borderline light and the curtains open. 'Once when I was sick in bed I woke up — ' Lex began, the recollection flat against her face like cold glass. 'The sun was going like — ' she ran her hand along the weatherboards, ' — *now*. It was the same window in our house. This window on this side.' Their houses were identical, but that the Keenes' was asbestos clad. 'The edges of the window were all yellow and the sky was blue. So blue — '

'Because you were shut in when everyone else had gone down to the river for a swim.' Thomas tried to help her out, this younger child who, as she spoke, blew up in his face, as gradual and fierce as a Mount Vesuvius, Fairy Rain, or Flower Pot.

'No, not fine, blue. Blue you can't breathe. Like, suppose there wasn't any air on the other side of the window. Or not much. Like on top of mountains. Like Sir Edmund Hillary and the oxygen tanks.'

'I've had oxygen.'

'Isn't it just another word for air?'

'No. It's special rich air.'

'Is it nice?'

'Yes.' Thomas seemed tired, he laid his head on his arms.

Lex looked at him with her mouth open — trying to imagine the different taste of oxygen to air, like cream to milk, then she went on: 'Suppose you are on top of a high mountain, without oxygen tanks — ' She made a swift search of her father's mountain stories and found, ' — the summit. You're on the summit and it's like a desert island. The air below you is the sea, the air above is the sky, freezing cold but not frozen and all blue. That was my blue.'

Thomas simply looked at her, quiet, his eyes cleared of colour by the dusk and curiously doll-like between their unfringed lids. Then he asked, with effort, 'Was it real?'

'I don't know.'

'Were you scared?'

'Not that something would happen, but I shut my eyes.'

Thomas moved his head to look along the gap between the house and the neighbour's fence. At, perhaps, some kin of Lex Keene's blue. The spindly hawthorn, each branch, twig, spine and blossom black against the sky, looked like the template of all flowering trees. There again was the other world that seemed, often now, to pull up and park beside his own.

Thomas felt four icy pressure points on his forehead and when he opened his eyes — they had been closed — he saw the palm of Lex's hand, a shallow rosy cave. She drew back. 'You went to sleep,' she said.

Pain ran a comb through Thomas's bones and he came apart, slid back without a word onto his bed leaving the window unlatched. Lex called his name and listened. Silence made an emphatic reply. The room's darkness seemed organic, and the furry mildew that dotted the windowsill like spores dropped of that darkness.

Frank caught his train well before the six o'clock swill. But it was still packed. He hefted his satchel into the luggage rack — already bulging, an overstuffed string bag — and stood holding on to a chrome knob on the end of a seat. The doors shut, the unit chirruped and set out from the shelter of platform five. The commuters flipped up the corners of their newspapers or narrowed their eyes against the glare from the platform of polished patches of old chewing gum, then the dazzle of broken glass between browned stones.

Frank stood facing a newspaper ad, a picture of Holyoake rising above a ripped-out headline: BRITAIN'S NEW MOVES TO ENTER EUROPEAN COMMON MARKET. The slogan read: More Than Ever Leadership Counts. Frank inaudibly advised leadership not to count its chickens but its days, then looked around for something better to read.

It was near dark when Frank got off the train. And when he turned the corner where Taita Drive curved to follow the river there was more light from the street lamps than the sky — and from kitchens, domestic yellow electricity. The houses hadn't yet drawn their blinds, so Frank could see into every kitchen (at the front left corner of every house, repetitiously, kids at kitchen tables, mothers at sinks). State houses, the street like a strip of film spooling between the shops at Pomare and those at Taita.

Frank saw Lex in her school clothes and pinafore cover-all. She ran towards him — all sprint, no skip — as if in fright. But she hadn't seen him and he watched her turn down the path to the house and pause, as he planned to, to look for people in their kitchen.

'Less', she had called herself when she was younger and lisping still. Less. No parent is as intimate with a second child as a first. Frank had no notebooks of Lex's odd, childish remarks, or folders of scribbles. He had misfiled the curl from her first haircut, and his camera had broken shortly before her second birthday and hadn't been replaced. Jo was odd and, as the IQ test confirmed, highly intelligent. It was Jo he played pieces of music and lectured on the composers' lives. Jo he read bits of Tolstoy and Proust. He hoped Jo would grow up able to appreciate the achievements of great men. He hoped she'd be a like mind — perhaps write him letters about concerts or museum visits from the great cities of the world.

But Lex — Lex was born by emergency caesarean. Hester was white and depleted and weaned the baby at six weeks. Lex was colicky and, while Hester slept, Frank would walk the baby — curled up around her gripe and crying in long, exhausted screams — walk her up and down the kitchen. Since then she would always at least pause to reassess her distress if he asked her, 'Don't cry, Curly.' It made him feel able, and he loved her. He had no plans for his second daughter but her happiness.

Frank's daughters were in the lounge, sitting in the cool animated light of the television. This was a recent shift in the polarity of half the houses in the street. At evening previously unused front rooms — polished pianos and wedding photos or, in the Keenes' case, the bookcases and radiogram in its oak cabinet — were now full of kitchen chairs, still children and the demons of these broached Pandora's boxes: *The Adventures of Rin Tin Tin, Travellers' Tales, Cameras on the Campus*.

Frank remembered standing hand-in-hand with Lex on the footpath outside a neighbour's house, at dusk, watching through a window the first television on the street. There was something wrong with the vertical hold and the image scrolled up and up. He had to explain to Lex that this wasn't how TV told its stories — like those toy televisions in vogue with children; made with a box, two sticks, and a roll of paper on which pictures were drawn — a scroll of comic panels (Lex: 'And then the children find a Martian hiding in a tree . . .').

Steph was picking her nose. Frank tapped on the window and all three girls started, then laughed.

3

The book Glenda had chosen for the week was about dreams. It was bedtime and Thomas was in bed, and dreamy. The people in the book — Marianne and Mark — their tiredness was catching. Thomas made to yawn, tried to gulp down sleepiness. But he was tired rather than sleepy — and frying in discomfort, hot, curling up at the edges.

'And sure enough,' Glenda read, and her voice waned like a radio slipping off the station, 'she had hardly lain down for the night before she was asleep, and asleep was dreaming.'

Glenda had once saved a life; Thomas was there and saw it. The previous summer, on perhaps his last long walk — he was tired then, but undiagnosed — Thomas had trailed along the river bank after Glenda and her boyfriend. The teenagers picked a spot by the rail bridge where the river was too swift for swimming, away from all the other picnickers, locals, the kids adrift on patched inner tubes. Glenda and her boyfriend laid their towels among the boulders, edge to edge on a mat of gravel. Glenda unfastened the back strap of her bikini and held its stiffened cups carefully against her breasts as she lay down. Her boyfriend smoothed Coppertone onto her back. 'Go away, droopy,' Glenda said to her brother, 'but not near the water.'

Thomas went the other way, clambered over progressively larger boulders, deposited by remote floods in the years before the city began to milk the Hutt's white headwaters. Under the rail bridge Thomas found Jo and Lex Keene, and Hayley Moynihan. They stood by the first cement pile, on a shelf hacked from the river bank. There was enough room for a tall man to stand upright, his head touching the steel girders of the bridge, or for children ten and under to stand on tiptoe reaching, without being able to touch. The shelf was completely dry and littered with broken glass (brown beer bottles) and charred wood from campfires. The bridge piles themselves were sticky and stank of urine.

The girls were waiting for a train, for the clamour of a train passing at speed above their heads. They had been swimming and were still damp, wet cotton togs gathered to their bodies by row after row of shirring elastic. They were grubby, uncomfortable, expectant.

The wind shifted and the children were warned by a gust of noise, the bells at the crossing on Taita Drive. The rails sizzled. Hayley began to shout; she covered her ears. The ground trembled. The noise bore down on them, full spate, and swept everything away. They yelled, Thomas too, and danced in terror, in exaltation.

Then it had passed; the bridge shivered into solidity and only the rails telegraphed back the sound of wheels dropping across each join — clank-clank, clank-clank — a quarter, then a half mile up the line.

'Let's wait for the next one,' Thomas said.

'Clickity-click, clickity-click,' Hayley chanted, 'sixty-six, clickity-click!'

Lex picked up a charred stick and began to draw on the pile — a cupboard and crockery; a rack with dangling kitchen forks, spoons, fish slice, potato masher; then, against the right angle of earth, a cat of snowman simplicity, two circles, ears, tail, whiskers.

Hayley had another blackened stick and was drawing, blasphemously, holes in her own hands while singing the peanut song:

> A peanut sat on the railroad track
> his heart was all a-flutter
> along came a train, the nine-fifteen
> toot toot, peanut butter!

As they waited someone walked by, overhead, limped from tie to tie — all the children recognised the wheezing hinge of David Hough's callipers. A minute after David passed the rails sizzled again, and Thomas and Jo's eyes met, alarmed. They ran out from under the bridge to see that — No! — David was only halfway across and had come to a halt looking up the line. He turned and began a hopping run back the way he'd come.

The children could see the train, a rattler, carriages drawn by a diesel engine — a big blunt front with a cow-catcher ploughing the air before it. Thomas and Jo began to shout encouragement to the limping boy. The train gave a blast of its horn, a megaphonic groan. Hayley stood gaping. The train horn sounded again, then the train began to brake. Lex ran back under the bridge and pressed her face into her imaginary kitchen cabinet; charcoal smeared her forehead and cheeks.

The train was on the bridge. David looked back over his shoulder and lunged forward, his shirt-tail flapped and the brace on his leg flashed in the sun. Then Thomas saw Glenda and her boyfriend stand up from among the boulders. The boyfriend put his hands to his head and pressed his skull; his eyes seemed to move farther apart, as if he was searching for an aperture through which an idea might make its way. Glenda had forgotten to hold herself together and Thomas stared at his sister's breasts. His eyes, in expectation of blood and violence, had never seen anything so tender and lovely. Glenda waved her arms and shrieked, 'Hang over the side!' She yelled this over and over, till David Hough, the train nearly upon him, veered to the edge of the bridge, caught hold of a protruding tie and dropped. The train crossed the place he had stood. He swung, shuddering with the bridge.

The train slowed to a stop, half of one carriage still on the bridge. The driver climbed out onto the footplate of the engine and looked back along the track. Glenda's boyfriend had scrambled up the embankment and onto the bridge to haul David to his feet. The driver began to shout, something about the police, prosecution. Glenda sat down on a rock and fastened her bikini; shook herself into it. The driver had a radio telephone — he shouted — that cretin had better stay put, the police would want to speak to him. Commuters had pushed their windows up and were peering out. 'You see to it!' the driver bawled. Glenda's boyfriend waved. David Hough sobbed and gasped, there were candlesticks of snot on his top lip and Glenda's boyfriend held him by the shirt — had done touching him for the moment.

'He'll get the belt, I bet,' Hayley said.

'Perhaps he'll be fined or sent to prison,' Thomas said.

'Borstal. Boys go to borstal.' Jo knew these things.

'His daddy will give him a good hiding.' Hayley relished the idea.

Thomas looked around. 'Where's Lex?'

Lex crouched halfway up the stopbank wiping her hands back and forth across the grass. Her hands were grey, reeking, and there was a streak of oil on her face, blacker than the charcoal. 'It came from the train,' she explained. 'It dripped down on me. I thought it was his blood.'

Glenda sat at the end of Thomas's bed. As she read she squeezed his foot through the covers — the counterpane. Peter Pan. She said he should try to put his pain into his shadow. But his shadow was a patch of mist, a warm breath shrinking on a cold windowpane. Was he confused? Hadn't they finished *Peter Pan* last week? Tonight it was *Marianne Dreams*. The book was face down on the bedspread. Glenda was at the door, calling, 'Mum! He's bad!'

This time the pain followed as the fever let go and left him settling slowly into a boy-shaped print of sweat, his pyjamas wet beneath him. He was like a piece of toast not put into a rack to cool but laid flat, left softening in its own steam. The fever relented but the pain followed, feeding still.

He wept — dry, weak, persistent — then slept for a short while. There was no gloss left in his young skin and his eyelids looked loose, crepey. The usual marvellous variations in colouring — blush, freckle, subterranean blues of venous blood — he had none of it, nothing but liverish yellow, contusions and pallor.

Thomas's mother folded the sheet back firmly, away from his face. He whined. If she could manage tonight, she thought. Only. If only she could manage only tonight —

The year had gone down in manageable pieces, and she had kept it down, days, nights, hospital visits. It was not an ordeal, it was — only — a dish she had not calculated was so burning hot, a dish containing tonight's dinner that she must not drop till she reached the bench. Not an ordeal — just one of her babies at three a.m. *Just necessary.*

Thomas's mother saw him to the lavatory in the early hours of the morning. When he had finished he wouldn't wipe himself, couldn't get up again. He slumped against the wall with his head hung. When she tried to move him he cried out — a piteous, angry, mindless complaint — as if he didn't know she meant the best for him; or didn't know her at all.

4

On the morning of Election Saturday Jo, Lex and Hayley took up a post on top of the cement milk-box at the gate to Pomare School. A sign stood on the path: *Polling Booth*. It had rained overnight and there were puddles on the asphalt, some filmed with oil and synthetically bright rainbows. The sun had been out for some time and the air was redolent of steam, solvents, car fumes.

The girls told everyone who came in at the gate to please vote Labour. Most laughed, a few frowned, one man asked them had their parents put them up to it. After half an hour Jo's Mr Heron appeared and gave each girl sixpence to take to the dairy and buy an ice-cream.

They strolled home licking their lime or tutti-frutti or orange and chocolate-chip triple scoops, and Jo advised Hayley to work her tongue around the ice-cream to prevent dribbles of melt softening its cone. A wind got up and Hayley's hair dabbled in the ice-cream. 'Yum,' she said, 'I like elections.'

Hester and Frank sat at the kitchen table looking over the architect's drawings of the Mairangi Road house, those and a bundle of papers: specifications, permits and builders' quotes.

'It has to be right if I'll be paying for it the rest of my life.'

The floor plan had pictographs: parallel bars for stairs; a small circle for the toilet; larger quarter circles to show where doors were hinged, which way they swung. Hester read 'window', 'ranch-slider', 'deck', 'basement', 'built-in shelving'. The frontage was 'north facing'. All the names, figures, symbols seemed charms to Hester. She would get up into the gallery above Churchill Drive and Wilton's Bush. It might not be the city's gallery, or a country seat, but it was still several degrees above the cheap seats of the Hutt Valley.

Hester had enjoyed her Pomare neighbours, although it had taken her some time to realise how different their lives and expectations were from her own. The differences surprised her, and she was surprised at herself for not anticipating such differences — not deficits, just departures.

Take the Robbs, who had lived next door when Lex was a baby. Each spring several litters of kittens got a start in life under the Robbs' house, and scrapped among the Robb girls' dismembered dolls, the boys' dismantled trucks and bits of a broken vacuum-cleaner Mrs Robb had bought — hire purchase — then let one son use to clean his bantams' cage. Hester's mother, up from Christchurch on a badly timed visit — Jo and Lex had mumps, followed almost immediately by chickenpox — said to Hester, one afternoon when the Robb children were charging up and down outside on bikes while Hester's spotty daughters soaked in a bath full of baking soda, that perhaps *her* girls would do better on Coca-Cola and chips like *that lot.*

Mrs Robb was a romancer. She would stand at the fence while Hester pegged out nappies telling Hester how the family's corgi was related to the Queen's; or how her Rolly was a war hero, unrecognised through some administrative oversight; or how scared she was for her youngest — a little girl in flounced nylon frocks whose top lip was frequently varnished with snot. Wendy was delicate, she said, and had been given extreme unction *twice* now.

This was all very diverting for Hester. She was mystified by the numerous salesmen who knocked at the Robbs' but always gave the Keenes the go-by. Then the Robbs moved, quite suddenly it seemed, and when Hester rang State Advances about a cat her neighbours had left behind, it turned out that State Advances had no idea their tenants had gone, or where they had got to. 'They did a flit,' another neighbour said, and laughed at Hester's account of the salesmen. 'Those were debt collectors.'

That neighbouring house, like their own, was a pool house for state servants. The Moynihans down the road lived in a Railways house; Pat Moynihan was a guard on the units. His wife, Queenie, kept every room dark, to stop the furnishings from fading — even the blinds in the kitchen were half-mast. Queenie sat in an umber twilight listening to 2ZB, Doreen dispensing advice. The radio somehow made her kitchen cheerful, even with the fine weather shut out; those callers, their rising inflections, the ease of Doreen.

The Keenes' other next-door neighbours had different surnames — Hester realised after having known them over a year. They were in a de facto marriage. 'Same as,' the neighbour said, 'half the street.' The neighbour was tolerant of Hester's raised brows, and her awkward attempt to back pedal. 'It hadn't even crossed my mind that you weren't — um.'

Hester had enjoyed the Hutt's different peoples, but not the valley's short winter days, the lawn that seldom dried, was filmed with water or smooth silt beads of worm-castings, that grew birds rather than daisies, so that her daughters learned as toddlers more than the generic 'bird' and could identify starling, sparrow, thrush, blackbird and, most discouraging, the gulls that mobbed sulkily on the stopbank in certain kinds of bad weather. Hester hated having to take in her washing at three in midwinter, when the sun went behind the hills; hated the flat, barren walks; the old bombs on front lawns and the more vulgar fads the children lent themselves to — like chewing tar picked off the road.

Hester left Frank in charge of lunch and went out to vote. When his older daughters didn't appear Frank called Steph in from the back yard. Her sleeves and trouser legs were wet. 'I've been riding my tricycle all morning,' she said. He sat her at the table and made her luncheon-sausage sandwiches, then taught her to take alternate bites of spring onion. She didn't talk but seemed happy to have him to herself.

Jo and Lex turned up at the same time as their mother. Hester looked troubled. Rumours of a disappointing result? But, of course, it was hours till the polls closed, Frank told himself.

Jo and Lex had been given lunch at Moynihans'. 'Because we helped pick the raspberries,' said Jo.

'We ate at a tray table in the garden. Saveloys and sandwich bread,' said Lex. 'And cordial. Pineapple, not lemon and barley-water.'

Jo relayed a message. 'Mr Moynie says you should come over later for a beer. Everyone else is. I've picked some fresh duckweed.' She went out to her tadpoles.

'Hayley taught me to play "Can you wash your Daddy's shirts" on the piano,' Lex said. 'And Mr Moynie's going to kill one of the chooks.'

Steph piped up. 'Mummy, I've been a good girl. I ate a onion.'

Hester sat down, still wearing her coat. Frank watched her as he filled the percolator, put fresh grounds in the basket and put the pot on. (This partiality to real coffee, rather than tea, or instant, was —

in their neighbours' eyes — the Keenes' greatest oddity.) The hot plate creaked as it warmed, and the coffee pot souffled like a man calling a cat.

Jo ran back inside, in tears. Big John and Mayflower were dead, floating belly-up. Little John had keeled over and was swimming in circles. The bucket was only half full.

They all went outside to see. Frank carefully removed the river stones and duckweed then squatted back on his heels waiting to speak to Jo. She continued to cry, hard.

'Do you think a dog got in and drank the water?' Lex asked.

Steph said, 'Maybe they fainted.'

No one responded.

'Little John doesn't have much life left in him, Snowy,' Frank said. 'You don't want him to suffer, do you?'

Jo shook her head.

Hester put out a foot and pressed it into the ground beside the bucket. Squelch.

'I should put him out of his misery,' Frank said.

Jo nodded; she felt that she was upsetting someone other than her parents, who didn't like to see her cry. Maybe Little John, who would perhaps prefer to be put out of *her* misery.

Lex watched the bands of sunlit water on the walls of the green bucket, and three shadows, two flotsam, one still under its own propulsion.

'Come inside and wash your face, pet,' Hester said. 'Wash your face and you'll feel better.' She took Jo's hand and led her in.

'What will you do with him?' Lex asked her father.

'While Jo's in the bathroom I'll pour them down the stormwater drain.'

'Maybe he'll get better,' Lex said. She imagined Little John making his way out of the drainpipe, as she had, to the outfall on the river bank, then somehow from the outfall to the river — no place for frogs, but she wasn't to know that.

'Maybe he will,' her father agreed.

Their mother had dressed her mouth with lipstick. She asked the girls whether they would all come along the road.

'I suppose so.' Jo stood, knock-kneed, her whole body unhappy and tending inward.

Jo's mother didn't remark on this; she was pulling at her own fingers as though adjusting a pair of gloves. 'Girls?'

Steph looked up, but Lex had just reached the part where Grendel 'rends' the men 'limb from limb to drink the warm blood'.

'Lex?'

'What!'

'Mind your tone, pet.'

Lex closed her book.

'Did you finish that book of puzzles Grandma gave you?'

'No. Only the connect-the-dots.'

Hester pulled up a chair and sat. She said, 'Thomas went to hospital last night. I met his daddy at the polling booth. I said I'd visit him tomorrow.'

The girls waited.

'And I thought it would be nice to take him some things to keep him busy if he has to stay there.'

Jo asked, 'Is that what they expect, that he'll be in hospital for a while?' Here was an opportunity to demonstrate a virtue — generosity. If only she could think of something she could bear to part with.

'I don't know where that book of puzzles is now,' Lex said.

'I've already found it. And I thought you might like to give him the space capsules you've been collecting.'

There were 'stages' of Gemini and Saturn rockets in Puffed Wheat packets. It seemed to take more breakfasts than three girls could get through to assemble a whole rocket. But they had four capsules already, so could practise splash-downs.

'No! Not those!' Jo protested.

'But you scarcely ever play with them, Jo.'

'Because they aren't *finished*.'

Hester lost her temper. 'How can you be so selfish! What selfish girls.'

Jo burst into tears. 'Let him have something else.'

Hester got up. 'Forget I even mentioned it.' For the next several minutes she banged about the kitchen, wrapping a batch of coconut roughs for Queenie. Then she stood at the sink, sighing through her nose.

Jo left the kitchen then returned with the rocket stages in her cupped hands — white plastic cones and cylinders stamped with red lettering, 'USA', and a stripe of chequered red and white. Jo deposited her offering by Hester's handbag. Lex looked at the pile sadly. There went most of the props for the space-race game. The Russians would win by default — the Russians flew cardboard cigar tubes.

'Thank you, Jo.' Hester put the parcel of biscuits under her arm and called Frank who was in the lounge listening to Mahler — the one Jo called 'Earwig, earwig' — *The Song of the Earth*. 'Just sing out when you're ready,' he had said.

Frank fetched two bottles of beer he'd had cooling in the fridge door and they all went over to Moynies'.

All the windows of the corner kitchen were open, there were beer glasses on the sills, and elbows, rolled sleeves and brown arms. Pat Moynie had just mown the front lawn; he hadn't a grass catcher so the lawn was thick with mulch, and the children were green of joint. Hayley's brothers were playing swing-ball — thwack — the whippy rod quivered as the shuttle-puppy reversed its orbit. Inside Lex and Hayley twisted to 'Do the Bluebeat': 'A-chicky-chick, a-chicky-chicky-chang-chang . . .' Laddie the collie pulled down the clothes prop and Queenie's washing lay muddled like bunting the day after some public celebration. Naomi Arapa looped the end of her elastics around the Moynies' letterbox. Jo stood in the other end while Naomi set out to master thighsies. Her parents were indoors being teased about the votes they'd wasted on Social Credit. Queenie moistened the chook she was slowly roasting, wrapped in layers of damp newsprint. The eldest Arapa boy drove his bomb up and down the road with children standing on its running boards. Mr Moynie moved the dial to listen to the news.

Lex put her hand on the shed door, the milled grip of its round handle.

She looked back. Her family were in the lounge watching an election special that had interrupted her programmes: *Thunderbirds*, *Mighty Atom*, *The Adventures of Robinson Crusoe*.

Honeysuckle grew about the door like kiss curls around a face. The sheet-asbestos of the shed walls still radiated warmth, and the flowers warm fragrance.

Lex's father stored empty beer bottles on narrow shelves formed by the shed's frame. They stood in rows up against the black builder's paper that lined the shed. Two new bottles were by the door, the only two still free of dust.

Lex liked beer and enjoyed draining dregs from the stored bottles, never mind that it was flat or warm — it reminded her of fresher swallows she might beg from Daddy's glass.

Lex tilted the first bottle. The beer was thicker than water — bitter spit. In the next bottle something rustled, but it was too late, Lex's lips already sealed the glass neck. Something tumbled into her mouth with the liquid, something resilient and living. It stung her tongue. She spat out onto the cement floor, a wasp, alive, sorting itself out from her spit and the sugary beer that was its temptation.

Her mouth was an agony in which she had no separate sensations of teeth, tongue, gums — it was all one pain. Lex stepped on the wasp, ground her foot, husked it of its hard skeleton. It was revenge and automatic; then, with more presence of mind, she stowed the bottle back on its shelf.

She hunkered down by the outside tap, held her tongue under its stream. The water cooled the hurt, but left a halfpenny-sized patch in the centre of her tongue that was completely numb. Numb, like a scab, to everything but pressure.

Inside Lex found her mother spooning peas from a colander onto five plates.

'I'm not hungry,' Lex said, achieving a perfect French 'r' in the back of her throat.

To Hester it sounded like babyish English. 'It's mock-chicken, Lex.'

Lex liked mock-chicken, salty ground meat, shaped like a drumstick and nicely caramelised at its thin end against the meat-skewer bone. But, tender of her mouth, she shook her head.

'No?' Hester said. She came and laid a palm against Lex's forehead, then the back of her hand as a second opinion. Lex was her usual pale olive shade, and ripe of eye.

'I can't eat because,' Lex began — and her thought flew, not towards the blurred green beyond the dartboard, or a wire at best, but towards the open-pored, painted cork of the dartboard proper, a bull's-eye — 'because Thomas is sick.'

'Oh, Lex,' her mother said, exasperated, but touched too.

'Really,' Lex said.

'I can't force you to eat. You go tell the others their tea is on the table.'

Lex fetched them all, then sat herself on the kitchen floor so that the food was out of her line of sight. Her father was telling Jo that the music to *The Adventures of Robinson Crusoe* was 'The Moldau' by Smetana. He promised to play it later. He and Jo were unusually quiet throughout the meal. Jo was mourning her tadpoles, and her father the election.

'General mourning,' he said to Hester.

'It's not yet absolutely certain.'

'What's *wrong* with this country?'

'They prefer strict parents.'

Frank smiled at his wife, then asked, 'Why isn't Lex eating?'

'She's upset about Thomas.'

'You should still eat, Curly.'

'I can't.'

'Don't lisp, pet. You're a big girl,' Hester reminded her.

'I told you she's the empathic one,' Frank said. He turned to Lex. 'Why don't you write Thomas a letter? Mummy can take it to him tomorrow when she visits. Or you could draw him a picture.' When Frank was in England at the end of '65 he had loved Lex's letters: 'Dear Daddy. I are on a Journal now. Grandmar has got the phone on now. Aunty Paulie is staying with us. Mummy bought some blue and white material for me. Paulie has cut my hair. Steph has her hair in a ribbon. Paulie cut Jo hair to. I have got a book from the library its name is how to oose. Are you good Daddy? Love from Lex.'

Frank said, 'Come sit up at the table. I'll get you some paper. Perhaps once you've written to Thomas you might feel more like tea?'

Lex sat at the table and swallowed the spit that had pooled under her tongue. Her father gave her some paper — not the usual waste-paper from his office with programme listings printed on one side, but a fresh sheet. Lex saw she would have to apply herself, at least till the gravy jelled in the dish where her mock-chicken drumsticks lay in reserve. She doubted her excuse could stand reheating.

She drew a car and tow-truck; as a boy Thomas would like that. Then she forgot her audience and remembered only letters — so wrote, 'Dear Thomas, I hope you are well ...'

5

Sunday, and Lex was at a loose end. Jo, still in mourning, had kept home to finish writing her book, *Honey and John on Windy Hill*. Jo planned to send it to Thomas on her mother's next visit — or take it to him herself; she liked the notion of a hospital visit.

The whole street was quiet, as if convalescing. Although it was a fine, still day very few adults were out-of-doors.

Lex spent her morning over the stopbank, by herself in her grotto — as Jo called it — a cavern formed by convolvulus which grew to cover the branches of a dead willow. The grotto was special to Lex because she had claimed the old sewing machine she found there — a treadle Singer a couple of decades older than her mother's own. There were a few rust spots on its black body, and its chrome was blistered, but the leather cord that drove its wheels was still whole and supple. Jo would say Lex liked to play at sewing, but Lex gave no thought to an imaginary garment, followed no phantasmal cloth through with her fingers. When she sat on her vine-upholstered branch to sew she wasn't being mother, she simply enjoyed the momentous resistance of the treadle against her foot, and the grotto's green, mitigated brightness, its tattered shadows.

Eventually hunger drove her home for lunch. Her father was

humouring Jo, who hadn't had to shift her book from the kitchen table, but ate with it open at her elbow, the more recent sentences of her composition hidden by her packet of Lakeland Coloured Pencils. Lex could see that Jo had been forced to make more 'monsters' from their father's scrawls. The book had been his, part of some indexing task. Most of its pages were blank, but on some were scattered stanzas of names and addresses — these Jo outlined, coloured in and gave eyes, ears, mouths and reasons for being: 'Honey and John met a monster. It looked like this.'

After lunch Hester put on lipstick, and her coat with three-quarter sleeves and daisy buttons. She said, 'Be good girls. I'll give Thomas your love.'

On her way back to the grotto Lex found Hayley. Hayley and two other girls were picking gorse flowers to scatter over a bride's head. They had a bowl full of the stuff, some petals crushed to transparency. It wasn't settled who was to be the bride. 'It was *my* idea,' said Hayley.

'But I'm the prettiest,' another girl said — and even Hayley was astonished by her confidence. Lex saw that Hayley was too surprised to lose her temper. The girl was persuasively dressed in a blue frock with a sateen cummerbund, and white shoes buckled across the instep — these gave off the fruity odour of fresh white liquid polish.

Lex thought it might be more fun to toss petals than be pelted by them. 'I'll do a ceremony. You two be bridesmaids.'

They sorted themselves into a small procession. Lex walked backwards before them. The petals streamed and the air smelled of buttered corn.

'What are you doing?' Three boys had appeared on the stopbank above them. One was around their age, two perhaps ten, like Jo.

'We're having a coronation,' Lex said, already changing the terms of the game.

'King Lippy the Lion,' Hayley added. Weddings were sissy and would shame them.

The two groups regarded each other. If the boys hadn't had some business in mind they would not have noticed the girls at all.

Apparently, having made contact, they were at a loss how to proceed. One wiped his nose on his forearm. 'It's your brothers built that fort, eh?'

Hayley nodded.

'They've gone off and left it uncovered. Want to go take a look?'

'I'm not allowed,' Hayley said.

'They're not there.'

'I'll go,' Lex volunteered.

The boys exchanged looks. Lex was a reinforcement, but Hayley was insurance.

'Come on,' Lex said to Hayley.

'Me too,' the bride said. 'Shake a leg.' She skipped off ahead of them all.

'She lives in Woburn,' Hayley told the boys — to explain the bride's peculiarities, and her disregard for the neighbourhood's delicately negotiated boundaries.

They all followed the bride, away from the open ground by the stopbank, the field of grass, dock, thistle and low gorse. They came on to a track through the broom. The sun cleared the high cloud and the heat doubled. The whole territory stirred; its tendons popped, then — adjustment made — it lay still again. The children walked single file through mounds of gravel left over from the Council's unfinished earthworks. Lex's father called it 'fill', and it did — stockpiled silence and did away with the usual horizons.

Before the willows and river was another strip of clear ground. And the fort. The children breathed freely again and looked about them. The stopbank had reappeared, a low green wall, nothing visible beyond till the Eastern Hutt hills.

Sheets of roofing iron had been propped up near the pit to make a kind of metal tent, the inside of which was blackened by smoke.

'They've been lighting fires,' the bride said. She stood a good few feet off but still twitched her skirt away from the sooty iron. Lex clutched at the hem of her own pinafore and tried to copy this fascinating feminine gesture.

Hayley and the boys went to the edge of the pit. 'Tunnels,' Hayley said. 'Tunnels, Lex.'

The reports were true. The children climbed down a knotted rope tied to a stake hammered into the ground.

The pit was deep, and five tunnels branched off level with its floor. The sides of the pit were straight, and showed their makers' spadework, neat chiselled cuts. The only untidiness was an occasional grubby, limp lace of fine tree roots hanging out of the soil. To Lex, looking up, the rectangle of sky was an old mirror, silver going a little at the edges — but less superficial than a mirror, a volume of vacancy. And blue; her blue.

David Hough appeared at the edge of the pit. He had either followed them, or had seized the opportunity to make his own investigations. Although he was a trespasser like them, the children snubbed David. He couldn't climb down into the pit, but limped around its edges talking to himself — or perhaps to them, without expecting an answer. Of the tunnels he wondered how far they went, straight or curved. He supposed one or more were emergency exits, or even the exits, concealed. Perhaps he expected the children to collect some of the information he wanted.

The boys had engaged in a debate — whether to explore the tunnels and, if so, who would go first — when something thudded into the bottom of the pit. David put his arms above his head and ran, doubled over. Lex looked up and saw a stone poised against the blue, compact and discrete, like a bird in the shut-winged, falling stage of flight. Something hit her on the side of the head and she fell forward, stunned. She closed her eyes and scuttled into the mouth of one of the tunnels.

The soil was cool and fragrant. Lex looked back from this throat of earth to see one boy follow her. He pushed her forward into the dark and dropping temperature. 'They're coming,' he urged. She crawled on.

Then the tunnel collapsed. Suddenly Lex was caught in smothering covers, stiff rough blankets. A warm ring — the boy's hand — encircled her ankle for a moment, then withdrew. The cold covered her. Soft, friable, airless, overwhelming soil fell between her face and the arms with which she had tried to screen her face — pushed against her eyelids, mouth and nose. A conquering weight pressed down on her body. She thrashed, immersed, blind, suffocated.

And thrashing — automatic now, with no apprehension, no thoughts, only reflex mobility, her last breath gone — her hand caught at something. Something sinewy and firm. A tree root. Lex held hard to this solidity, she pulled herself forward then up.

It was as though light, not earth, sifted down. Grey mealy light. The hole was everything. And pewter-coloured, increasingly coarse grains of crumbled light.

Lex pulled herself out of the earth, hand over hand, and the dirt around her, still tending down, dragged at her body, like peristalsis, tried to swallow her again.

Lex unearthed herself.

Lex lay on the far side of the willow and listened to the sound of a rout. When the big boys finished throwing rocks, the smaller children swarmed out of the pit and scattered. Hayley's brothers singled Hayley out. Lex heard one shout, 'Scrag her!' then scuffles, a shriek. David Hough called out, 'Wait!' then went under — Lex heard body-blows, the grunts of attacker and victim.

Lex lay still. Her eyes and nose streamed. Each breath stank of earth, or of nothing, the air that had no savour, until, as her sinuses filled, she came to smell only the soapflake stink of snot. Lex lay where she was till the big boys saw the children off their property and didn't come back. Then she began to wipe at her face, where there was nothing now, no mask over her eyes or nose or mouth but air. She scoured with her palms, as if clearing clotted web, a memory of obstruction.

At the river Lex cleaned up; took off her sandals and squatted in the shallows to wash her legs, arms and face.

The sun had gone behind the Western Hutt hills. On the far bank the scar of quarry drained of colour then put itself forward, like something nasty in a ghost story staring at a small girl, the hem of whose dress dipped into the water, then dripped. The river moved but made no sound. Lex looked up at the bared rock, and if she had been a rabbit she would have stopped chewing. She stilled; then realised it wasn't the rock that watched her.

David Hough stood on the river bank twenty feet behind her. He didn't say anything, but seemed relieved when she turned to face him. Relieved to recognise her, as if, till then, his inventory wasn't complete. He raised a hand to hail her, an unimposing wave that didn't climb higher than his breastbone, then he turned and bobbed off through the willows.

Lex went home. It was dusk, and though the lounge was alight with pale aquatic television radiance, there was no light in the Keenes' kitchen.

Lex paused in the kitchen doorway. Her mother was there, standing at the sink, in the half-dark, peeling potatoes. The cold tap ran and Hester's hands were red to the wrist. Her eyes were red too.

Lex took a step into the room, but her mother failed to notice her. Lex went forward another step to identify the jumble of whiteness on the kitchen table. Jo's bird bones, she thought. Then she saw it was the collection of rocket parts, capsules and stages. The objects gathered what light remained and glowed like — perhaps — the sky coming apart in mealy pieces.

Lex went to the bedroom and shut herself in, left it dim. She fetched her hairbrush and sat, feet tucked under her, on the end of her bed. She began to brush the earth out of her hair.

biographical notes

Katherine Mansfield (1888–1923)

Katherine Mansfield was born Kathleen Mansfield Beauchamp in Wellington, to a prominent business family. She completed her education in London, returning after a short sojourn in New Zealand 1906–1908, to settle permanently in Europe. After several years of illness she died of tuberculosis at Fontainebleau in France. Her major publications during her lifetime were *In a German Pension* (1911), *Bliss and Other Stories* (1920) and *The Garden Party and other Stories* (1922); several other volumes appeared posthumously. Her *Collected Stories* were first published in 1945. The best of many biographies is Antony Alpers, *The Life of Katherine Mansfield* (1980). Four of a projected five volumes of her *Collected Letters* have been edited for Oxford University Press by Vincent O'Sullivan and Margaret Scott (1984–96). *The Notebooks of Katherine Mansfield* were edited in two volumes by Margaret Scott (1997).

Prelude was first published by the Hogarth Press, London, in 1918 and included in *Bliss and Other Stories* (Constable, London, 1920). The text used here is from *The Stories of Katherine Mansfield*, edited by Antony Alpers (Oxford University Press, Auckland, 1984).

Frank Sargeson (1903–82)

Frank Sargeson was born Norris Davey in Hamilton and trained as a solicitor. He travelled to Europe in 1926, returning to New Zealand in 1928 and eventually settling in Takapuna on Auckland's North Shore where he spent the rest of his life. His first book, *Conversation with*

My Uncle and other Sketches, was published in 1936, followed by *A Man and His Wife* (1940) and *That Summer and other Stories* (1946). His *Collected Stories* were first published in 1964. He wrote several novels including *I Saw in My Dream* (1949), *Memoirs of a Peon* (1965), *The Hangover* (1967), *Joy of the Worm* (1969), and *Sunset Village* (1976). *Man of England Now* (1972) is a collection of three novellas. He also wrote a celebrated autobiography in three volumes: *Once is Enough* (1973), *More than Enough* (1975), and *Never Enough* (1977), collected in one volume as *Sargeson* (1981). His critical writings were edited by Kevin Cunningham as *Conversation in a Train* (1983). Michael King's *Frank Sargeson: a Life* (1995) is a biography.

That Summer was first published in *Penguin New Writing*, Numbers 17–19, 1943–44, and included in *That Summer and Other Stories* (John Lehmann, London, 1946). The text used here is from *The Stories of Frank Sargeson* (Penguin, Auckland, 1982).

Maurice Duggan (1922–74)

Maurice Duggan lived his whole life in Auckland apart from three years in Europe in the early 1950s. Duggan suffered much from ill health including osteomyelitis, tuberculosis, alcoholism and cancer. In later years he worked in advertising. Duggan wrote sparingly and published only three collections in his lifetime: *Immanuel's Land* (1956), *Summer in the Gravel Pit* (1965) and *O'Leary's Orchard and other Stories* (1970). He also published some children's stories and a collection of his poetry, *A Voice for the Minotaur*, was published posthumously in 2001. His biography is *To Bed at Noon: The Life and Art of Maurice Duggan* (1997), by Ian Richards.

O'Leary's Orchard was first published in *Landfall* 81, March 1967 and included in *O'Leary's Orchard and Other Stories* (Caxton Press, Christchurch, 1970). The text here is taken from his *Collected Stories*, edited and introduced by C.K. Stead (Auckland University Press/Oxford University Press, Auckland, 1981).

Patricia Grace (born 1937)

Patricia Grace was born in Wellington; she is of Ngati Raukawa, Ngati Toa and Te Ati Awa descent, and is affiliated to Ngati Porou by marriage. She is the mother of seven children and worked as a schoolteacher in various parts of the North Island before becoming a full-time writer. She lives in Plimmerton. Her story collections are *Waiariki* (1975), *The Dream Sleepers* (1980), *Electric City* (1987), *Selected Stories* (1991), *The Sky People* (1994), and *Collected Stories* (1994). Her novels are *Mutuwhenua: The Moon Sleeps* (1978), *Potiki* (1986), *Cousins* (1992), *Baby No-Eyes* (1998), and *Dogside Story* (2001). She has also written several books for children.

Valley was first published in *Waiariki and Other Stories* (Longman Paul, Auckland, 1975); the text here is taken from *Selected Stories* (Penguin, Auckland, 1991)

Albert Wendt (born 1939)

Albert Wendt is of the Aiga Sa-Tuaopepe of Lefaga, the Aiga Sa-Maualaivao of Malie and the Aiga Sa-Patu of Viaala of Samoa. He first came to New Zealand in 1953 where he attended high school, teachers training college and Victoria University. Later he returned to Samoa as principal of Samoa College, became professor of Pacific Literature at the University of the South Pacific in Suva, and came back to live in New Zealand as professor of English at the University of Auckland in 1988. His story collections are *Flying-fox in a Freedom Tree* (1974), *Birth and Death of the Miracle Man* (1986) and *The Best of Albert Wendt's Short Stories* (1999). His novels are *Sons for the Return Home* (1973), *Pouliuli* (1977), *Leaves of the Banyan Tree* (1979), *Ola* (1991), and *Black Rainbow* (1992). He has also published four books of poetry and edited several anthologies of Pacific literature. A film version of *Flying-fox in a Freedom Tree* was released in 1990.

Flying-fox in a Freedom Tree was first published in *Flying-fox in a Freedom Tree* (Longman Paul, Auckland, 1974). The text here is taken from *The Best of Albert Wendt's Short Stories* (Vintage, Auckland, 1999).

Peter Wells (born 1950)

Peter Wells has lived most of his life in Auckland. He has published two collections of stories: *Dangerous Desires* (1991) and *The Duration of a Kiss* (1994). He has also published a novel, *Boy Overboard* (1997) and a memoir, *Long Loop Home* (2001). He is also a film maker: among his best known films are *A Death in the Family* (1986) and *Desperate Remedies* (1993). He edited (with Rex Pilgrim) *Best Mates: Gay Writing in Aotearoa New Zealand* (1997). A film *Memory and Desire*, based on Wells' novella, and directed by Niki Caro, was released in 1998.

Of Memory and Desire was first published in *Dangerous Desires* (Reed Books, Auckland, 1991). The text here is taken from this edition.

Elizabeth Knox (born 1959)

Elizabeth Knox was born and lives in Wellington. She has published six novels: *After Z-Hour* (1987), *Treasure* (1992), *Glamour and the Sea* (1996), *The Vintner's Luck* (1998), *Black Oxen* (2000), and *Billie's Kiss* (2002). *Pomare* (1994) is one of a trio of autobiographical novellas, the others being *Paremata* (1989) and *Tawa* (1998); the trilogy was published together as *The High Jump: a New Zealand childhood* (2000).

Pomare was first published by Victoria University Press, Wellington, in 1994. The text here is taken from *The High Jump: a New Zealand childhood* (Victoria University Press, Wellington, 2000).

acknowledgements

The editor would like to thank the publishers of the following books in which the works listed first appeared or were printed.

Every effort has been made to locate copyright holders or their agents. The publisher would be interested to hear from any copyright holders who have not already been acknowledged.

Katherine Mansfield, 'Prelude': *The Stories of Katherine Mansfield*, edited by Antony Alpers. Oxford University Press, Auckland, 1984.

Frank Sargeson, 'That Summer': *The Stories of Frank Sargeson*. Penguin, Auckland, 1982.

Maurice Duggan, 'O'Leary's Orchard': *Collected Stories*, edited and introduced by C.K. Stead. Auckland University Press/Oxford University Press, Auckland, 1981.

Patricia Grace, 'Valley': *Selected Stories*. Penguin, Auckland, 1991.

Albert Wendt, 'Flying-fox in a freedom tree': *The Best of Albert Wendt's Short Stories*. Vintage, Auckland, 1999.

Peter Wells, 'Of Memory and Desire': *Dangerous Desires*. Reed Books, Auckland, 1991.

Elizabeth Knox, 'Pomare': *The High Jump: a New Zealand childhood*. Victoria University Press, Wellington, 2000.